THE SEWING
FACTORY GIRLS

THE SEWING
FACTORY GIRLS

Posy Lovell

ORION

First published in Great Britain in 2023 by Orion Fiction,
an imprint of The Orion Publishing Group Ltd.,
Carmelite House, 50 Victoria Embankment
London EC4Y 0DZ

An Hachette UK Company

1 3 5 7 9 10 8 6 4 2

A CIP catalogue record for this book is
available from the British Library.

ISBN (Paperback) 978 1 3987 1877 7
ISBN (eBook) 978 1 3987 1455 7

Typeset by Input Data Services Ltd, Somerset

Printed and bound in Great Britain by Clays Ltd, Elcograf S.p.A.

www.orionbooks.co.uk

For my grandma Jess, who's not here to read this story but whose spirit runs through Ellen, Bridget and Sadie.

Chapter One

Ellen stood on the top step, hands on her hips, barring her sister from coming any further.

'Don't even think about it,' she said. 'It's awful bad luck to see your wedding dress before it's finished.'

On the step below, Bridget frowned. 'I don't think that's the saying, Ellen. Isn't it bad luck if the groom sees the dress? Not the bride.'

Ellen thought for a moment, realised her sister was right and shrugged. 'Well, you can't come in anyway.'

'My feet hurt and I need to sit down.'

Ellen grinned at her sister. 'Sit down somewhere else.'

'I live here.'

'Not for much longer.'

A brief shadow crossed Bridget's face and Ellen wondered if she'd annoyed her. Bridget, normally so stoic and no-nonsense, had been a bit prickly lately.

'I'm in your sewing bee, too, you know,' Bridget said with a tut. 'I've got to mend my blue blouse.'

Privately Ellen thought Bridget's blue blouse was only fit for the bin, faded from too much washing, and the plain cut of the practical shirt made Ellen want to scream with frustration.

1

'I've got a ribbon you could stitch into the collar of that blouse,' she said. 'You could tie it in a big bow under your chin, and it would look so pretty.'

'Ellen . . .' Bridget sounded exasperated.

'Anyway, we've got two wedding dresses to finish.'

'*Two* wedding dresses? Oh Ellen, I thought we'd agreed not to do the parade?'

Realising she'd let the cat out of the bag, Ellen threw her head back and groaned. 'You have to do it. It's a Wentworth tradition.'

'I don't want to.'

'It's not up to you.'

'I'm the bride,' Bridget said through gritted teeth. 'It's my dress.'

'Dresses,' said Ellen.

Knowing she was pushing her usually amenable sister to her limit, but quite curious to see how far Bridget would take it, Ellen spread her arms out, bracing herself against the cold stone walls of the stairs trying to fill the doorway to the flat. 'You can't come in.'

They stared at one another for a minute, like they had when they were wee girls and were bickering over a toy or a sweetie, until Ma would say, 'Oh Bridget, come on,' and Bridget would hand over whatever it was Ellen wanted. Every time.

Just like now.

Bridget sighed. 'Can I come in if I say I'll do the parade?'

Ellen gave a little bounce of delight and clapped her hands. 'Yes! Come in!' She stood aside and let her sister walk past her into their flat. 'I knew you'd agree to do it in the end,' she muttered under her breath, then regretted it as Bridget turned and gave her a withering look.

The kitchen was a hive of activity. Bridget's real wedding dress – the one she'd wear to walk down the aisle to marry Malcolm in just a few weeks' time – was on a mannequin by the fireplace. Ellen's best friend, Janet, was on her knees, with a mouthful of pins, fastening up the hem.

Ellen's and Bridget's mother, Gert, was sitting in a chair by the window – where the light was best – stitching Bridget's veil. And Gert's own mother, Sal, was sitting next to her, keeping a close eye on what she was doing and offering 'helpful' suggestions. Ellen could feel her mother's irritation growing from where she stood.

The dress was rather beautiful. It was perfect for Bridget, being absolutely plain, without any fuss or frippery. Just a simple long gown, high-necked and long-sleeved, the only addition being a small lace trim on the bodice. Ellen thought it was terribly dull, but she had to admit it would look well on her sister, who didn't suit flounces or frills.

Fortunately, Ellen had indulged her love of embellishments elsewhere. Because on another mannequin, on the opposite side of the room, was the other dress. The parade dress. Ellen watched as her sister's gaze landed on the enormous flouncy gown, made from worn pillowcases, a couple of torn petticoats, ribbons, offcuts of lace, and, Ellen hid her grin, their mother's old brassieres.

'Ma's underwear?' Bridget said, closing her eyes briefly.

'Uh huh.' Ellen gripped her sister's arm. 'It's tradition, Bridget.'

Bridget took a deep breath and Ellen watched, waiting for her response.

And then her sister laughed – a slightly forced laugh admittedly – but Ellen knew she'd won.

'If I cut you, Ellen Kelly,' Bridget sighed, 'you would bleed Wentworth.'

'Aye, you're probably right,' Ellen said unapologetically. 'But aren't we all the same?'

She looked around at the other women in the room, most of whom worked at the huge Wentworth factory too, except for Sal, who had given up work now, but who'd been a Wentworth girl once herself, and their ma, who did dressmaking and mending at home on the Wentworth machine that had pride of place in their kitchen.

Bridget made a face. 'Go on, then,' she said. 'I'll try it on.'

'Good girl,' said Ma. 'Ellen's worked really hard on this dress, you know.'

'I have,' Ellen agreed cheerfully. 'Pushing that needle through the elastic on Ma's underwear wasn't easy.'

Bridget gave a tiny smile and shrugged off her coat. 'Where do you want me?'

Ellen found the small stool her mother used to get things out of the high cupboards, and positioned it so Bridget could stand on it.

'Here,' she said. Obediently, with a slight air of resignation, Bridget dropped her coat onto an empty chair and balanced on the stool.

'Go on, then.'

'You should really take off your skirt and blouse,' Ellen began, then changed her mind as Bridget glared at her. 'But it's fine as it is.'

With a bit of help from Janet, because Bridget was taller than Ellen even when she wasn't standing on a stool, Ellen managed to drop the dress over her sister's head and then stood back to admire her handiwork.

'It's perfect,' she said, giggling.

'It is.' Janet stifled a snort. 'I think it's the puffy sleeves, Bridget.'

'Or perhaps it's the frilly neck?' Ellen said.

'And all the petticoats,' Ma added. She nudged Ellen fondly. 'I wondered where my Sunday petticoat had gone, but I can see it peeking out from under Bridget's hem. I'll have that back after the parade, please.'

Bridget was smiling but Ellen wasn't sure the smile reached her eyes, which were shiny with what could be tears, but surely no one would make such a fuss over a silly frock? Ellen felt a flush of annoyance with her sister, who was always so reluctant to have fun. If she just let herself enjoy the parade, it might make her realise that she didn't have to be so dull all the time.

'Can I take it off now?' Bridget asked. 'It's so itchy round my chin. I'm not sure how Mary Queen of Scots coped with her ruff.'

Ellen chuckled, her brief irritation with her sister forgotten. 'Go on then, take it off.'

Bridget wriggled out of the dress and Janet put it back on the mannequin.

'Do you want to try the other one on?' Ma asked. 'The real dress?'

'It's not hemmed yet,' Bridget said. 'It's full of pins. I'll wait.'

Ellen thought that if she was getting married, she would wear her wedding dress all the time. Just around the house, or to work. Maybe even to bed. Even if it was full of pins, she'd still wear it. She almost admired Bridget's self-restraint.

Throwing herself onto the saggy armchair, she said: 'Give me your blouse, Mary Queen of Scots, and I'll mend it for you.'

'Don't put the ribbon on it,' Bridget said, smoothing her hair down and straightening her skirt, dishevelled from pulling the dress over her head. 'I know that's what you're planning.'

'I was not,' said Ellen indignantly, even though that was exactly what she'd been planning.

'Girls,' said Ma. 'Bridget, Ellen's just being nice.'

Bridget rolled her eyes. 'I'm twenty-one, Ma,' she said. 'I'm not really a girl anymore.'

'You'll always be my wee girls,' Ma said. 'Now Ellen, are you sitting on my order book there, doll? Don't crumple it up, will you? If Mrs MacKay doesn't get her new blouse, she'll not ask me again.'

Ellen leaned to one side and her mother pulled the notebook out from underneath her and tutted to see it bent from Ellen's behind. She tucked it behind the clock on the mantelpiece and Ellen saw her bite her lip as she glanced at the time.

'Da will be home soon,' she said.

'Right enough.' Ma sat back down on her chair by the window and picked up Bridget's veil again, though Ellen could see her casting worried looks along the street as she sewed.

5

'Bridget,' she said loudly, making Janet jump and prick her finger on a pin, 'is there any more news about Mr Beresford?'

Bridget rolled her eyes. 'What kind of news are you expecting?'

'Like why he came to Wentworth,' Ellen said.

'He came to Wentworth because there was a management vacancy,' said Bridget. 'Because old Mr Driscoll died.'

Ellen groaned. 'Bridget, don't spoil it,' she said. 'I think he has come to transform the factory. He's so young and charming – I imagine he has lots of ideas.'

'He's forty-five,' Bridget said. 'He's the same age as Ma. And I can assure you, he's got just the same idea as everyone else – to make a profit for Wentworth.'

Ellen tutted. Bridget was rather too fond of reminding her that she worked in the clerical department on the top floor, mingling with the factory bosses, while Ellen worked her fingers to the bone in cabinet polishing at the bottom.

'Do you know if he's married?' Ellen said.

'I don't know.'

'Do you know if likes blondes or brunettes?' Janet said, pointing from her own blonde head to Ellen's dark mop of curls.

'Janet, honestly,' Bridget said, but Ellen could tell she was amused. 'He's just another manager like all the others.'

'But he's so handsome.' Janet clutched her heart. 'Surely even you can see that, Bridget?'

Bridget shrugged. 'He has nice hair.'

'Nicer than Malcolm's,' Ellen said with a flash of wickedness. Poor Malcolm was only in his twenties but his hair was thinning already. Bridget glowered at her.

'Where did he come from?' Ma asked. 'Another factory?'

'Yes,' Bridget began, but Janet jumped in.

'He came from heaven,' she said. 'He is too handsome to be from this world.'

'Janet Lang,' said Ellen's gran, laughing. 'I remember your ma talking about your da like that.'

'Urgh, Mrs Douglas,' said Janet half giggling, half groaning.

Ellen laughed too. Janet wasn't the only one to have been taken aback by the new manager at work. Ellen had been won over by his handsome face and charming manner, too. The rumours on the factory floor were that Mr Beresford was a reformer. Younger than the rest of the older managers and ready to make changes. Ellen loved being part of Wentworth, but there was no denying it was hard work. Perhaps Mr Beresford would change that, she thought. And then perhaps one day she would catch his eye when he was on the factory floor, and he would ask someone – Bridget perhaps because she worked for him, after all – who she was. 'Who is that vibrant young woman with the dark hair and mischievous eyes?' he would say. Ellen's grandpa had always said she had mischievous eyes, and Ellen liked the idea of being a woman who had mischievous eyes. So, Mr Beresford would ask Bridget who she was, and Bridget would say, 'That's my wee sister, sir,' and Mr Beresford would ask her to introduce them . . .

'Ellen?' Janet said. 'You're away with the fairies. I said I've got some news.'

'Sorry,' Ellen muttered, feeling her cheeks flame and hoping no one would notice. 'What's your news?'

Janet tucked a final pin in the hem of Bridget's dress and stood up. 'I've put my name down for the job that's going in clerical.'

Ellen stared at her. 'You're leaving cabinet polishing?'

'Aye, I am. Well, that's the plan.'

'But clerical is so boring,' Ellen said. She couldn't imagine Wentworth without her friend by her side. 'Why would you want to work there . . .' Realisation struck and she prodded Janet's arm. 'Is it because of Mr Beresford?'

'No,' Janet said firmly, but her reddening cheeks told Ellen she was fibbing. 'Of course not. You know I've been wanting to learn to type. I've been talking about it for ages.'

'I've never heard you utter the words until this very minute,'

Ellen said. She felt oddly betrayed, as though Janet had taken something from her she didn't realise she had wanted.

She turned to her sister. 'Do you think it's a good idea, Bridget?'

Bridget looked horrified to be asked.

'Well I, well, if Janet . . .' she stammered.

'Och, you just want Beresford to yourself,' Janet said cheerfully. 'Well, now you'll have to share him with me. Right, shall I put the kettle on, Mrs Kelly?'

Chapter Two

Bridget felt her sister's eyes on her, as Janet headed over to the kettle.

'Bridget Kelly, you're virtually a married woman,' Ellen teased. 'But there's you keeping Mr Beresford for yourself.'

Bridget shook her head. 'That's not what this is, Ellen. Don't be silly.'

'Bridget, be kind to your sister,' Ma said, and Bridget swallowed a retort that would demand to know why Ellen was never asked to be kind to her. Though she knew why, of course. Her mother had lost all of the babies that had come between her and Ellen and after. Tiny scraps who never drew breath and wee Aggie, who the whole family had doted on and who lived just a few weeks before she died in their ma's arms. And then, just when everyone had thought Ma would fade away with sadness, along came Ellen with her laughter and her curls and her flashing, sparkling eyes. Their wee miracle. Their beloved. And, of course, Bridget adored her sister. Of course she did. She'd do anything for Ellen because she loved every bone of her body. And she did. She did everything Ellen asked of her.

But sometimes she just wished she didn't have to.

Now she forced herself to smile at Ellen, who was looking at her indignantly.

'Does Malcolm know about this?' Ellen asked, waggling her eyebrows.

'There is no "this", Ellen,' Bridget said, more sharply than she'd intended. Feeling bad to have snapped at Ellen, she softened immediately and in a conspiratorial tone she said: 'Malcolm's Mr Beresford's biggest fan. Bigger than you. Bigger than Janet, even. He thinks he's wonderful.'

Ellen giggled. 'Because the first thing he did when he arrived was promote Malcolm.'

'That's it,' Bridget said, feeling slightly disloyal towards her future husband but unable to resist the chance to make Ellen laugh. 'And because of what he said when he did it.'

Ellen's eyes were like saucers. 'What did he say?'

'He said that Malcolm reminded him of himself when he was younger.'

'NO!' Ellen looked positively gleeful. 'He said that?'

'Apparently.'

'Mr Beresford with the lovely hair, and the tweed suits and the shiny shoes and the charming manner, said baldy Malcolm reminds him of himself?'

'I don't think he meant because of how he looks,' said Bridget, bristling. 'It's more because Malcolm's a very hard worker.'

'It must be,' Ellen said, and Bridget had the overwhelming urge to give her a shove just as she did ten years ago when Ellen was annoying her.

'The best thing about marrying Malcolm is not having to live here with you anymore,' she hissed, hoping their ma wouldn't hear.

'I'll have the bedroom to myself,' Ellen said with a broad grin. 'I can't wait.' Then her face fell and she screwed her nose up. 'It'll be funny without you though.'

This time Bridget did give her a shove, but it was much more good-natured than it might have been.

'Malcolm's done well to get promoted,' Ellen said.

Bridget nodded. 'He really has. When you think of what things were like for him . . .'

She trailed off. She didn't generally enjoy talking about Malcolm. It made her feel awkward and uncomfortable. The idea of their wedding made her cringe with embarrassment. But she liked the idea of being married to him. It seemed to be, what was that expression her old teacher had used? The path of least resistance. That was it. Though that sounded awful. It wasn't that she didn't like Malcolm. On the contrary, she liked him a lot. She admired him greatly and she was fiercely protective of him. But sometimes – often, in fact – she wondered if they'd fallen into agreeing to get married just because it was the easy thing to do.

She shook herself, aware of Ellen watching her. 'Right, where's that tea, Janet?'

Janet brought the teapot over to the table and Ma helped set out some cups and then Gran poured, and Bridget felt her discomfort easing. After all, if she had to marry anyone – and surely she did, because she didn't know any unmarried women much older than herself except for Margaret at work, and her spinster-status consumed her every waking thought – then Malcolm was the best man for the job.

Ma looked at the clock again. 'Where's that father of yours?' she said with false jollity.

'Was he at the football?' Janet asked. 'The big match?'

'He was, aye.'

Janet made a face, which Bridget thought wasn't especially helpful. Her ma always worried about Da when he went to the football in Glasgow and knowing it had been Celtic playing Rangers today only added to her concerns. And while they usually accepted that their ma worried about them whatever they were doing, Bridget thought she did have a point today. There were always scuffles at the games.

'He'll be home any minute, doll,' said Gran.

And just then, they heard the heavy main door of their tenement block open and slam shut, someone climbing the stone stairs, and Bridget could feel her mother holding her breath.

The door to the flat opened and Da came into the kitchen. His shirt was splattered in blood, his eye was swollen shut and his lip was puffy.

'Hi, girls,' he said cheerfully, pulling his green and white scarf from his pocket – he never wore it while he was travelling to and from the match – and hanging it up.

'Allan, what on earth?' Ma said, rushing over to him. She held his face in her hands and examined him. 'Are you all right?'

'Aye,' said Da. 'Not bad.'

'You shouldn't go to those games,' Ma said, biting her lip.

'Gert, I've been saying that since he was a wee boy,' Gran said. 'He goes every time and every time he comes back with a battle wound.'

'It wasn't the football,' Da said, shaking off Ma's attentions and going to wipe his face. 'It was that wee sod Frankie Briggs and his pals. He was waiting for us to get off the train. He's not even a football fan – he just uses it as an excuse to get physical.'

'He is out of control,' Ma tutted. 'Someone needs to take him in hand.'

'He's getting worse,' Da agreed. 'He's got that gang of younger ones who think he's the big man, and it's made him worse.'

Ma took the cloth from Da's hand and dabbed his lip gently. 'Aye, well, some folk are just looking for an excuse to start.'

'When it's really us that has the excuse,' Da said.

Bridget and Ellen exchanged a glance. They knew where this was heading.

'Don't I have more skills than half the men employed in the shipyard?'

'You do, Al.' Ma's voice was soft and soothing. 'Of course you do.'

'But will they employ me?' He didn't wait for an answer. 'They won't. And why not? Because my name is Kelly, that's why, and there's no jobs for Catholics there.'

Ma caught his face in her hands again and kissed his swollen mouth.

'But aren't you better off being in charge of your own work?' she said. 'No boss to answer to. And wasn't it your carpentry skills that got us this flat instead of all being crammed into one room, eh?'

Bridget breathed out slowly. Ma certainly knew how to calm their father when he was getting hot and bothered about us against them – Catholics against Protestants.

'Al, why not go and see if any of the boys are in the pub,' Ma said. 'I think you deserve a drink after the day you've had.'

'Och, I'm not really in the mood now,' said Da, but he was already heading to the coat hook and shrugging on his jacket. 'Though maybe I'll just pop in for one.'

'Good man,' said Ma.

Da blew her a kiss over his shoulder and headed back out into the evening chill, while the women – except Ma – all chuckled softly.

'His face was such a mess,' she said.

'Ah, he's had worse,' Gran said. 'He can look after himself.'

'I thought he'd grow out of these scuffles,' Ma said, sitting down in the window again and peering out, obviously looking for Da in the dim street.

Bridget thought that rather than growing out of scuffles, her father was doing the opposite. He seemed to be getting more set in his ways as he got older, more convinced that his way was the right way, with no argument likely to change his mind.

'Ma,' she said, wanting to cheer her mother up, 'shall I try on my dress? Would you check the hem is the right length now Janet's finished pinning it up?'

Her mother smiled gratefully and Bridget felt glad. 'Of course I will,' she said. 'Come on, then, let's see how it looks.'

Chapter Three

One month later

The bridal parade was a Wentworth tradition that went back decades. Ellen's grandmother Sal had told her she remembered it happening to her when she'd wed her husband, Peter. And when a Wentworth girl married another Wentworth employee, as Bridget was doing, then the celebrations were doubled.

The bride-to-be was dressed up in a funny gown – though Ellen was sure the one she'd created for her sister was the best yet – and pushed around the factory in a trolley, while the employees cheered and wished her well for the future. It was a lot of fun. And, Ellen had to admit, if there was one thing the factory was short on, it was fun. She thought that was why the bridal parades were so popular – they provided a brief break from the monotony of the day.

Ellen had dragged herself out of bed when it was still pitch-dark, and now she was on her way to work early because she had a list as long as her arm of things to do before Bridget's big day. She wanted to ask Janet to help her get Bridget into the flouncy dress for the parade, which was happening later that afternoon, and get someone to find a trolley to push Bridget around in.

Walking through the large factory gates, Ellen stifled a giggle as she thought about her strait-laced sister being stuffed into the gown and then wheeled around the factory. It would do Bridget good to have some fun. For someone who was about to get married, she was always so serious.

'You look pleased with yourself.'

Ellen turned to see Bridget's fiancé Malcolm standing by the gate. She was almost half an hour early but he was still there before her. Typical Malcolm. She forced a smile onto her face. 'Just thinking about the plans for the parade later,' she said.

Malcolm frowned. 'Oh, I'm not sure that's a good idea, Ellen.'

'It's all arranged.' Ellen gritted her teeth.

'Well, maybe you should unarrange it? I'm management now, Ellen, and it's important that I give the right impression.'

'What impression is that?' Ellen said innocently, thinking that if he meant the impression of being a pompous know-it-all then he was doing very well.

Malcolm glared at her. 'Management,' he said again. 'You might be happy staying on the factory floor, Ellen, but I've got plans, and I don't want anything to stop me. I'm on my way to bigger things. Better things.'

'Good for you,' Ellen said, brimming with false jollity. 'Do you know what? I'm pretty sure Mr Beresford said he'd come along to the parade too.'

'Mr Beresford did?' Malcolm looked thoughtful. Ellen had no idea whether Mr Beresford would come; it was simply wishful thinking on her part. But Bridget worked in the clerical department and now so did Janet. Surely Mr Beresford would have heard them talking about the parade? It was going to be the first bridal parade since he'd arrived at the factory and Ellen thought he was bound to be curious. She was almost certain he'd be there. So certain, in fact, that she'd slept with her hair in rags last night so it would curl softly under her headscarf and frame her face, and she'd worn her good skirt with the wide waistband that she thought made her look particularly sleek, even though it would be hidden under her pinny.

She smiled at Malcolm, even though it took quite an effort. 'He said he's looking forward to it.'

'He told you that, did he?'

Should she lie? She thought about it, then dropped her gaze from Malcolm's. 'Not directly,' she muttered. 'But I'm fairly sure he knows about it.'

Vague though she was, it was enough. Malcolm stood up a bit straighter. 'What time will it be?'

'Four o'clock,' said Ellen, starting to walk away before he changed his mind again. 'Bring your management pals.'

She hurried on, past the offices and round to the entrance to her bit of the factory. This was where the magic happened, she always thought. Where bits of metal and wood were brought together to make the beautiful Wentworth sewing machines that were sent from here in Clydebank, all around the world. Ellen herself was a cabinet polisher. It was skilled work and it was so rewarding, seeing the dull wood transformed into a piece of furniture anyone would be proud to have in their home.

She looked up at the huge factory clock that hung overhead. Her shift would start soon, but first she had to find a trolley. The parade would be a disaster if that wasn't sorted out.

Pulling her hat down over her ears because the wind was bitter, Ellen darted across the courtyard.

'Ellen Kelly?' a voice said. She turned to see Mr McIver, the factory foreman, with a young woman who was gazing around her with wide eyes.

'Yes?'

'This is Sadie Franklin,' he said. 'New in cabinet polishing.'

'Replacing Janet?' Ellen said with a frown. She was still a little cross about Janet going to work in clerical.

'That's right,' Mr McIver said. 'Can you give her a wee tour, show her where everything is, before the bell goes?'

'All right,' said Ellen reluctantly, because she hadn't had a chance to find a trolley, but she did love giving tours of the factory and it was a good chance to meet the new girl. And, of course, no one ever said no to McIver.

'I'm Ellen,' she said, holding out her hand to shake.

The other woman went to take Ellen's hand then pulled back and wiped her fingers on her skirt. 'Sorry,' she said. 'I'm so nervous my palms are sweating. I'm Sadie.'

Ellen grinned at her. 'Let's start down here, shall we?'

Mr McIver nodded his thanks and headed off across the court-yard. Ellen glanced up at the big clock.

'We've only got about a quarter of an hour, so we'll have to be quick,' she said. 'Come on.'

She hurried off towards the timberyard, with Sadie following.

'How much do you know about Wentworth?' she asked over her shoulder.

'Only that it's so much bigger than I thought it would be,' Sadie said in an awed tone. 'It's like a city.'

'Aye it is.' Ellen stopped at the edge of the timberyard. She clambered up onto a low wall and held her hand out for Sadie. 'Come up, and you'll get a good view.'

Sadie hauled herself up, and stood open-mouthed, staring at the yard.

'Right,' said Ellen, getting into her stride because she really was proud of Wentworth. 'They say it takes forty-one pairs of hands to make a Wentworth machine. Our sewing machines are sent all over the world and they're twice as fast as the most experienced seamstress.'

'Goodness,' said Sadie faintly.

'We've got our own train line,' Ellen said, pointing across to where the tracks were just about visible, glinting in the early morning gloom. 'And the canal, of course. So you're right, it is like a city. There are twelve thousand people working here and we make everything, even the packing crates that the machines are sent out in.'

She took a deep breath. 'It's quiet now, but once the bell goes, this yard will be full of men. This part of the factory is all men and it's so noisy and dusty. The foundry's over there – that's where they make the metal parts of the machines. You wouldn't believe the heat of it, Sadie. And you can't hear yourself think when it's all going. Turn around.'

Sadie obediently turned and Ellen tugged her a little further along the wall, to where there was a clear sightline down to the street. 'Look.'

Coming along the road, towards the factory, were the workers. Hundreds and thousands of them, ready to start their shift. Like a wave of people, flowing towards the gates.

'Those folk are all coming from Clydebank,' Ellen said, amused by Sadie's startled face. 'But on the other side of the factory will be the ones coming from the station. Lots of workers come through from Glasgow every day.'

'I live in Glasgow,' said Sadie.

'So you'll come in the other way, but there will be just as many folk streaming in. You wouldn't have seen them today because you were early.'

She jumped down off the wall, and gestured for Sadie to follow. 'Over there is where the machines are moulded, then they're dipped and sprayed in there – I hate it in that part of the factory because the smell gets in your nose and your throat and you can taste it for days.'

Ellen pushed open the door into the main factory hall and they were hit with warm air and the hum of the start of the day. The workers were arriving now and there was a buzz as machines started up and conversations were had.

'So this is where the serial numbers are put on, and the Wentworth names and the designs transferred to the machines. Hiya, Marion.'

'Hi, Ellen,' said a woman who was tying on her pinny. 'How's your ma?'

'Not so bad, thanks.'

They walked on, Ellen hurrying Sadie a little because there was a lot to see, and the bell would be going any minute.

'The machines are so beautiful,' Sadie said, looking around her.

Ellen beamed with pride. 'Aren't they? And they're all checked and double-checked. Every bit of them.' She gestured to one side. 'Shuttles and spindles over there,' she said, waving to a man starting up one of the huge saws. 'Hello, Uncle Bobby.'

'Hi, Ellen. How's that da of yours? I heard he was in a bit of trouble at the match?'

'Aye, well, you know what he's like.'

'Don't I just?'

Ellen chuckled. 'Down there are the furnaces – that bit of the factory is right on the canal because they use the water for cooling. And over there is needle-making. That's a tough job, that is. Fiddly.'

'It all looks tough,' Sadie said in a small voice. 'I've never seen anything like it.'

'You'll get used to it soon enough. Come on, you've still got to see the best bit.'

Ellen led Sadie down a corridor, along to another enormous part of the factory.

'This,' she said proudly. 'This is the cabinet department.'

The air felt gritty with sawdust and the smell of shavings was in the air. Ellen loved the smell of wood. It was in her blood.

'My da used to work here,' she said. 'He was a cabinet maker. It was him who got me and my sister our jobs.' She breathed in deeply, savouring the smell. 'Here's where they make the covers for the machines, and the cabinets. Then the treadles and tables are assembled and the machines are put inside. Then the cabinets are varnished through there.'

She went through another set of doors. 'And here's where we do the most important job of all,' she joked. 'This is cabinet polishing.'

'Right,' Sadie said, looking a little stunned. 'This is us?'

'This is us. We polish the cabinets. There are fifteen of us.'

'And this is the last bit?'

'Not quite,' Ellen said. 'Here, follow me but we need to be quick.'

She and Sadie hurried outside again.

'From here, the machines go to the packing department, then they're loaded into cases and put on the trains to the docks.' She looked round and sighed in relief to see a familiar face. 'Oh, thank goodness, there's Jock. Uncle Jock!'

'Hiya Ellen. What are you up to out here? You don't belong in packing.'

'Just showing Sadie round,' Ellen said. She gave Jock what she hoped was a winning smile. 'And I'm hoping for a wee favour, actually.'

'Oh aye?'

'Can I have a trolley later?'

'What for?'

'Bridget.'

Jock let out a hearty laugh. 'That poor lass puts up with a lot from you, Ellen Kelly.'

Ellen rolled her eyes. 'I put up with a lot from her too.'

'Come and see me when you're ready and I'll sort one out,' said Jock, 'Go on, get off. Bell's about to go.'

Pleased to have got a trolley arranged, Ellen led Sadie back to cabinet polishing.

'So that's it,' she said. 'Wentworth.'

Sadie shook her head. 'It's so enormous, and we're such a tiny part of it all.'

'We are, but every bit of the factory is important. None of it works without the rest of it.'

'I like that,' Sadie said. 'Being part of something.'

Ellen grinned. 'Exactly.'

She took off her coat and hat and showed Sadie where to hang hers. Then they put on their headscarves and pinnies, Ellen tucking in the crucifix she wore because she wasn't really supposed to wear jewellery at work. Her gran had given the necklace to her and she never took it off.

'So you're not a Bankie?' she said to Sadie.

'A what?'

'You're not from Clydebank? You said you live in Glasgow?'

'That's right.' Sadie smoothed down her pinny.

'What made you come to work here, then?' Ellen asked.

'More money,' said Sadie frankly. 'I was working in a shop in the Gorbals. But the hours were short. Wentworth pays more, though it's a lot more work.' She swallowed. 'I didn't realise . . .'

Ellen felt a bit sorry for her. 'It is hard work, but you'll be fine.'

Sadie nodded. 'I hope so,' she said. 'We really need the money.'

She pressed her lips together and Ellen had a horrible sense that she was trying not to cry. 'My da died,' Sadie said all in a hurry.

Ellen felt awkward, unsure how to react. She wished Bridget was here because she'd say just the right thing to make Sadie feel better.

But Bridget wasn't here, so instead Ellen patted Sadie on the arm in a clumsy way, and said: 'You'll be grand.'

Sadie took a breath and gathered herself. 'Aye.'

'You'll be one of us in no time,' Ellen reassured her. 'In fact, I'd say you already are.'

The women smiled at one another, and Ellen felt a little rush of warmth. She would miss Janet alongside her, but she felt she'd just made a new friend.

'Come to Bridget's parade later, that'll be fun,' she said. 'It's a hoot.'

'Parade?' asked Sadie with a frown. 'What is it?'

'My sister Bridget – she works in clerical up on the top floor – she's getting married, so we're going to put her in a ridiculous dress and push her around in one of Jock's trolleys,' Ellen explained. 'It sounds silly but it's a good way to see the fun side of the factory.'

'There's a fun side?' Sadie said wryly.

Ellen laughed. She liked this woman, who clearly had a sense of humour despite the sadness in her eyes. 'Every now and then,' she said.

'Sounds like I shouldn't miss it, in that case.'

'And if you like, you could join our sewing bee. There's me, and Bridget, and my friend Janet, and a few others. We say we sew, but really it's just a chance for a cup of tea and a blether once a week.'

'I'd like that,' Sadie said. 'I've got little ones at home I need to help see to, but I'll come when I can.'

'You've got children?' Ellen was surprised because Sadie really didn't look any older than she was, and she was only nineteen.

'Three,' Sadie said, nodding earnestly.

'THREE?'

'Two brothers and my wee sister.' Sadie laughed and Ellen did too.

'I thought you meant your own weans,' she said, rolling her eyes at her misunderstanding.

Sadie shook her head vigorously. 'Ma's doing her best but she's not well, and she's missing Da, you know?'

Ellen squeezed Sadie's arm in empathy and was pleased when her new friend smiled in appreciation.

'I do,' she said.

Sadie jumped as the factory bell rang loudly.

'That's us, then,' Ellen said. 'Ready for it?'

'As I'll ever be.'

Chapter Four

Bridget didn't want to do the stupid parade. She didn't want to wear the stupid underwear dress. At this very moment she didn't want to get married at all. The whole thing was getting out of hand.

She jammed a fresh sheet of paper into her typewriter and turned the dial violently to feed it through.

'Easy does it,' said her colleague Maggie, who sat next to her and who was always far too interested in what Bridget was doing and not nearly interested enough in her own work.

Bridget turned to glare at her. 'Shh,' she said crossly. 'I'm very busy doing letters for Mr Beresford and I need to concentrate.'

She peered at her notepad, but the little shorthand scribbles danced about in front of her eyes. She was so tired. She'd not been sleeping for worrying about the wedding, and if she was honest, about what came afterwards. She liked Malcolm. She did. He was nice. He would make her a good husband even if he could be a bit stuffy. It wasn't that she didn't want him to be her husband. It was more that the closer the wedding came, the more she understood that she didn't really want a husband at all.

She began typing, clattering the keys in the hope that it would put Maggie off talking to her again.

It didn't work.

'It's your parade today,' Maggie sighed. 'I love the parades. Are you excited? I'm just green with envy about it. You'll make a beautiful bride, Bridget.'

Bridget glanced at Maggie. She'd spent years caring for her mother who'd not long passed away. Now Maggie was thirty and lived alone, desperately ashamed of her spinster status. Bridget, though, thought Maggie was the lucky one. Even when she was wee, she would dream at night of waking up in the empty flat, prowling the rooms alone and stretching out in bed. And then when she woke up for real and found Ellen's cold feet on her shins, and heard her father's snores in the room next door, she would feel horribly disappointed. Now she looked at Maggie's eager face and felt embarrassed.

'I'm very excited,' she said. 'I can't wait for the wedding.'

'And your Malcolm's been promoted, I hear,' Maggie said, clasping her hands together by her heart. 'You must be so proud of him.'

'I am,' Bridget said truthfully. Then a moment of mischief overtook her, and she leaned slightly towards Maggie and whispered: 'I just wish he'd stop mentioning it every hour of the day.'

Maggie looked shocked for a second, and then she giggled, covering her mouth with her hand so their boss – Mrs Whittington – wouldn't hear their chatter.

Bridget smiled and turned back to her work.

Some days at Wentworth dragged, but today had sped by so fast Bridget was surprised when she heard the bell that announced the end of the shift.

She put the cover on her typewriter slowly. Maggie was already wearing her coat and gloves when she looked up.

'Come on, Bridget,' she said, tugging on Bridget's sleeve. 'It's going to be a hoot.'

'I'm coming.' Reluctantly, she followed Maggie out of the large room where the typists sat and down the stairs through the parts department where the men were all packing up.

'Looking good, girls,' one of them called.

Bridget tutted, but Maggie – who was really rather pretty – gave him a glance over her shoulder and swayed her hips as she walked on.

And then they were outside and there was Ellen looking like she was about to burst with excitement, alongside Janet, and just about everyone Bridget knew at Wentworth.

She wanted to turn tail and run, hide under her desk until everyone had forgotten this silly parade, but Ellen was so excited and happy, Bridget couldn't bear to ruin this for her. So once more, she forced a smile onto her face and threw her hands out wide.

'Here I am,' she said.

'Bridget,' Malcolm appeared at her elbow, 'Have you really thought about this?'

She froze and turned slowly to see her fiancé, his brow furrowed and his thinning hair ruffled as though he'd been scratching his head. Which he probably had been doing. Malcolm always scratched his head when he was worrying about something.

'I spoke to Ellen earlier and I mentioned that I was concerned that this might reflect badly on us.'

Bridget gave Malcolm a disdainful look.

'On us?'

He did, to his credit, wince a little sheepishly. 'On me.'

She glared at him for a second and then she gave him a quick kiss on the cheek.

'It's fine,' she said. 'You're making your mark at the factory and nothing I do – not even this silly parade – can spoil that. You're too clever.'

Her heart twisted a little bit because she hated Malcolm worrying about things and yet worry he did. She couldn't blame him, really. He'd grown up with nothing. His da had died very young, and his ma was a devil for her nerves – made worse by her fondness for a drink – and would often take to her bed, leaving the wee ones to fend for themselves. And there was no money, ever. Malcolm and his siblings had often been hungry. They'd gone without food, shoes, clothes and bedding, and when all was said and done, without love.

Bridget had met him one day after another of Ma's babies had died and she was staying out of her way because she hated to see her cry. She'd felt sorry for him and had given him a hand with the little ones that were crowding round him. They'd hardly been more than babies themselves then, but they'd become firm friends. When Malcolm's ma died, the weans went to live with a cousin in Paisley, and Malcolm was left alone. He was working by then, living hand to mouth on a meagre salary, and teaching himself bookkeeping at night, though he was still only fourteen. Bridget used to take him home for tea and her ma would sneak extra slices of bread and jam into his bag. At some point, everyone had just started talking about when Bridget and Malcolm would get married. And now it was happening. She was still a little surprised by it all.

Bridget knew better than anyone that Malcolm getting the job at Wentworth, and his sharp brain and head for figures being noticed by management, had changed his life utterly.

She knew all that. She understood why he loved the factory and why he wanted to impress. It was still a little annoying when he told her what to do, but she understood.

Feeling a rush of affection for him, she looped her arm through his and squeezed it.

'Ellen is convinced that Mr Beresford is coming,' she said in a quiet voice. 'I think she truly believes their eyes will meet over the parade trolley. She has curled her hair and I think that's her favourite skirt she's wearing. She thinks Mr Beresford will fall head over heels in love with her.'

Malcolm gave her a small smile. 'Chance would be a fine thing.'

'He's here.' Bridget nodded over to the back of the gathering crowd where she'd spotted Mr Beresford.

'Maybe I should go and make sure Ellen doesn't bother him?'

'That's an excellent idea,' Bridget said. 'Go on.' She gave him a tiny push and to her relief, Malcolm took a deep breath and nodded.

'Right.'

He weaved his way through the crowd and Bridget turned her attention to Ellen, who was hovering close by, clutching the huge billowing cloud of the underwear dress.

'Is he all right?' she asked.

'He's fine.' Bridget smiled at her sister. 'He's gone to speak to Mr Beresford.'

'Is he here?' Ellen's eyes gleamed and she stood on tiptoes trying to see over the crowd. 'Maybe I should go and introduce myself?'

'Don't even think about it,' Bridget said, laughing. 'Malcolm would faint with the shock of it.'

Ellen chuckled. 'That's true,' she said cheerfully. 'Come on, then. Are you ready?'

Bridget screwed her face up. 'No.'

'Bridget,' warned Ellen.

'I'm ready.'

Ellen gave a little squeal of joy and suddenly Bridget was surrounded by lots of excited women, pulling the dress over her head and laughing and calling to one another, and strange as it was, she began to enjoy herself.

She let them tie ribbons into her hair and daub her cheeks with rouge like a china doll, and then an unfamiliar woman with very dark, very shiny hair and sharp, flashing eyes, appeared with a trolley and Bridget found herself wedged into it with her legs dangling over the edge in a most ungainly fashion.

'Let's go,' Ellen called.

She and Janet, and the woman with the sparkling eyes, began to push Bridget, and others joined in and there was cheering and laughter and shouts of 'Congratulations!' and 'Good luck!'.

She sped past Malcolm and Mr Beresford, who were chatting like old friends and they both clapped, and Mr Beresford slapped Malcolm on the back, and he beamed with pride, and Bridget was glad.

Round and round they went until she started to feel queasy and begged Ellen to stop.

'Please,' she begged, laughing and hiccupping at the same time. 'That's enough.'

Ellen and Janet stopped the trolley and Bridget clambered out, so desperate to be back on firm ground that she didn't care if she was looking unladylike. She glanced over at Malcolm just in time to see a flash of disapproval in his eyes before he turned back to Mr Beresford, so she took her time adjusting her skirt as she pulled off the silly gown.

'Did you enjoy it?' Ellen said, gathering up the flounces of the underwear dress.

'I did.' Bridget was telling the truth – it had been fun. 'But I'm not in a hurry to do it again.'

Ellen laughed. 'Well, that's lucky, isn't it? Because you'll never have to do it again. Marriage is forever. I'll give the dress to Mrs Ross and they can use it in the testing department for scraps.'

Bridget felt light-headed. She steadied herself against the wall as Ellen dashed off again, and the dark-haired woman looked at her with concern.

'Are you all right?'

'Just a bit dizzy,' she said, trying to sound cheerful. 'Too much twisting and turning.'

'I'm Sadie, by the way,' the woman said. 'Ellen told me I should come along. I'm new.'

'New to Wentworth?'

'That's right. I'm in cabinet polishing with Ellen.'

'Are you settling in?' Bridget was glad of the distraction of making small talk with Sadie.

'It was a little overwhelming at first but now Ellen's taken me under her wing, I've got a feeling I'll be fine.'

Bridget chuckled fondly. 'That's Ellen all over. She's very welcoming and the only thing she loves more than meeting new people is Wentworth.'

'She's been telling me all about it.'

'Bending your ear?'

'A bit, but it's nice she enjoys her work so much.'

'It is.'

'You don't feel the same?' Sadie looked at Bridget and she dropped her gaze, feeling uncomfortable.

'Ellen and I have always worked here,' she said, choosing her words carefully. 'My father used to work here. My gran worked here. Ellen's friend Janet works here. Malcolm works here.' She breathed out. 'Sometimes it's a bit much, that's all.'

Sadie nodded. 'It's much bigger than I'd expected.'

'It's like a whole world,' Bridget said. 'But sometimes I'd like to see what else is out there.'

Sadie snorted, much to Bridget's surprise. 'It's not up to much,' she said, and Bridget saw a shadow behind her eyes.

'No,' she said thoughtfully. 'I'm just being silly. Worrying about the wedding and everything changing overnight.'

'I understand that,' Sadie said. 'Change is frightening.' And then to Bridget's surprise, Sadie reached out her hand and squeezed her fingers quickly. 'You'll be fine,' she said. 'I know it.'

Bridget hoped she was right.

'Come to the wedding,' she said on a whim. 'It's next Saturday – a week tomorrow – at St Joseph's. It's not until four o'clock, so you'll have time to get changed after work.'

'Really?' Sadie looked at Bridget with a sharp gaze that made Bridget feel like she wasn't totally convinced that the wedding was going to happen at all. Or perhaps that was just her imagination running away with her.

'It would be nice if you could make it.'

'I'd like that,' Sadie said with a smile. 'Thank you. I'll be there.'

'So will I,' Bridget said firmly, ignoring the odd glance Sadie gave her. 'So will I.'

Chapter Five

Since Sadie's father had died, her mother had lost her enthusiasm for religion. Well, for anything really. Sadie thought her ma had always assumed she'd be the first to go – she suffered badly with her chest and the wet Glasgow winters played havoc with her breathing. So when her husband Gerry had just dropped down dead at work one day, it had fair knocked the stuffing out of her. Out of all of them to be honest.

Sadie still wasn't sure how it was that her huge, healthy da – a solid, beast of a man who could lift up all three of his younger children at the same time even though Daniel was almost twelve – could suddenly stop existing. It made no sense to her that he could be there one day, waving them all goodbye and doing the silly thing he always did when he walked past the window of their ground-floor flat, pretending to be rowing in a boat, and then just not come home again.

But that was what had happened and as much as Sadie couldn't quite understand it, her poor ma was in a worse state.

Da had died in October and now it was February and this winter had been cold, hard and bleak.

Now though, walking home from the station after Bridget's parade, she felt brighter. She'd enjoyed herself today. She liked Ellen and Bridget and she'd been touched to have been invited to the sewing bee, and to Bridget's wedding.

She looked up at the darkening sky. The streets were quiet here because this was a Jewish neighbourhood and it was Friday. Sadie hunched down in her coat, hoping she'd not be spotted coming home from work after sunset, but of course as soon as she rounded the corner, there was Mrs Henson, the rabbi's sister, of all people, carrying a challah loaf for her Shabbat dinner. The smell made Sadie's mouth water.

'Sadie Franklin,' Mrs Henson said. How did she even manage to make Sadie's name sound like an insult?

Sadie pulled her coat round herself a little tighter. 'Good evening, Mrs Henson. You're out late for a Friday evening.'

'I got chatting,' Mrs Henson said. 'You know how it is?'

Sadie smiled and went to walk past, but Mrs Henson hadn't finished.

'I've not seen you in a while, Sadie,' she said pointedly. 'You've not been to Shul.'

Sadie closed her eyes briefly. 'No,' she said. She knew that actually no one much cared whether she went to the synagogue or not – it was the men's attendance that really mattered – but Mrs Henson liked to make herself feel important.

'Will you be there tomorrow?'

Sadie shook her head. 'I've got a new job and I have to work on Saturdays now.'

Mrs Henson pinched her lips together.

And because Sadie was tired, and because the wind was cold and her fingers ached, and she didn't want to go home and be thrown back into the worries that awaited her, she sighed heavily. 'My da died, Mrs Henson,' she said, speaking slowly and clearly as though Mrs Henson might be hard of hearing. 'And I am the only person earning in our family. And Ma is ill, and Daniel and Joseph just don't stop eating and growing, and Rachel's shoes are worn right through. And our flat is too small, too cold and too damp, but it still has to be paid for or we will be on the streets. And so, no, I haven't been to Shul. But I'm sure the rabbi understands.'

Mrs Henson's jaw dropped and feeling slightly better, Sadie left her gawping and walked home, thinking about her mother. She hoped she'd had a good day because recently she'd had more and more times when she couldn't even get out of bed. Sadie knew her ma suffered with her chest, but she also knew that sometimes Ma just couldn't cope with her grief and staying in bed was easier when that happened.

Once upon a time their weekends would have been full of chatter and laughter, then they were quiet and sad. But Sadie was hoping they'd turned a corner; that the worst, most shocking part of their grief was over, and now they could get on with feeling sad and missing Da, while also living. At least, that was what she hoped.

'I'm home!' she called as she let herself through the front door. Daniel was wandering past with a book in his hand – he always had a book in his hand – and he looked up at her for the briefest of seconds and mumbled 'hello' then disappeared into the bedroom where all four children slept, even though Sadie was eighteen and really not a child any more.

Smoothing down her hair, which was ruffled from the wind, Sadie went into the warm kitchen where her mother was sitting at the table playing cards with her best friend Miriam. Miriam's husband Jack was sitting beside the fire reading the newspaper. Ma looked pale and wan next to Miriam, who was positively glowing with health – or perhaps just from the cold wind outside that had reddened her cheeks – but she wasn't in bed, which Sadie took as a good sign.

'Hiya,' she said, kissing her ma's cheek and squeezing Miriam's hand. 'I just saw that Mrs Henson. She was giving me bother about working on Saturdays and not going to Shul.'

'Och,' said her mother in disgust, waving her hand as though flapping away an irritating fly. 'She's a nudnik. Ignore her.'

Sadie grinned at the Yiddish phrase that summed up Mrs Henson so precisely, then turned to Miriam. 'Is Noah not here?'

she asked, smoothing down her hair again and trying to be casual.

'He's working,' said Jack, rolling his eyes as if to say, 'What can you do?'

'That boy's always working,' Miriam added.

Sadie grinned as she shrugged off her coat and hung it up. She knew Miriam and Jack were fiercely proud of Noah, who was a schoolteacher. He would be doing extra classes at the synagogue for his students. But she suddenly realised she'd been hoping to see him and that she was disappointed he wasn't around. What was this? She'd known Noah forever and saw him almost every day. Why was she suddenly making sure her hair looked nice and hoping he'd turn up? Flustered at the thought, she pulled out a chair and sat down.

'Deal me in?' she asked. 'How are you feeling, Ma?'

Her mother patted her hand. 'Better, I think.'

'Glad to hear it.' Sadie caught Miriam's eye and gave her a questioning look. She was reassured as Miriam nodded. Ma really had been all right without Sadie. She hoped it would be the same on Monday, when her hours were longer. 'Have you eaten?'

'Miriam made some oatcakes. I put a couple aside for you – hid them from the boys.'

Sadie laughed. 'Is Rachel here?'

'She's out playing with Joseph.'

Happy that everyone was fed and accounted for, Sadie settled back in her chair.

'How was your first day at Wentworth, Sadie?' Miriam asked, shuffling the cards deftly.

'It was good. I made a friend. Two, in fact.'

'Two friends,' Miriam said, throwing her hands up in delight.

'Stop teasing her,' Sadie's mother said fondly. 'Tell us about your new friends, Sadie.'

34

'Ellen and Bridget,' Sadie said. 'Bridget's getting married next weekend and she's invited me.'

'That's nice,' said Miriam. 'Isn't that nice, Jack?'

From behind his newspaper, Jack muttered something.

'What's going on the world, Uncle Jack?' Sadie asked, picking up her cards and looking at her hand.

'Nothing very exciting,' he grumbled. 'Suffragettes making trouble.'

'Good for them,' said Sadie and her mother together and they both laughed.

Jack rolled his eyes. 'And some instructions for the census,' he said.

'When is it?' Miriam asked. 'April?'

'Aye. April the second.'

'And what are we to do?'

Jack scanned the page. 'We'll be sent a form to fill in. We are to write down everyone who is under our roof,' he paused, 'and alive, at midnight on the second. Then the forms will be collected.'

'That's not too difficult,' Sadie said.

'Not for us, but some folk can't write,' Jack pointed out.

'Maybe once they see how many families are crammed into flats smaller than ours, or into single-ends, something will be done,' Miriam said.

Sadie looked at her mother whose face was even paler than it had been. 'What's wrong, Ma?'

'I'll have to put myself down as head of the household,' she said, looking stricken. 'I won't put your da's name this time.'

Sadie winced. 'Oh Ma,' she murmured, taking her mother's hand. 'I can fill the form in for you.'

Ma gave her a small, sad smile. 'Thanks, doll.'

Sadie remembered that as she walked up the path to St Joseph's on Bridget's wedding day. She wondered if she'd ever find someone she wanted to spend her life with, the way her ma had found her da. The way Bridget had found Malcolm. Though from what Ellen had said, Bridget and Malcolm had just grown up together, like the roots of two trees intertwining.

Just like she and Noah had.

She'd not seen Noah for ages, because she seemed to have spent every waking moment at Wentworth this week. Or on the train, travelling to and from Wentworth. She even dreamed about Wentworth. But she missed Noah. And she wondered why she missed him. Though she quite liked missing him, because it reminded her how well they got on and how much she enjoyed spending time with him. And the whole thing was like a confusing tangle in her head.

She shook her head gently to dislodge the thoughts of Noah and gazed up at the church. It was another bitterly cold day, but the rain had stopped at least, and she was pleased for Ellen, who'd been fretting about Bridget's dress getting soaked. Bridget hadn't seemed too worried, mind you.

Sadie couldn't wait to see her new friend in her wedding gown. Bridget wasn't what you'd call pretty, not exactly. Sadie thought 'handsome' would be a better word. Whereas Ellen was small with delicate features like a little fairy or an elf or some other woodland creature, Bridget was taller – sturdy, Sadie's mother would say – with a nose that was a little too big to be dainty and a mouth that was a fraction too wide. But Sadie thought Bridget was rather striking, so she knew that what Ellen called the 'simple' dress and the headband trimmed with silk flowers that Ellen had patiently stitched by hand, would flatter her perfectly.

She didn't know anyone in the church except Janet, who was at the front with a woman who she assumed was Mrs Kelly because she looked so like Ellen, so she slid into a pew at the back on the bride's side and took the chance to have a good look around at the other guests.

Everyone was very nicely turned out. The women were all wearing hats and the men's hair was neatly slicked down, their moustaches neat. And there was a little buzz of excited conversation that Sadie liked.

'How do you know Bridget?' asked a woman in the pew in front, turning round to look at Sadie. She was about the same age as Mrs Kelly, and she was wearing a hat that had obviously been squashed on top of a wardrobe or in a cupboard because it was bent out of shape on one side. But she had a lovely smile and Sadie warmed to her immediately.

'Work,' she said. 'Wentworth.'

'Are you in the clerical department?' The woman looked impressed.

Sadie shook her head. 'No, I'm in cabinet polishing with Ellen. I've only been there a little while.'

'How are you getting on?'

Sadie glanced around and lowered her voice. 'It's really hard work.'

The woman laughed loudly and the sound echoed up into the arched roof of the church making Sadie feel self-conscious, but no one seemed to mind. 'I worked at Wentworth for years,' she said. 'First in shuttles, then needles for a while. It's all hard. But you're settling in, are you?'

'Ellen's looking after me.'

'Nice,' the woman said in approval. 'She's a smashing girl, Ellen. She sees the good in everyone and everything.'

'She's been very kind.'

'I've known her since she was born – before she was born.' The woman laughed again. 'She's like a wee ray of sunshine, that girl. I wish I could see the world the way she sees it, you know?'

Sadie nodded. Ellen was so happy all the time, and she really did find the good in every situation. She'd even confided in Sadie that she wasn't overly fond of Malcolm but had added, 'As long as Bridget's happy, so am I.'

The woman patted Sadie's arm and turned back to face the front of the church. Sadie followed her gaze to where Malcolm stood. He was alone apart from the priest, and Sadie looked round to see if he had a best man, but she couldn't see anyone. She felt a little bit sorry for him. Malcolm's side of the church was much emptier than Bridget's, too. And, she couldn't help but notice, much quieter and less chatty than where she sat.

A loud chord on the organ startled her out of her thoughts, and she sat up straighter as the 'Wedding March' began to play. The doors opened and in came Bridget on the arm of her father.

Mr Kelly looked proud and happy. Bridget's face was covered by her veil, but Sadie could tell she was anxious from the way she walked with her shoulders up beside her ears and her knuckles were white where she was gripping her da's arm a bit too tightly.

Ellen walked behind carrying a basket of foliage. She was wearing a pretty, pale-pink dress and she was virtually skipping down the aisle, beaming at all the guests and even waving or saying 'hello' to some as she passed. Sadie smiled as she passed because Ellen's grin was so infectious.

There was, Sadie thought, a lot of talk and a lot of standing up and sitting down again, before they got to the actual wedding ceremony. By then Bridget seemed more relaxed. She even laughed a tiny bit when Malcolm stumbled over his vows and muddled up the order of her names, calling her Ruth Bridget instead of Bridget Ruth.

Then it was all done and the congregation stood up as the newlyweds walked down the aisle together, with Ellen bouncing along behind them.

The woman Sadie had been chatting to earlier turned to watch the bride and groom go by and gave her hearty chuckle again. 'You'd think Ellen was the bride, with how happy she looks,' she said. 'Bridget's much harder to read.'

'Bridget's lovely,' Sadie said loyally. 'I like her.' She watched as the couple reached the door of the church and Bridget took her hand from the crook of Malcolm's arm. 'I think they'll be very happy together.'

But she wasn't sure she meant it.

Chapter Six

A few weeks later

Ellen knew she'd asked these questions before but she loved hearing the stories about the factories in Glasgow. Sadie had proved to be full of knowledge about how other factories worked and Ellen was hanging on her every word. She was absolutely convinced that Mr Beresford was going to change how Wentworth operated and make everything a bit less . . . well, hard.

'So they have football matches? Every week?'

'Not in the summer,' Sadie said. 'How about this colour of thread?'

Ellen shook her head and rummaged in the basket to find a darker shade of blue. 'This one.' She threw it at Sadie, who caught it in one hand.

'Perfect,' Sadie said, holding the thread against the skirt she was mending. Sadie always did mending at the bee – she seemed to have endless bags of her siblings' clothes that needed darning, or hems let down, or taken up. 'How do you do that? Match colours without them even being next to each other.'

'Ellen's always had a good eye for colour,' Janet said with a devilish glint in her eye. 'Though you'd never tell to look at her clothes.'

'Oh shush,' Ellen told her happily. She leaned back against

the chair where she was sitting and sighed with contentment. She loved these regular get-togethers where they could sew and chat and have a giggle. Her da always went for a drink on the nights the women gathered for their sewing bee, so it was just the girls. Janet, Sadie, and Ma and Gran, along with a couple of Ma's friends who were all huddled beside the fire just now talking about something in fierce whispers. Ellen thought it was probably that Isobel's rotten husband Neal had disappeared again, and good riddance to him. Poor Isobel worked all hours, and didn't Neal just spend all the money she made on drink? Isobel was much better off without him and thank the lord for her friends because they'd look out for her and wasn't it better to have good girlfriends than a waste-of-space husband anyway?

She turned her attention back to Sadie. 'And did you say there's a factory that has a choir?'

'Oh aye, I think so. I'm sure someone said so,' said Sadie, tutting as she examined the hem of the skirt. 'This is terrible. I'm not sure what Rachel does to her clothes.'

'And tell me, do you know if any of the Glasgow factories have summer picnics? There was a picnic at the factory Mr Beresford came from, you know? In Lancashire.'

'I know.' Sadie gave Ellen an exasperated, but, Ellen thought also, affectionate, glance. 'You've told me enough times. I think the weather must be nicer down in Lancashire.'

'I just really hope Wentworth does something similar,' Ellen said. 'There are so many of us, it would be a wonderful thing to have a picnic for the whole factory. Imagine everyone out on the green?'

'Actually, that does sound fun,' Janet admitted.

Ellen clasped her hands to her chest. 'It sounds wonderful. I can't wait.' She was convinced it was only a matter of time before Mr Beresford and the rest of the bosses introduced all the things that had worked so well elsewhere. 'And tell me more about the choirs. Was there ...'

'Ellen, stop blethering for five minutes because I really need to mend this skirt,' Sadie said, mock-sternly. 'Rachel needs it for school.'

'Right you are.' Ellen nodded. She picked up the stocking she was supposed to be darning, then put it back in her lap because she had more to say. 'How are you liking Wentworth?'

'I like it,' Sadie said. 'It's . . .' She thought for a second and Ellen jumped in.

'Satisfying?'

'Yes, that's it. I like seeing the cabinets looking so beautiful and imagining them in someone's living room.'

'For a hundred years,' Ellen said proudly. 'Maybe even longer.'

'Right.' Sadie didn't look convinced, but Ellen knew the craftsmanship on Wentworth sewing machines would last forever.

Once more Sadie turned to her mending and Ellen looked at her stocking.

'I've barely had a chance to miss Bridget,' she said after a second of quiet. 'And it's actually quite nice that she's gone because I get the bedroom all to myself and I can be as untidy as I like without her nagging me. And she's here all the time anyway.'

'She comes home a lot, does she?' Janet asked.

Ellen rolled her eyes dramatically, even though she really enjoyed it when her sister came back with her after work. 'Malcolm's always at the factory now he's management. So Bridget comes for tea some days.' She thought about it. 'Most days, actually. But not tonight because Malcolm's home tonight so she wanted to cook for him. Mince, I think she said she was doing. Or was it fish? Anyway, she said she might pop in . . .'

And as if she'd made it so, there was the sound of the front door opening and Bridget came in.

'Hello,' she said. Her cheeks were rosy with the cold air, even though spring was on its way, and Ellen thought she looked very pretty, though her eyes looked a little red. Perhaps it was the wind.

'Mending a skirt, Sadie?' Bridget said, taking off her coat and hat.

'Trying to.' Sadie glared at Ellen and she made a face at her in response.

Janet giggled. 'Ellen's distracting her.'

'I know how that feels,' Bridget said. She sat down next to Sadie and held her hand out. 'Give it here, I'll have a look.'

Sadie handed the skirt over with relief, and Ellen saw her chance to get back to her favourite subject.

'I expect the football teams and whatnot are very good for building a real friendly feeling in a factory. People looking out for each other. Helping each other. Wentworth's like that already, mind, but a bit more fun can only be a good thing.'

Sadie nodded. 'I suppose so. Not everyone gets along the whole time, mind you.'

'Well, that's to be expected. It's like a family, isn't it? And families don't always get on.'

Bridget made a funny noise that sounded a little bit like a snort but when Ellen glanced in her direction, she was bent over the skirt, her needle flying in and out as she deftly mended the hem.

'I think Mr Beresford is going to make a real difference at Wentworth,' Ellen sighed. 'I imagine he's just been getting to see how it all works for the last few weeks, but now he's settled in he'll start making some changes.'

This time the noise Bridget made was very definitely a snort.

'What?' Ellen said, exasperated. 'What's wrong?'

Bridget shrugged. 'I'm not sure Mr Beresford is quite the knight in shining armour you think he is.'

Ellen glared at her. 'A new broom sweeps clean, Bridget. Everyone says he was brought in to shake things up.'

'Right.' Bridget looked back at the mending. 'If you say so.'

Ellen looked at Janet. 'What do you think, Janet?'

Janet shifted on her chair. 'I've not seen much of him, to be honest,' she muttered. 'Sadie, are you done with that blue thread?'

Ellen frowned at her friend, who just a few days ago had been telling her every detail of every moment that she'd seen Mr Beresford. How he'd walked past her desk last Wednesday and she'd smelled his cologne. How he'd been standing beside the window and she'd seen his face in profile and wasn't his nose a thing of beauty? How he'd smiled at all the typists and said 'good morning' on Saturday. How he rubbed his earlobe between his thumb and forefinger when he was reading. And suddenly she didn't want to talk about him? If Janet had announced she was a witch and turned herself into a frog, Ellen couldn't have been more shocked.

'Janet?' she began.

Janet stood up. 'Mrs Kelly?' she called over to Ellen's ma. 'Can I use the machine? I've got a skirt all cut and pinned but it'll take me ages to stitch it by hand.'

'Go ahead, doll,' said Ma.

Janet sat herself down at the Wentworth machine in the window and began to sew. Ellen knew she wouldn't be able to hear over the noise of the motor, so she turned back to her sister and Sadie and made a face to show that she thought Janet was being a bit strange about Mr Beresford.

'Have you seen much of him?' she asked Bridget.

'Just a normal amount,' her sister said. 'Just the usual.'

'And how was he?'

'Gosh, Ellen, give it a rest,' Bridget said. 'You need to get over this obsession with Beresford.'

'It's not an obsession,' Ellen said, affronted. 'I just think it's exciting, that's all. A new, young member of the team, ready to make a difference.'

'A new, young, handsome member of the team,' teased Sadie.

'Well, yes, that too,' Ellen giggled. 'Come on, Bridget, what do you think of him?'

'Honestly?' said Bridget. 'I don't like him.'

There was a stunned silence. Even Janet stopped sewing for a moment. Ellen gawped at Bridget, who rarely said a bad word about anyone.

'What do you mean you don't like him?'

'I just don't.' Bridget looked up at the ceiling. 'He's awfully pleased with himself, that's all.'

'Well, wouldn't you be,' Ellen said, 'if you had a face like that, and the brains to match?'

'Perhaps,' said Bridget tetchily. 'Perhaps not.'

'I know why you really don't like him.' Ellen sat up straighter.

'Oh please tell me,' Bridget said.

Ellen sighed. Bridget could be very annoying when she wanted to be.

'Because he's a rule breaker.'

'That's not the reason.'

'It is!' Ellen was triumphant. She knew her sister almost better than she knew herself. 'You hate people who don't follow the rules.'

Bridget didn't say anything. She just kept sewing, even though Ellen could clearly see that she'd already finished what she was mending.

Annoyed at not getting a response, Ellen got to her feet. 'Mr Beresford is a reformer,' she announced to the room. 'Everyone says so. Brought in to make changes – that's what we heard. And that's why Bridget doesn't like him.'

'Shut up, Ellen,' Bridget said.

'Bridget, be nice to your sister,' said Ma, pausing in her conversation with Isobel.

Bridget flung her head back in exasperation and Ellen felt another rush of triumph.

'Shut up,' Bridget said again, so quietly that Ellen barely heard her this time. Her voice sounded odd. Wavery. Tearful even. Ellen peered at her sister, whose eyes were bright.

'What's wrong?' she said, slightly defensive now. 'What's the matter? I'm only teasing you, Bridget.'

'It's fine,' Bridget said, closing her eyes as though she was gathering herself. 'You're just so . . .'

'Annoying?' Ellen said with what she hoped was a winning smile. 'Irritating? Infuriating?'

'Naïve.'

That was a new one. Startled, Ellen looked at Sadie, who shrugged.

'I'm not naïve. I don't even know what you mean by that,' Ellen said. She hated it when Bridget threw big words around and pretended she knew more than everyone else.

'I mean you just trot along in your own world thinking everything's sunlight and roses, and you're wrong.'

Ellen felt her stomach twist. 'Wrong, how?' she said. 'Is something the matter, Bridget? Are you ill?'

Beside her, she felt Sadie and Janet grow still and quiet, and her stomach lurched again. 'Tell me, Bridget.'

Bridget folded her arms, looking bullish for a moment, then her expression softened. 'I'm not ill,' she said. She shook her head gently. 'I just don't like Mr Beresford. But I'm sorry for being so crabbit.'

'Sure?' Ellen had the oddest feeling that Bridget was hiding something.

'Sure.'

There was a pause as Ellen wondered if she should push it. But then Bridget smiled. It wasn't quite genuine, Ellen could tell, but it was an improvement.

'But please don't tell Malcolm I said that,' she said, sounding more upbeat. 'He'd probably drop down dead from the shock.'

'You're not fighting again, girls?' Ma said, coming over with a plate of wee biscuits made by Isobel to share.

'No, Ma,' Bridget said, turning to her with a smile. 'Just teasing.'

'That's right, teasing.' Ellen pinched a biscuit as her ma passed her and grinned. 'It's all fine.'

She sat back again, trying to stay cheerful, even though she had a gnawing feeling inside that there was something Bridget wasn't telling her. She watched her sister through narrowed eyes. No one kept secrets from Ellen for long. She was determined to find out what was going on.

Chapter Seven

Bridget was feeling wretched. A mixture of sadness and worry and sheer, red-raw rage. She'd never felt that way before and frankly she didn't know what to do about it. She was trying to listen to Janet's story about a coat she was planning to make, but she couldn't concentrate. Partly because she could feel Ellen's eyes on her, and partly because she couldn't stop thinking about the document she had in her bag. A document she'd taken from work.

She'd get the sack if anyone found out she'd taken it, that wasn't in doubt. She'd be escorted from the premises without being allowed to so much as time to stop and pick up her hat and gloves. She remembered it happening to that Mulvey boy who'd worked in the canteen. Bridget had never quite worked out what he'd done wrong, but she remembered him being half carried, half dragged out of the factory by two large men whom Bridget had never seen before or since. Everyone had watched in shocked silence as they opened the gates and virtually threw him onto the pavement outside. And when he turned and spat at them, there were gasps from the assembled workers. Rumour was he'd gone to work in Newcastle after that. Bridget remembered Malcolm saying it was the only place he could get work because his bad reputation had followed him across Scotland.

And here she was doing something that was perhaps even more than what the Mulvey boy had done, and she wasn't even sorry.

Well, not really. She was just angry. And worried. So very, very worried.

She looked over at her bag again and imagined the document inside, fighting the urge to pull it out and look again at the figures she'd been typing that afternoon.

She knew, deep down, that they weren't wrong. The whole report had been carefully put together and it had been going back and forth between managers for days – she'd just not seen it altogether until now. And she'd not really grasped what it meant for Wentworth. And for Ellen.

When the whistle had gone for the end of the day, she'd pulled the paper from her typewriter and tucked it inside the folder where she put documents for Mr Beresford's signature. And for some reason that she still didn't quite understand, she'd put the folder into her bag.

Where it still was. She could see the outline of it through the fabric.

'And I'm thinking if I make it in wool, then it'll be warm enough,' Janet was saying.

'Good idea,' Bridget said, because Janet seemed to be waiting for a response. 'Good thinking.'

She had thought she'd take the papers home and show Malcolm. She was pretty sure he'd be as shocked as she was, and the good thing was, he was management now. Junior management, of course, but still. Perhaps he could do something. Speak to someone. Double-check the figures. Double- and triple-check them.

Change them, if possible.

Bridget knew Malcolm had his faults, but he was nothing if not fair. He didn't like injustice and he liked hard work to be rewarded. Bridget was as sure of that as she was that the sun would rise each day. And Mr Beresford liked him. Perhaps he could have a word, get him to reconsider the changes the report spelled out . . .

Malcolm will sort this out, she thought.

Making a sudden decision, she stood up.

'I have to go,' she said to Janet and the room in general.

'So soon?' her ma asked.

'Malcolm will be home,' she said vaguely, aware that Ellen was staring at her again. 'I said I'd cook.'

'Good luck, Malcolm,' said Ellen and everyone laughed.

Bridget tried her best to join in, but it wasn't easy to force gaiety when she felt the way she did. She picked up her bag and virtually ran to the front door, wanting to escape.

Ellen, though, was faster.

She was beside Bridget before she even had her coat on.

'What's the matter?' she said.

Bridget looked at her sweet, kind little sister and wanted to cry. Or at least to wrap her up in her arms and protect her from the horrible things that the world had to offer. Ellen was always so happy. So full of sunshine and positivity. Bridget hated to think that could be taken away one day.

She pulled Ellen into a hug and squeezed her tightly. Ellen protested but only for a second, then she relaxed and hugged her back.

'Is there something wrong?' she asked as Bridget finally let her go. 'What aren't you telling me?'

'I'm all right,' Bridget said truthfully. 'I'm fine. Honestly.'

'Are you having a baby?' Ellen tilted her head and examined her. 'You're definitely a bit thicker around the waist.'

Despite her mood, Bridget laughed. 'No, I'm not having a baby,' she said, her cheeks reddening just a little at the very thought.

'Do you want to have a baby? Is that it?'

'Ellen, stop it.'

'But something's wrong?'

Ellen's face was so sweet and crumpled with worry that Bridget hugged her again. 'Nothing's wrong,' she lied. 'Nothing at all.'

She untangled herself from her sister's arms, hurried through the door and down the stone stairs, her footsteps echoing as she went.

After the wedding, Bridget had moved into Malcolm's flat. It was on the fourth floor – the top floor – of a tenement just round the corner from where her parents stayed, and Bridget didn't like it very much. It was in shadow most of the day, so despite its big windows and high ceilings, it was dingy and cold. It was a single-end, so it was just one room and they had to share the WC, which Bridget didn't like at all. Their bed was in an alcove, and Bridget had made it quite cosy, screening it off from the rest of the room by hanging a curtain from the ceiling. But it didn't really feel like home. Not yet, anyway. Bridget hoped that it would one day.

She opened the main door, then trudged up the stairs letting the door slam shut behind her even though she knew Malcolm hated it when she did that. Or maybe because she knew he hated it.

Inside, Malcolm was sitting on his chair by the fire, listening to the wireless with his eyes closed. For a strange, terribly disconcerting moment, Bridget thought it was her da sitting there because that was how he relaxed in the evening after work. And then she blinked and it was Malcolm and she felt that anger rise up in her again.

'I need to talk to you,' she said, not even bothering to say hello in her eagerness to speak. 'I've done something a bit silly, but I wanted to tell you, to show you . . . I typed up a big report today – it's been going around for weeks but it's the first time I've seen it properly all in one place.' She took off her coat and hung it up. 'It's awful, Malcolm. Awful. When they said Beresford was coming to make changes, I had no idea they meant this. They're going to make folk work harder and faster, for less pay.'

She turned back to Malcolm, who was standing up, looking worried. Bridget stared at him as realisation hit her.

'You know this already?' she said, aghast. 'You bloody know.'

'What?' he said, defensive. 'No. I don't know. How could I know?'

But his protests were too late. Bridget had seen his face. She reached into her bag and took out the folder and calmly found the document she'd typed. Then she held it up so Malcolm could see.

'This,' she said. 'You know about this?'

Malcolm was a terrible liar. His face reddened and he shifted from foot to foot. 'I know,' he said. 'I've seen the financials.'

'Oh, it's not just financials,' Bridget said. 'It's a whole new way of working.'

'It's called scientific management,' explained Malcolm. 'It's what they brought Beresford in for. It's like an experiment to make things more efficient.'

'An experiment?' Bridget was stunned.

'We were asked to do the sums,' Malcolm said, rubbing his nose. 'Beresford's been working on it since he arrived.'

'And you didn't think to mention it to me? Your wife?'

'No, of course not. It's . . .' He trailed off and Bridget glared at him.

'It's what? None of my business? Ellen and Janet have been talking about all the exciting changes Mr Beresford's going to bring in for weeks. You've heard them. And all the time you knew . . .' She took a deep breath. 'You knew this was all about them.'

Malcolm sat down again and sighed.

'I knew,' he admitted. He squeezed his lips together. 'This restructuring makes sound financial sense, Bridget. Let me show you.'

Reluctantly, Bridget sat down next to him and he took the document from her. 'See here? Department Six is very overstaffed. Half the time they're sitting around doing nothing.'

Bridget raised an eyebrow.

'Well, perhaps not half the time, but even if we lose one salary it's enough to make a difference.' He was beginning to look animated. 'And then there's Department Fourteen – it's a disaster when it comes to people. If they increase their output by just a third, we can reduce staffing numbers.' He jabbed the paper. 'See?'

Bridget took the paper back from him and turned the pages until she found what she was looking for.

'And what about this?'

'Ah, yes.' Malcolm nodded as he took the document and peered at it. 'That department has fifteen employees. If we cut it back to twelve, and drop their hourly rate, it'll make a huge difference to the bottom line.'

'And that department is?'

'Cabinet polishing.' There was a sudden silence as Malcolm met her gaze. 'It's cabinet polishing,' he said again more quietly.

'Hmm.'

'You don't need to worry, though. It won't affect Ellen. They can lose those employees from natural wastage. Enid Travers, for one. She's been muttering about leaving for years and she's almost sixty. Then there's Jackie Burns. She just needs a wee nudge and she'll be gone. Then there's Molly . . .'

'Natural wastage?' Bridget was appalled. 'These are people. My sister.'

'It's just business, Bridget. It's not personal.'

'Oh it's personal all right.'

But Malcolm shook his head. 'It's just making the numbers balance.'

'Enid Travers lost her husband last year,' Bridget said. 'How do those numbers balance? And you know Jackie Burns's daughter is in a wheelchair? She's got a lot on her plate as it is.'

Malcolm's face was reddening again. 'Don't do this, Bridget.' He was firm. Unapologetic. And that annoyed Bridget.

'What about the women who are left?' she demanded. 'Ellen and Sadie and the others?'

'Well, their hours will increase slightly to cover the workload,' Malcolm began.

'And their pay will drop?'

'Yes.'

'The departments affected are all women,' Bridget said. 'It's that what you meant by an experiment? Trying it out on the women because they're not the breadwinners?'

Malcolm screwed his face up. 'Well, it's true they won't be as troubled by this as the men.'

'Sadie's the only person working in her family,' Bridget said. 'She's the only one bringing in a wage and she looks after her mother and her siblings. And now you want her to work more hours for less money?'

Malcolm looked straight at her and he gave an exasperated sigh. 'Yes,' he said. 'I do want that, and do you know why, Bridget? Because I want the Wentworth Factory to continue. If they don't make these cuts now, then perhaps the whole company will go under. And what then? Sadie can't support her family on no job at all, can she?'

'No, but . . .'

'There is no but,' Malcolm said. He thrust the paperwork back at Bridget. 'Just business.'

Bridget had nothing to say. She looked at her husband in shock.

'Why did you bring this home, Bridget?' he asked.

'I thought you might be able to stop it,' she admitted. 'I thought perhaps you'd be as shocked as I am and tell Mr Beresford that it's not a good idea.'

'But it is a good idea.'

'For Wentworth. Not the workers.'

'Is there a difference?'

'You're not the person I thought you were,' Bridget said, shocked to her core at how unemotional he was being.

Malcolm sighed. 'You're being rather overdramatic,' he said. 'I'd have expected this from Ellen, but not you. I think the problem is that you've not heard the explanations properly. Beresford is a real visionary, you know? These working practices are being used in America and he's learning from that.'

Bridget tried to dampen down the anger she was feeling. 'And you really think it's a good thing?'

'I do.' Malcolm took her hand. 'I understand that things might be a wee bit harder for your sister but it'll be worth it in the end.'

'Right.' Bridget wasn't sure, but she nodded.

'Does Mr Beresford know you took that?' Malcolm said, pointing at the report Bridget was still clutching.

'No.'

'Well, you'd better make sure it's on his desk first thing,' he said. 'You wouldn't want anyone to tell him you took it.'

Bridget turned away from him and put the document back in its folder, hiding her face so he wouldn't see the tears that had sprung into her eyes. How could he be so cold?

'We'll say no more about it,' Malcolm said in a softer voice, obviously realising she was upset. He rubbed her back as she fumbled with her bag. 'You'd understand if you knew more about how the business works.'

Bridget didn't reply. She pushed the folder into her bag and went to hang it up with her coat and hat.

'What's for tea?' Malcolm asked, picking up his newspaper.

For a second, Bridget thought about taking her coat from the peg, walking out of the door and never coming back. She took a deep breath.

'Mince,' she said to her husband. 'I'm cooking mince.'

Chapter Eight

When Bridget woke the next morning she felt as though she'd barely slept. She'd tossed and turned all night, worrying about the report and what it contained.

Malcolm had slept like a baby. Bridget had stared at his back as he snored softly and she'd made a decision.

She was going to take the document to Mr Beresford and ask him to explain what was in it. Malcolm was adamant that if she only understood the numbers and the thinking behind this new approach – this 'scientific management' – then she'd see that it was the right thing to do.

So Bridget was going to find out more.

She was tetchy and edgy at work, telling Maggie she had a headache and hadn't slept well so she wouldn't bother her, while she thought about what to say to Mr Beresford. She had other jobs for other managers to do first which didn't really calm her nerves, but eventually, later that morning, she took the report and headed for Mr Beresford's office.

Clerical was on the top floor of one side of the factory. There were large rooms where the typists and accountants and other worker bees spent their time, and then big wood-panelled offices where the managers were.

Mr Beresford's office was at the end of the corridor. Bridget had been in there lots of times, taking documents and papers for him to look at, but today she felt different. More nervous. She hoped Mr Beresford would answer her questions.

As she approached his office, a young woman Bridget vaguely recognised came out. She had two red spots on her cheeks and she looked rather dishevelled. She looked at Bridget as she walked past her and Bridget thought she saw tears in her eyes.

'Are you all right?' she asked, wondering if the woman had received some bad news. But the woman didn't answer. She simply hurried off down the corridor.

Bridget boldly walked on, taking the documents into Mr Beresford's office. He was sitting at his large desk, reading some notes as she entered and he didn't look up immediately, which gave her time to study him.

He was handsome, Ellen was right about that. He had a good head of hair, which waved slightly and gleamed with good health. His suit was beautifully cut and hugged his broad shoulders and she thought, as he looked up at her and smiled, he had an easy way about him. A manner which put people at ease and made them feel they were the most important person in the room.

'Miss Kelly,' he said. 'My report, I assume?'

Flustered by him using her maiden name, Bridget stepped forward and put the report on his desk. He caught her hand as she put the folder down and looked at her wedding ring.

'I'm so sorry. Mrs Walsh, isn't it?' He gave her a dazzling smile.

'Just Bridget is fine,' she muttered, caught off guard.

'Thank you for the report, Just Bridget,' he said. He dropped his gaze back to the notes and Bridget took a deep breath.

'Actually, sir,' she said. 'Actually . . .'

He looked up again, raising an eyebrow.

'Yes?'

'I read the report, of course, because I was typing it. And I found it . . .' She searched for the right word. 'Fascinating.'

'You did?' Beresford looked pleased and Bridget realised that, like everyone, he responded to praise.

'I really did, sir,' she said. 'You're very clever.'

He preened. 'Did you understand it? I imagine it wasn't easy for you? Women, in my experience, lack the capacity to grasp concepts of this sort.'

Bridget bristled inwardly but shook her head and widened her eyes. 'It was a wee bit complicated,' she said. 'I wondered if you'd explain it to me?'

'Now?'

'Well, I asked my husband but he said I'd be better asking you, as it's your idea.'

'Take it to the top, as it were?' Beresford said. 'Wise chap, your husband. Does he work for me?'

'Malcolm Walsh, sir. He's my husband. He works in accounts.'

Beresford looked blank and Bridget felt a sudden stab of sympathy for Malcolm who had so much respect for this man, and whose existence and hard work was barely acknowledged.

'Walsh?' Beresford said thoughtfully. 'Yes. Tall chap? Clever?'

'That's him.' Bridget's sympathy turned to pride.

Beresford looked at Bridget. 'He's your husband?'

'Yes, sir.'

He snorted, gesturing at her with his pen. 'He's going places. You might need to smarten yourself up a bit.'

Shocked, Bridget looked down at her clean, neat skirt and blouse. 'Right.'

'And smile a bit more. You're almost pretty when you smile.'

Bridget pursed her lips together and then forced herself to grin broadly at Beresford, who smiled back.

'That's the ticket,' he said. 'Lovely. Good girl.'

For a second, Bridget almost felt better about herself thanks to his flattery. Then she thought again.

'About the scientific management . . .' she said.

'It's quite straightforward,' Beresford began. 'It's all about streamlining. Using our workers to be more efficient. More like machines. They can work harder and we intend to make it happen. Wentworth will be the envy of the world.'

Bridget nodded.

'We've had efficiency engineers in,' Beresford said, puffing his chest out. 'That was my idea.'

'Well done, sir,' said Bridget through gritted teeth.

Beresford smiled again. 'Americans. They looked at the bottom line, and the costs, and worked out how to make things work better.'

'And this plan is the result?'

'Indeed.'

Mr Beresford got up from his desk and came round to where Bridget was standing.

'What do you think of it?' he asked. 'The plan?'

He moved slightly closer to her. A fraction too close, Bridget thought. She could smell his cologne and she fought the urge to move away.

'What do I think of scientific management?' she said. She wondered what would happen if she told him that she thought very little of it. That a plan to work folk harder and for longer would surely backfire in the end? But then again, people had few choices. Perhaps the man was right.

'I'd like to know your thoughts,' Mr Beresford said.

She knew he didn't really want to hear what she thought. He wanted her to flatter him. To tell him how clever he was.

So she did.

'It's a little difficult for me to understand, like you said.' She gave a tiny laugh and hated herself for it. 'But it sounds very . . .' She thought for a second. 'Innovative.'

'Yes,' Mr Beresford said, looking pleased. 'I agree.'

He nodded just once, giving himself approval and dismissing Bridget all at once.

'Thank you, sir,' she said. And as she turned to go, Mr Beresford slapped her on the behind. It took Bridget so much by surprise that she gasped aloud, and Beresford chuckled.

'Keep that husband of yours happy,' he said. 'He's going places. And smile, for heaven's sake.'

Chapter Nine

Usually Ellen could get Bridget to tell her anything. Where the Christmas presents were hidden. What mark she'd got for her school assignment. How it felt when Malcolm kissed her for the first time (though actually Bridget had been annoyingly unexcited by that, and it had been rather a disappointing conversation). But this time, Ellen couldn't get her to spill the beans.

In truth, she'd barely seen her sister for days and she was beginning to think she was avoiding her.

'I don't think she was annoyed with me,' she said to Sadie as they ate their lunch together a few days after the sewing bee. 'What did you think?'

They were sitting outside because Sadie liked having fresh air, even though it was still freezing cold, and the clouds were heavy with snow.

Sadie shrugged. 'She seemed more cross with herself.' She looked up at the sky, thoughtfully. 'Or with the world.'

Ellen put her sandwich back into the bag she'd carried it to work in. She'd lost her appetite suddenly. 'I asked her if she was having a baby but she said she wasn't. Now I'm worried she might be ill?' she said, feeling a rush of fear. 'Maybe she's sick.'

'She doesn't look ill,' Sadie pointed out. 'And you asked her if she was ill and she said no.'

'She might have lied.'

'Not Bridget,' Sadie said. 'Look we can talk about this until the cows come home but the only way to know for sure what's wrong is to ask her.'

'I can't,' she said.

'Oh come on, you two are so close. Surely you can speak to her about anything?'

'I can,' Ellen said, nodding furiously so Sadie understood just how close she and Bridget were. 'I just meant that I can't speak to her because I've not seen her.'

'You work in the same place and you live round the corner from her,' Sadie said with a chuckle. 'How have you not seen her?'

Ellen brushed crumbs from her skirt and stood up. 'Because I think she's avoiding me.'

'Really?' Sadie put the last piece of bread into her mouth and stood up too. 'Why do you think that?'

'*Because* we work in the same place and she lives round the corner and I've not seen her,' Ellen said in frustration. 'I always see her. But it's like she's vanished. She's not been round to see Ma. She's not walked home or to work at the same time as me.' She glanced up at the big factory clock. 'And we all work the same hours, Sadie. I always see her.'

Sadie bit her lip. 'That does sound a wee bit strange.'

'It's a big bit strange,' Ellen said. 'And do you know what the strangest thing is?'

'Tell me.' Sadie tugged Ellen's sleeve. 'But tell me while we walk because we need to get back to work.'

They began heading for the cabinet polishing room.

'Yesterday, I went to take a message to Department Fifteen for Mrs Taylor and I saw Bridget going up the stairs beside Department Ten,' Ellen began. 'And I hurried along the passageway so I could catch up with her, and when I got to the top of the stairs, she'd vanished.'

'Vanished?' Sadie looked astonished. 'Like a ghost?'

'Like she'd ducked into a cupboard or one of the departments off to the side, just so I didn't catch her,' Ellen said darkly.

'Surely not? She must not have seen you.'

'I've thought about it a lot and it's the only explanation,' Ellen said. She felt a lump in her throat and tried to swallow it away, but her voice came out thin and squeaky. 'I don't understand why she's being this way.'

Sadie looped her arm through Ellen's and gave her a comforting squeeze. 'I'm absolutely sure it's nothing you've done,' she said. 'But why don't we wait for her after work. If we wait on the corner then she'll have to walk past us eventually, even if she stays late. Then we can force her to tell us what's up?'

'Don't you have to be home for your ma?' Ellen gave Sadie a grateful, if a little tearful, smile.

'I'll get a message to her. I'll find Nigel in Department Three. He lives in our street and he can let her know I'll be late.' She looked up at the clock. 'I'll run and find him now. Tell Mrs Taylor I've got a family crisis if she asks.'

She hoiked her skirt up and hurried off towards Department Three. Ellen went back to cabinet polishing, feeling a little bit better. She was definitely going to get to the bottom of this.

Later, after the whistle had blown for the end of the day, Ellen and Sadie dashed to the corner by the bridge over the canal. There was only one way to cross, so they knew if Bridget was going home, she'd go that way. Eventually.

It was freezing. The women were wearing gloves, hats and winter coats as well as knitted stockings and heavy boots and they still had to stamp their feet and jump up and down to keep warm. At first there was a steady stream of workers going by, lots of them saying goodbye as they passed. Then the stream slowed to a trickle as people made their way home. And eventually there was just Ellen and Sadie on the corner feeling a bit silly.

'Maybe we missed her,' Ellen said. She looked at the clock. 'We've been waiting here an hour. You should go home. Your ma needs you.'

Sadie shook her head. 'She's fine. My Auntie Miriam will be there.' She hugged herself, and Ellen reached out and gave her shoulders a brisk rub, hoping to help warm her up. 'This is more important.'

Ellen's teeth were beginning to chatter. 'I hope she comes soon,' she said. She looked down the road, towards the factory gates, and to her relief, she saw a figure hurrying along, hunched down in a coat.

'That's her,' she said.

Sadie squinted through the twilight. 'Are you sure?'

'Of course, I'm sure. I know Bridget's walk.' Ellen was nervous suddenly, not sure what to say to her sister, which was ridiculous because she'd never had a problem talking to her before.

'Bridget!' she bellowed. 'Bridget!' Beside her, Sadie rubbed her ear with a grimace, and across the street, the figure stopped walking.

Ellen waved. 'Bridget!'

Bridget looked behind her, as though she was considering walking back the way she'd come, then slowly she came towards Ellen and Sadie.

'Hello,' she said as she approached. 'What are you doing here?'

'Waiting for you,' Ellen said.

'Why?' Bridget carried on walking and after exchanging a glance, Ellen and Sadie scurried after her.

'Because I want to talk to you,' Ellen said to the back of her sister's head. 'Have you been avoiding me?'

Bridget stopped and sighed, then she turned round. Ellen thought she looked sad. 'Yes,' she said.

'Why?' Ellen said. The word came out like a wail.

'Because I have to tell you something that'll upset you and I don't want to,' Bridget said. She scrunched her face up. 'Sorry.'

'What is it?' Ellen felt that lurch of fright again. 'What?'

'Erm . . .' Sadie tugged on Ellen's sleeve. 'Could we talk about it inside, maybe? I'm freezing.'

'Can we go to yours?' Ellen asked Bridget, but she shook her head.

'Malcolm will be there.'

'Come home, then.' Ellen looped her arm through her sister's and gave her what she hoped would be a reassuring smile. 'Come home, Bridget.'

They walked the short distance to their flat, talking about anything and everything. Ellen was jabbering about how her stockings always fell down inside her boots and made walking uncomfortable and Sadie was saying how her sister hated stockings and would wear their brother's trousers under her skirts when she could get away with it, but Bridget was quiet. When they reached the flat, Ellen opened the door.

'Ma?' she called. 'Gran?'

It was quiet inside.

'Must be at the shops,' Ellen said. 'That's good – we won't be disturbed.' She steered Bridget inside and pulled off her own hat and coat, waiting impatiently for Bridget as she did the same, much more carefully.

'Shall I make some tea?' Sadie asked, heading to the kettle. Ellen thought she was really just giving Bridget some space to say whatever she had to say in private, and she loved her friend for being so thoughtful.

'Sit down,' she said to her sister, who was standing awkwardly in the middle of the room, looking like an uninvited guest rather than someone who'd lived there all her life until a few weeks ago. 'What is it?'

Bridget sank down onto the couch and took a deep breath. 'Mr Beresford . . .' she began.

Ellen stared at her. 'Is this all about Mr Beresford?'

'No,' Bridget said. 'Well, yes, in a way.'

Bewildered, Ellen shook her head. 'What about him?'

'You were right, he does want to make changes,' Bridget said. 'And those changes mean some people are going to lose their jobs.'

Ellen gasped. 'Are you losing your job, Bridget? Is that why you're so worried?'

But Bridget shook her head. 'No, my job is fine. And yours is too,' she added, much to Ellen's relief. 'They're saying it'll be folk who want to leave – natural wastage, they call it. And I said to Malcolm that there was nothing natural about it, but he said it's just the words they use.'

Ellen couldn't quite follow her sister's train of thought.

'Who's going to lose their jobs, Bridget?'

Bridget grimaced. 'Three people from cabinet polishing.'

'Three?' Ellen shook her head. 'No, that can't be right. There's only fifteen of us as it is.'

'And the rest of you will have your hourly rate cut.'

'What?' Sadie stood at the door of the kitchen. 'What do you mean?'

'I mean, you're going to be doing more work for less pay,' said Bridget.

Ellen looked at her. Surely she was joking? Though frankly, she didn't think it was very funny and neither, by the look of it, did Sadie. The colour had drained from her face and Ellen wasn't surprised because she knew that Sadie was the only one in her family earning now and with her ma sick and her siblings to care for, it was a big responsibility . . .

'Ellen?' Bridget said. 'Are you all right?'

'Sorry.' She shook her head. 'Are you joking?'

'I'm not.' Bridget looked wretched. 'It doesn't make any sense to me, but I went to Mr Beresford and I asked him about it, and he said it was to do with efficiency.'

'Efficiency?' Sadie said. 'So this is about profits?'

Bridget nodded. 'It's business,' she said quietly.

'It's wrong.' Sadie folded her arms. 'I may not have been at Wentworth as long as you have but I value what I do here. I've got a skill. A skill that's worth them paying for. I can't go back to my old job now, anyway – it's long gone. And even if I could, the hours aren't long enough for me to earn as much.' She shook her head. 'And Ma's not working . . .' Her voice cracked and Ellen jumped to her feet.

'It's fine, Sadie,' she said. 'Honestly, Bridget's got this wrong. You must have misunderstood, Bridget.'

Bridget shook her head. 'I've not. I saw a document, and then Malcolm confirmed it. And like I say, I went to speak to Mr Beresford.'

She almost spat the name and Ellen saw a look of distaste cross her face.

'You've got this wrong,' she said again. 'You don't like Mr Beresford and that's fair enough. We can't all like everyone. But you can't go around saying such awful things about him.' She laughed, even though it sounded a bit thin and unsure. 'They'd hardly have brought him into Wentworth just to sack people, Bridget. It makes no sense at all.'

'Ellen, listen. He said he'd . . .'

But Ellen didn't want to hear it. She was annoyed with her sister for making something out of nothing. 'If Mr Beresford is making changes, then I'm sure they're for the best and you've just got the wrong end of the stick somehow. He won't sack people. We're skilled workers – you know that as well as we do. No one would expect us to do more work for less pay – not unless they want the cabinets to go out unpolished. It's silly.' She scoffed. 'I thought you were cleverer than that, Bridget.'

Bridget was still and quiet. Realising she'd got it all wrong, Ellen thought.

'I have to go,' Sadie said. She picked up her coat and straightened her skirt. 'I need to see to the children's tea.'

'It'll all work out,' Ellen said, hoping to reassure her friend. 'I promise. This is all just a big misunderstanding.'

But Sadie didn't reply. She gave Ellen a small wave and headed out of the door, her head down.

'Bridget, this is surely just a mistake . . .' Ellen began and then stopped when she saw her sister's face. Bridget looked stricken. 'You honestly think this is going to happen?'

'I think so.' Bridget nodded. 'Beresford told me so. They're using these new techniques to work out how best to maximise output.'

'Beresford is really clever, you know?' Ellen said slowly. 'He must be, to be in charge when he is so young. And he's so charming and funny, Bridget.' Her sister looked as though she was going to be sick and Ellen gave her a reassuring squeeze. 'Do you know what I think has happened? I think maybe they've had a look at how efficient everyone is being – which is a good thing to do, actually – and they're checking everything's working as it should be. And I really believe this is great for us, you know? Because maybe they want to cut some corners and I'm sure that looks good on paper, when they add up all the figures and take away the . . . well, the costs and whatnot . . . but when they really think about what's involved – the skills and the training that's needed to keep Wentworth going, those forty-one pairs of hands to make one machine – when they really think about it – and I know Mr Beresford will really think about it – they will realise we're actually worth a lot more than they're paying us now.' She sat back against the sofa. 'In fact,' she said, feeling faintly triumphant, as though she'd averted a huge disaster, 'they'll probably pay us more.'

Chapter Ten

The next day was Friday. Sadie was very quiet at work and Ellen knew she was stewing over what Bridget had told them. She tried to talk to her, to reassure her that Mr Beresford wouldn't cause them any bother, but Sadie clearly didn't want to chat.

'It'll be all right,' Ellen whispered to her during the afternoon. 'Things always work out in the end.'

Sadie had simply looked at Ellen for a long moment and then she'd said: 'That's not true.'

In that second Ellen remembered that Sadie's father had dropped down dead one day and that was definitely something that would never work out in the end, and she'd felt awful, but when she'd tried to apologise, Sadie had got up from her cabinet and walked away.

Wentworth was a big place with a lot of staff, and rumours spread quickly. People had been talking about Mr Beresford bringing in changes for weeks so it wasn't a surprise to Ellen to hear folk talking about what could happen as they all left the factory at the end of their shift.

'Whole departments closed down,' said someone up ahead. 'Hundreds out of work.'

'I heard the opposite,' another man said. 'Big expansion. Hundreds of new jobs.'

'There's no one left in Clydebank that's not already working here,' said someone else and everyone laughed.

Ellen felt a little more positive. Everything was wild rumours and whispers. Bridget's news was just another part of that.

She glanced up as they filed out of the factory and saw, on the stairs to one side, Mr Beresford and two stern-looking men, watching everyone. They were talking earnestly, and one of the other men had a clipboard. Ellen thought Mr Beresford was looking especially handsome today. He was wearing his hat and coat and she liked the way he tilted the brim down over his forehead.

She looped her arm through Sadie's and wondered what the men were talking about.

Nothing bad, she thought confidently. Nothing awful like making them work harder for less pay. She looked over her shoulder, back at the men who were now all laughing. Mr Beresford slapped one of them on the back. There. Surely that proved that any changes he was planning were positive.

Outside the gates was a group of men, stopping people from walking by and handing out leaflets.

'What's this?' said Sadie, taking one of the pamphlets.

'We're the Industrial Workers of Scotland,' said the man who seemed to be in charge. 'We're forming a group here at Wentworth to look after the interests of the workers.'

'Isn't that what the managers are for?' asked Ellen, and then she was taken aback as the men all laughed loudly.

Feeling a bit silly, she tugged Sadie's sleeve. 'Let's go.'

But as they turned to walk away, the man shushed the others.

'Sorry, doll,' he said. 'This lot have forgotten their manners. Take a leaflet, eh? Read about how we need protection from the folk at the top who are only interested in profits.' He nodded towards where Mr Beresford and the others were still standing. 'Like those ones over there.'

Ellen raised an eyebrow at this man, who was insulting Mr

Beresford. He looked back at her unapologetically. She glanced down at the leaflet which said 'Rights For All' along the top. It looked a bit dull, she had to say.

'I'll read it later,' she said. 'Come on, Sadie.'

Sadie held her hand out for her own leaflet. 'I'll take one,' she said. She tucked it into her bag and the pair set off again.

'Ellen, isn't it?' A younger man fell into step with them. Sadie recognised him because he worked on the motors, near where cabinet polishing was. 'I'm, erm, I'm James.'

'Aye, I know you,' she said. 'This is Sadie.'

The young man looked a bit nervous. He took his cap off and swapped it from hand to hand as they walked. 'I just wanted to say you should come along to our meetings,' he said. 'Get to know us. We could . . . we could do with some more younger members.' He swallowed. 'And some women.'

Ellen shook her head. 'I'm not really one for meetings,' she said honestly. 'But thanks for asking.'

'Maybe I'll ask you again,' James said.

'Maybe I'll say no again.'

'See you around?'

'Maybe.'

Ellen speeded up, with Sadie hanging off her arm, and the lad – James – watching them go.

'Ellen,' hissed Sadie. 'What was that?'

'What?'

'He likes you.'

Ellen stopped walking and looked back at James, who was still standing on the pavement. He gave her a tiny wave, and she nodded at him.

'He does not.'

'He's watching you.'

'I've never even spoken to him before,' Ellen said.

'Aye, but everyone knows you, Ellen.' Sadie grinned and Ellen felt a little bit flustered. She tried to look back at Mr Beresford, but they'd gone round a bend in the road and he couldn't been seen any longer.

'What about you?' she said to Sadie, a little rudely, if she was being honest. 'Who do you like?'

Sadie flushed bright red up to the roots of her hair and Ellen was delighted.

'There is someone!' she said. 'Who? Someone at work? Is it Angus in packing? He's always giggling away when you go past.'

'Noooo, not Angus,' Sadie admitted. 'But there is someone I like.'

'Who is it?' Ellen stopped walking. 'Does he like you back?'

Sadie took a deep breath. 'It's my friend Noah,' she said. 'And no, I don't think he does.'

For a second she looked so miserable, Ellen wanted to fling her arms round her. But instead she said, 'Tell me about him.'

Ellen looped her arm through Sadie's again, and they walked towards the station, and Ellen's flat.

'I've known him my whole life,' Sadie said. 'His parents – Miriam and Jack – they're Ma's best friends. Their parents came from Poland together.'

Ellen made a face. 'He's practically your brother.'

'I know,' Sadie groaned. 'That's why this is so odd. I've never thought of him in that way, but since Da died, he's been so caring and he's just there for me, you know?'

'He sounds like a good man,' Ellen said.

'He is.' Sadie breathed in and then spoke in a rush. 'I was finding that I looked forward to seeing him more and more, and then one day we'd been out and it was raining so hard we got absolutely drenched. So when we got back to the flat – his family live a wee bit further along our street – our clothes were all wet and his shirt was soaked through and he took it off to hang it in front of the fire, and I'd been in the bedroom and when I came back in he was just about to put on an old shirt of my da's, and I just ... well, I saw him differently, that's all.'

'Sadie Franklin,' Ellen said in glee. 'He stripped off and it made you feel things?'

Sadie looked half embarrassed, half thrilled to bits. 'Don't,' she said, burying her face in her hands, which made her walk off at an angle because she couldn't see where she was going.

Ellen righted her friend. 'Have you told him how you feel?'

'Heavens, absolutely not!' Sadie said, appalled.

'You should tell him. What's the worse that can happen?'

'Well, he could be disgusted. I could be humiliated. And the friendship between our families that's lasted for three generations could be smashed to pieces.'

Ellen thought for a moment, and then she nodded. 'Aye, you're right. Not worth the risk. You'll just have to join me in yearning after him from a distance.'

Sadie looked shocked. 'You're yearning after Noah?'

Ellen burst into laughter. 'No, you goat, I'm yearning after Mr Beresford.'

And in fits of giggles, they went on their way.

The following morning, there was a strange atmosphere in the factory. A sort of buzz of expectation. Nothing ever stayed quiet for long at Wentworth, so Ellen was pretty sure that feeling of waiting for something to happen came from knowing Mr Beresford and the rest of the managers were about to make their changes. Cabinet polishing was in a part of the factory from where they could see people arriving. And the managers were gathering like storm clouds in winter.

Ellen felt a bit sick. She was trying to stay confident and believe that the changes would be good. But the rumours flying around – and Bridget's inside knowledge – meant her conviction was wavering. It came as almost a relief when an unfamiliar man, in a smart suit, appeared in their area and asked them all to come to a meeting outside in the courtyard.

He vanished as quickly as he'd appeared, while the women all paused in their work and found their hats and coats, because even though it was March already, it was still bitterly cold outside.

To get to the outdoor area, the cabinet polishers had to walk through some of the male-dominated departments. Ellen didn't like walking that way when everyone was working because as soon as a woman set foot on the factory floor, the men all had something to say. Something lewd or rude, usually. All the women walked through those departments with their shoulders hunched, bracing themselves for the shouts and comments.

Today was no different. Ellen was leading the department as they walked, with Sadie close behind her, and a man – old enough to be her da – shouted: 'Come to make our dinner, doll?'

Ellen glared at him, and he whistled.

'Oooh, she's a nippy one. I'd no stand for that if she was my woman.'

Ellen, who could normally ignore comments like this, felt oddly wounded today. She dropped her head, and felt Sadie snake her hand into hers. She squeezed her fingers in gratitude.

And then, across the floor, a voice spoke.

'That's enough, Don.'

Ellen turned her head a little and saw James, the lad who'd been giving out leaflets. He looked annoyed.

'Got something to say, James?' Don demanded.

Ellen wanted to run away but she also wanted to see what would happen. She slowed down, just a bit.

'Aye,' said James. 'Don't speak to the women that way, Don. It's not right.'

There were a few 'ooh's but then another man shouted: 'Leave them be, Don. They might be your boss one of these days.'

'That'll never happen,' said Don. But he turned his attention back to his work and Ellen was pleased. She glanced over at James, who was smiling at her. She liked the way his eyes crinkled up as he grinned. He gave her that wee wave again and this time, she waved back.

Through the doors of the factory, she could see the managers gathered in their wool coats and posh hats. Mr Beresford was there, looking as handsome as ever. But as the women drew nearer, Ellen noticed for the first time that his mouth was, perhaps, a little too thin and his expression was, maybe, a little too stern.

'Ladies,' he said as they gathered. 'Good morning.'

Chapter Eleven

The case had been made for scientific management. The managers were very pleased with themselves and Bridget was feeling wretched. She'd taken minutes at a meeting where Mr Beresford had introduced one of his 'efficiency engineers', an American called Mr Toms. Bridget still wasn't entirely sure what an efficiency engineer did but she knew he was very different from the engineers at the factory. She'd given him a cup of tea and his hands were pale and smooth. Not working hands. Indoor hands, she'd thought.

Mr Toms had declared that it was possible to train a gorilla to be more efficient than the workers at the factory. Bridget had expected everyone to laugh at that, but they hadn't. They'd all murmured in approval and talk had turned to maximising profits. It had taken all Bridget's self-control for her to stay quiet as they talked about increasing output and reducing costs. 'What about pride in your work?' she'd wanted to ask. 'How about treating your employees like people with skills rather than trained animals?' But she'd kept her mouth shut, and she hated herself for it.

And so, now, it was with a knot of worry in her stomach that she watched the members of management coming together. Malcolm wasn't there and she was glad. He was only an accounts clerk when all was said and done. He may have been in charge in his department, but he didn't make decisions. Not like these chaps in their dark suits, like undertakers, who kept walking past the door of the clerical department and down towards the management offices.

There were a few departments they were focusing on – for now, they'd said. It was, as Mr Beresford had said, an experiment. Bridget thought they were trialling this new way of working on the women only, because they weren't as important as the men. The thought made her want to scream in frustration.

Mr Beresford had said in the meeting that if these changes went well, there would be more. Bridget didn't know what they meant by 'well'. She didn't want to know.

'What's happening?' Maggie spoke in an undertone because Mrs Whittington was lurking. 'What are they all doing?'

Bridget closed her eyes briefly. 'Restructuring,' she said.

Maggie made a face. 'Thought so. I did some letters the other day.'

'Me too.'

'Rotten.'

'Yes.' Bridget swallowed. 'Cabinet polishing.'

'Your Ellen?'

'Yes.'

'What else? Do you know?' Maggie pretended to be looking through some notes as Mrs Whittington glanced in their direction, then she thumped at the typewriter keys to muffle the sound of her voice. 'How many people are going?'

'About twenty altogether, I think.' Bridget bent down and scratched her ankle as she spoke. She and Maggie had been carrying on conversations this way for ages and Mrs Whittington hadn't spotted them yet. 'For now, that is. I think they're testing these changes on some departments to see how folk react, then they'll do it elsewhere.'

Maggie picked up a sheet of paper and held it in front of her face so it seemed she was reading. 'Bloody Nora.'

'I feel sick about it all,' Bridget admitted. 'Like I'm responsible somehow.'

'Och away with you, it's not your fault.'

'Feels that way,' Bridget sighed.

Under the desk Maggie reached out and touched Bridget's fingers briefly in a tiny gesture of solidarity. 'I know, doll,' she said. 'We're all part of a bigger thing, aren't we? Hurt one of us, hurt us all.'

Mrs Whittington cleared her throat and Bridget busied herself turning the wheel of her typewriter. 'It feels like an axe is falling,' she said. 'Ellen's going to be so upset.'

She'd expected Ellen, always so dramatic, to be wailing and shouting about the unfairness of it all. But she wasn't. She was resigned. Which was worse, actually, Bridget thought. She'd gone back to her parents' house after work wanting to see her sister. She'd found Ellen sitting in the window, looking out at the road below, one hand resting on the smooth, polished surface of the Wentworth machine next to her.

'Where is everyone?' Bridget asked. On the floor next to the chair was some mending that Ellen must have pushed off the seat before she sat down. Bridget picked it up and started examining what needed doing.

'Don't know,' Ellen said in a dull voice. 'Ma's not here.'

'Does she know?' Bridget went to the sideboard where Ma kept her sewing kit and found a needle, the wooden darning mushroom, and some wool. Then she sat down with Da's socks in her lap and began to sew, finding the repetitive movement quite soothing.

'Aye, Johnny told her.' Johnny was their cousin, who also worked at Wentworth. He worked with the furnaces, so wasn't affected by the changes. The news had spread fast.

'Is Johnny all right?'

'Aye, course he is. But his Flora isn't.'

Flora was a defect repairer in cabinet polishing. Bridget had forgotten all about her in her worries about Ellen. She concentrated on the needle moving in and out. Flora and Johnny had been planning to get married. She wondered if the wedding would go ahead now or if they would wait for Flora to find another job.

'All three of the defect repairers have been sacked,' Ellen went on. 'All of them.'

Bridget nodded. In and out went her needle. The hole had disappeared now, but she kept sewing.

'Are you all right?'

Again, Ellen shrugged. 'No choice really.'

'You'll be doing extra work. Taking on the jobs of Flora and the others.'

'Yes.'

'And you'll be paid less.' She almost didn't want to know. 'How much less?'

Ellen turned to look at her for the first time.

'At the moment we make fourteen shillings a week.'

'Right.'

'From Monday, it'll be twelve shillings.'

'Oh, Lord.'

Ellen was grim-faced. 'It's all right for me, isn't it? Because working is good for me. It's fun. It gives me independence and Ma doesn't take all my wages. It's hard work, but I've got pals.'

'Yes.'

'But it's not like that for everyone. Sadie's the only one earning a wage, Bridget. She's got the weans to look after, and her ma's sick and she's two shillings a week down. She's almost lost a whole day's pay.'

'It's not right.'

'No,' said Ellen simply. 'It's not right. And you know they're going to be timing us? We have to do a certain amount of work in a set amount of time.'

'That's ridiculous.'

'I know,' Ellen sighed. 'You know what Da always says?'

'There's dignity in work,' Bridget parroted.

'He's right. Or he was right. But not now. There's no dignity in this, Bridget.'

Bridget felt the rage within her building from her toes to the tip of her head. She threw her father's mended sock down on the chair beside her. 'It makes me so cross,' she said, standing up. 'Furious.'

'Me too,' said Ellen.

'I feel completely helpless,' Bridget said. 'And there's absolutely nothing we can do about it.'

Chapter Twelve

It wasn't so much that she was tired, Ellen thought, because work had always been tiring. It was that the tiredness never went away now, no matter how well she slept every night. And the ache in her knuckles never faded, nor the knots in her back from bending over half the day, nor the burning in her eyes from peering at defects in the cabinets.

The new system had been in place for almost a week, and it was worse than Ellen and Sadie had expected it would be. It was relentless. They'd worked hard before but there'd always been time for a quick chat, a pause to straighten up, flex their fingers, shake out their arms. Not now. Now, as soon as one cabinet was done, it was on to the next one. And they had to look out for any defects, and repair them, just as fast. And quality control hadn't changed – they had to make the cabinets just as good as they'd always been or they were forced to redo them. And now their daily targets were tighter, so there was no time to make any mistakes. It was horrible.

And it was all for two shillings less every week.

Despite all the evidence to the contrary, Ellen was still convinced none of this was Mr Beresford's doing. She preferred to blame the efficiency engineers who'd come up with the plan. And Malcolm. Not that he'd had anything to do with it really, but Ellen enjoyed holding a grudge against her brother-in-law, unfair though it might be.

Every day it was a relief when the bell went at the end of their shift and they dragged themselves outside. Today was no different. It was supposed to be their sewing bee later, but Ellen really wasn't in the mood.

She packed away her equipment, pulled on her coat, then she and Sadie walked arm in arm – Ellen had the distinct feeling they were propping one another up – outside, following the stream of people down towards the railway station.

Just beside the factory gates was a group of men – the Industrial Workers of Scotland. They were giving out leaflets again, but this time there were more of them and they even had a small banner with their name stitched along the top.

'That last S isn't sewn on right,' said Sadie, running a critical eye over the banner. 'It'll not last the day.'

As if she'd willed it, the S suddenly drooped and then dropped gently to the ground, making both women laugh.

'Hiya, girls,' said the older man they'd met before. 'I was hoping we'd see you. You're cabinet polishers, am I right?'

'Aye,' said Sadie. 'And you're the Industrial Workers of Cotland.'

Ellen chuckled but the man looked confused.

'We met the other day,' he said. 'I'm Walter.'

'I'm Sadie,' said Sadie. 'And this is Ellen.'

'Did you read the leaflet?' he asked.

'Every word,' fibbed Ellen, who didn't even remember where she'd put it. But Sadie nodded.

'Some interesting stuff in there,' she said. Her eyes gleamed. 'Rebellious.'

'Aye, it is,' said Walter. 'And we think it's even more important now, with these changes that Beresford's brought in.'

'Not Beresford,' Ellen said. 'The Americans. The efficiency engineers.'

'Right.' Walter nodded but he looked unconvinced. 'Anyway, we wanted to know how it's all going. Is it working?'

Sadie and Ellen looked at one another, then both shook their heads very firmly.

'It's not,' Ellen said. 'I've worked at Wentworth for a long while now, but I've never been so tired.' She held out her hands. 'My knuckles are sore already, and my fingers are stiff. We've got our sewing bee this evening and I don't even know if I can hold a needle.'

'We're working much harder, covering the jobs of the defect repairers,' Sadie added. 'And we still have to pass quality control.'

Walter was writing notes furiously. 'Anything else?'

'The worst bit is that we get paid less. We're down two shillings a week.'

Ellen felt that surge of injustice again.

'They're treating us like machines,' she said. 'Not people.'

Walter looked around at the other men and for the first time, Ellen noticed James standing at the back of the group. She met his gaze and he gave her a little smile. She smiled back, finding herself pleased to see him.

'Leave it with us, girls,' said Walter. 'We're having meetings and we're discussing what we should do about all this. Don't worry.'

'Right you are,' said Ellen, who was fairly positive that nothing would change. 'Here, give me your banner.'

'Why?' Walter looked round at the fabric flapping in the cold spring breeze. 'Oh, Cotland. I see why you were laughing now.'

The women giggled again. Ellen held her hand out. 'Give it here and I'll mend it at our sewing bee this evening.'

'That's kind of you,' James said. He took the banner from its pole, folded it up and handed it to Ellen. Then he picked up the S and handed that to her, too. 'Can I walk you home?'

'Och, no, I'm walking with Sadie,' Ellen said. 'Will you be here tomorrow? I'll bring the banner back then.'

'We'll be here,' said Walter.

'See you then,' Ellen said.

They walked away, with Sadie shaking her head at Ellen.

'What?' said Ellen. 'The banner was torn and we're sewing this evening anyway.'

'Not the banner,' said Sadie, slapping her forehead with her palm. 'James.'

'What about James?'

'He offered to walk you home.'

'Yes.' Ellen screwed her face up. 'So?'

'He likes you,' Sadie said. 'I told you he likes you. And you just brushed him off like he was an annoying fly or something.'

'Oh no,' said Ellen, feeling bad. 'I didn't mean to be rude. I just didn't need him to walk with me because I'm with you.'

'He's a nice lad,' said Sadie. 'Quite handsome, too.'

Ellen glanced back to where James was talking to Walter. He was quite handsome in a sort of rough way. His hair was a wee bit messy, and his clothes were a little worn – not like Mr Beresford, who was sleek and well put-together. James did have a nice smile though, she thought. He smiled with his whole face. Mr Beresford smiled widely and dazzlingly, but really he only smiled with his mouth.

'He's not as handsome as Mr Beresford,' she said to Sadie, who rolled her eyes.

Up ahead, they saw Janet leaning against a wall, waiting for them.

'Hiya,' she said as they approached.

'Ellen's got an admirer,' Sadie said immediately. 'James.'

'James McCallum?' Janet said. 'He's liked you for ages, Ellen.'

Ellen was startled. 'Has he?'

Janet tutted and Sadie laughed. Ellen felt a bit prickly. She didn't like it when her friends ganged up on her, no matter how good-natured the teasing.

'Ellen, you must go around with your eyes closed,' said Janet. 'Of course he likes you. He follows you around like a lovesick puppy.'

'There's no such thing as a lovesick puppy,' said Ellen, who knew that she didn't go around with her eyes closed at all – she went around with her head full of daydreams about Mr Beresford but she was too embarrassed to say so.

'Ellen's only got eyes for Mr Beresford,' said Sadie, who had no such qualms.

Ellen expected Janet to swoon and say she felt the same, but instead Janet screwed her nose up.

'He's not worth the bother,' she said.

'What do you mean?' Ellen was surprised.

Janet shook her head. 'Nothing,' she said. 'Listen, I'm going to skip the sewing bee this evening. I'm not really in the mood.'

'Are you all right?' Ellen asked, looking at her friend's drooping shoulders and faded smile.

'Aye,' said Janet, clearly lying. 'I'm grand.'

She hurried away, with Ellen and Sadie watching.

'What was that all about?' Sadie said as they carried on walking.

'No idea.' Ellen shrugged. 'It might just be me and you at the sewing bee, then. And maybe Ma's friends.'

'Is Bridget not coming?'

'She says not. Malcolm's being funny with her because she took that folder from work – you know the one that had the details about scientific management?'

'She put it back though. No one knew she'd taken it.'

'Malcolm likes to follow the rules,' said Ellen. 'Bridget says it makes him feel safe.'

'I understand that,' Sadie said. 'The world can be a scary place.'

Ellen looked at her friend, impressed by her empathy. 'I suppose so. Malcolm's got no family, so Bridget says Wentworth gives him the support he needs.'

Sadie snorted. 'Not sure he's right to rely on Wentworth.'

'Well, Mr Beresford's taken him under his wing,' Ellen said. 'And he's doing well.'

'Nothing's ever certain,' Sadie said darkly. 'Look at what they've done to us.'

They'd reached Ellen's tenement so she opened the main front door and they went inside and up the stairs, their boots scuffing on the stone steps.

Inside, the flat was quiet. Sadie and Ellen took off their coats and settled down at the table to wait for the others.

'Are you worried?' Ellen asked Sadie. 'About money? Now they've cut our wages. Will your family be all right?'

Sadie bit her lip. 'We'll have to be. Daniel's getting older so he could be working soon enough, and when Ma is better she might be able to find something to do from home.' She swallowed. '*If* she gets better.'

There was a pause and Ellen squeezed Sadie's hand in sympathy.

'My ma says she's glad she and Da work for themselves,' Ellen said. 'Da's got a couple of lads he uses on big jobs and he says he'd never treat them how Wentworth have treated us.'

'They're right,' Sadie said. 'Once the bosses elsewhere see what they're doing at Wentworth then they'll do it too. And soon everyone will be working harder for less pay.'

'No, that won't happen,' Ellen said. 'Will it?'

'What's to say it won't?'

Ellen had a sudden vision of a picture in one of her schoolbooks of an ant colony with the wee soldier bugs scuttling around the tunnels beneath the ground.

'I wonder if they just don't understand?' she said, unfolding the banner from the Industrial Workers of Scotland and examining the stitching. 'The Americans?'

'What don't they understand?'

'What we do. That we have skills and that we can't rush our work without things going wrong.'

Sadie raised an eyebrow. 'You don't think they know?'

'No,' said Ellen. 'Maybe I could go and speak to Mr Beresford. Explain to him that our work isn't easy and that if we carry on this way, people will be forced to stop working because their hands will be too swollen, or their backs too stiff.'

'Perhaps,' said Sadie, but she didn't sound convinced. 'Do you think he'd care? Because if you stopped work tomorrow, they'd just find someone else to take over.'

'Not someone who's been doing the job as long as me,' said Ellen, a bit affronted that Sadie thought she was so easily replaceable. 'Not someone with my skills. That's what I think they don't understand.'

Ellen got up and went to the sewing basket, looking through it for the right thread to mend the banner.

'Do you know what a strike is?' Sadie asked, smoothing out the banner and positioning the S in the right place for Ellen to sew it on.

'Not really.' Ellen screwed her face up. 'Is it something to do with miners?' She thought again. 'Or match girls?'

Sadie shook her head. 'Did you read the leaflet? The one from the IWS?'

'What's the IWS?' Ellen found the thread and brought it back over to the table, looking at the banner and wondering how best to stitch it.

Sadie pointed to the first letters of each word in front of them. 'Industrial Workers of Scotland,' she said with a laugh. 'You didn't read the leaflet, did you?'

Ellen chuckled. 'It was a bit boring.'

'It mentioned strikes,' Sadie said. 'It's when the workers just stop.'

'Stop what?'

'They stop working.'

'Why?'

'To make management realise how important they are.'

Ellen scoffed. 'But that's what I'm saying. Management know how important the workers are. They know nothing would happen without us. It's these efficiency engineers that are the problem.'

Sadie put her hands on the banner. 'Maybe,' she said. 'Maybe not.'

'What are you saying?'

'I'm saying, maybe we don't have to put up with these changes.'

Ellen threaded her needle. 'Sadie, I think you're great,' she said, 'but this is one of the silliest things I've ever heard.'

Sadie looked deflated. 'I suppose so.'

'Maybe it'll get better?' Ellen said. 'Perhaps they'll realise it's not working and change things? Or perhaps it would be a good idea for us to go and speak to Mr Beresford? But don't worry, Sadie. I'm sure things can't carry on the way they are. Trust me. They'll look after us.'

'All right,' said Sadie, looking slightly brighter. Ellen was heartened to see that she'd cheered her up, even just a little bit. 'We'll wait and see if things improve.'

Chapter Thirteen

Things did not improve.

Working at Wentworth had never been a picnic. Sadie may have only been there a short while, but she'd learned quickly that it was hard work, with few breaks and little time for chatter or fun. But she thought it was worth the hard work because she got genuine satisfaction from doing her job well and seeing the cabinets gleaming. And because she was earning well. Putting food on the table, caring for her mother, and looking out for her little brothers and sister. She'd stepped up, and she was proud of herself.

But somehow none of that mattered any more. Sadie was exhausted. Her fingers were beginning to swell from the constant repetitive movement of polishing, her eyes were prickly, and her kidneys ached because they no longer had the chance to be relieved as often.

And when her mother's brow furrowed when Sadie gave her twelve shillings instead of fourteen, it made everything worse.

On the way home, a few days after their sewing bee, she walked slowly from the station to the flat, wondering if she should try to change jobs again. But she knew she'd had her chance. Many of the factories in Clydebank and Glasgow were cutting staff, increasing workers' hours or reducing their pay. Even if there were plenty of jobs to be had – there weren't – chances were they wouldn't be any different. And though she'd enjoyed her work in the shop, she also knew it simply wasn't enough to support the family.

'Better the devil you know,' she muttered under her breath.

'Talking to yourself again? You know it's the first sign of madness?'

Sadie whipped round to see Noah grinning at her, and immediately – ridiculously – felt flustered at the sight of him. She'd known Noah her whole life. She couldn't imagine him not being around all the time and yet she was reacting like this whenever he showed up.

'You gave me a fright,' she said, feeling her mood lift just because he was there. Noah never failed to cheer her up. He was so energetic all the time. Sparky and clever and interested in everything. She thought he must be a very good schoolteacher because he could explain anything in a way that made it easy to understand. Trying not to show quite how pleased she was to see him, she grinned at him.

'Madness, eh? You'd know about that,' she said.

'Oh, I'm totally mad.' Noah looped his arm through hers. 'That's probably why I like spending time with you.'

Sadie nudged him affectionately and together they started walking towards home.

'Busy day?' Noah said, looking down at her with concern. 'You look tired.'

Sadie's throat closed up as she tried not to cry. Why did a little bit of kindness always make the tears come? 'I'm fine,' she mumbled. 'It's just a bit difficult at the moment.'

'You're doing a great job,' Noah said. 'Working hard. Earning money. Supporting your whole family.' He chuckled. 'I heard Mrs Henson was giving you a hard time about working on Saturdays?'

Sadie gave a small smile at the memory. 'I was quite rude to her.'

'Ach, she deserved it.'

Sadie smiled properly this time, basking in the glow of Noah's approval.

'How was school?'

'Today we talked about weddings,' Noah said, chuckling. 'And Jacob – he's six – was very interested in my marital status.'

'Jacob sounds a wee bit nosy.'

'He is. He wanted to know what my wedding was like and when I said I'd not had a wedding, he wanted to know why not.'

'And did you tell him it was because there isn't a woman in all of Glasgow brave enough to take you on?' Sadie said, enjoying the distraction.

'I did not,' Noah said. He tightened his arm in hers and pulled her a little closer. 'I told him it was because I'd not plucked up the courage to tell the woman I want to marry how I feel about her.'

Sadie felt her stomach lurch. She'd been half enjoying, half tormenting herself with the feelings she had for Noah, and this whole time he'd been falling in love with someone else.

Suddenly, she was acutely aware of how close they were. She could feel the firm muscles of his arm in hers and the warmth from his torso. She could smell the soap on his skin and hear his breathing.

'I have to go,' she said, pulling her arm from his.

The still evening quiet was suddenly shattered by Daniel's frantic shouts. 'Sadie! Sadie!'

Frightened, Sadie turned to her brother who was running towards them.

'You need to come. It's Rachel. She's awful sick and Ma says to get the doctor, but I saw you coming and I thought I should check with you.'

Sadie's heart twisted in fear at the thought of her wee sister being ill and her brother waiting for permission to go for help. He was only young, but he already knew the reality of money being tight.

She grabbed Daniel's shoulders. 'What's wrong with her? Is it her chest?'

Daniel nodded, his face grey and drawn. 'She's coughing something bad, Sadie, and she can't get her breath.'

'Right.' Sadie's mind was racing. 'We don't need the doctor. Not yet.' She turned to Noah. 'Can you get your ma, Noah? Get her to bring bowls. And her kettle.'

He was already heading away from them, towards his own flat and Sadie felt the relief of having someone to share the burden with.

'Come on,' she said to Daniel. 'Hurry.'

Inside the flat was dark and quiet.

'Ma?' Sadie called. 'Rachel?'

The only reply was an awful, barking cough. Poor Rachel. She suffered with her chest just like their ma.

'She's really bad this time,' Daniel said quietly. 'Ma's scared.'

'Ma's just worried because she knows how it feels,' Sadie said, rubbing his hair in reassurance.

She found her mother and Rachel curled up together in Ma's bed in the kitchen. Rachel was asleep – or at least her eyes were closed – but horribly frequently her little body was racked with awful coughs.

'She's bad this time,' Ma said, stroking her daughter's hair. 'I thought the doctor might help.'

Sadie thought about her pay packet being two shillings down and shook her head. 'We know what to do, Ma. Don't worry.' She reached out and squeezed her mother's hand, then dropped a kiss on Rachel's clammy forehead. 'Try to prop her up a bit if you can. You know lying flat makes it worse.'

Hoping she seemed efficient and in control, she bustled around the tiny kitchen area and began filling the kettle, and whatever pots she could find, with water, lighting the fire and putting them on to boil.

Miriam appeared in the doorway, holding two saucepans and

her kettle. 'Is she bad?' she said in a low voice, kissing Sadie on the cheek.

'It's not good.' Sadie took a pan from her and filled it with water. 'Daniel's in a state.'

'Noah's with him,' Miriam said. 'He'll be all right now.'

Once again Sadie felt the sheer relief of having someone to rely on, and her heart swelled with affection for Noah. Misplaced affection, she told herself, when he was in love with someone else. But she had no time to think about it now as the kettle began to whistle.

She and Miriam put the pots of hot water around the bed, which was set in an alcove, then they pulled the curtain across, so it could fill with steam. Sadie knew the warm, damp air would help Rachel to breathe and as she watched the kitchen windows fog up, she was pleased to hear her sister's rasping coughs lessen.

She kissed Miriam on the cheek and whispered 'thank you', then ducked into the alcove and sat at the end of Ma's bed to keep a watchful eye.

Rachel stirred with each cough, panicking as she tried to catch her breath. Sadie took her hand and with Ma on the other side, they helped calm the frightened little girl and encouraged her to breath in the steamy air.

It seemed like hours later when finally Rachel slept peacefully, Ma next to her, also asleep, and Sadie felt it was safe to leave the alcove. She took two of the now cool saucepans and pulled back the curtain, jumping in surprise to see Noah sitting beside the fire, reading a book. She stood for a second watching him, his glasses perched on the end of his nose, his hair ruffled and his collar squint. Then she pulled the curtain across again, leaving Ma and Rachel sleeping in the dark.

'You didn't have to stay,' she said quietly, glad he had.

He looked up at her and once again his smile made her heart skip.

'I took the boys to ours and gave them a jam sandwich each.'

He stood up. 'Then I brought them home. They're in bed now but I can hear them chatting. My ma's gone home to get my da's tea.'

Once again, Sadie felt herself close to tears because of his kindness.

'Thank you,' she whispered.

Still holding his book in one hand, Noah put his arm round her shoulders. She stiffened, not wanting to relax and let herself enjoy his embrace.

'Tough day, eh?' he said.

'Uh huh. Work's awful.'

'Tell me why.'

'Really? It's awfully boring.'

'It's not.' Noah looked at her. 'Not if it's important to you.'

Sadie sat down at the table. 'What do you know about scientific management?' she began.

When she'd finished explaining what was happening, Noah was cross. Crosser than she'd ever seen him.

'I can't for the life of me understand why they think it's a good idea,' he said, running his fingers through his hair.

Sadie shrugged. 'It saves money.'

'But it's not right.'

'No.'

'No?'

'No, it's not right.'

Noah sat up straighter and looked at Sadie with suspicion. 'What are you going to do?'

'What makes you think we're going to do anything?' Sadie said.

He raised his eyebrows. 'I know you, Sadie, and I know that glint in your eye. What are you planning?'

Lowering her voice, even more, Sadie said: 'Ellen and I have been talking about stopping work. She's not keen – well, that's an understatement really. She's not on board at all. But I think it's the only way.'

'There's no other jobs, though,' Noah said.

94

Sadie shook her head vigorously. 'I don't mean leaving Wentworth. I mean downing tools and stopping work. Withdrawing our labour.' She stood up and went to her bag, digging about for the IWS leaflet. She'd read it over and over again. 'Look. These men have been organising themselves into a group – they're calling themselves the Industrial Workers of Scotland. They want more rights for workers and because there are a lot of them, people are paying attention.'

She handed Noah the leaflet and was pleased to see him look at it with interest. 'If I stop work, no one will care,' she said. 'If we all stop . . .'

'The whole factory?'

'No, just us. Just the cabinet polishers.'

'Do you think it'll work?'

'I'm really not sure.' She screwed her nose up. 'Maybe. I think Ellen will be easy enough to persuade in the end as she's very upset by it all, but I don't know about the others. It has to be all of us.'

'How will you persuade them?'

'I don't know.'

Noah adjusted his glasses. 'Can I keep this?' he asked, waving the leaflet.

'Yes.' Sadie knew it off by heart now anyway. 'What do you think, Noah? Do you think we should try?'

'If I said no, would you stop?'

Sadie thought for a moment.

'Probably not.'

Noah whooped with laughter and Sadie shushed him in case he woke Rachel or Ma.

'You're amazing, Sadie,' he said. 'You should absolutely fight this. Fight it with everything you've got. And I'll be right by your side.'

Chapter Fourteen

'So he didn't actually say who it was he wanted to marry?' Ellen frowned.

Sadie sighed. 'I think he was going to, but then Daniel came to find me and the moment was lost.'

Ellen looked at her friend. She looked glum and fed up.

'He might have meant you,' she pointed out.

Sadie looked at her feet. 'Don't be silly. If he'd meant me, he'd have said so.'

'Perhaps,' said Ellen. 'Maybe you should ask him who he meant?'

But Sadie shook her head. 'Och, no. It would be awful if he said some other woman's name and I'd have to pretend to be interested in it all.'

They were approaching the factory gates, so Ellen paused and pulled Sadie's arm to get her to stop walking. 'Listen, I want to talk to you about work,' she said. 'I was awake half the night, thinking about the changes, dreading going in today. I just couldn't settle. And so . . .' She took a deep breath. 'I read the leaflet.'

'You did?' Sadie looked pleased.

'It makes a lot of sense,' Ellen said. 'I thought that going to see Mr Beresford was the way to make him realise how important we are, but the stuff about everyone speaking with one voice made me think differently. It's like sewing.'

'Is it?' Sadie frowned.

'Aye, it is. You can break one thread, but hundreds of threads? That's a rope.'

'Or a banner,' Sadie said with a grin.

'Yes.' Ellen felt a little shiver of excitement. Or was it fear?

'And I was thinking rather than me just going to tell Mr Beresford how important we are to Wentworth, we should show him.'

'By stopping work?'

'Yes,' said Ellen simply. 'What do you think?'

Sadie looked thoughtful. 'We couldn't do it for long because if we're worried about losing two shillings, think how bad it would be to lose a whole week's pay?'

'I know. I thought if we talk about it today, persuade the others that it's the right thing to do, then perhaps we could walk out tomorrow – I think it will have more effect if we just stop in the middle of our shift. And then management will understand what we're trying to tell them and perhaps we'll be back at work by Wednesday.'

Sadie stared at her and Ellen grinned at her startled expression.

'You really have thought about this.'

'I told you, I was awake half the night,' Ellen sighed. 'I don't want to cause trouble or make things difficult for Mr Beresford, but we can't keep going the way we are. It's just not possible.'

'So we stop work?'

'Aye.'

'Do you think it will work?'

Ellen bit her lip. 'Honestly? I've got no idea. But I really believe they've made a mistake when it comes to changing our work and if we can just show them how hard we work, then they'll put it right.'

'I'm not sure, Ellen . . .'

'About walking out, or about them changing their minds?'

'Both.' Sadie rubbed her nose.

'Sadie! You were the one who told me about strikes and who read the leaflet first. I can't do this without you.'

Sadie looked a little tearful. 'I just don't want to lose a day's pay,' she said. 'Rachel's better for now but I'm sure she'll have another turn soon – they're getting closer together now – and she'll need a doctor. And Daniel's worn through his shoes again . . .' She gave Ellen a small, brave smile. 'He's getting cold feet and so am I about doing this.'

Ellen took her friend's hand. 'I honestly believe it'll be over in a day or so. And we can help out with Daniel's shoes. I bet someone's got a pair that one of their boys has grown out of. I'll find something.'

'I don't want pity,' Sadie said fiercely.

'Och, it's not pity. It's being practical,' Ellen said. 'Don't be silly.'

Sadie screwed her face up and then to Ellen's relief, she nodded. 'All right, then.'

'Great.'

'And you definitely don't want to speak to Mr Beresford first?'

Ellen shook her head. 'No, I don't think it's worth it.' She thought about seeing Mr Beresford on the stairs with the Americans. 'But I do honestly think that it's just that he's not been at Wentworth for long, you know? Maybe he thinks this new idea will work in our factory but he's not understood exactly what we do here? That's why we need to show him.'

'We need to get everyone in cabinet polishing to stop work, or it won't have any effect,' Sadie said.

'That's the plan.'

'How will you do that?'

'I'll speak to them.'

'One at a time?'

'Maybe.' Ellen felt a glimmer of nerves at the thought of trying to convince her fellow polishers that this was the right thing to do. But wasn't Sadie on board despite her worries, and Ellen was nothing if not persuasive. Her da always said she could sell coal to a miner. She just had to talk to them all. But when? And how? 'It might be better to get everyone together.'

'Yes. In fact, I think you should do it now,' Sadie said, glancing up at the clock. 'We've got time. Get everyone together just outside the gate and explain.'

'Now?' Ellen was alarmed but it made sense. 'I suppose so.'

'Quickly, there's Mary Jones coming. And Jackie Burns.' Sadie gave Ellen a little shove. 'I'll fetch them. You get a pallet or something to stand on so everyone can see you.'

Without stopping to think, because she knew that she'd talk herself out of it if she thought too much, Ellen marched over to just outside the huge factory gates. There were always boxes and pallets stacked outside, so she took one, and stood on it, as Sadie appeared with Mary, Jackie and the other women from their department.

With her knees knocking, Ellen cleared her throat. 'Hello,' she squeaked.

'What's going on, Ellen?' Jackie Burns snapped. 'I've not got time for a chat. Not with this new workload.'

'That's what I wanted to talk about,' Ellen said.

'Speak up!' Helen Butcher shouted from the back. Sadie sprang into action, herding the women forward until they were closer to where Ellen stood.

She tried again. 'We're all working harder than ever. Too hard,' she began.

'Got that right,' said Jackie, folding her arms. 'I've been envying those defect repairers that were sacked, just because they'll get a rest.'

'It's impossible,' Ellen said, nodding. 'They sacked our friends and now we're doing their jobs as well as our own. And the added insult is we're doing all this hard work for less money in our pay packets at the end of the week.'

Out of the corner of her eye she saw some of the workers streaming past, towards the gate, slowing down to listen.

'I think this whole thing is a mistake,' she went on. 'Management think they're doing the right thing, but they're not. And so we need to show them how important our department is.'

'How will we do that?' someone said. Ellen wasn't even sure that the person who spoke was from cabinet polishing because more people seemed to have gathered at the back. But she replied regardless.

'We're going to stop work,' she said. She held her hand up to quell the chatter that immediately erupted. 'Not for long. Just for today, perhaps, or maybe tomorrow too. But we need to make them see that this scientific management won't work. We have to make them see that they've made a mistake. So, cabinet polishers, I think we should walk out. We should leave work in the middle of the day.'

'Just go home?' One of the youngest members of the department, a girl called Christina, gasped in shock. 'And what would we do?'

'Anything you want,' Ellen said vaguely, because she hadn't really thought that far ahead. 'We'll lose a day or so's pay, but the way I see it is it'll be worth it in the end.' She looked from face to face, seeking approval. 'But everyone needs to agree because we need to speak as one. We're stronger together – like threads, you know? But I know it's not easy.'

To her absolute relief, everyone was nodding, some more eagerly than others, and some with very definite reluctance. But everyone seemed to agree.

Beside her, Sadie got onto the pallet too, treading on Ellen's toes.

'We should organise,' she said.

Ellen glanced at her, and Sadie took her hand.

'I read it in one of the leaflets,' she said in an undertone. 'Trust me.'

She turned back to the crowd again. Ellen was certain it had grown bigger. To the side, she spotted James leaning against the factory wall, watching her from under the peak of his cap. She caught his eye and he winked at her, giving her an approving nod. Ellen felt surprisingly pleased to have impressed him. She felt her cheeks flush as she turned her attention back to Sadie, who was still talking.

'Once we've stopped work, we'll need someone to go to management on our behalf, to explain what we want,' she said. 'I think that should be Ellen.'

'Agreed,' shouted Helen Jones and there was a murmur of agreement. Ellen stood up a bit straighter and imagined herself going in to speak to Mr Beresford as a representative of the whole department. He was bound to be impressed by that. Perhaps he'd even suggest taking her out one evening to talk about it properly.

'We really need support from everyone,' Sadie went on. 'There's no point in us stopping work if they're just going to bring in extra polishers from another department.'

'Sadie's right,' Ellen said, forcing her attention away from daydreams of Mr Beresford and back to the here and now. She looked over the top of the heads of the women she knew, to the unfamiliar faces at the back. 'Spread the word, will you? Make sure everyone understands what we're doing.'

'What about the rest of us?' a woolly-hatted woman shouted. 'Can we stop work, too?'

'Why?' Ellen said. 'It's cabinet polishing that's affected by these changes.'

'Aye, but they could do the same to us any minute, couldn't they?' said the woman. At the back of the gathering, Ellen spotted Walter nodding and unfurling the banner she'd mended and began to wonder if this whole thing was getting out of hand because the crowd was still growing, and she felt a bit like a performer at a music hall.

'I suppose so,' she said to the woolly-hatted woman. 'But it has to be everyone. Just speak to your department – make sure they're all in agreement.'

She looked down at the cabinet polishers. 'So, we're all agreed?' she said. 'We're going to stop work at . . .'

'Two o'clock,' said Sadie.

'Two o'clock.' Ellen took a deep breath. 'When the clock chimes, we'll all put down our tools and leave. We'll meet on the other side of the bridge, where the wee green is, and we can have a chat about what I'll say to management.'

The women of the cabinet polishing department all nodded, and Ellen felt a rush of excitement mixed with fear.

'Good luck, everyone,' she said. 'Change is in the air.'

She jumped down from the pallet and came face to face with Janet.

'Are you sure this is a good idea?' Janet asked without even saying hello.

'What?' Ellen was surprised by her friend being so negative. 'Why not? We have to do something.'

'It's just a job, Ellen. Why do you want to make trouble?'

'I'm not making trouble.'

'You really are.' Janet looked around. 'You'll lose your job, you know?'

'Why?' Ellen felt a little bit sick. She'd not thought that was a possibility. 'They can't sack me, can they?'

'Of course they can. Especially if you're costing them money.' Janet shook her head. 'The bosses only care about the money.'

'The efficiency engineers care about the money,' Ellen assured her. 'Mr Beresford—'

'Mr Beresford isn't as nice as you think he is,' Janet snapped.

Ellen stared at her and Janet hung her head, looking wretched. 'He isn't as nice as *I* thought he was,' Janet said, more quietly.

Ellen thought Janet was probably upset because Mr Beresford hadn't paid her any attention since she'd moved to clerical, but she wasn't going to say that.

'Listen, Janet,' she said, wanting to make her feel better. 'It's nice that you're worried, but you don't have to be. It's just an easy way of showing those efficiency engineers how important we are to Wentworth. I expect we'll all be back at work tomorrow morning.'

'I doubt that very much,' Janet said.

Ellen was cross. 'We're doing this for the good of Wentworth,' she said. 'A bit of support would be nice.'

Janet rolled her eyes. 'Fine,' she said in a very grudging tone. 'But don't come crying to me when you lose your job, and you can't get another because everyone in Clydebank thinks you're a troublemaker.'

'Everyone in Clydebank thinks that anyway.' Ellen turned to see Bridget next to her, and thought she'd possibly never been so pleased to see her sister.

'Well done,' Bridget said. 'I think you're doing the right thing.'

'Really?'

'Really.' Bridget paused. 'I was wondering why the changes started with cabinet polishing.'

Ellen thought about it. 'Sadie says they're experimenting on us.'

'Exactly. I think it's because you're all women and they think you won't kick up a fuss.'

'They're wrong about that.' Ellen grinned.

Janet huffed and puffed beside her. 'My ma always says you Kelly girls would run towards a fight instead of away,' she said. 'Reckon she's right about that.'

'Reckon she is,' Ellen said in defiance, feeling as bold as anything with Sadie and Bridget by her side.

Janet opened her mouth and Ellen thought she might have more to say about why they were doing the wrong thing. But instead she simply said: 'I hope it works out, Ellen.' Then she hurried off towards the factory gates.

Ellen raised an eyebrow at Sadie, who shrugged.

'We need to hurry,' Sadie said. 'Our efforts won't be appreciated if we're locked out all morning.'

Bridget leaned forward and kissed Ellen's cheek, much to Ellen's surprise. 'Good luck,' she said, then she walked away too.

'She's not normally so affectionate,' Ellen told Sadie.

'Change is in the air,' Sadie joked.

The two women linked arms and together they walked through the gates.

'This feels like the beginning of something,' Ellen said, looking around at the familiar factory buildings that suddenly felt very different.

Sadie smiled at her. 'I think you're right.'

They walked through the courtyard towards cabinet polishing and as they reached the entrance, a gust of cold wind made Ellen shiver. 'I just hope it's the beginning of something good.'

Chapter Fifteen

The morning dragged. Ellen felt every tick of the clock like a heartbeat, counting down to something bigger than she was.

She focused on her work, concentrating hard and trying to ignore the slight tremble in her hands as she polished the wood.

The foreman of the cabinet polishing department was a woman. Her name was Miss Browning and she was a small, meek woman with mousy hair and a nervous smile. But she could be vicious if she was annoyed. Ellen always thought of her as a cornered rat – ready to attack. It was Miss Browning she was worried about now, more so than about Mr Beresford or the efficiency engineers.

Ellen knew Miss Browning liked a cup of tea in the afternoon. The tea trolley didn't come to cabinet polishing – it went to the bigger departments staffed by the men, something that had always faintly rankled with Ellen – but Miss Browning usually listened for the rattle of the cups and ducked out of their department for five minutes to grab herself some refreshment. Ellen was hoping that, today, the trolley would arrive just at the right time.

And perhaps someone, somewhere, was listening to her prayers because as the clock ticked on, she heard the wheels of the trolley rumbling down the corridor. Miss Browning heard it too – she tilted her head, like a dog who'd scented a rabbit, then she said, 'As you were, girls,' and off she went, scurrying out of the department.

Almost as soon as she'd gone, as though they'd planned it, the factory clock rang out twice for two o'clock, and quietly, Ellen folded her cloth and put away her tools. She glanced at Sadie and the pair exchanged a tiny nod. Without making a fuss about it, they caught the eye of their colleagues, who all began packing away too. And then, scarcely able to believe she was doing it, Ellen led them out of the cabinet polishing department, down the stairs and out into the cold air. They went through the main gates and out into the street, Ellen feeling like she was playing a strange version of 'follow the leader' as the women followed her, still quiet and focused, along the road, across the bridge and on to the green.

It felt, Ellen thought, almost like a funeral procession. Sombre and silent. And as they went, the people they passed stopped to gawk.

'Look at them staring,' Ellen murmured to Sadie, who was walking by her side, head held high.

'Why?' she asked, keeping her eyes to the front. 'Why are they all looking at us?'

Ellen glanced over to where a mother with a baby in a pram was standing still, watching them, her mouth hanging open.

'They know the factory shifts,' she said. 'Everyone knows. Seeing us leave in the middle of the day will be strange for them.'

They'd reached the green, the meeting point they'd arranged. Ellen walked across the grass, feeling it squelch beneath her boots and it was only then that she turned and saw, to her astonishment, that it wasn't only the cabinet polishers who'd been following her. The tall woman with the woolly hat was leading the testing department, and behind them were ten or so women from quality control.

'Sadie,' Ellen said. 'Look.'

Sadie turned and Ellen watched as her jaw dropped.

'More of them,' Sadie said in wonder. 'There are more of them.'

'What have we done?' Ellen was half thrilled, half terrified to see the women who'd followed her out of the factory.

'We've done the right thing.' Sadie looked proud. And more

than a little fearful. Ellen looked over the women again and thought how desperate they all must be to be willing to lose a day or maybe two days' wages to come here and show management what a mistake they had made. The thought filled her with energy.

'Now,' she said to Sadie. 'We organise.'

Sadie grinned. 'Go on, then.' She looked round. 'Here, there's a tree stump there. Get up on that and everyone will see you.'

Taking a deep breath, Ellen nodded. She clambered up on to the stump and shouted: 'Hello, everyone.'

The women, who'd been chatting quietly among themselves, all stopped their talking and looked at her. Ellen smiled.

'This is it,' she began.

It wasn't easy to talk to such a big group, There must have been at least thirty women there with the polishers, and the other departments who'd followed. Sadie helped out by darting among the crowd, speaking to people who wanted to contribute and rushing back to where Ellen stood and repeating what had been said. After a bit of discussion, they agreed that Ellen should speak to management.

'Our desires are simple,' Ellen said. 'We want a return to how things were before scientific management was brought in. We want our weekly wage returned to what it was, and we want the workers who were sacked to be brought back.'

'I don't think Jane Cruikshank wants to come back,' said Jackie Burns. 'She says she should have retired years ago.'

'Then we need someone else to cover her work,' Ellen said, hiding the scowl she wanted to direct in Jackie's direction.

'Aye, that's right,' said the woolly-hatted woman. Ellen made a mental note to find out her name. 'We just want things back to the way they were.'

'No, we don't,' said a voice from the back of the crowd. 'We want to make them better.'

Ellen saw, huddled behind the women, a group of men that

included James and Walter, and some of the other members of IWS. James caught her eye and nodded again and she felt a tiny tug towards him. Like she was being drawn to him by an invisible thread.

'Let's just start with things being put back the way they were, eh?' she said to the woman who'd spoken. 'I'll go to speak to Mr Beresford – to management – this afternoon, with Sadie, and if we meet back here at five o'clock, I'll let you know how things went. With any luck we'll be back to work tomorrow morning.'

There was a ripple of applause and a few shouts of encouragement and feeling quite proud and a bit nervous, Ellen went to find Sadie. She was talking with the men who had joined the back of the crowd.

'Ellen, these men are from the Industrial Workers of Scotland,' she said. 'There's Walter, and Stan, and you know James.'

'Hello,' Ellen said. The men all nodded. James smiled at her from beneath his cap.

'You sounded good,' he said. 'You're a natural speaker.'

Ellen's cheeks flamed. 'Och,' she said, embarrassed by his praise. 'Just saying what I think.'

'That's what makes it good.'

'So, girls,' said Walter. He was about the age of Ellen's da, with ruddy cheeks and kind eyes. 'Want us to come to see management with you?'

'With us?' said Ellen, taken aback. 'Why?'

Walter chuckled. 'Because we're the Industrial Workers of Scotland,' he said, matter-of-factly.

'I think Ellen and Sadie can do this alone,' James said. 'This is their fight.'

Ellen shot him a grateful glance. She felt like they were muddling through, and she didn't want to look silly in front of these men.

'Right enough,' Walter said cheerfully. 'But we're here if you need us.'

'We won't,' said Ellen, sounding more confident than she felt, but somehow boosted by the faith James had in them. Then she paused.

'What should we do?' she asked. 'Go and speak to Mr Beresford? And then what? Come back here and tell everyone what they said?'

'Sounds good to me, girl,' said Walter. 'You said you'd be back at five, right? Off you go, then. We can keep everyone entertained while you're away.'

'Right,' Ellen said, her courage draining away with each second that passed. 'Off we go, then.'

Sadie gripped her arm and together they left the green and walked back to the factory.

'What do you think Mr Beresford will say?' Ellen asked, wondering if he'd simply agree to put things back to how they were, or if she'd have to use her best skills of persuasion to convince him. She remembered once talking Bridget into handing over her favourite doll. If she could do that . . .

Sadie was frowning. 'Not sure. I was thinking they might try to compromise. Maybe give us one shilling a week back instead of two? Or not all three of the staff? Especially if Jane Cruikshank doesn't want to come back. So then we'd have to decide whether to agree or not.'

Ellen thought about it. 'We're not in charge though. *All* of us have to decide.'

'I suppose we say we'll think about it, then go back to the green and tell them what they said?'

'Yes.' Ellen felt a lurch of nerves. She'd been so convinced that Mr Beresford would realise what a mistake he'd made and want to put it right, that she'd not really considered any alternatives. 'Good.'

The factory gates loomed up in front of them. Large and very definitely locked. They paused for a moment looking up at them. Ellen found Sadie's hand and held it tightly.

'We'll be clear about what we're asking,' she said. 'We want things back to how they were.'

'And we'll be polite,' Sadie added. 'Not aggressive or demanding. Just calm and firm.'

'All right.' Ellen's heart was thumping. 'Let's do it.'

They went to the little gate hut, where Ossy, one of the guards, was sitting.

'Hiya girls,' he said. 'Bit late, aren't you?' Then he grinned. 'Only joking. Saw youse all leaving a wee while ago. What's that all about, then?'

Ellen swallowed. 'We're on strike,' she said. The words sounded odd to her, like she was reading aloud from an unfamiliar book.

'Are you, aye?' Ossy looked unimpressed. 'What are you doing here, then?'

'We'd like to see someone from management, please. Mr Beresford, perhaps?'

Ossy nodded. 'Wait here.'

He disappeared through the little door in the wall that led to the factory. Ellen and Sadie waited quietly, pacing up and down.

'We believe you've underestimated the skills needed to work in cabinet polishing,' Ellen muttered under her breath, walking ten steps in one direction, then turning and walking back. 'We'd like to ask you to give the workers you sacked their jobs back, and to put our wages back to what they were.' She turned again. 'We believe you've underestimated . . .'

'Here you are, girls.' Ossy was back, followed by – Ellen groaned – Malcolm.

Malcolm bustled over to where they stood, looking rather disgruntled.

'Ellen, this is putting me in a very difficult situation,' he said.

'It's nothing to do with you.' She glared at him.

'Mr Beresford has asked me to come and speak with you,' he said. 'And to tell you . . .'

'Why did he send you?' Ellen interrupted. 'Did you just decide you wanted to be involved?'

'No.' Malcolm looked a little put out. 'Like I said, he asked me to come.'

'Where is Mr Beresford?' Ellen said.

'He's busy.'

Ellen glanced up at the high windows where she knew the clerical offices were, and thought she saw Mr Beresford standing watching them down below. But as quickly as she spotted him, he vanished. Was he hiding from them? Surely not.

Annoyed, she turned back to Malcolm.

'Look, we can't talk out here,' she said. 'Let's go up to the offices and we'll explain what it is we want. And Mr Beresford can come . . .'

'He won't see you,' Malcolm said. Ellen got the distinct impression that he was glad to be passing on that news. 'He asked me to come and tell you that management aren't going to speak with you.'

'What?' Ellen was shocked. That hadn't been in the plan. 'They can't just ignore us.'

'No, they can't,' Sadie said, putting her hands on her hips. 'Workers have rights, you know? They can't treat us like this.'

'Oh, but they can,' said Malcolm with a smirk. 'In fact, I think you'll find they have.'

He turned around sharply, and walked back through the little door in the wall, next to the big factory gates. Ellen watched him go, thinking she'd never hated anyone as much as she hated Malcolm at that moment.

'He's a snivelling, disgusting wee . . .'

'Easy, Ellen,' said Sadie, nodding towards Ossy who was watching everything with a glint in his eye. 'Polite, remember?'

Ellen knew Sadie was right. Reluctantly, she took a few deep breaths, trying to calm herself down.

'How can we talk to them if they won't let us in?' she groaned. 'I didn't think this would happen. Probably Malcolm didn't even tell them we were here, the wretch. I bet he just sneaked off to see us without letting Mr Beresford know.'

'Perhaps,' said Sadie but Ellen didn't think she sounded convinced and really, she wasn't convinced either, because she was pretty sure it had been Mr Beresford she'd seen watching them from the window – she'd recognise him anywhere.

'What should we do now?'

'Go home, girls,' said Ossy. 'And come back tomorrow and get to work.'

'We bloody well will not,' said Ellen, bristling again. 'If Malcolm wants a fight, he's got one.'

She marched off, with Sadie following behind, back to the green, where someone was playing a fiddle and the crowd were singing. There was a slight festive atmosphere, and Ellen felt sad that she was about to burst their bubble.

She made her way to the front of the group, beside the fiddle player and signalled for him to stop.

'How did you get on?' someone called.

Ellen exchanged a nervous glance with Sadie. What if the women thought she'd let them down? What if they got angry or even turned on her?

Sadie patted her arm reassuringly. 'It's fine, just tell them what happened.'

'Really?'

'Go on.'

Ellen cleared her throat. 'Everyone?' she called. The women fell silent. 'I'm afraid we've not got very far. We weren't allowed into the factory.'

'Not at all?' someone said.

'Not at all.'

'Did they know you were there and wanting to speak to them?' Walter asked, his brow furrowed.

'Aye. Well, Malcolm Walsh came out and said they wouldn't be talking.'

'That wee goon,' huffed Walter. 'He's got no authority.'

Ellen hid her smile. 'What should we do now?' she asked the group.

'We could all march together and break down the gates,' shouted someone from the back.

'I really think we need to keep things civil,' said Sadie. 'If we don't misbehave then they can't criticise us, can they?'

'She's right,' said Ellen. She looked at Walter. 'What can we do?'

Walter grinned. 'We need everyone behind us.'

Ellen felt both relieved and a little prickly at his use of the word 'us'. As though they had someone on their side who knew what to do, but also as though they were handing over control of the situation to this man they'd only just met.

'He's a good man,' a voice said in her ear. She turned to see James, standing close enough that he could speak without being overheard. 'He can help.'

She was touched that he'd obviously realised how she was feeling and wanted to help. Ellen nodded. 'All right,' she said to Walter. 'Tell us what to do.'

'Leave it with me, doll. I'll spread the word.' He raised his voice. 'Come back tomorrow at noon,' he said to the gathered women. Then he and the fiddle player both weaved through the crowds. Ellen saw them chatting to women as they went, laughing and nodding.

'What's he going to do?' Ellen asked James, confused.

'He's telling everyone to tell everyone,' James said with satisfaction. 'That's how this works. Word of mouth.'

'How what works?'

'The fight for workers' rights.'

'Oh.' Ellen felt a bit silly suddenly. 'Is that what this is?'

'Of course.' He smiled at her and she felt her heart pound,

so she looked away. Goodness, how fickle she was – admiring Mr Beresford one minute, then fluttering her eyelashes at James McCallum the next.

But James was here, in the thick of things, while Mr Beresford was hiding away upstairs at the factory and it didn't matter how hard Ellen tried to put a positive spin on that, she couldn't help feeling disappointed.

'Come with us to the factory,' he said. 'We'll speak to people on the way out after their shift.'

'All right,' Ellen said, pleased to be asked.

'I can't.' Sadie looked annoyed. 'I have to get home.'

Ellen kissed her on the cheek. 'See you tomorrow.'

Sadie nodded. 'Keep fighting,' she said cheerfully. Ellen thought this action had lit a flame under her friend. Given her something to focus on apart from just getting through the days and going home to care for her siblings and her sickly mother and yearn after Noah, who wanted to marry someone else. Ellen was glad.

As the crowd began to drift away, she and James strolled towards the factory together.

'You really think more people will support us?' she asked. 'Even though it's cabinet polishing that's affected?'

'We're all one, though, aren't we?' James said. 'You can't treat one department badly and expect it not to affect the rest of us. Injure one of us, injure us all.'

'Oh that's good,' Ellen said, impressed. 'We should tell the bosses that, if they ever speak to us.'

James snorted but Ellen had been thinking.

'I think I know a way to get in to see Mr Beresford,' she said. 'My sister, Bridget, works in the clerical department. She knows him well. In fact, it was her who put us on to what was planned with this whole scientific management thing, because she was typing a letter about it.'

'Good contact to have,' James said. 'She'll be useful.'

Ellen thought about telling him Bridget was married to

Malcolm but decided against it. She liked having James's approval and she found – to her surprise – she didn't want to disappoint him.

'How did you get involved in all this, then?' she said, to distract him from talk of Bridget. 'This workers' rights stuff?'

'The lad who lived downstairs from us, David Harris, he worked at the shipyard, right?'

'Right,' said Ellen without any real interest.

'And he was a slight wee chap. Narrow shoulders, you know? And so obedient. Not like me.' He smiled briefly. 'So the bosses, they made him work on the rudder because he was so wee. But they didn't bother to teach him how to be safe and he slipped down in between the hull and the side of the wall, and he died.'

Ellen put her hand over her mouth. 'That's awful.'

James looked distraught. 'It was his first day on the shipyard.' He took a deep breath. 'They fished him out and took him home to his ma. And his head was all, you know . . .' He gestured vaguely with his hands and Ellen nodded, not wanting to know the details. 'And they gave her twenty shillings.'

'They gave her twenty shillings?'

'A week's wages and a wee bit extra for the inconvenience.' He ran his finger round his collar. 'I still hear her crying at night, and she doesn't go out now. She's not the same as she was.'

His voice cracked and Ellen put her hand on his arm in sympathy.

'Some other lad's doing that job now. Nothing's changed.' He looked fierce suddenly. 'It's the same all over. The shipyard, the factories – everywhere. No one should be treated like they're just another cog in the wheel. And it doesn't matter whether it's wages you're worrying about, or safety, or working hours, or whatever. You deserve to be listened to.'

'Injure one of us, you injure all of us,' Ellen said, impressed by his fervour. She looked up into his eyes, which were flashing with passion, and suddenly thought that he was perhaps the most interesting person she'd ever met. And Sadie was right. He was quite handsome, albeit with a broken nose that gave him a look of a man who wasn't afraid to fight to get what he wanted. It was at odds with the tears Ellen had seen in his eyes as he talked about his pal. The factory bell rang loudly, signifying the end of the shift and making Ellen jump.

'Come on,' James said. 'Let's go and spread the word.'

Chapter Sixteen

Bridget had heard what was happening. It was all everyone was talking about in the factory.

Maggie shoved a bit of paper off her desk with her elbow and both women bent down to pick it up.

'Your Ellen led them out of the factory,' Maggie said under her breath. 'Three departments. What do you think of that?'

Bridget thought that she'd never been prouder of her wee sister. She wished she'd seen her at the head of the crowd, like the Pied Piper leading the children out of Hamlin. She couldn't concentrate on her work because she was wondering what Ellen was doing now. Where was she? Where had she taken the women who'd all downed tools because of this new unfair way of working?

She didn't say that to Maggie, though. Instead she smiled and said: 'Ellen's Ellen.'

As she straightened up again and turned her limited attention back to her typewriter, she wished she could be more like Ellen. She had a knot in her stomach like a lump of coal. Or rather, she thought, like an ember from a fire. She felt aglow with rage, ready to spark into flame at any moment. Or at least she could, if Malcolm and − she sighed, knowing she was being a little overdramatic − society itself didn't keep pouring water on her smouldering anger.

Ellen, though, was doing something about it. Ellen was taking action.

'Bridget, could you take these letters to the post room, please?' Mrs Whittington was next to her desk, holding a bundle of mail.

Bridget looked up at her in surprise. Normally the porters came to collect the post.

'I'd go the long way round,' Mrs Whittington said. 'Along the top corridor.'

The top corridor had large windows with views across Clyde-bank. Was Mrs Whittington letting Bridget have a peek to see where Ellen had gone? Would she do that? Bridget met her gaze, and gave her a tiny, barely noticeable nod.

She scurried off before Mrs Whittington had time to change her mind, rushing up the stairs to the top floor and along to where the windows were.

At first she couldn't see anything. Or nothing unusual, at least. The streets beside the factory were quiet. And then some move-ment caught her eye and she saw across the river, on a patch of grass known as 'the green', a group of women. They were all chat-ting and – Bridget blinked – a couple of them looked as though they were dancing. She strained her eyes to see and thought she could make out someone playing a fiddle, right at the edge of the group.

What she couldn't see, though, was Ellen ... until she looked down again, closer to the factory and saw her sister, arm-in-arm with Sadie, both talking furiously and marching towards the group on the green.

Bridget frowned. Where had they been? To the factory? But they'd not long walked out, according to the whispers she'd heard. What was going on?

She watched them go back across the bridge and then realised she was still holding the envelopes. Mrs Whittington may have given her an excuse to see what was going on, but Bridget was fairly sure her patience had a limit, and she didn't want to push her luck.

So she delivered the letters and considered, for a second, going back the way she'd come to see what was going on now. But she'd taken a long time already. She headed down the lower corridor and bumped into Malcolm coming the other way.

'Hello,' he said cheerfully.

He looked very pleased with himself, and Bridget smiled to see his puffed-out chest.

'Are you having a good day?' she asked. Malcolm didn't always like to chat at work because he didn't like to risk the bosses spotting him socialising, but today he grinned at her and nodded. 'Very good.'

'Me too,' said Bridget, thinking about Ellen and how proud she was, and about Mrs Whittington and her unexpected leniency. 'Why is yours good?'

Malcolm opened his mouth and then shut it again. 'It's just good.'

But Bridget knew him better than anyone and she knew when he was hiding something.

'What?' she said. 'What is it?'

'I've been dealing with some stuff on behalf of Mr Beresford,' he said. 'And he said he is pleased with how I handled it.'

'What stuff?' asked Bridget, though her head was filled with the image of Ellen and Sadie walking away from the factory and she absolutely knew what Malcolm was going to say.

He shifted slightly on his feet. 'Strike stuff.'

Bridget fixed him with a fierce glare. 'Ellen?'

'Yes.' Malcolm glared back at her. 'I know she's your sister, Bridget, but she has to understand that this type of action won't work.'

'Won't it?'

'No. Management aren't going to be dictated to.'

'Dictated to?' Bridget was shocked at the words he was using.

'That's not what they want, they just want to be heard – to put their point across.'

Malcolm lifted his chin. 'Well, that's not happening.'

In a flash, Bridget understood why Ellen and Sadie had been walking away from the factory. 'They came here to talk to Mr Beresford?' she said. 'And they were sent away? Without even speaking to anyone?'

'They spoke to me,' said Malcolm. 'And I told them to go.'

'Why?' Bridget felt the ember of rage within her burn a little stronger as though someone had jabbed it with a poker. 'Why would you do that?'

'Because Mr Beresford asked me to.'

For one ridiculous moment, Bridget remembered one of the nuns at school who would always say, 'If your friend told you to jump off a bridge, would you do it?' and she was tempted to ask Malcolm the same thing. But she knew the answer would be yes. He followed the rules. He did as he was told. He didn't question or complain. If Mr Beresford asked Malcolm to jump off a bridge, Malcolm would jump.

The realisation struck her dumb for a moment, which Malcolm clearly took as conciliation.

'They're not going about this the right way, Bridget,' he said more gently. 'Workers can't just march in the gates and demand to speak to the people who run this factory.'

Bridget had recovered herself. 'Whyever not?'

Malcolm's jaw dropped.

'Well, because Mr Beresford is more important . . .' he began.

'I speak to Mr Beresford all the time,' Bridget pointed out.

'But that's different.'

'Why?'

Malcolm rolled his eyes. 'I can't talk to you when you're like this, Bridget,' he said.

'Like what?' Bridget said.

He tutted. 'Like Ellen.'

Bridget felt a tiny flush of pride alongside her rage. She glared at her husband.

'We'll speak more at home.' He checked his watch. 'Why are you in the corridor at this time, anyway? I hope Mrs Whittington's keeping an eye on your output.'

He hurried off and Bridget watched him go, her eyes burning with anger and unshed tears of frustration.

Back at her desk, she took her fury out on the typewriter keys and more than made up for the time she'd spent looking out of the window because she was working so quickly. But even so, the afternoon dragged and when the bell finally rang, she was up and out of her seat in no time at all.

'Come on,' she said to Maggie, who'd had the cover on her typewriter almost before the shift ended. 'Let's see what's happening.'

Together, they joined the crowds of people streaming towards the factory gates and Bridget filled Maggie in on what she'd seen from the windows – and what Malcolm had said. Though she didn't mention how smug he'd been. Or how he'd scolded her for asking questions. She was a little embarrassed about that.

'I expect everything's normal now,' Maggie said. 'It seems just like every other day.'

'You're probably right,' said Bridget, disappointed. 'Maybe they've even gone back to work.'

'I hope not.' Maggie gave her a quick, cheeky smile. 'I always thought your Ellen had more about her than that.'

Bridget beamed with pride. And sure enough, when they got outside the gates, there was a feeling that things were different. Instead of everyone heading in the same direction like a wave of people going into town, there were workers milling about, talking and calling to one another.

'What's going on?' Bridget breathed. 'What's happening?'

Maggie was watching everyone, her sharp eyes taking it in.

'They're planning something,' she said. 'Passing on information. Look – everyone's moving. They chat and then they move on.'

Bridget watched for a few seconds and realised Maggie was right. 'What are they saying?' she said. She felt a shiver of excitement. 'Let's go and find out.'

'They're saying that everyone's going to stop work.'

Bridget turned to see Ellen's friend Janet standing next to her. 'Everyone?'

Janet nodded. 'Yes, apparently. Or at least, that's what they want. Everyone's saying they're going to walk out to support the cabinet polishers.'

Bridget breathed out in awe.

'Every department?'

Janet shrugged. 'Seems that way.'

'I thought it would be over after a day,' Bridget said. 'I didn't expect it to come to this.'

'Management wouldn't talk to Ellen and Sadie,' said Janet. She looked a bit smug. 'I knew this would happen.'

'She's your friend,' Bridget snapped. 'She's doing a brave thing.'

Janet waved her hand. 'Och, of course she's brave. Ellen's always brave. But this is too risky, Bridget. They could be the next ones to be sacked.'

'Have you seen Ellen?' Bridget asked. 'Where is she?'

'I don't know,' Janet said. She sounded quite sad about it. 'I've not seen her.'

'If you find her, tell her I'm here,' said Bridget. 'We have to go.'

She tugged Maggie's arm and together they weaved their way through the crowds, looking for Ellen, but not seeing her.

When they reached the edge of the crowd, Maggie tapped Bridget on the arm.

'Are you going to do it, Bridget? Will you stop work tomorrow?'

Bridget didn't have to think twice.

'I will.'

*

'Over my dead body,' said Malcolm. His face was red and Bridget thought – though she didn't say it – that she'd never seen him look so angry before. 'Absolutely not.'

'It's only for a day,' Bridget said. She'd been chatting with lots of other workers who'd decided to stop working and she was even more convinced that this was the right thing to do. 'Just to show how valuable we are and make them see we all support the cabinet polishers.'

Malcolm sniffed. 'This isn't the way to do it, Bridget.'

They'd just finished eating tea and now he pushed his empty plate away. Usually, Bridget would pick it up when he did that and take it to their tiny sink to wash the dishes and make a pot of tea. But not today. Today she leaned forward with her elbows on the table, and frowned. 'Then what is?'

'What is what?'

'What is the way to do it?'

Malcolm stared at her. 'Well, the best way would be . . .'

Bridget waited, as he trailed off.

'There are better ways,' he finished lamely.

'Are there?' She got up and started clearing the plates. 'Right.'

As she stretched for one of the dishes, Malcolm reached out and took her wrist.

'I forbid you to stop working,' he said.

Bridget's ember of rage flared and flamed. She pulled her arm away from Malcolm's grip.

'You can't tell me what to do,' she growled, dropping the plates onto the table with a clatter. Malcolm looked startled and Bridget picked up the crockery again, noticing with annoyance that her favourite plate had cracked when she'd dropped it. Then, without speaking, she walked over to the sink and leaned against it, feeling her heart thumping, and tried to steady her breathing. How dare Malcolm try to stop her supporting her sister? And really, this wasn't just to do with Ellen. She very much understood what they were trying to do here. How could it be fair that the women were doing more work for less pay? Ellen was just trying to show the bosses that they'd made a mistake. What was it the suffragettes said – 'Deeds not words'? Ellen was just putting that into practice.

'You made promises.' Malcolm was standing behind her.

'What?' Bridget turned to look at her husband.

'You stood in church on our wedding day and you promised to honour me.'

Bridget felt cold. 'Well, yes. But surely that's not relevant . . .'

'Going against my express wishes. Humiliating me? That's not honourable.'

'No, Malcolm. I didn't mean . . .'

'You didn't mean what you promised?' Malcolm said. He sounded bleak. 'Was that the only part of our marriage vows that you didn't mean?'

'No,' Bridget said. 'That's not what I said.' She rubbed her forehead. 'I meant our vows.'

'Did you? Because it doesn't feel that way.'

Bridget felt the ground shift beneath her feet, like she was on a ship. 'Of course I did, Malcolm.'

'I don't believe you.' His defiant demeanour crumpled and he suddenly looked like a little boy. Bridget's heart went out to him. He'd had such a hard upbringing, and she knew all he craved was stability, security and a family, just like the one she'd been lucky enough to grow up in.

She went to him and put her hands on his upper arms. 'Malcolm, I love you. I don't want you to think that my supporting Ellen means I don't want to be your wife. Not one bit.'

He looked at her for a second and then he wrapped his arms round her. 'Do you promise?' he said into her hair.

'Och, get away with you. Of course I promise.' Bridget wanted to lighten the mood but Malcolm was serious. He pulled away from her and looked straight into her eyes.

'Promise me you won't stop work,' he said.

Again Bridget felt her world tilt. How could she choose between her sister and her husband?

'Malcolm . . .' she began.

'Promise me.'

She sighed. 'I really don't think this stopping work is the big thing you're making it out to be.'

'Of course it's a big thing. It's unrest.'

'Unrest?'

'I could lose my job. Just imagine how it will look if the bosses see my wife walking out with those rebels.'

'Rebels? Oh, for heaven's sake, Malcolm, don't be so dramatic.'

'Promise me you won't join in,' he said.

Bridget's mind was racing. She didn't want to cause problems for Malcolm. Maybe he could lose his job. Maybe Ellen could. She wasn't sure. But she knew Ellen would be expecting her to stand by her and support her.

'She's my sister.'

'And I'm your husband.'

There was a loaded silence. Bridget was suddenly very aware that whatever she said next could change her life forever. She shook her head. Now who was being dramatic?

'I promise I won't stop working,' she said.

Then she put down the dishcloth she'd been gripping in her hand all this time, walked past Malcolm and went to bed without saying another word.

Chapter Seventeen

It felt odd not going to work the next morning. Ellen got up and dressed as usual, just as early as she did when she was going to Wentworth. But she wasn't planning to head to the factory. Instead, she'd arranged to meet Sadie, Walter, James and the others on the green.

Her father was in the kitchen, holding a mug of tea and looking out of the grubby window, when she wandered in, hoping the pot wasn't empty.

Ellen hesitated when she saw him. He worked long hours, her da, and she'd been fast asleep when he got home last night. She didn't know what he'd think of the strike. Her ma had said: 'Oh, Ellen.' And she'd sort of sighed and shaken her head, but then she'd put her arm round her and given her a little squeeze that made Ellen sure she approved of what she was doing. And her gran, well, she'd been even more supportive. She'd put her fists up, like she was taking part in some sort of boxing match, and said that if she was twenty years younger . . . Ellen had laughed at that, relieved the women in her family were behind her. Janet was right: the Kelly women ran towards fights, not away from them.

Her gran had even said she wasn't to worry about being short on what she brought home, even though they were missing Bridget's wage now she'd got married.

'Away with you worrying about money,' she'd called from her

seat in the window. I'm not flush, but I've got a wee bit put by. I'll help out.'

'Really?' Ma had looked relieved. 'Are you sure?'

'Course I'm sure,' she'd said. 'I don't want those swines at the factory getting their own way.'

But while Ma and Gran were right behind her, Ellen wasn't sure her da would feel the same way. He had a fierce work ethic, and he was proud of doing a good job to earn his wage and support his family.

'Da?' she said now, going into the kitchen.

He turned to look at her.

'Not working today?' he asked.

Ellen paused, not knowing whether to try to justify her decision. But then she simply shook her head. 'No.'

'Right enough.' Her father turned his gaze back to the window. 'Proud of you, doll.'

Ellen felt tears prick her eyes. Da was a typical Clydebank man. Big and strong and a hoot when he'd had one too many beers, but he didn't say much and he didn't show his emotions very often.

'Thanks, Da,' she said.

When it happened, when everyone stopped work, it happened so fast that Ellen could hardly believe it.

Some people had not gone to the factory at all that day. There were all the cabinet polishers and the other women who'd stopped working yesterday in support, and a few others too. The green was crowded when Ellen got there and at first she couldn't even see Sadie among all the people.

Most people, though, had gone to work as normal. The plan was to wait and see if anything happened – if any of the bosses came to speak with the strikers on the green. And if not, then Walter said he had ways of getting messages to workers once the factory gates were closed. He'd give the nod and they'd down tools and walk out.

Ellen, though, hoped it wouldn't come to that. She hoped that the three departments that had walked out yesterday, as well as the new strikers who'd joined in today – more women, she noticed with satisfaction – would make their point clearly enough. She really expected Mr Beresford and the others to appear almost as soon as the bell sounded to start that morning's shift.

She saw Sadie, standing slightly to the side of the group, looking at the gathered crowd with something rather like awe, and went to speak to her.

'What a sight, eh?'

'It shows this is the right thing to do,' Sadie said. 'I've been counting and I think there are a thousand people here.'

'A thousand people?' Ellen was struck dumb for a second. She looked around her. 'A thousand people?'

Sadie grinned. 'All because of you.'

'And you.'

'But mostly you.'

Ellen gave her a good-natured punch on the arm. 'Surely this will work?' she said. 'Surely Mr Beresford will see this and understand what we're trying to show them?'

'You'd hope so.' Sadie shrugged. 'Not sure what else we can do if it doesn't.'

Ellen felt a little shiver of nerves. She'd not thought about what they'd do if this strike didn't pay off.

'I saw your Bridget,' Sadie said.

'Here?' Ellen was astonished and also rather pleased. 'Is she here?'

Sadie screwed her face up. 'Don't think so. She was heading towards the factory. I thought she saw me, but she didn't stop so maybe she didn't.'

'Perhaps she'll come later,' Ellen said hopefully.

'Perhaps,' Sadie said. She didn't sound very certain, which annoyed Ellen a wee bit. But she didn't say anything.

'Noah's right behind us,' Sadie added. 'He says if he wasn't teaching, he'd come along too.'

'He doesn't work at Wentworth,' Ellen pointed out in a slightly sulky tone because she was still a bit annoyed about Bridget. 'Why would he come?'

'Just to give us support.'

'We won't need it,' Ellen said. 'By lunchtime, we'll be back at work, I've got no doubt about it.'

But lunchtime came and there was no sign of any of the bosses making an approach to the workers.

'They're not coming, are they?' she said to Sadie.

Sadie shook her head. 'Doesn't look like it.'

'I really thought we'd be back at work by now.' Ellen was feeling a little sick. What had started as a way of reminding the bosses that they mattered, was growing and swelling and it seemed almost out of control. It felt much bigger than they were.

'Hello, girls,' Walter said. 'All set?'

'All set for the next stage?' Ellen said. She put her arm through Sadie's because she felt dizzy suddenly. 'For everyone else stopping work?'

'That's right.' Walter's eyes gleamed with excitement.

Ellen looked at Sadie, who gave her a little nod.

She took a deep breath. 'All set,' she said.

'Good stuff.'

There was an awkward pause.

'What should we do? Should we just wait?' Ellen asked Walter, glad he was there, as she really didn't have a clue what to do next.

'You just wait,' he said, looking over at the factory clock. 'I'll give the nod.'

'Right.' Ellen bounced a little bit on her toes because even though spring had arrived, it was still a bit cold. 'You give the nod.'

James was standing slightly to the side of Walter, and as the older man walked away, he came over to Ellen. She was pleased to see him and even more pleased when he gave her a little nudge with his shoulder.

'Hiya,' he said.

'Hiya.' She beamed at him, ignoring Sadie's knowing look. 'I'm pleased you're here.'

'Me too,' he said. He jigged about a bit on the grass, looking like he had something to say and, for a second, Ellen thought he might ask her to go for a walk one Sunday, or maybe even to a dance or for a drink.

But instead, he screwed his nose up. 'Don't let Walter take over, will you?' he said.

Surprised, Ellen frowned. 'He's helping.'

'Aye, he means well, but you know what they're like, eh?'

'What who's like?'

James gave her a broad, very cheeky smile. 'Men.'

Ellen let out a bark of laughter. 'I do.'

'He's really passionate about workers' rights and that. And he's great. But you started this, Ellen. Don't forget that.'

Absurdly pleased with his praise, but a little embarrassed too, Ellen ducked her head.

'Ellen?' Walter called from across the green. 'We're ready.'

Ellen looked from Sadie to James and back to Sadie again.

'Do you think anyone will come?'

Sadie crossed her fingers. 'I really hope so.'

'They will,' said James with confidence. 'I absolutely believe they will.'

And then a strange thing happened. The factory hummed with noise, as a rule. From morning to night, Clydebank buzzed with the noise of the machines. It wasn't something you heard, so much as something you felt. Like a thrum deep inside your chest. It was always there when the factory was working. And the people of Clydebank barely noticed it because it was as much a part of the town as the river, or the rain.

But now, it was gradually fading away. Quietening. And then it stopped. And as it stopped, the crowd stopped too. All the chatter died away and there was silence.

Ellen clutched Sadie's arm.

'What is this?' she breathed.

Everyone on the green was turned towards the factory, watching and waiting, though Ellen wasn't sure what for.

Then suddenly, there was a new sound. A tramping, thudding noise that rang around the tenement blocks and reverberated off the buildings.

Footsteps.

'Oh my goodness,' Sadie said. Then louder: 'Oh my goodness, Ellen. Look!'

Streaming down the street from the factory were hundreds and hundreds of workers. Thousands. Ellen could see people looking out of their windows as they passed, bemused by why so many folk were leaving work early.

'You did it, girls!' Walter was looking thrilled. 'You bloody did it!'

Thrilled and scared and full of excitement, Ellen and Sadie ran to the edge of the green and clambered up onto a wall outside a tenement block so they could see.

The road from the factory was full of folk, their footsteps making a rhythmic beat that sounded like drums. It was as busy as the end of the day, or a football crowd at one of Da's matches. There were people as far as Ellen could see, way back to the factory gates and beyond. She squinted at the clerical office windows but they were too far away now and the windows simply looked back at her blindly.

And the people kept coming, filling the green until they spilled onto the street too.

Sadie and Ellen stopped talking and simply watched in awe as the people kept streaming in. It took a long time for everyone to leave work – well over an hour – because there were just so many people, but the women didn't get bored. They stayed perching on the wall, and watched as the workers kept coming.

In one of the windows of the nearby tenement, a wee boy watched, his mouth open in surprise.

'He'll remember this day forever,' said Sadie. Ellen thought they would all remember it. Every one of the thousands of people who were here on the green – they'd all remember the day the factory stopped, and the workers walked out.

She shivered. And they'd started it. All these people were here because of her and Sadie. Two women with no power, not really. They'd done this.

Someone was playing music. Ellen could hear singing and chatter, and a chant of 'fair pay for fair work' and she felt so very, very proud that she could barely believe it. It felt like a party. A celebration of sorts.

Sadie nudged her and pointed over to where Walter and a group of men were busy, grabbing pallets and piling them up to make a platform.

'We should go and help,' Ellen said. They both jumped down from the wall and weaved their way through the crowd, which wasn't easy because there were so many people dancing and milling about.

Eventually they reached the men.

'Here they are!' Walter exclaimed, and to Ellen's absolute astonishment, the men all cheered and slapped them on the back and lifted Sadie up on to their shoulders, shoogling her about until she screamed with laughter and told them to let her go.

Walter put his arm through Ellen's and gave her a broad smile. 'This was all you, doll.'

But Ellen shook her head. 'It was all of us.'

Walter winked at her. 'You've got it.' He passed her a megaphone. 'Go on, then,' he said. 'Off you go.'

Ellen looked down at the cone in her hands in confusion.

'No one will hear you if you speak without it,' said Sadie, who'd finally managed to extract herself from the men's shoulders. 'Come on.'

Walter and the others lifted first Sadie, then Ellen onto the platform and even though it was a bit wobbly, and even though Ellen's heart was pounding at the sight of so many people, she felt alive. Alive in a way she'd never felt before.

'Hello,' she said into the cone, feeling a little bit silly. But she was heartened that the crowd fell quiet, the hush falling across the people in a wave.

'You're all heroes and heroines,' she said through the megaphone, reeling at the sound of her voice being projected across the crowd. 'We just want to show the efficiency engineers that this new style of management isn't fair. We don't want to work longer and harder for less money. We can't. In fact, it's not efficient at all. And now, thanks to you all supporting us, they'll understand how valuable we are to Wentworth.' She paused. 'It's no surprise that we've been thinking about this like threads. Individually we can be broken, like a single thread, but together? Well, we're strong as anything.'

The crowd cheered and Ellen clambered down again, passing the megaphone to Walter, who clearly had something to say too.

As he began talking, Ellen caught sight of her mother, standing with her cousin Johnny and his fiancée Flora, one of the defect repairers who'd been sacked. Dragging Sadie with her, she made her way through the crowds and threw her arms round them.

'You're here,' she said. 'Thank you.'

'Ah shush,' Ma said. 'Not going to let my wee girl do all this on her own now, am I?'

Ellen grinned at them, and then a thought struck her.

'Where's Bridget?'

Johnny made a face. 'She's not coming.'

'What?'

'Some of the secretaries are here,' he said. 'But I saw that Maggie, you know? Sits with Bridget?'

Ellen nodded slowly. 'I know Maggie.'

'She said Bridget just kept typing when everyone else stopped.'

Ellen's stomach dropped. 'She did?'

'Aye.' Johnny shrugged. 'I saw that Mrs Whittington too, who runs their department. She's here.'

'She is?' Ellen was astonished.

'Bridget must be the only one left.'

'Why wouldn't she come?' Ellen said, to herself really. 'She was the one who started this. Why wouldn't she support us?'

'Malcolm,' Sadie said. 'He's her husband after all. Perhaps she felt she had to be loyal to him?'

Ellen snorted but her mother nodded. 'Sadie's right, doll. Poor Bridget's in a tricky position. Don't take it personally.'

Rationally, Ellen knew she was right. Of course Bridget was in a bind, what with that idiot Malcolm being her lawfully wedded husband and all that. But, but, but, Bridget had always been there for Ellen. Always. She'd always had her big sister at her side, like when she started school. She remembered learning to read and how proud Bridget had been. And when she started working at Wentworth – in fact, it had been Bridget who'd got her the job in the first place. It was always Bridget who was there, cheering her on. Propping her up.

Today seemed like it was the most important day in Ellen's life, but Bridget wasn't there.

Chapter Eighteen

Bridget wasn't working. She had been. She'd kept her head down and her fingers flying across the typewriter keys when a murmur went around the room and her colleagues began tidying their desks and putting on their coats.

It was a never-ending source of mystery to Bridget how messages spread through Wentworth. You never really saw anyone talking or passing notes or giving someone else a nod, but somehow it happened and suddenly everyone knew it was time to go. Time to stop work and join the women who'd walked out yesterday. To go and add their voices to Ellen's and to ask for things to return to normal.

Bridget felt like she was being ripped apart. Malcolm, her husband, the man she'd made promises to in church, in front of God and her family, had asked her not to join the strike. He'd *told* her not to join the strike. And more importantly, she'd seen in his face how much this meant to him and how much her support meant to him. She'd always felt this way about Malcolm – like he'd been so sad as a wee boy that she didn't want to do anything to make him feel that way again. And she didn't want to upset him now. She loved him.

Didn't she?

And yet that ember of rage was still there, smouldering away inside her, making her feel like at any moment she could burst into flames and scream: 'This isn't fair!'

She didn't though. She just kept typing.

'Coming?' Maggie said in a low voice.

Bridget had glanced at Mrs Whittington, who was sitting, stock-still at her own desk, staring straight ahead.

'I can't.'

'Sure?'

Bridget gave a little nod. Maggie looked at her for a second, then joined the others leaving the room until there was no one left except Bridget and Mrs Whittington. Looking up, Bridget caught her boss's eye.

'It's your sister doing this, isn't it?' Mrs Whittington said. 'Your Ellen?'

Mrs Whittington had been at school with Bridget's ma. Ma had always said she had a good heart and Bridget had always screwed her face up and doubted it very much because she worked them hard. But now she wondered.

'Aye, it's Ellen.'

There was a pause and then Mrs Whittington got to her feet.

'Right,' she said. 'That's me going.'

Bridget's jaw dropped. 'You're stopping work?'

'I think it's important.'

'So do I.' Bridget was wretched.

'Come on, then.'

For a second, Bridget was tempted. She thought how easy it would be to simply get up and walk out of the room with Mrs Whittington. But she shook her head.

'No.'

She and Mrs Whittington looked at one another for a moment and Bridget was certain she saw disappointment on the older woman's face. She'd disappointed her. The thought was almost unbearable. But still she sat.

'Good luck,' she muttered.

'You too,' said Mrs Whittington.

Of course, as soon as the factory had emptied and the clatter of feet faded away down the street, Bridget abandoned all pretence of working and instead grabbed some paperwork – just to have an excuse if she bumped into anyone from management – and hurried along the top corridor to the big windows.

From there she watched in absolute amazement as thousands of workers streamed along the street towards the green. Ellen was down there somewhere, she knew. And Sadie. And Johnny. Everyone.

If Mrs Whittington's disappointment had been hard to take, Bridget didn't want to think about how difficult it would be to see the same expression on her sister's face. But she'd made her choice and now she had to live with it.

She watched for ages, seeing the crowd move and sway like it was one huge beast. And then slowly, she turned and went back to her desk, her feet echoing around the empty corridors.

The factory wasn't completely deserted. She could tell. She could hear that some machinery was still running. And there were occasional shouts or calls. And, of course, she knew that management would all still be in their department. That Malcolm would still be working.

But it still seemed very much as though she was the only one there. She gave a little snort, thinking of her childhood longing to wake up and be alone. Now she was alone, rattling around in this enormous building, thousands of times bigger than their flat, and she didn't like it. She was a fickle one, indeed.

She took a breath and fed a clean sheet of paper into her typewriter. She had work to do.

What Bridget hadn't thought about was leaving work when her shift was over. She'd not considered that the striking workers would still be on the green, chatting and listening to each other talk, and singing and dancing.

But there they were. And she and the other employees who'd not stopped work – there were more of them than Bridget had expected actually, but they were still vastly outnumbered by the strikers – had to walk past them on their way home.

She pulled her hat down over her face, and walked quickly, her skirt flapping round her ankles because she was striding so purposefully.

She expected questions. Hostility even. But what she got was friendly shouts. A group of young women had made silly trumpets from paper, and they danced around her, tooting their paper horns and calling to her to join in.

Bridget walked on.

And then, at the corner of the street where she would turn away from the green and head to her wee flat, she saw Ellen.

Bridget's heart skipped a beat at the sight of her sister, so small and delicate but so fierce. She had her hands on her hips and she was wearing her best blouse and her Sunday skirt, her crucifix glinting at her neck. The thought of Ellen choosing to dress up today – to put on her special clothes because today was a special day – made Bridget want to cry.

She paused for a second, gathering herself, and then she walked towards Ellen, ready to take whatever was coming.

'You stayed in work?' Ellen said before Bridget had even reached her. 'Why would you do that? You're the one who started this whole thing, Bridget. You told us about the scientific management before it even began. Why wouldn't you see it through?'

'I'm sorry,' Bridget said, knowing that Ellen didn't want to hear apologies.

'Are you, aye?' Ellen folded her arms, looking so much like their gran that Bridget wanted to laugh, but she didn't because she knew that wouldn't go down well.

'Ellen, you know it's hard for me.'

'Is it?'

'Stop replying to everything I say with a question.'

'Why?'

Bridget let out a gasp of frustration. Was there anyone alive more annoying than her sister? She doubted it.

'I can't talk to you when you're like this.'

'Like what?'

'Ellen!'

There was a pause, then Ellen said: 'I just don't understand why you didn't come.'

She looked so sad and bewildered that Bridget felt horribly guilty.

'Because of Malcolm, Ellen,' she said. 'I couldn't come because I'm married to Malcolm.'

Ellen sighed. 'He's not in charge.'

'No.'

'So why does he get to decide?'

'He doesn't get to decide. I decided.'

Ellen shook her head, clearly despairing and Bridget sighed.

'I know you find Malcolm difficult,' she began. Ellen snorted and Bridget glared at her. 'He's had troubles in his life,' she went on. 'Things haven't been easy for him.'

'Sadie's da just dropped down dead one day,' Ellen said. 'One day he was there and working and the next day he wasn't. And her ma can't work because she's too sick.'

'Yes, but . . .'

'And all those babies Ma lost, Bridget. The ones before me, and the ones after. All those times we heard her crying at night-time and then she'd be up making breakfast for us before school the next morning.'

'Malcolm had an awful time of it, Ellen,' Bridget said. 'And it's changed the way he feels. The way he acts.'

Ellen, though, wasn't moved. She curled her lip with disdain. 'He's using his bad times to make you do what he wants you to do.'

'No!' Bridget was appalled. 'That's a terrible thing to say! Don't say that. He'd never do that.'

'Wouldn't he?'

So they were back to the questions again, it seemed. Bridget rolled her eyes.

'I have to go.'

'Will you work tomorrow?' Ellen met her gaze and Bridget stared back and then, slowly, she nodded.

'I will.'

'What if I asked you not to?'

'I still have to work, Ellen.' Bridget had that feeling again, as though the very ground beneath her feet was tilting. 'I have to.'

Ellen looked like she was about to cry. Bridget averted her gaze so she didn't have to see her sister so upset. 'It's a choice between me and Malcolm,' Ellen said. 'And you've chosen Malcolm.'

Bridget tried to swallow. Her throat was dry and scratchy. 'Yes,' she said. 'I've chosen Malcolm.'

'Then you're no longer my sister.'

Bridget watched as Ellen turned and walked away, never once looking back, and then was swallowed up by the crowd, vanishing from view.

She felt hollow inside. And light-headed, suddenly. She hurried away from the crowds, down the street towards their flat. Then as she approached home, she changed her mind. She couldn't face Malcolm at the moment. She had a horrible feeling if he so much as mentioned Wentworth – and let's face it, when did he talk about anything else? – she would snap.

Instead, she walked right past their front door, along the road to the railway station, where she sat down on a bench to gather herself together. There was another woman sitting there already. Bridget vaguely recognised her as the woman who worked in McKinley's General Shop, and she clearly wasn't one of the strikers – her dress was a little too well made and her hat a little too well cared for.

She nodded at Bridget as she sat down and moved her carpet bag so there was more room for her, and Bridget nodded back, glad of the tiny kindness after such a horrible day.

The sky was darkening overhead, and she knew she couldn't sit outside all evening, but her mind was racing and she wanted to get her thoughts in order.

She hadn't chosen Malcolm over Ellen. That was a ridiculous thing to do, so ridiculous she couldn't even consider it. And yet, she'd just done exactly that. And now Ellen was upset, and she was feeling awful and she saw no way round it. If she went to work, then Ellen would feel betrayed. If she stopped work, then Malcolm would feel the same.

'It's an impossible thing,' she said aloud.

'And one can't believe impossible things,' the woman sitting next to her said.

Bridget turned to her in surprise.

'I daresay you haven't had much practice,' she added.

The woman hooted with laughter.

'I'm sorry,' she continued. '*Alice* was my favourite book when I was wee, and it just popped into my head when you spoke. How nice that you knew immediately what I was talking about.'

'It was my favourite, too.' Bridget smiled. 'I liked the talking flowers the best.'

'I liked the sleepy dormouse.'

'My sister Ellen liked the Cheshire Cat,' Bridget said and then, to her mortification, she burst into tears.

'Heavens,' said the woman. She shuffled along the bench so she was closer to Bridget and gave her a handkerchief, which was edged with lace and smelled of lavender. 'Is your sister . . . did she . . . did you lose her?'

Bridget wiped her eyes with the hanky and feeling more than a little silly, said: 'No, she's alive. We just had a row, that's all.'

The woman looked relieved. 'Well, thank goodness for that,'

she said. 'I have no biological sisters, but I fall out with my friends at least once a week. Often more.'

'But you're still friends again afterwards?' Bridget said hopefully.

'The best of friends.' The woman touched Bridget's arm and though she was wearing gloves, and though Bridget had her coat on, Bridget felt the warmth of her hand.

'I'm Ida,' the woman said. 'Ida McKinley.'

'Bridget Walsh. Nice to meet you, Ida.' Bridget gestured with the handkerchief. 'Thank you for being so nice.'

Ida huffed. 'Not at all,' she said. She took off her hat and held it in her lap and in the dim light, Bridget saw her face properly for the first time. She was a little older than Bridget, closer to thirty than twenty. She had wide, clear eyes and she would have been very pretty had it not been for a scar down one cheek, which ran over the side of her mouth and turned it down even when she smiled. Bridget tried not to stare. Somewhere in the back of her mind she remembered hearing folk talk about 'that poor McKinley girl' and 'wasn't it all just awful what happened' but Bridget couldn't remember exactly what had gone on, and she wasn't about to ask.

'Now,' Ida said. 'Do you have somewhere you need to be?'

Bridget thought about Malcolm, who would be sitting at home, wondering where she was, and she shook her head.

'I am waiting for a train to Glasgow and I am impossibly early, as I always am, and I still have at least a quarter of an hour to kill,' Ida said, with her curious, lopsided smile. 'Why not tell me all about your sister? A problem shared is a problem halved, after all.'

Bridget opened her mouth to say she was absolutely fine and didn't need to talk, but she suddenly found that she very much wanted to tell Ida about her troubles with Ellen. And so instead, she nodded.

'Ellen's the boldest girl I know,' she began.

Chapter Nineteen

Sadie hadn't known Ellen very long, and she'd never seen her upset – not really. She'd seen her happy, and angry and nervous and excited, but not upset. Until now.

Sadie was standing with Walter when Ellen came to find her. The crowd was thinning out a bit now, with people drifting away back to their houses for the evening and Ellen came weaving her way through, without looking round, ignoring the folk who stopped to say something to her. Which was very unlike her.

'What's the matter?' Sadie asked, taking in her friend's stricken face and red-rimmed eyes.

Ellen took her arm and tugged her a little away from Walter. Sadie gave Walter a nod to let him know she wasn't just walking off rudely, and then, worried, followed Ellen.

'Ellen, tell me what's happened?'

They stopped beside a tree and Ellen, looking exhausted suddenly, leaned against the trunk for support.

'I saw Bridget.'

'Right.'

'And I asked her why she didn't stop work.'

'Because of Malcolm?'

'Yes.' Ellen's lips were pinched together tightly.

'Ellen,' Sadie said gently, 'it's hard for Bridget. She's in a difficult position.'

'She's my sister.' Ellen's eyes filled with tears again. 'I really wanted her to be here.'

Sadie put her arms round Ellen. 'I know. It's tough.'

Ellen wiped her eyes with the back of her hand and took in a long, shuddery breath.

'What were you talking to Walter about?'

'Next steps,' said Sadie. 'Now we've all stopped work, what should we do?'

Ellen made a face. 'What should we do?'

'I don't know because you came along,' Sadie said with an affectionate squeeze of Ellen's arm to make sure she knew she was joking. 'Shall we go and find him?'

Ellen nodded. 'Am I all puffy?'

'Not at all,' Sadie said, which was a bit of a lie because it was quite obvious Ellen had been crying. 'Come on, let's find Walter and make some plans.'

'Wait,' said Ellen. 'Is it just Walter, or . . .'

'Walter and Stanley, and James,' Sadie said.

Was Sadie imagining it or was Ellen blushing? Perhaps she was beginning to see the good things about James. As far as Sadie could tell, there were a lot of them for Ellen to see.

Ellen smoothed her hair down and blinked her eyes a few times. 'Better?' she said.

She looked exactly the same, but as Ellen always looked nice because her enthusiasm and zeal for life shone from her face, Sadie just nodded. 'Better.'

Walter took them to the pub, which Sadie pretended was absolutely normal for her, but actually it was a bit of a thrill. She asked for a beer because that was what everyone else asked for, but she didn't really like it, so at first she took small sips, and then she was so caught up in the conversation, she didn't drink the rest of it.

Walter, along with James and Stanley, sat on one side of the table and Sadie and Ellen sat on the other. Sadie felt a little bit like she was in school, and that made her think of Noah, which made her wish he was there. She saw Ellen studying James from under her eyelashes and smiled to herself. He seemed like a nice lad. Thoughtful and careful. Sadie liked that.

'I didn't for one minute think that everyone would stop work,' Ellen said.

Walter smiled. 'You've tapped into something there, girls. A feeling we've been trying to harness for a couple of years, isn't that right, Stan?'

Stan had been by Walter's side since the first day Sadie and Ellen met him, but Sadie hadn't heard him say more than a few words and it seemed he wasn't about to start now. He just nodded. 'Aye.'

'What this has proved is that we need to stick together,' Walter went on. 'Like you said, Ellen, we're stronger together. There were thousands of folk out there today and we can't be ignored.'

'So what do we do?' asked Sadie, leaning forward.

'We have to get organised. We need a list of demands . . .'

'We've got a list of demands,' Ellen said. 'Well, not demands. We've got a list of what we want.'

'Good girl,' said Walter, and Sadie felt herself bristle a little at the term of affection. She knew he meant well, but this was only happening because of Ellen and it sounded a little . . . she thought for a second . . . demeaning.

Ellen clearly felt the same because she caught Sadie's eye and raised a brow. Sadie screwed up her nose in response and Ellen smiled, and Sadie thought how glad she was that they were doing this together.

'We need to picket,' said James, clearly picking up on the women's irritation and jumping in.

'Picket?' said Ellen, but Sadie had been reading more leaflets and she knew what it was.

'We stand outside the factory and speak to anyone going in – try to persuade them not to go to work,' she said. Ellen snorted, obviously thinking of Bridget, and Sadie put her hand on her arm, showing her she understood.

'It makes us visible, too,' James said. 'Management go in the same gates as we do.'

'We can't all picket,' Ellen pointed out. 'There are too many of us. We won't fit.'

'No. We'll have a rota,' Walter said.

'What will the rest of us do?' Ellen frowned. 'Stay on the green?'

Sadie was thinking. 'We should divide into groups,' she said. 'There's too many of us altogether.'

'Well, that's our strength,' said Walter, sitting up a bit straighter.

'Yes, in some ways, but it also makes us unwieldy.'

'Unwieldy, eh?' said Walter. He looked amused and that annoyed Sadie, too. She glared at him.

'Yes.'

'We've thought of that,' said Walter. 'We'll divide according to where we live, with each division having a representative who can pass on information and anything that's happened.'

'You've planned all this very quickly,' said Sadie, who was still feeling a bit prickly.

James looked proud. 'We've been organising for months,' he said. 'The Industrial Workers of Scotland are going to change the way we all work.'

'Well, the Industrial Workers of Scotland wouldn't be in this position if it wasn't for Ellen,' Sadie snapped. 'And they'd do well to remember that.'

James looked chastened but Walter whistled. 'Aye, you're a feisty one, that's for sure.'

Sadie took a slug of her beer to stop herself saying anything rude and regretted it as the bitter liquid hit the back of her throat.

'What about Mr Beresford and the other managers?' Ellen said. 'All this will be for nothing if they won't speak to us.'

'Negotiations will take place,' Walter said. 'But on our terms.'

'Well, they're not taking place at all at the moment,' Ellen pointed out.

'They will. Once they see we're serious.' Walter drained his drink and pushed his empty glass away. 'We're working on the principle of collective bargaining,' he said.

'What's that?' Sadie was still annoyed with him, but she was interested.

'Like I said, we're stronger together. We believe if you injure one of us, you injure us all. That's why, when you girls were treated badly, we all stopped work.'

'Right,' Ellen said.

'So, we'll negotiate on behalf of all the Wentworth workers. Ask for an improvement for all of us.'

'Good,' said Sadie. 'As long as the bosses will listen.'

'We'll go and see Beresford again tomorrow.' Walter looked determined.

'Who's we?'

'Stanley and me.'

Stanley silently nodded and Sadie wondered if he'd speak when he was face to face with Mr Beresford and the others, or if he'd let Walter do all the talking.

'They wouldn't see me,' Ellen said.

'No . . .' Walter left the word hanging in the air, clearly implying that they'd take him more seriously than they'd taken Ellen.

Sadie pushed her chair back from the table. 'I have to go,' she said, standing up.

Ellen glanced at her, then pushed her chair back too. 'I'll come with you.'

'Actually, Ellen, could you stay five minutes and just go through what happened with management on the first day?'

Ellen looked from Walter to Sadie, and Sadie shrugged. 'See you tomorrow, Ellen,' she said.

She picked up her coat and walked quickly to the door of the pub.

Outside, the evening air was cool and the sky was dark. Sadie quickened her pace, thinking about Ma. Miriam had promised to look in on her and the children, and Daniel was more than capable of buttering some bread for their tea, but Sadie still felt guilty for not being there. She hurried towards the station and stopped as she saw Noah, waiting under a streetlight.

'What are you doing here?' She virtually skipped to him, so pleased was she to see him. 'Why are you in Clydebank?'

Noah grinned at her, pushing his glasses up his nose. 'I came to see you.'

'Why?'

'Because of this.' He opened his satchel and took out the evening newspaper. On the front page was the headline WENT-WORTH STOPS WORK with a write-up about the strike and an astonishing photograph of Ellen and Sadie balanced on the stage made from pallets.

Sadie stared at it in awe. 'It's about us.'

'It is.'

She took the newspaper from him and began to read.

'Listen to this bit,' she said. 'The well-behaved strikers gathered at Clydebank Green, led by the girls from the polishing department.' She grinned at Noah. 'That's us.'

'I'm not sure anyone could ever call you "well behaved",' he said. 'But they don't know you like I do.'

Sadie flapped the newspaper at him and carried on reading. 'This is wonderful,' she said. 'People are really taking notice.'

'How could they not? I heard a woman down the road saying it had taken more than an hour for all the strikers to walk past her front door. This is huge, Sadie.' Noah looked right at her. 'I'm really proud of you.'

Sadie felt warm inside from the tips of her toes to the very top of her head.

'Are you?'

Noah turned to face her. 'You are one of the cleverest, funniest, bravest women I know,' he said.

'Stop it,' Sadie said, wondering if he said that to the mysterious woman he wanted to marry and wondering – again – if she had the chutzpah to ask him about her.

'And the most modest,' Noah joked.

Reluctantly, because she was still a bit grumpy, Sadie smiled at him. 'It's a shame those men from the IWS don't see it,' she said.

'Are they being difficult? I'd have thought they'd support the strike.'

They began to walk towards the station. 'They're almost too supportive,' Sadie said, trying not to sound like she was complaining, even though she was. 'They're taking over. They want to speak to Mr Beresford, and they're organising pickets, and divisions ...' She put her hands in her pockets. 'It's annoying, that's all.'

Noah gave her a little amused glance, which annoyed her too. But the sound of the approaching Glasgow train interrupted her just as she was about to snap at him.

'Quick,' she said instead. 'We don't want to miss it.'

Together they ran up the steps to the station and onto the platform, just as the train pulled in. Then they collapsed into a carriage, breathless and laughing, and Sadie felt her prickly feelings about the strike begin to disappear.

Her improved mood didn't last, though. In fact, it faded as soon as she opened the front door and heard Rachel crying. Her stomach lurched. She found Ma sitting in her chair with Rachel curled up in her lap. Her sister had never been big but Sadie caught her breath at how small and shrunken she looked. At nearly thirteen, she was too old to be sitting on Ma's lap now, but she looked like a wee girl. She was crying quietly, but her eyes were closed.

'Is she sleeping?' Sadie whispered.

Ma shook her head. 'Dozing off and on. She says everything hurts.'

'She needs to see the doctor,' said Sadie. 'I'll sort it.'

'Thank you.'

'Where are the boys?'

'Gone to play football.' Ma looked a little sheepish. 'Daniel said the man who organises it always brings food for the boys to eat afterwards.'

'There's food here,' Sadie said, feeling her prickles again. 'They should have eaten here.'

Her ma looked at her over the top of Rachel's head. 'Daniel gave Rachel the last bit of bread.'

'What did you have?'

'Och, I'm not hungry,' her mother said. Sadie knew she was lying, and she felt a twist of annoyance, embarrassment and fear all at once.

She dropped a kiss on her ma's head and stroked Rachel's hair. 'I'll take some money from the pot and go to get some bread, and I'll call in at the doctor and see if he can come and see Rachel.'

'You're a good girl, Sadie,' Ma said. Sadie smiled, thinking how odd it was that when Walter said 'good girl' it sounded like an insult but when her ma said it, well, she was proud as punch.

She went into the kitchen and opened the biscuit jar where they kept the money. There wasn't much in there. She tipped it out onto the counter and did some sums in her head. She could buy some food now, and hopefully Dr Cohen would let her pay half now and half on Friday when she got her wages ...

With a sudden realisation that made her shiver as though she'd been doused in a bucket of cold water, Sadie remembered that there would be no wages on Friday. From the way Walter was talking, the strike would carry on for much longer than she and Ellen had ever considered. There would be no work for days and that meant no money.

What on earth was she going to do?

Chapter Twenty

Ellen knew that she was younger, much younger, than Walter. And she knew that she was a woman, which meant he felt he had to explain everything ten times, but she was beginning to get fed up with him telling her things she already knew.

'I understand,' she said, as he tried to talk her through the management structure of Wentworth for the second time.

'Mr Beresford isn't in charge of the whole factory, but he does look after the employees' side of things . . .' Walter said.

'My sister works in the clerical department,' Ellen said for the third – or was it the fourth time? 'She knows Mr Beresford. He came to her bridal parade.'

'Aye, right,' said Walter without interest. 'He's a tricky customer, Beresford. He's very devoted to the American way of doing things. Scientific management all came from there, you know.'

'The efficiency engineers were American,' Ellen told him. 'One of them was called Mr Toms.'

'Is that so?' Walter said. 'How do you know that?'

'Well,' Ellen said with a smirk. 'My sister works in the clerical department . . .'

'Shall I walk you home, Ellen?' James jumped in. Ellen had been quite enjoying his company all evening – he was sharp and funny and passionate about workers' rights and she liked being with him. But now she glared at him.

'I don't need to go home yet,' she said.

He leaned forward towards her and spoke in an undertone. 'No, but I think Walter might.' He tilted his head to where the empty glasses were stacking up on the edge of the table and winked at her. Ellen felt her cheeks flame and she grinned at him.

'All right,' she said. 'That would be good.'

As they left the pub, however, Walter was ordering more drinks for him and Stanley, the older men clearly settling in for the evening. Ellen found she was glad to be out of there, and even gladder when James offered her his arm.

'Where do you live?' he asked.

'Just round the corner, beside St Joseph's,' she said.

'Is that where you go to church?' James asked, sounding casual.

'Yes. What about you?'

'I live across the way,' James said, waving his hand vaguely. 'Towards the shipyard.'

'Then you're going out of your way to walk me home.' Ellen realised it was inconvenient to him to accompany her and she thought that perhaps Sadie and Janet were right. Perhaps James did like her.

She sneaked a glance at him as they walked. He was nice, she thought. Better than nice, in fact. She was finding that she liked being with him.

The evening air was chilly – this spring was taking a while to get started – and she shivered, holding James's arm a bit more tightly.

'I think it's brilliant, how you've got everyone to stop working,' James said as they strolled along.

'It is.' Ellen bit her lip.

'You don't sound very sure.'

'No, I am. It's just that it all got a bit bigger than we intended.'

'That's what will make management come round to your way of thinking, though,' James said.

They began to walk across the green, which was dark under

the trees. Some movement to the side caught Ellen's eye, and for a second in the dim light she thought she saw Frankie Briggs, watching her from under a tree. After the trouble at the football match back at New Year, Da had been in a few run-ins with Frankie and his hangers-on, though from the sound of things Da and his pals had always had the upper hand. Even so, Da had warned Ellen and Bridget to watch out for Frankie because he held a grudge. Ellen had been looking out for him but she'd forgotten him in all the excitement of the strikes.

She kept her eyes fixed ahead and when she looked round, as they reached the pavement, Frankie had gone.

'The factory can't function with so many workers on strike and they're going to have to close down,' James said. 'Once it starts costing them money, they'll realise they have to do something.'

'I hope so.'

On the corner was a newspaper stand. Ellen blinked at the headline on the front page and tugged James's arm. 'Look at that.'

A broad grin split his face and he darted over to buy a paper. Then they both sat down on a bench and put their heads together to read.

'Well behaved,' Ellen said with a chuckle. 'We are so well behaved.'

'And good-natured,' James pointed further down the page. 'They've said we're good-natured, too.'

'We're extremely good-natured.' Ellen was thrilled with the article. She sat back against the bench in satisfaction. 'And what was the best bit?'

James scanned the page. 'Where they list what you want? Clear messaging is really important.'

'No.' Ellen shook her head vigorously. 'Where it says the strike is being led by women.'

'Ahh.' James sat back too, and Ellen allowed herself to enjoy the feeling of his leg touching hers. 'Walter annoyed you, did he? I thought he was getting on your nerves. Sadie's too.'

Ellen sighed.

'I don't want to be unkind because I know he's really passionate, and we need him to help us organise and that, but I can't help feeling he's taking over a wee bit.'

'He knows his stuff.'

'Clearly.'

'And he knows everyone at Wentworth.'

'He proved that when he got everyone to stop work,' Ellen said with grudging admiration. She groaned. 'I'm being mean, don't listen to me.'

'You're not,' James said. He thought for a moment. 'If collective bargaining is going to work, then we have to listen to everyone. Everyone should have a voice and that includes the women. Especially the women, considering you're the ones who started this whole thing. And we're all equal after all.'

Ellen stared at him. 'My da is the nicest man you could ever meet,' she said. 'He thinks the world of me and my sister and my ma. And he loves my gran, even though she can be a wee bit snippy. He's surrounded by women at home and I've never once heard him say a bad word about us.'

'He sounds like a good man.'

'He's a very good man,' Ellen said, pleased. Then she made a face, thinking of Frankie Briggs. 'Though he does sometimes get into fights when he's been to the football. But only wee scuffles really.' She sighed. 'Anyway, I don't think that deep down he thinks women are the same as men. I think that if push came to shove, he'd say men should earn more money. Or take on different jobs. He thinks men should be in charge.' She frowned. 'And he wouldn't mean it in a bad way. Just because that's how it is. Or how it's always been.'

James nodded. 'Until now.'

Ellen grinned at him. 'Do you really think men and women are just as good as each other?'

'I look around at the people I grew up with,' James said. 'And it's the women I see holding it all together. Going to get their husband's wages on a Friday, so they don't drink it all away. Making every penny count. Altering clothes and passing them down to younger siblings, and cousins and friends. Making pots of soup when someone dies. Or when someone's ill. Or just if someone needs soup.'

Ellen chuckled. 'Right enough, the women do all that. And they've got jobs too, most of them.'

'How can I live among women like that and not think they're as valuable as men?' James said, as if it was the most obvious thing in the world, like night following day or the sun rising in the east.

'Bridget thinks women should be allowed to vote.'

'What do you think about that?'

'I think she's right.'

James nodded. 'I do, too.'

Ellen felt a rush of emotion. She'd never heard a man speak this way before. It stirred something deep within her; a sense of injustice that had been festering there for a long time but she'd never managed to properly identify.

And something else, too.

She looked at James, who was looking at her, his sludgy green eyes narrowing as he studied her. Suddenly she wondered what she'd ever seen in Mr Beresford.

And then it started to rain.

It started with a couple of fat drops, sliding down Ellen's neck and making her shiver. Within moments it was a proper downpour and James's cap was drooping under the weight of the water pelting off its brim.

'We need to get out of here,' he said. He jumped to his feet and held his hand out to Ellen, and together they ran along the street.

'I hope it stops before tomorrow. More folk will come to protest if it's dry,' James said as they hurried along. 'Walter says summer strikes are the best.'

'No guarantee it'll be dry in summer in Clydebank though,'

Ellen pointed out through raspy breaths. 'Yuck, look at me, I'm drookit.'

'Me too,' said James laughing.

They were outside Ellen's flat now and she was torn between wanting to be inside in the dry, and wanting to spend more time with James. But a crack of thunder overhead made her mind up.

'Thank you for walking me home,' she said.

'Any time.' James grinned at her, and then he walked away, splashing through the puddles as he went.

Chapter Twenty-One

Bridget was having a horrible day. She wasn't the only worker in the clerical department, but it felt that way. It was dreadfully busy, and she wondered if Mr Beresford and the rest of the management men were deliberately creating work for her to do because surely, if the factory was hardly functioning, her usual tasks weren't necessary.

Despite all the extra chores she had to do, she was very bored and her mind kept drifting to her conversation yesterday evening with Ida McKinley.

They'd only sat on the bench together for about ten minutes, before Ida's train had hooted in the distance. But in that short time Bridget felt she'd made a new friend. It had been, she thought, a meeting of minds. And then she scoffed at herself because how could it be, when they'd barely had a proper conversation.

And yet, it had felt that way. Bridget had told Ida about Ellen and her fervour for the strike. She'd confessed that she agreed with the striking workers, but had been forced back to work by her husband, feeling only the briefest wince of disloyalty when she mentioned Malcolm. And then she'd told Ida all about her row with Ellen.

Ida had looked impressed.

'Your sister is fiery young woman, by the sound of it,' she'd said with a smile. 'Perhaps you could introduce me when you have time?'

'You'd like her,' Bridget had promised with a certain amount of pride. 'She's really something.'

Ida had looked at Bridget with what seemed to be an appraising eye. 'I believe it runs in the family.'

Feeling absurdly pleased for such a compliment, Bridget had blushed. 'I'm not nearly as strong as Ellen,' she admitted. 'She acts on her feelings. I just . . . feel them.' She'd clenched her fists and pushed them into her solar plexus. 'Here,' she said. 'I feel this rage inside me and I just ignore it.'

'What has caused the rage?' Ida asked.

Bridget put her head back and looked up at the darkening rain clouds overhead as she finally put what she'd been feeling into words.

'Being born a woman.'

She'd expected Ida to look surprised, or even confused. But actually her new friend looked like she understood exactly.

'I used to put my fist in my mouth and bite my own knuckles,' Ida said softly. 'It stopped me from screaming in frustration.'

She pulled her glove off and showed Bridget the tiny silvery scars that crisscrossed her fingers.

Bridget's eyes widened. 'You were angry too?'

'Angry. Indignant. Sad.'

'But you're not now?'

'I am, but now I use my anger.'

Bridget leaned towards her.

'How? How do you use it?'

There was a pause and somewhere in the distance a train hooted.

Ida leaned forward too, so their faces were almost touching. Bridget could feel her warm breath on her cold cheeks.

'I use it in the pursuit of malicious mischief,' she said.

A thrill went through Bridget like a bolt of lightning.

'What malicious mischief?' she whispered.

Ida got to her feet, looking over towards the railway line where the train was puffing into the station.

'Come to a meeting tomorrow,' she said. 'We have a room above the bookshop on Sauchiehall Street. Seven o'clock.' She reached out and cupped Bridget's cheek in her hand. 'Don't be late.'

Now, sitting at her desk in the quiet office, Bridget put her own hand on her cheek in the same way as Ida had touched her.

'Malicious mischief,' she whispered to herself as though it was a magical spell, brewing up trouble.

But malicious mischief wasn't a charm or an enchantment. She knew exactly what malicious mischief was. It was the charge levelled against the women who were fighting for the right to vote – the suffragettes.

Bridget had read about their protests in the newspapers with a mixture of admiration and envy, and a smattering of shame. She thought she'd never be brave enough to do as they did and battle so hard for women's suffrage, though she wished she could be.

And now she'd met Ida, who was exactly how she'd imagined a suffragette to be, and she was wondering if perhaps she was brave enough after all.

'Bridget?'

Mr Beresford was there, beside her desk, startling her from her imagination.

'Sorry, sir,' she said. 'I was miles away.'

He put his hand on her thigh and squeezed it. 'Dreaming of that husband of yours, eh? I can see it in your eyes.' He squeezed again and moved his hand upwards, just a tiny bit. Bridget moved her leg away and shook her head.

'Just thinking about what to make for tea,' she lied.

Mr Beresford frowned. 'I'll thank you not to think of domestic matters while you're at work. You need to be on top of things more than ever.'

Bridget had noticed how none of the bosses mentioned the

strike directly. They were all pretending that everything was normal, more or less. It amused her because it reminded her of Ellen when she was wee. When, on her birthday one year, she'd been so poorly with a streaming cold and a sore throat she could barely speak, but she'd been determined to enjoy her special tea. 'I'm fine,' she kept rasping. 'I feel good.'

Until she'd fainted at the table and banged her head on her plate.

They all still talked about Ellen's disastrous twelfth birthday, and it kept popping into Bridget's head now as management bustled about trying to look busy.

'Could you take a letter for me, please,' Mr Beresford was saying. 'In my office?'

Bridget picked up a notepad and a pencil and followed him. She sat down on the chair and he stood beside the window, looking out, as he liked to do when he was thinking. She knew he'd have a good view of the green from there. He'd be able to see the strikers, who all seemed much more organised today. They had banners saying 'Injure One, Injure All', which Bridget thought was rather clever. And they seemed to have divided up into smaller groups that were much easier to control. She wondered if that was all Ellen's doing or if she was getting help from the men she'd seen around. Not that Ellen needed the help of men, but Bridget knew they'd been forming groups for a while in Wentworth. Meeting and organising and discussing the rights of the workers. She suspected this strike might only be the beginning of changes in the factory, but she'd not said as much to anyone.

Mr Beresford could undoubtedly see all that was going on over at the green but if he did, he didn't react. Instead, he said: 'The letter needs to be addressed to the Home Secretary.'

'To Winston Churchill?' Bridget blinked in surprise – she normally typed letters to suppliers and stockists and the like, not politicians.

'Yes,' Mr Beresford said with an impatient tut. 'Mr Winston

Churchill, at the Home Office. And please send a copy to his constituency office in Dundee, too.'

Bridget made a note, wondering what on earth Mr Beresford was doing. Was this letter about the strike? Churchill was Home Secretary and that meant he was in charge of the police. Perhaps Mr Beresford was asking for more police officers to stop the workers protesting? She wrote Mr Churchill's name obediently, with hands that trembled slightly, and waited for more.

Mr Beresford paced up and down beside the window as he thought and then began dictating. And to Bridget's relief it was nothing to do with the strike whatsoever. As it turned out, Churchill was going to visit Ireland and would be coming back via a trip to his constituency in Dundee, which meant changing trains at Clydebank. Apparently, he would be visiting the shipyard while he was there, so Mr Beresford wanted to take the opportunity to invite him to visit Wentworth.

'We are a first-class operation,' he said, and Bridget wrote. 'And we would welcome the chance to show you around our factory.'

He carried on for a few more sentences, then stopped.

'Yours sincerely, etcetera.'

'Do you think he'll come?' Bridget asked, genuinely interested.

Mr Beresford shook his head. 'He's not in Scotland for long and I can't imagine he's got time to spare if he's already committed elsewhere. But it's worth a try. I want to show the world that Wentworth is an important company and that it's a real pat on the back for Clydebank that its factory is here.'

'Definitely worth a try,' Bridget said, though frankly she thought it was a terrible idea, given everything that was going on. Churchill's trip was next week, and she wondered why Mr Beresford was so confident that things would be back to normal by then. Was he imagining the workers would be back in their departments next week, happily getting on with the job and all grievances forgotten? It didn't seem likely.

But what did she know?

The day dragged on and eventually five minutes before the whistle blew, Malcolm appeared in the office.

'Mr Beresford suggested I should walk you home,' he said. 'We have to walk past the strikers and they're dangerous.'

Bridget snorted. 'They're not dangerous. They're Ellen and other women like her.'

'Aye, but they've been riled up, Bridget. They're angry.'

All day, Bridget had been hearing cheers and shouts, and music playing. It hadn't sounded like anger to her.

'They're determined,' she said. 'That's different.'

'We'll go out the south gate, then we won't have to walk past.'

Irritated, Bridget put the cover on her typewriter. 'But we will have to walk half an hour more to get home because the south gate's in totally the wrong direction.'

'It's safer.'

'You're being a baby, Malcolm,' she said. 'Nothing will happen to us if we walk by the strikers.'

But Malcolm looked bullish. 'That's the way we're going.'

And so Bridget picked up her things, said goodbye to Mr Beresford, and followed her husband out of the office, down the stairs and across to the south gate.

It was silly, really, how annoyed she was about it. She didn't mind walking further. She liked walking. Last night's rain had gone, and the air had a hint of spring in it. And yet, knowing she was heading away from home made her want to scream.

So, as they crossed the courtyard with the handful of workers who were also leaving, she stopped.

'I'm going the other way,' she said. 'If you want to use the south gate, that's fine. But I'm going the usual way.'

'Bridget, I forbid you to walk past those rebels,' Malcolm said.

'Rebels?' Bridget laughed. 'It's my sister and her pals.' She didn't mention how wounded she'd been by Ellen's words yesterday. He didn't need to know about that.

'Bridget,' Malcolm said again.

But she turned on her heel and walked away, feeling like she'd done something much bigger than chosen which gate to leave by.

As she reached the exit, she turned to see where Malcolm was, but she couldn't catch sight of him.

Of course, there was no danger. She walked past the green without incident, though she strained to see Ellen and couldn't catch a glimpse of her through the group that was gathered there. She'd been correct, though, in her assumption that it was good-natured. Some people were dancing; others were sitting in small groups, seemingly having rather heated – but friendly – discussions. She felt a longing to be a part of it all. To channel her anger, like Ida had done.

Her steps slowed as she remembered Ida inviting her to the meeting in Glasgow this evening. She'd dismissed the idea as soon as Ida had said it, knowing Malcolm would be less than impressed.

But now she wondered if she could go. Should she go? Dared she go?

She considered all those things as she walked past the strikers, but as she approached home, she thought that perhaps not. She would find something else on which to focus her rage. Housework, perhaps. She could do marvellous things with a cloth, some elbow grease and a fraction of the angry energy she had.

Or sewing. She'd barely picked up a needle for ages and the mending pile was getting bigger. Malcolm seemed to go through socks like nobody's business, and she had that skirt that needed its hem fixing. She held her hand out in front of her as she walked and watched how it trembled, ever so slightly. Perhaps not sewing then.

But this rage was fizzing through her, making her senses tingle and pop. She had to do something before she burst.

At home, she took off her outdoor clothes and hung them up and went to see what food they had for tea, just as Malcolm came in.

He didn't speak to her, just took off his hat and went to sit by the fire.

Something inside Bridget snapped. And suddenly, inexplicably, the rage was gone, replaced by an icy cold determination to change things.

Calmly, she walked out of the kitchen to where Malcolm was unlacing his boots.

'There isn't much food,' she said. 'Make yourself a sandwich if you're hungry. I'm going out.'

Malcolm, with one boot on and one off, sat up and stared at her. 'Where are you going? It's not sewing bee night.'

'No, it's not.' Bridget lifted her chin wondering whether to tell the truth then lost her nerve. 'But I'm going to Ma's anyway.'

Malcolm looked as though he might argue, so Bridget added: 'I need to hurry. I'm not sure what time I'll be home.'

Malcolm sat, open-mouthed, one boot in his hand, as she put on the coat she'd just taken off, found her bag, and left the flat, closing the door quietly behind her.

She stayed calm while she walked down the stone steps to outside, but as soon as the heavy tenement front door was shut, she felt a rush of exhilaration and nerves. Was she really doing this? She paused for a second on the step, wondering if she should go back. She could apologise to Malcolm. Make something for them to eat and life would go on as normal.

She turned slightly towards the door. But then a train hooted in the distance and feeling giddy as a schoolgirl, Bridget hitched up her skirt and ran to the station as fast as she possibly could.

Chapter Twenty-Two

By the time she'd found the bookshop in the centre of Glasgow, Bridget had talked herself into and out of going to the meeting a hundred times. But somehow, she'd still got off the train and walked up the hill.

She knew where the shop was because she'd been past it before, though she'd never been inside. They weren't really the sort of family who bought books, though they were all fond of words. Bridget liked to read the newspaper and Ellen loved novels, but she didn't buy them. She and her friends passed them round between each other like treasure. There was talk of a library opening in Clydebank. Ellen was pleased about that.

Bridget stood in front of the bookshop, which had a closed sign on the door, and looked up. The windows on the first floor were glowing with light and she could hear muffled conversation filtering down to where she stood.

'Come on, Bridget,' she muttered to herself. 'This is what you wanted.'

Taking a deep breath, she pushed the door, and nothing happened. It was locked.

She knocked quietly at first and then louder but still nothing happened. No one came to let her in.

A burst of laughter came from upstairs, and she suddenly felt like an outsider. Perhaps this was a bad idea, after all.

But she didn't want to go home. Not now. She took a step back and gazed upwards again, working out if there was another way in.

'You came!'

Flooded with relief, Bridget turned to see Ida hurrying up the street towards her.

'I did.'

'I'm so pleased.'

'Me too.' Bridget beamed at her. 'But I can't get inside.'

'Oh Lord, I forgot to tell you where to go. What a silly woman I am. Follow me.'

Bridget followed Ida with far more willingness than she'd followed Malcolm earlier, past the shop next door, then down a narrow alley to the back entrance of the bookstore. They went inside and up the stairs to the room that ran down the whole length of the shop. There were about fifteen women inside, which meant the room – large though it was – was crowded.

'Ida,' one woman called as they entered. 'We were about to give up hope.'

'I was early,' Ida said. 'So I went for a wander and ended up being late. But how lucky that I was because I bumped into my new friend Bridget and helped her find her way inside.'

The woman who'd spoken got to her feet and came over to where Bridget stood, slightly tucked behind Ida, like a little girl hiding behind her ma on her first day of school.

'Helen Cranbourne,' she said, holding her hand out for Bridget to shake. 'Pleased to meet you.'

'Bridget, erm,' said Bridget, pausing slightly on her surname then making a decision. 'Bridget Kelly.'

'Bridget lives in Clydebank,' said Ida. 'Her sister organised the strike at Wentworth.'

Helen looked impressed. 'Come and tell us all about it.'

She bustled Bridget over to a battered sofa and someone took her coat, someone else pressed a mug of tea into her hand, and an older woman sat down next to her and began talking to her as though she'd known her forever, and suddenly Bridget felt completely at home. It reminded her of their sewing bees with women everywhere chattering and sharing their views. No need to temper their opinions or bite their tongues. She liked it a lot.

'Tell us, was the strike really led by women?' Helen asked.

Bridget nodded proudly. 'My sister Ellen, just as Ida said. Ellen started it. She and her friend Sadie discovered they were being asked to work harder and longer for less money.' She looked around at the women, who were, as far as she could tell, a real mixed bag. She let her expert eye fall on their clothes, noticing that though some were dressed well in good-quality skirts and blouses, whereas others had outfits more like hers – darned and mended many times.

'Lots of women in Clydebank work at Wentworth,' she went on, finding her stride. 'And it's great, you know? We've got money in our pockets and we've got independence. Ellen and me, we owe it a lot.' She paused. 'But they owe us, too. And the bosses need to realise we're not just working to improve their lives.'

'Well, that sounds very familiar,' Helen said, raising an eyebrow and Bridget laughed.

'Are you striking?' another woman asked.

Not wanting to admit to these fierce women that she wasn't because her husband didn't let her, Bridget felt a flush of shame followed by huge relief as Ida jumped in.

'The first departments to stop work were all women,' she said. 'That's right, isn't it?'

Grateful, Bridget nodded. 'All women, aye. Now the men have stopped as well, though.'

'I've heard it's thousands of workers,' Helen said.

'That's right.'

'You must be very proud of Ellen.'

'I'm so proud of her,' Bridget said, feeling hot tears in her eyes as she thought about their argument. 'I don't think she really understands how proud. I honestly believe this action will make the managers realise how important we are.'

'Perhaps we need to go on strike in our households, and make our husbands realise the same,' one woman called and everyone laughed.

After a few minutes of chatting and teasing and a good many sharp, thoughtful observations about what was happening at Wentworth and whether it could happen in other places too, Helen stood up and tapped a teaspoon against her mug.

'I'm calling the meeting to order,' she said. 'Bridget, we're just a small sub-committee of the main Glasgow branch of the WSPU.'

Bridget nodded. She had wondered why there weren't many women there, because from what she'd heard of the Women's Social and Political Union, it was gaining members by the day.

'We're planning some activity,' Ida said. Bridget felt that little shiver of excitement again.

'Malicious mischief?'

There was a ripple of laughter around the room and Ida smiled. Bridget thought again how pretty she was, despite the scar on her face.

'Actually, no, not this time,' she said.

'Well, let's not rule it out,' said the older woman who'd been talking to Bridget and everyone laughed again.

'Thank you, Mary,' Helen said, but she was laughing too. She leaned against the mantelpiece of the room they were in. It had obviously once been a home, but was now full of mismatched, dusty furniture and boxes of books, and the fire was full of bits of twigs making Bridget wonder if a bird or two had built a nest in the chimney.

'Listen,' Helen said. Her eyes gleamed. 'I'm sure you all know that the 1911 census will be taken on April the second?'

The women all nodded.

'That's just over a week away,' Helen continued. 'And we've

been talking to our friends in London and all over the country about it and we've made a decision.'

'About the census?' said Ida, looking confused. 'What's the decision?'

'We suffragettes are going to use the census to register our views. If women don't count, then why should we be counted?'

'Oh, that's very good,' said Mary. 'I rather like this civil disobedience. I've been writing "Votes for Women" on every ten-shilling note I have in my purse and passing them on.'

Bridget made a mental vow to do the same. She liked Mary with her sharp mind and a glint of humour in her expression. She liked all of these women, who were now eagerly debating how best to approach this new protest.

'So we simply don't write our names on the census forms?' Ida asked. 'Is that legal?'

'No,' said Helen and the women all chuckled softly. 'But the idea is to go elsewhere on the night of the census. According to the letters we've all received, we are to note down everyone at a particular address, who is living at midnight.'

'We could stay out all night and then we wouldn't be at any particular address, so it wouldn't be illegal,' Bridget suggested. 'We could walk round and round Kelvingrove Park, perhaps? Though it would be dark and cold and perhaps not much fun.'

'Some of our sisters in London are planning to walk around Trafalgar Square,' Helen said. 'But I agree with you about the weather.'

'We could hide out somewhere instead,' Ida suggested. 'Here, perhaps? It's a shop so they're not expecting anyone to be here. If we all spend the night together and tell no one, then we won't be counted.'

Bridget thought that sounded like a much better idea than braving the cold in the park and so, clearly, did most of the others who all added their voices of approval.

'We'd have to keep it quiet,' Helen said. 'It's a legal requirement to fill in the census if we're indoors. But we could bring some food to share, and blankets. It might be rather fun.'

'Count me in,' said Mary.

'And me,' said Ida.

Without any thought of how Malcolm would react to her staying out all night with a group of women she hardly knew – and on census night, too – Bridget nodded. 'And me.'

'I need to be home,' said a worried-looking woman who was leaning against the wall in the corner of the room. 'I can't leave the baby overnight.'

'You've got a husband,' said Mary crossly. 'Why can't he help?'

The woman frowned. 'I do have a husband and he does help.' Then she grinned, putting her fingertips on either side of her chest, and thrusting her bosom towards Mary. 'But he can't provide everything can he?'

Mary chuckled. 'Fair enough. You could always bring the wean with you. No one would mind.'

'Course not,' said Ida. But the worried woman shook her head.

'Honestly, she's a nightmare. Barely sleeps. None of us would get any rest.' She thought for a moment. 'Should I just not fill in the census form? Or fill it in for the rest of them, but not for me?'

'How about you write something else instead of your name?' Helen suggested.

'Ooh yes, something rude,' said Mary. 'Maybe you could say that all politicians are full of . . .'

'We get the idea,' Helen interrupted. 'Thank you. I was thinking more along the lines of "No Vote, No Census", or even just "Votes for Women".'

'I could do that,' the woman said. 'At least we know it'll get read. I've got a lot of things I'd like to say to the people in power, let me tell you.'

'You have told us, Vera,' Mary called. 'Many, many times.'

Ida perched on the arm of the sofa next to Bridget. 'Vera here is convinced that if we just got to talk to the politicians, then they'd come round to our way of thinking.'

'That's how my Ellen feels about the bosses at the factory,' Bridget said. 'She just wants them to listen to her.'

'I simply feel that it's such an obvious argument that they can't argue against it,' Vera said, looking more animated and lively than she had done. 'If I could sit down with the Prime Minister, Mr Asquith, or with Mr Churchill, the Home Secretary, and explain why women should be given the vote, then surely I'd be in with a chance of convincing them.'

'Wouldn't that be lovely, to have five minutes with one of them,' Ida said wistfully. 'To have them really listen to us?'

'I'm afraid there's little chance of that,' said Helen. 'Even Mrs Pankhurst gets short shrift from our politicians.'

'We should find a time when they're in a room together, then barricade ourselves in with them and tell them all our demands,' said Vera. 'Then they'd have to hear what we said.'

She laughed, but Bridget didn't. She was too busy thinking. 'How about on a train?' she said. 'They couldn't get away if they were on a train.'

'A train would be perfect,' Vera said. 'We could sit down next to them and chatter about women's suffrage all the way to London.'

'No, not all the way to London.' Bridget was still thinking. 'From Stranraer to Dundee.' She grinned. 'Via Clydebank.'

Ida looked at her. 'Do you know something, Bridget?'

Excited now, Bridget clutched Ida's hand. 'Winston Churchill is visiting Ireland next week. And he's coming back to Stranraer on the boat, then travelling to visit his constituency in Dundee by train. If we – or some of us – bought tickets for the same train, then perhaps we could sit near him and talk to him. He couldn't walk away, could he? Because he'd have to stay on the train until Clydebank.'

Ida squeezed Bridget's fingers. 'How do you know this?'

'Because earlier today I typed a letter from Mr Beresford, my boss, asking for Churchill to come and visit Wentworth while he's in Clydebank. He knows all the details of his trip.'

'You're not striking, then?' said the woman who'd asked earlier, but this time Bridget didn't care. She simply ignored her.

'I can find out all the timings, and then we can make sure we get on the right train.'

'This is a very clever idea,' said Vera. 'I'd like to speak to Churchill. Can I be a part of it?'

'Of course,' said Helen. 'Who else?'

'I think Bridget should go because this is all down to her,' said Ida.

Chuffed, Bridget ducked her head modestly. 'I'd like to, but I don't know all the arguments. Perhaps Ida could come too?'

'Agreed.' Helen clapped her hands. 'Bridget, I know I speak for us all when I say we're very glad you've joined us.'

The women all murmured their agreement and Bridget sat back against the saggy couch, proud and happy to be a part of this.

Chapter Twenty-Three

Sadie was hungry. Not starving, not yet. But she was hungry enough that her belly was growling, and she was irritated by it because she knew there was nothing she could do about it.

Rachel had seen the doctor, who'd done very little except tell Sadie to carry on with the steam when her chest was bad, and to keep Rachel warm. Then he'd handed Sadie his bill, and waited patiently for her to pay.

Sadie had swallowed.

'Dr Cohen?' she said. 'Would it be all right if I just pay half now?'

Dr Cohen was a friendly man and he'd been very kind when Sadie's da died. But it was still a relief when he nodded.

He took out his little ledger where he jotted down all the money that was due to him, and scribbled something.

'Will you pay the rest tomorrow when you get your wages?'

Sadie had crossed her fingers behind her back, feeling bad about lying. 'That's right.'

Dr Cohen looked at her. 'Are you doing all right?'

'We're grand,' Sadie said, forcing a smile.

'My wife said to tell you she has a few pairs of trousers that our Jacob has grown out of. If they would be of any use to your boys?'

Sadie wanted to shake her head and say, 'No thank you, that's not necessary,' but instead she nodded. 'Thank you,' she whispered.

She tried to smile again. 'Noah tells me your Jacob has been quizzing him about why he isn't married.'

Dr Cohen let out a hoot of laughter. 'He's very nosy, that boy.'

'Curious,' said Sadie. 'Curious sounds better.'

Dr Cohen patted her shoulder. 'You're right. Perhaps we could all be more curious, eh?'

Sadie was glad that people weren't more curious. She didn't want anyone knowing about the empty biscuit jar in the kitchen. She felt sick at the thought of being pitied. Or, worse, judged for not providing for her family.

They'd got through Thursday thanks to the boys playing football and getting food there, and Sadie scraping together enough money to buy a loaf of bread and some cheese. But she could only afford a tiny bit of cheese and she herself didn't eat anything at all, because she couldn't bear to think that she might eat a piece that Ma or Rachel might want later.

But now it was Friday morning. Rachel was looking brighter again and the boys were at school. Ma had got up, dressed and was sitting reading in her chair. Sadie should have been happy. But all she could think about was that empty biscuit jar and Dr Cohen's bill, and the rumbling in her stomach.

'It's strange you being here during the day,' said Ma. 'I'll miss you when you go back to work.'

Sadie gave her a tiny smile. 'It doesn't look like that's happening anytime soon, Ma. Management won't talk to us.'

Her mother sighed. 'Typical men. Your da was the same. Never wanting to admit when he was wrong.'

This time Sadie's smile was genuine because that was exactly how Da had been. 'It's not helpful, though. We can't negotiate if they won't speak to us.'

'They've not communicated at all?'

'They sent a letter,' Sadie said, rolling her eyes.

'To the strikers?'

'No,' said Sadie, irritated at the thought. 'They sent it to the

Glasgow Herald and it was published. The letter said that if we had a genuine grievance then they'd admire our tenacity.'

'If?'

'Well, exactly. They seem to think we're making a lot of fuss about nothing.'

'Tsk,' said Ma. 'Playing the big man. Your da did that, too – he hated admitting he was wrong, but he always realised I was right in the end.'

'Walter and the others have written a letter in response. He says he thinks this is how management want to negotiate, through the newspapers.'

'You should go and speak to them, Sadie. You and Ellen.'

'We tried, Ma. They wouldn't let us in.' Sadie grinned. 'But it makes me feel a wee bit better to know they wouldn't let the men in either. The way they were talking, you'd think they were just going to knock on the gate and management would welcome them with open arms. But it didn't happen.'

'Course it didn't.' Her mother looked thoughtful. 'Next week, I think, things will change.'

'Really?'

'At the moment, they're still functioning, aren't they? More or less?'

'Hmm, more or less. But it can't keep on this way.'

'Exactly. Right now, they've probably managed to get some deliveries out because you worked at the start of the week. And actually, they're making money from you because you're not there to get your wages, so at the moment they're sitting pretty. By next week, though, it'll look very different.'

Sadie stared at her mother. 'What did you say?'

'It'll look very different?'

'No, about our wages? You said we're not there to get them?'

'Well, no. You're here.' Ma looked a little concerned, as though Sadie was having a funny turn. 'You can't collect your wages because you're not at work.'

'But we've worked two and a half days since Saturday,' Sadie said. 'Some people worked longer. We're owed that money.'

'Yes, you are,' Ma said. 'But what can you do about it?'

Sadie darted over to her mother and gave her a hug. 'I can go and get our wages.'

'But they won't let you in?'

'No,' she said. 'They won't let me in if I turn up alone. But I'm not going to go by myself.'

It was warmer today and thank goodness because the strikers were spending a lot of time outdoors. The Glasgow division of the strikers were gathered by the Gorbals Cross. Sadie hadn't realised quite how many workers lived near her. Some were Jewish like her, some were Irish immigrants like Ellen's family. All were waiting patiently to hear what the response to management's letter was going to be.

The organiser of the Gorbals division was a chap called Brody. Sadie didn't know if that was his first name or his last, so she'd avoided speaking directly to him. But today she had something to say.

She found Brody sitting on the clock at the centre of the cross-roads, talking animatedly to another man. Both of them were looking annoyed.

'Don't ask,' Brody said as she approached. 'Yes, we're working out what to say. And yes, I know that if we're going to get our response in tomorrow's *Herald* then we need to get it to them by midday.' He looked up at the time and then glared at the other man. 'But they're still arguing.'

'Oh, for goodness' sake,' said Sadie. 'They simply need to point out that there are ten thousand of us.'

'Eleven,' said the other man.

'Pardon?'

'There are eleven thousand of us,' Brody explained.

'Even better. They need to point out that there are eleven

thousand of us and would so many people cause ourselves and Wentworth such hardship if it wasn't a genuine grievance?'

'That's good,' Brody said. 'What do you think?'

The other man, who was a big lumbering chap, shrugged. 'It says what we need to say.' He wrote it down on a sheet of paper. 'I'll go through to speak to them. But this needs to go quicker.'

Brody turned to a wee boy wearing a jacket that was much too big for him. 'Take this message to Clydebank Green,' he said. 'To Walter. You know Walter?'

'Everyone knows Walter,' said the lad. He held his hand out and Brody dropped a coin into his grubby palm.

'Go quickly,' he said. 'Get it to him by ten and I'll give you another penny.'

The boy shot off, swerving through the crowd, with the big man following him at a much slower pace. Brody looked at Sadie. 'You're one of the cabinet-polishing lasses that started this thing, aren't you?'

'Sadie Franklin.' She put her hand out and he shook it. 'I need your help.'

'What do you want?' He eyed her suspiciously. 'I'm as new to all this as you are.'

'We're owed money,' Sadie said. 'All of us.'

Brody looked more interested. 'What money?'

'Our wages.'

'We've stopped work.'

'Aye, but we worked Saturday, Monday and half of Tuesday before then. And some folk worked all of Tuesday and some of Wednesday. We need to get what we're owed.'

'You know Walter and Stanley tried to get in and couldn't?'

'I do know that.'

'So why do you think you'll be different?'

Sadie grinned. 'Because I think we should all go.'

'What?'

'All eleven thousand of us.' She emphasised the 'eleven'. 'We can march back to the factory just like when we walked out. They can't turn us all away and they can't refuse to pay us, surely? It's our money.'

Brody nodded thoughtfully. 'Take some organising,' he said.

'I know. It won't be easy.' Sadie felt desperate to make him understand how important this was. 'But we need the money. We all need those wages.'

'Aye,' said Brody.

'So will you organise the Glasgow division if I go back to Clydebank and speak to the others?'

Brody stayed quiet for so long that Sadie thought he'd lost interest. But then he took the cigarette from his mouth and said: 'My pal, Stuart. He's a piper.'

'Right,' Sadie said, confused. 'Good.'

'He'll lead us if you want. Pipe us through the streets.' He grinned suddenly. 'Let folk know we're coming.'

'We're doing it, then?' Sadie did a little bounce on her toes.

'Aye.'

Resisting the urge to give him a hug, Sadie thanked him.

'Sadie Franklin, you said?' Brody looked at her.

'That's right.'

'Gerry Franklin was your da?'

Sadie screwed her nose up. Unexpected mentions of her father always made her remember all over again that he was gone.

'Yes.'

'I was sorry to hear what happened,' Brody said. 'He was a good man.'

Tears pricked Sadie's eyes and, unable to speak for a moment, she just nodded.

'He'd have been proud of you, I think.'

Sadie nodded again, touched by his words.

'We'll walk from here,' Brody said, obviously having shared enough platitudes.

'It's a long way.' Sadie rubbed her nose. 'Are you sure?'

'We'll leave at midday and get to Clydebank by three. You get everyone to join us when we arrive.'

With a flutter of excitement, Sadie nodded. 'Right. See you later.'

It was astonishing really, how fast they got things organised. It felt like a matter of minutes, though actually it was a few hours – time just sped by because Sadie was so busy, dashing around and spreading the word about what was planned, making sure all the divisions knew what to do.

Walter, to her surprise, was impressed with what she'd suggested.

'You're a proper wee rebel,' he said approvingly. Sadie laughed. She liked being a rebel, she'd discovered.

And then Walter surprised her again.

'You should lead the march,' he said. 'James is right. This is your fight. Yours and Ellen's. You go at the front.'

'Well, Brody's piper pal's going at the front.'

A ghost of a smile crossed Walter's face. 'Always have to be right, eh?'

Sadie thought about what her ma had said about Da and nodded.

'Brody's piper pal at the front, then you and Ellen.'

'All right.'

'Well done, lass,' Walter said. 'We'll all be following on behind.'

'Where is Ellen?' Sadie hadn't seen her all day. 'Is she here?'

'James will know – the pair of them are thick as thieves,' Walter said. 'He's over at the side, there.'

'I'll go and find him. Thanks, Walter.'

Walter gave Sadie a little salute and she made her way over to where James was listening to someone talking about workers' rights. Though, thought Sadie watching him closely, he didn't actually look as if he was listening at all. He was watching something a little way away. Sadie followed his eyeline, hoping he was looking at Ellen, but he was watching another young man who was standing apart from everyone else, in the shadow of the trees.

She waved to James and he came away from the group a little to speak to her.

'All right?' he said.

Sadie nodded. 'I'm sorting out this wage march, but I need to find Ellen. Do you know where she is?'

'Aye, she's over there.' He pointed towards another small group. 'She's running about here, there and everywhere.'

'I'll go and speak to her.'

'Tell her . . .' he began. Sadie looked at him and he grinned. 'Tell her I'll see her later.'

Smiling to herself, Sadie carried on through the crowd, which was still, as the newspaper had said, well behaved. There were far fewer people here now they'd organised the divisions but there was still a bit of a party atmosphere with music playing and small groups – like the one James was in – talking about various issues. Sadie felt a little rush of pride that this had grown from their determination to do something about the unfair practices at Wentworth.

'Sadie!' Ellen was waving madly at her through the crowd. The women hurried towards one another and hugged. 'Everyone's talking about this wages march, you clever thing. What a good idea.'

'We did that work, we need to get paid for it.'

'You're right.'

'Walter says we should lead the march,' Sadie told her friend. 'Do you want to?'

'Of course we should.' Ellen puffed her chest out. 'This is all our doing. Well, the march is your doing, but the rest of it is both of us.'

Sadie threaded her arm through Ellen's. 'We're a team.'

'We are.'

'The Glasgow division are walking through. We just need to wait for them. There's a piper.'

'So we'll hear them coming?'

'Exactly.'

'Then let's go to the road so we get a good view,' Ellen suggested.

Still arm in arm, the women walked slowly round the green to where it met the street.

'I saw James,' Sadie said. 'He said he'll see you later.'

Ellen's cheeks flushed and Sadie gave a little squeal. 'I thought Mr Beresford was the only man for you?' she teased.

Ellen nudged her as they walked. 'I've gone off Mr Beresford a wee bit,' she admitted.

'And gone on to James?'

'Maybe.' Ellen gripped Sadie's arm a little tighter. 'I really like spending time with him.'

'He clearly likes spending time with you too,' Sadie said, wriggling her arm so Ellen loosened her grip a wee bit. Sadie was thrilled that her friend had found someone she liked, but she couldn't help feeling a twist of envy. Was this excited longing Ellen was feeling the same way Noah felt about his mystery woman?

'Tell me about this wages march,' Ellen said, jolting Sadie from her gloom.

'We're going to get our wages,' Sadie said simply. 'Every single one of us.'

As they reached the road, the sounds of a distant piper reached them. Sadie bounced on her toes. 'It's them!' she said. 'They're coming!'

Sadie clambered up onto a nearby tree stump. 'Get ready!' she called to the crowd. 'They're here!'

It was just like the day everyone had walked out of the factory. It was a truly impressive sight. Hundreds of people were walking along, behind the piper, chatting a bit but mostly quiet, their faces set in determination. And that was just the ones who'd come from Glasgow; all the Clydebank strikers were yet to join the hordes of folk walking towards Wentworth. Even without them, the march was impressive, with people as far back as Sadie could see. She felt a huge wave of relief. The bosses couldn't possibly refuse to pay them – not with this many people going to ask. There would be a riot if they so much as tried to wriggle out of this.

Sadie could see Brody at the front and as the marchers approached the green, he waved to her.

Walter had come up behind the women, and now he gave them a gentle push. 'Go on, then, girls,' he said. 'Take your places at the front.'

Sadie and Ellen exchanged a glance and then, as the strikers approached, they fell in with them, matching their pace as they walked along behind the piper.

Sadie looked round at the swell of people following them. No one was talking. The only sound was the tramp of their boots and the lonely wail of the pipes. She felt tearful all of a sudden and was glad when Ellen sneaked her hand into hers.

'It's really something,' Ellen whispered.

Just as when they'd left work, people were coming out of their houses to watch. Sadie lifted her chin and fixed her gaze on the factory gates.

Ossy was at the gate in his hut.

'Hiya, girls,' he said, just like it was a normal day.

'We've come for our wages,' Sadie said.

He nodded. 'They've set up tables inside for you.'

'They knew we were coming?' Ellen was surprised, but Ossy laughed.

'Everyone knew you were coming, doll. We heard you all long before we saw you.'

'So we can go in?'

'You can.'

Sadie felt sheer, blinding relief. She could pay Dr Cohen's bills and buy some more food. And as for next week, she could work that out when they got there.

'They're going to do it,' she said to Ellen. 'They're going to give us our wages.'

Ossy opened the gates for them, and they saw four long trestle tables inside, each marked with department numbers, and each staffed by a slightly alarmed-looking member of the accounts department. Malcolm was there, on the first table.

Sadie and Ellen exchanged a glance.

'No management?' Sadie said.

'No.'

The crowd behind them – the thousands of staff waiting to pick up their money – noticed it too. The women heard the news being passed backwards through the marchers.

'Cowards,' the people whispered. 'Cowards.'

Sadie took Ellen's hand, and together they walked to the desk where Malcolm stood.

'Ellen Kelly and Sadie Franklin,' Ellen said. 'Cabinet polishing.'

Malcolm rolled his eyes, and Sadie stifled a laugh as he leafed through the wee brown envelopes and handed them over.

Sadie couldn't help but notice that his hands were shaking as he gave her the money and she felt sorry for him.

'They made you come out, huh? Beresford and the others didn't want to face the crowd?'

'It's our job,' Malcolm said, though he didn't sound quite as sure as Sadie thought he might once have done.

'Well done, Malcolm,' Ellen said, in a slightly grudging tone that made Sadie smile. 'This can't be easy.'

Malcolm looked over their heads at the advancing crowd.

'Is it safe?' he asked. 'They won't riot?'

'We just want the money that's owed,' Sadie said. 'No one's going to riot.'

She crossed her fingers behind her back and hoped the crowd would stay as good-natured as they'd started.

It took hours and hours for all the workers to collect their wages. They streamed through the factory gates one after another, while Sadie and Ellen stood to one side and watched – and stepped in when Malcolm and the other accounts staff got barbed comments, insults and, on a few occasions, threats.

Towards the end of the queue, when the sun had long since set and the sky had darkened, a couple of men approached the desk.

'Malky Walsh,' said one of them with disgust. 'Ya wee sook.'

'You're such a jessie, Malcolm,' said the other. 'A feardie jessie.'

Pointedly ignoring the men's insults, Malcolm found the men's envelopes and held them out. Sadie's respect for Malcolm had been growing throughout the afternoon and she admired him even more as he shouldered the rude comments and abuse without reacting. She may not have agreed with the way he obeyed orders from management, but she couldn't deny he was bolder than he looked.

The men took the envelopes from Malcolm and stuffed them into their jacket pockets. And then, one of them looked across the courtyard towards the factory building.

'Lookit,' he said in glee. 'It's Beresford.'

Sadie and Ellen both looked and sure enough, there was Mr Beresford. He was hunched down in his coat, hurrying towards the south gate. He'd obviously waited until it was dark, and the crowds had eased, before deciding to leave.

'BERESFORD!' bellowed one of the men. 'OI! BERESFORD!'

The few people left waiting for their wages all took up the shouts.

'Beresford! Come here and have a wee chat, eh?'

'Beresford! BERESFORD!'

'Do you think he'll come over?' Ellen breathed, clutching Sadie's arm. 'This could be our chance to talk to him.'

The crowd's shouts were echoing around the courtyard. 'I don't think so,' said Sadie. 'Look!'

The women watched as, to their utter amazement and disappointment, Mr Beresford glanced round at the crowd, then took to his heels and ran away.

There was a brief moment of shocked silence from the watching workers and for a second Sadie thought someone – the men who'd insulted Malcolm, perhaps – would give chase. But instead a huge wave of laughter spread through the crowd.

Sadie wondered what Mr Beresford thought, as he scurried away, hearing the hoots of hilarity as he went. She hoped he was ashamed of himself.

Next to her, Ellen was watching him go with a look of disdain on her face.

'Still the only man for you, is he?' said Sadie, beginning to chuckle.

Ellen shook her head, laughing. 'Absolutely not,' she said, struggling to catch her breath because she was giggling so much. 'Not if he was the only man on Earth.'

Chapter Twenty-Four

Sadie was a hero and Ellen was so very proud of her, as well as grateful because she was so relieved to have been given her wages. But despite her pride, she was feeling a little lost now the strike was into its second week. Everyone had a job to do, it seemed, except for her.

In the few days since she'd had the idea to march for the wages, Sadie had been in demand. Her quick brain and cleverness with numbers meant she was helping Walter and the others with their letters to management via the newspaper, and she'd been rushing between Clydebank and Glasgow. Sadie said Rachel was on the mend and that she wasn't nearly so worried about her as she had been, but still she hurried back to Glasgow each evening. And Ellen knew she was always hopeful she'd see Noah. Sadie was still convinced he was involved with some mystery woman, even though he'd not mentioned her again.

Ellen adjusted her seat on the tree stump where she'd plonked herself to listen to yet another man wittering on about employees' rights and what they hoped to achieve from the strike.

Ellen could tell him a thing or two about what they hoped to achieve from the strike, seeing as she was the one who'd thought of the idea in the first place, but no one wanted to know what she thought. No one had even asked her opinion.

Well, to be fair, Walter had run a few things by her, and Sadie made a point of mentioning her every time she spoke, but still . . . Ellen felt neglected. Abandoned.

And to add to her worries, it turned out her head was full to bursting with thoughts of James. She couldn't imagine what she'd seen in cowardly Mr Beresford now, with his thin lips and his refusal to engage with the striking workers.

Instead it was James who kept sneaking his way into her daydreams. She couldn't stop thinking about his green eyes, and the way he looked at her as if she was something to be admired and protected.

Ellen liked that. Though she wasn't sure how to deal with these feelings. Mr Beresford was so distant and out of reach, it was as though he wasn't a real person. But James. Living, breathing, laughing, handsome James was so real that Ellen almost couldn't bear it. The thought of acting on the way she felt gave her a thrill and also scared her half to death. What if she made it clear that she thought he was – you know – all right? And he didn't feel the same? Ellen wasn't sure she could cope with him rejecting her. But she also wasn't sure she could cope with him never knowing the way she felt. The delicious torture of it all had her lying awake until the small hours every night.

But that wasn't the worst of it. The worst of it was that she still hadn't spoken to Bridget. She'd not even seen Bridget, in fact. Not since their argument. She missed her so badly, but didn't want to admit it. Well, not unless Bridget admitted it first. But how could she admit it if Ellen hadn't even seen her?

In fact, it was strange because her ma hadn't seen her either. She'd not even been at church. Ma just said she thought Bridget was busy but she didn't know what with. Ellen had felt a bit guilty at that, wondering if Bridget was working harder because of the strike. But actually, there wasn't really anything for the remaining workers to do now, because the factory had pretty much stopped functioning.

It was strange, being in Clydebank just now. The factory dominated everything in the town. In normal times, the noise it made could be heard from everywhere – the rattle of the trains and the hum of the machinery, the shouts of the workers, and the bell ringing for the shifts to start. The trains to and from Clydebank ran according to the factory timetable so the workers could arrive when they needed to. If you didn't work for Wentworth then chances were you lived with someone who did. Or you worked in a business that relied on Wentworth for its trade. Or you used a Wentworth machine, like Ma did.

But now nothing was happening. The barges were tied up at the bank. The trains weren't running. The factory was quiet. The bell still rang twice a day, but the streams of people walking to and from Wentworth had stopped. Instead they were all down on the green or on the picket line. Everything had changed.

So Bridget couldn't have been working longer hours at the factory because the honest truth was, there was no work for her to do. And she wasn't protesting or coming along to the strikers' meetings. So what was she doing? It made no sense to Ellen. But still it swirled round and round in her head.

'Ellen?'

She turned to see James and tried not to look too pleased to see him in case he got the wrong idea. Or the right idea. Whichever it was.

'Oh,' she said, very casually. 'It's you.'

James smiled and Ellen's heart gave an extra strong thump. 'I saw you sitting here,' he said. 'You looked so sad I thought I'd come and check you were all right.' He swallowed. 'Are you all right?'

Ellen gazed at him. His clear, bright eyes were full of worry, and his cheeky smile had vanished.

She opened her mouth to say she was fine, thank you very much, but instead she wailed: 'I miss my sister!'

James looked startled. There was a brief pause and then he

darted over to where Ellen sat, plonked himself down next to her and put his arm tight round her.

'Now, now,' he said. 'There's no need for tears.'

Ellen sniffed loudly. 'Bridget's not worth my tears,' she said.

'I'm not sure that's true.' James moved slightly and Ellen thought he might take his arm away so she put her hand on his, anchoring him in place. 'See me and my brother?' he said. 'We fight like cat and dog.'

'You've got a brother.'

'I do, aye. Well, he's my stepbrother. My ma married his da.'

'Is he older than you?'

'Three years older.'

'Same as me and Bridget.'

'He's a funny one, my brother. He's had a hard time,' James said.

'What kind of hard time?'

'He used to work at Wentworth, actually. But he had an accident when someone stacked a shelving unit too high and it fell on him. His leg's not been right since. He doesn't work there anymore.'

'That's sad,' Ellen said. 'Where does he work now?'

James shrugged. 'He just does this and that. Not always on the right side of the law. It's not easy for him.' He breathed in. 'And he takes his frustrations out on me. And my ma. And his da.'

Ellen made a face and James carried on. 'My brother annoys me more than anyone else in the world.'

Ellen laughed. She knew exactly. 'Bridget's the most infuriating person I know.'

'But when push comes to shove, he's family,' James snorted. 'And that matters.'

'I feel the same about Bridget.'

James took his arm away from Ellen's shoulders and the sudden cold air made her shiver. 'You'll make it up,' he said. He reached out and tucked a loose strand of hair behind Ellen's ear. 'No one could stay cross with you for long.'

'I'm cross with her for not striking,' Ellen said, sitting up straighter. 'She's not cross with me. Well, she is now, but she wasn't at first, until I said I was cross with her.'

'Och, Ellen, you know it's not easy for her.'

'Everyone keeps telling me that,' said Ellen, with a sudden flash of annoyance. 'It's not easy for any of us, is it?'

James shook his head. 'No, it's not. But it's not easy for the ones who stayed behind and Bridget's got a good reason for not striking too.'

'That's what my ma says.'

'She's right.'

Ellen groaned. 'Stop being so reasonable. I like bearing a grudge.'

'Well, don't bear it too long or you might find Bridget's got fed up of waiting for you to say sorry.'

'I'm not ready to apologise yet,' Ellen said, feeling a tiny niggling worry that Bridget had already got fed up of waiting. Maybe that's why she was so busy. Though doing what, Ellen didn't know. 'But I'll get there.'

James grinned. 'Good.'

They looked at one another for a second and Ellen had the strangest urge to tell him all the feelings she was having but she didn't. She just smiled at him, and he smiled back and then James looked at the factory clock and slapped his forehead.

'I'm supposed to be seeing Walter and the others,' he said.

Ellen tutted. 'Walter.'

'What's Walter done to upset you?'

'Oh nothing,' Ellen said with a sigh. 'You know what he's like, though. He's sort of taken over. Which is fine, because he's got the knowledge and the expertise and that. But . . .' She stopped talking, suddenly worried she sounded like a whinging schoolgirl, wanting attention.

'What?'

Ellen screwed up her nose. 'I was part of this and now I feel like I'm not.'

James laughed. 'You weren't just part of it, Ellen – you were the reason it all got going in the first place.'

'I know.'

'And weren't you at the head of the march to collect the wages?'

'Yes, but that was Sadie's idea.' Ellen sighed again. 'I feel like I'm not needed now. I'm not being useful.'

'Of course you're useful.' James nudged her with his shoulder affectionately.

'Really? Then why are you going to this meeting, when I've not even been told about it?'

James looked sheepish. 'You've got a point there,' he admitted.

'Is it all men?' Ellen was feeling riled up all over again.

'Aye, it will be. Me, Walter, Stanley. Some lad called Brody, from the Gorbals.'

'A man from the Gorbals?' Ellen was outraged. 'A man? From the Gorbals?'

'Yes?'

'Sadie lives in the Gorbals.'

'Ah,' said James.

'Ah, indeed.' Ellen stood up, brushing dust from the tree stump from her behind. 'Do you see what I mean? The men have taken over.' She rolled her eyes. 'As usual.'

'Och, Ellen. Walter's got his faults, but he's a good man. He wouldn't have done it deliberately.'

'That's no comfort,' she snapped. 'It's like we don't even figure in his plans. We do all the work and get none of the credit.'

'Want me to speak to him?' James asked, getting to his feet, too. 'Point out that you and Sadie deserve a seat at the table?'

'Yes,' Ellen said. 'No. I don't want you speaking for me. But yes, I do want to be there.'

'I'll speak to him,' said James, trying but failing to hide the smile that had crept to his lips. 'I'll remind him how determined you are.'

'I'm determined all right,' said Ellen. 'You'd do well to remember that.'

James looked slightly alarmed 'I will.'

'What are you even discussing at this meeting?'

'They're going over their next letter.'

'Oh those blasted letters,' Ellen said.

'You don't think they're doing things the best way?' James looked interested. 'How would you do it?'

'I think the letters are good because they're getting everyone talking,' Ellen said. 'Da says everyone he meets is talking about the strike, because they've read it in the paper. And they're all on our side.'

'Right enough,' said James. 'I can hear a but coming, though.'

'I understand this whole collective bargaining thing,' Ellen said slowly. 'I really do. And I completely agree that we're stronger standing together. But I can't help wondering if we've put a distance between us and the bosses that was never there before.'

'That's inevitable, surely?'

'I don't know.' Ellen frowned, thinking about Mr Beresford fleeing from the workers collecting their wages. 'I think they're scared of us. But we've got a problem and they can solve it. Surely we'd be better off asking them for help?'

'Ellen, that won't work. They won't even see us.'

'Yes, because we've been going about it all wrong. We've gone in with demands and insults. Maybe we need to be a bit more . . . humble.'

'Absolutely not.'

'I don't mean going cap in hand,' Ellen said. 'Just be a bit nicer, is all. We've got a relationship with these men. A personal relationship.'

James stood up, looking a bit affronted.

'Not you as well?'

'Me as well what?'

'Going all doe-eyed over Beresford. I know he's handsome and charming and blah blah,' James said. He sounded a bit het-up and Ellen was quite pleased about it. Was he jealous? She hoped so. 'But he's not thinking about us, Ellen. He's not.'

She hid her smile. 'I'll admit I did admire Mr Beresford for a wee while,' she said, waving her hand as if she'd barely noticed his good looks. 'But not now. No one who saw him running away the other day could admire him.'

James laughed.

'That's not what I meant by personal relationship,' Ellen continued.

'Glad to hear it,' said James, and Ellen felt a flush of happiness.

'What I mean is, perhaps we approach this not as workers and management, not as big clumps of people,' she explained, forcing herself to stay focused. 'I mean approaching it as me, Ellen Kelly, having a chat with Mr Beresford.'

'I'm not sure . . .' James began, but Ellen interrupted.

'I know him,' she said. 'Well, I don't know him as such, but Bridget does. And he came along to her bridal parade, for goodness' sake. If we – if I – could speak to him and just tell him exactly how much we were struggling before, then perhaps together he and I could work out a solution together. No confrontation or demands. Just two people talking.'

'Perhaps,' said James doubtfully. 'Could you even get in to see him, though?'

Ellen's mind was racing, Perhaps she could go via Bridget's office? 'I could try,' she said. She felt a little rush of excitement. 'I will try. I'll go to the factory and talk to him. One to one. Appeal to him as a person rather than as a manager.'

'I'm not sure this is a good idea,' James said, shaking his head. 'Beresford can be a nasty piece of work. I've heard stories about him . . .'

'Nonsense,' said Ellen, caught up in the idea of saving the strike. 'The two of us having a chat can do more than twenty of Walter's letters.'

'Walter won't be happy.'

Ellen glared at him. 'I don't care. Walter didn't start this strike and Walter's not in charge.' She put her hands on her hips. 'I am.'

Chapter Twenty-Five

Bridget was doing very little work. She'd barely so much as typed a letter, and she'd discovered that no one really paid any attention to what she was doing so long as she was at her desk.

So what she'd been doing was her own brand of malicious mischief.

She had spent a long time looking at train timetables between Stranraer and Clydebank, reading news stories about Mr Churchill's trip to Ireland and his journey home again, and working out the best place to get on board his train to give them the most time to talk to him.

She had drawn a wee diagram of the train, which she was rather proud of, and she'd written down all the timings to make sure everyone was in the right place at the right time.

Every time she'd had a bank note in her purse, she'd carefully written 'VOTES FOR WOMEN' along the top and yesterday, when she'd been especially bored, she'd written it hundreds of times on hundreds of tiny scraps of paper, then she'd sneaked up to the very top of the factory and dropped them all out of the window, watching them swirl on the breeze like rice at a wedding.

What she hadn't done was speak to Malcolm. Not really.

They were living and working together and yet she barely saw him. Except on Friday when he'd come home late, ashen-faced.

Bridget knew why, of course. She'd seen her sister and Sadie being piped along the street to pick up their wages. Everyone in Clydebank had heard and seen them – it had been a truly wonderful sight and Bridget had thought she might burst with pride.

She'd watched from the window until it got too dark to see, then she'd gone home through the south gate because she didn't want to see Ellen and have to answer her questions again. Not when Ellen was being so wonderfully brave and she, Bridget, was simply writing slogans on bank notes, and sneaking around behind her husband's back.

Later, when Malcolm came home, Bridget expected him to be annoyed with the workers for going to the factory in such a showy way.

But he'd been sad.

Sad and sort of disillusioned.

He'd sat by the fire and Bridget made him a cup of tea, and he looked at her and said: 'Am I on the wrong side, Bridget?'

Bridget sat down opposite him. 'No,' she said simply. 'I don't think it really matters which side you're on, as long as you're sure of your opinions.'

'That's the thing,' Malcolm said, shaking his head. 'I'm not sure I am sure anymore.'

Bridget's jaw dropped. 'You think the workers are right to strike?'

'No.' Malcolm sounded uncertain. 'I don't think so, not exactly. But they are right to object to the changes that have been made. And ...' he swallowed. 'Mr Beresford ran away.'

'What?'

'He came out when some of the workers were still there and they shouted at him and he ran away.'

'Heavens.'

'All afternoon I sat at that desk, handing out wages,' Malcolm said, through gritted teeth. 'All afternoon, taking the insults and the abuse and the ...' He spat out the words. 'The shit, from the workers. And Beresford just ran away.'

Bridget took his hand.

'You are a good man, Malcolm Walsh,' she said. 'You are worth ten Beresfords. A hundred of them.'

Malcolm had looked at her. 'I feel like everything's changing,' he said. 'The world isn't what I thought it was.'

'No.'

Bridget had thought about telling him then that she had joined the suffragettes and that the world was changing and it was a good thing. But Malcolm had shaken his head.

'But I have you, Bridget. And you stay the same. Thank goodness. Because where would I be without you?'

And Bridget felt herself shrink back inside her secrets once again.

Now Bridget was off for a walk. It was a bright, sunny late March day, though the breeze still had a chill, the evenings were lengthening, and she wanted to get some fresh air. Or so she'd told Malcolm.

Really she was going to see Ida.

She knew where McKinley's General Shop was, and she set off with a definite spring in her step. She wanted to tell Ida all about the plans to corner Mr Churchill. And she'd heard the census forms were to be distributed tomorrow, so she wanted to talk about those plans too.

And, most of all, she realised, she wanted to see Ida.

Bridget had seen Ida once since the meeting last week. She'd been waiting for her outside the factory yesterday evening and Bridget had felt a tiny shiver of excitement when she saw her new friend there. Ida was wearing trousers. TROUSERS! And she'd been leaning on a bicycle.

'I've been delivering some bits and bobs to a chap on Caledonian Road,' Ida said. 'And I heard the bell, so I thought I'd swing by and see if you were coming out.'

'In normal times, you'd never spot me among the throngs of people.'

'Ah,' Ida had said. 'But these are not normal times.'

They'd walked along together, Ida wheeling her bicycle, chatting about the suffragettes, with Ida filling in Bridget on all the characters in their group.

'They're a good bunch,' she said. 'Except for Christina, who is a sour-faced woman and who I think has a longing to join the army.'

And Ida had asked Bridget about the strike, so she'd told her about the march for the wages – though she knew about it already of course – and Mr Beresford running away. She didn't mention Malcolm's odd reaction. She wasn't sure how she felt about that.

'He actually fled the scene?' Ida said, chuckling. 'He ran away from your wee sister and her pal?'

'That's what happened.'

Ida grinned. 'I can't say I'm surprised, Bridget. I've long suspected that men are simply terrified of women.'

'I wonder if Mr Churchill will be frightened of us?' Bridget had said with a laugh.

'Well even if he is, he won't be able to run away,' Ida pointed out. 'Which is why speaking to him on the train is such a wonderful idea.'

Bridget had basked in the praise.

Now she was going to the shop to fill Ida in on the final arrangements. She strolled along the street, admiring the different shop fronts and noticing the store next door to Ida's was boarded up.

'Mr Kennedy died,' Ida said when she opened the door to let Bridget in and noticed her looking. 'He was the greengrocer, remember? No family to take over his shop, poor sod.'

Bridget followed her inside, looking in admiration at the rows of tiny drawers, the shelves of tools and candles, blankets, pots and pans, just about everything.

'My father always said he wanted people to say "McKinley will have it", no matter what "it" was,' Ida said.

'It's marvellous,' Bridget said, honestly. 'And your father is . . .'

'Long dead,' Ida said, looking up to the sky. 'God rest his soul. Lovely man.'

'So the shop belongs to you alone?' She bit her lip. 'I assumed a man must own it,' she admitted, shamefaced.

Ida locked the shop door behind Bridget. 'That's not your fault,' she said. 'It's just the way things are. I know there aren't many like me. And as you know, my shop was my father's before me, so I really only have it because of a man.'

'You should still be proud of yourself for running it,' Bridget said.

'Oh believe me, I am,' said Ida with a smile.

She showed Bridget out the back of the store, and then up some narrow steps that led to her flat. It was small but rather lovely. Just right, thought Bridget, like Baby Bear's porridge in the story about Goldilocks. Just the right number of chairs, the right amount of furniture and the right size rooms.

'So what's new at the factory?' Ida asked, as she bustled about making tea.

Bridget made a face.

'It seems since Beresford ran away, everyone – well, those of us still in the office – they've all got something to say about him,' she said. 'And none of it's good.'

'Like what?'

Bridget told Ida about the young woman she'd seen coming out of his office a while back, adjusting her clothes, and how he'd touched her own thigh and slapped her behind.

'What an awful man,' Ida said, handing Bridget a mug and sitting down.

'I think I got off lightly compared with some,' Bridget said. 'We have a sort of unspoken agreement that we don't let anyone be alone with him, with the door closed at least. Not if we can help it.'

'Looking out for one another like sisters,' Ida said. 'Speaking of which, we have a problem with the census protest.'

'What sort of problem?'

'The bookstore roof has fallen in.'

'Oh, that's terrible.'

Ida nodded. 'All that rain the other day proved too much. So we're on the hunt for another place to stay.'

'I'll think of somewhere,' Bridget said. 'I really don't want to have to walk round and round the park all night.'

'Me neither,' said Ida, with an exaggerated shiver. 'Right then, show me these plans you've made for Mr Churchill.'

Bridget took out all the notes she'd made, and as she sat there with Ida, sipping her tea and making plans, and laughing, she thought it wasn't the flat that felt just right.

It was Ida.

Chapter Twenty-Six

Sadie's wages did not stretch very far.

She paid Dr Cohen's bill and bought some food, but the boys were so hungry all the time, and Ma was under the weather again, and Rachel wasn't getting better as fast as Sadie would have liked.

She'd been helping Walter with the letters to management about the strike. Walter had a real talent for words, but he liked Sadie to check the numbers before he sent the letters. She'd discovered she had a flair for understanding the figures. A business brain, Walter had called it, which had pleased Sadie.

And finally, management had replied to the strike committee directly, though they still sent letters to the newspaper, too.

Sadie had read through the offers sent from management, which they'd made sound like enormous concessions, and worked out that they were simply taking a bit from one and giving it to another and overall no one was going to be better off at all. Quite the opposite, in fact.

Walter had been terribly grateful, though she had a slight suspicion he was taking her numbers to his meetings and 'forgetting' to mention she'd done all the working out, but she was too exhausted to care. When the strike committee told the workers about the offers, they all laughed at the cheek of the managers and agreed to keep fighting, thanks to Sadie's hard work in deciphering what the deals really meant. She was proud of that.

Today she'd decided not to even go to the Gorbals Cross to hear the speakers or show her face. She wanted to clean the flat because she had a horrible feeling the dust wasn't helping Ma's chest, and the spring sunshine that had finally arrived was shining through the windows and lighting up every dirty mark. She longed to buy a whole chicken from Benson's the fancy butcher, but she didn't have enough money. So instead, she planned to loiter in the market at the end of the day and perhaps manage to get some cheap cuts of meat from Mr Barnett's stall that wouldn't last until tomorrow. A bit of mutton perhaps. And she could get some carrots and potatoes from the greengrocers at the end of the afternoon too. Mr Mackenzie on the stall often sold them at a good price if they weren't going to last another day. She could boil it all up in a soup and maybe it wouldn't be as good as chicken, but it would be hot and comforting and, most importantly, filling. Her stomach rumbled at the thought of some tasty soup and she wrapped her arms around her abdomen, hoping Ma wouldn't hear. She'd not eaten yet today but if she could hold on until later, that would be better.

They'd been on strike over a week now. A week and a day. And things weren't going to plan at all. Sadie had never thought for one minute that it would have gone on this long. And worst of all, it showed no sign of ending.

Sadie was a proud woman. She had stepped up to care for her family when her father had died and she'd not asked for help. She wasn't about to ask for help now, either. Not yet. Not while there were still a few coins in the biscuit jar and while she could get by on small amounts of food each day – or even no food because wasn't she young and healthy and fine to last a wee bit longer than the others – as long as Ma and the children were fed.

She knew Noah was worried about them, and so were Miriam and Jack. But things weren't easy for them either. They had a shop – a tobacconist – but Noah had said their rent had gone up and their takings were down, and times were hard. Sadie suspected that if it wasn't for Noah's contribution to their household they'd not have been managing at all.

And Noah himself was stretched thin. There were so many children at the school where he taught who were in the same boat. Lots of their parents worked at Wentworth too and were out on strike. Sadie knew Noah was taking bread to work with him every day just to give the hungry children something to fill their empty tummies with each morning. He was spending his own money on helping those children and she loved him for it. Even though she tried not to.

She took the mop from the kitchen cupboard and set about cleaning the floor, keeping half an eye on Ma, who was dozing in her chair. She looked pale and thin, and Sadie could hear her raspy breathing even on the far side of the room. But another visit from Dr Cohen was out of the question.

Soup would help, Sadie thought. Most definitely.

In fact, maybe she'd go to the market now. Ma and Rachel would be all right for a while and the boys always went to play football after school, so they'd not be home yet. She could get the ingredients for soup and get it all in the pot, and then perhaps they could all sit round the table together for once.

She glanced at her mother, who was slumped sideways in the chair, and for a moment she felt awful, icy-cold dread. Was she breathing?

Cautiously, Sadie took a step towards her ma, and then jumped as she breathed in deeply. Thank goodness.

She found her coat, and stuck her head round the bedroom door. Rachel was asleep, too, but her breathing had eased now. The winter had been long and bleak but it seemed warmer weather was on the way. Spring was definitely here, and Sadie had to hope it would help her mother and her sister return to better health.

Outside, it was raining, and the number of people gathered at the Gorbals Cross had definitely reduced. No surprise really.

It was a lot less fun to stand outside and listen to speakers when there was cold rain running down the back of your neck.

Sadie hurried past the group, not wanting to see Brody and have to answer questions about why she wasn't there today.

She found a spot beside the market where she could see the butcher and the greengrocer, and paused. If she timed it right and went to the stalls just before they started packing away for the day, she'd get more for her money. She turned over the coins in her pocket. And that way, she'd have enough to make soup for all of them.

'Sadie?'

She glanced round and saw, to her astonishment, Ellen walking towards her. She looked flushed and happy, and Sadie immediately felt sallow and wan next to her.

'I've been looking for you everywhere,' Ellen said, throwing her arms round her. Sadie hugged her back, glad to see her friend despite her woes.

'Everywhere?' Sadie raised an eyebrow.

'Well, I looked at the green in Clydebank, and then I thought you must have stayed in Glasgow so I asked that Brody one, and he said he'd not seen you this morning but he thought you'd be here now, so I came through on the train and I went to the Cross but I couldn't find you there either, and I was going to come to your flat . . . but here you are.'

Sadie grinned. 'What's so urgent that you had to put all that effort in?'

Ellen looked round. 'Is there somewhere we can sit down?'

But Sadie didn't want to lose her spot beside the butcher. So she just shook her head. 'Just tell me, Ellen,' she said, more sharply than she'd intended.

Ellen made a face, but she didn't comment. Instead, she said: 'I was fed up with Walter and that ignoring us, so I've made a plan to get more involved in the strike again. I'm going to sneak into the factory and go to see Mr Beresford. I think if I can talk to him face to face, on a personal level, we'll get somewhere.' She clutched Sadie's arm, making her jump. 'And, oh Sadie, I think I like James.'

Sadie stared at her friend, trying to process everything she'd just told her.

'Hold on,' she said, laughing. 'Let me deal with this one step at a time. You want to go and speak to Mr Beresford?'

'I do.'

'And say what?'

'Just explain what the problem is, person to person rather than striker to employee.'

'He wouldn't speak to us before.'

'Aye, I know, but this will be different. I'll be a bit nicer, rather than giving him a list of demands.'

'You want to be nicer?'

Ellen sighed. 'Yes. My gran always says you catch more flies with honey than with vinegar.'

Sadie couldn't argue with that.

'I suppose . . .'

Ellen looked annoyed. 'You've got the same expression on your face as James had when I told him. Neither of you think this is a good idea. I know I'm not as quick with numbers as you are, and I don't understand the way companies work like Walter and James, but I do understand people, and I understand Wentworth, Sadie. It's part of me. I'm the third generation of our family to work there.'

Sadie looked at Ellen's eager face and smiled. 'Wentworth's in your veins,' she said, nodding. 'I think it's worth a try.'

'Oh, thank you!' Ellen squealed, throwing her arms round Sadie. 'I wouldn't have done it if you hadn't approved.'

'Sure you wouldn't.' Sadie untangled herself from her friend's arms and prodded her. 'Tell me about James.'

'He's lovely,' said Ellen dreamily. 'I really like him, Sadie. He's so handsome. Don't you think he's handsome?'

Sadie thought Noah had the edge when it came to looks, but she didn't say so. She just nodded.

'And he's funny. And he's clever. And he's so kind and thoughtful. What's that word when someone can imagine themselves in someone else's shoes?'

'Empathetic.'

'That's it, exactly. He really thinks about other people, you know? Oh, and did I mention how handsome he is?'

'You did.'

'Funny, clever, handsome. He's perfect,' Ellen said.

'It's not that long ago you thought the same about Beresford.'

'He's not a patch on James,' Ellen said, with a chuckle. She leaned against Sadie. 'What about you and Noah?'

'What about us?'

'Has he said anything else about the woman he wants to marry?'

Sadie frowned. 'No,' she said. 'Nothing at all.'

'You have to tell him how you feel,' Ellen said, but Sadie shook her head. She looked at Ellen, all starry-eyed and giddy over James, and thought that flush of excited first love was so different to how she felt about Noah that perhaps she had this all wrong.

She loved being with Noah, there was no doubt about that, but their relationship didn't have the excitement of first love. Instead she simply relied on him for support with her sick sister and invalid mother. There was hardly room to start a romance when you had to stay up all night propping Rachel up with pillows to stop her coughing, and you couldn't sleep for worry about how to make sure your ma was warm enough, or how you were going to afford to buy food for two hungry lads. She felt a sudden, uncharacteristic and frighteningly fierce burst of envy towards Ellen.

'Stop it,' she said sharply. 'It's not like that with Noah and me. We're not like you and James. Stop it.'

Ellen looked startled. 'Sorry,' she said. 'I must have misunderstood.'

'Well don't.' She clenched her fists by her sides. 'Don't.'

'Evening, Sadie,' said a cheery voice and she turned to see the butcher, Mr Barnett, walking by.

'Oh no,' she said desperately. 'Have you closed up already? I wanted some mutton. Just for soup.'

'Sorry, Sadie. It's all gone. I just gave the last of it to Mrs Wexler. Come back tomorrow.'

Close to despair, Sadie watched him walk away. The green-grocer's stall was boarded up, too, with no sign of Mr McKenzie – she'd not noticed him close because she'd been talking to Ellen. And now it was too late. She had no food for this evening and Ma would be hungry, and poor Rachel needed something to keep her strength up, and as for the boys, well, they'd be home soon and they'd be desperate for more than just a piece of bread.

She wanted to cry. She'd let them all down, and now she didn't know what to do.

'Sadie?' Ellen touched her gently on the shoulder. 'Sadie, what's wrong?'

Sadie felt that rush of envy again, because Ellen was fine. Her da was still alive and he was strong and healthy and he was working. Earning. Bringing home his pay every week. And her ma was busy doing her mending. Being paid for it, too. And yes, of course they'd be missing Ellen's wages, and Bridget's too, but they weren't starving, were they? They didn't have small hungry mouths to feed, nor doctors' bills to pay.

She clenched her fists again and then she shook Ellen's hand off her shoulder.

'Shut. Up,' she growled.

Ellen looked shocked. 'Sadie?'

'Shut up,' Sadie shrieked. 'Shut up and leave me alone. You don't understand, Ellen. You don't know anything about my life and I don't want you to. Just . . .' She took a deep breath. 'Just go away.'

Ellen stared at her, eyes wide.

'Sadie, you don't mean that.'

'I mean every word,' Sadie said. 'Just go away. I never want to see you ever again.'

And leaving Ellen standing beside the closed-up stalls, she turned and marched away, back to the flat where there was no food, and no wood for the fire, and no hope.

Chapter Twenty-Seven

Ellen couldn't quite believe what had just happened. She watched Sadie marching away towards her flat and thought about chasing after her. But what if she shouted at her again? She rubbed her forehead. She seemed to have developed quite a knack for upsetting people recently – first Bridget, now Sadie.

But whereas her row with Bridget had come from both of them being annoyed with the other, this argument had blown up out of nowhere. She may not have known Sadie as long as she'd known her sister, of course, but she knew her well enough to know that this was very out of character.

She began to walk in the same direction as Sadie had gone, keeping her distance because she didn't want another public shouting match. She couldn't see her anymore because the street was bustling with people going home from work, but Ellen knew Sadie was heading for her flat. Should she ring the bell, perhaps? Ask Sadie if she wanted to talk? She wasn't sure. She crossed the road and walked down a side street and now she caught a glimpse of Sadie. Ellen watched as her friend strode up the path to the flat then paused for a second outside, as though she was readying herself to go inside.

Something wasn't right, Ellen was sure of that.

'Sadie!' Footsteps behind Ellen made her jump and a tall man with dark hair and glasses hurried by, waving in Sadie's direction. 'Sadie!'

But up ahead, Sadie either didn't hear or didn't want to hear. She opened the door and went inside, and the man paused, a little way ahead of Ellen on the street, looking disappointed.

Ellen went towards him. 'Excuse me?' she said. 'Are you Noah?'

He looked surprised and slightly alarmed. 'Yes?'

Relieved, Ellen put her hand to her chest. 'Oh thank goodness,' she said. 'Sadie's upset and I think it's my fault, but I don't know why, and I wondered if you might know, because I don't want to leave her like this, but also I'm not sure she'll want to see me. Though, like I said, I'm not sure why.'

Noah pushed his glasses up his nose and looked at Ellen. 'Sorry,' he said. 'Could you start again? Who are you?'

Ellen tutted. 'Sadie said you were clever.'

'She did?' Noah looked pleased.

'Well, she was clearly wrong.'

'Bit rude,' said Noah. 'But go on.' He looked at Ellen through narrowed eyes. 'You must be Ellen.'

'I am,' Ellen nodded, 'and I'm sorry I was rude. I'm just worried.' She sat down on a nearby wall. 'She's really not herself, Noah, and I'm not sure why.'

Noah sat down next to her, adjusting the straps on his satchel as he did. Ellen thought he looked a little like an overgrown schoolboy, but he also looked very concerned and she was pleased he was listening to her worries. He obviously cared about Sadie, too.

'We were just chatting in the market, and then she got so cross with me, completely out of the blue,' she explained. 'And it's really not like her to be so blunt. So I think there must be something else going on.'

Noah nodded thoughtfully. 'Was she shopping? In the market?'

Ellen shrugged. 'I don't think so, she didn't have any bags. But she did get upset when she saw that the man on the meat stall had packed up while we were chatting.'

'She didn't buy anything from him?'

'He'd sold out.'

'Ah,' said Noah. 'Right.'

'Ah, what? There are lots of other stalls.'

'Mr Barnett always sells his leftovers off cheap at the end of the day,' Noah said, turning to her and speaking earnestly. Ellen could see herself reflected in his spectacles. 'Sadie was probably waiting to buy some meat but then missed him packing up.'

'Because I'd distracted her.' Ellen slapped her forehead with her palm. 'No wonder she was annoyed.'

Noah shook his head. 'I think Sadie's really struggling,' he said slowly.

'Struggling with money?' Ellen felt a bit sick that she'd been so clueless.

'Yes.' Noah rubbed his nose and knocked his glasses askew, but he didn't straighten them. 'I've asked and asked if she's all right, and she says she's fine, but how can they be?'

'She's the only one working,' Ellen said, realisation dawning. 'Except she's not working, is she?'

'Exactly. And Rachel's had Dr Cohen out again, and the boys just eat and eat.'

'She's so pale.'

'I don't think she's eating properly,' Noah said. 'If I know Sadie, she'll make sure everyone else is fed first and leave herself until last.'

Ellen wanted to cry. 'I didn't realise things were so hard.'

'Me neither, and I'm right here all the time,' said Noah, patting her hand.

'We need to help her.'

Noah nodded, but he looked grim-faced. 'I haven't got much myself but I can buy some bread now, and perhaps some cheese. I can't run to meat, but it'll be better than nothing.'

'Here . . .' Ellen dug about in her pocket and found a couple of coins. 'Get some milk, too.'

Noah took the money. 'She'll be furious, though. She's so proud of looking after the family since her da died.'

'Then lie,' Ellen said simply. 'Tell her you found the food somewhere.'

'She won't believe that.'

'Could you say that someone gave it to you?'

Noah made a face. 'I don't think so.'

'How about if you left it somewhere for her to find? Like on the doorstep?'

'That's not a bad idea.' Noah nodded. 'I'll do that. She might guess it's from me, but I can brazen it out.'

Ellen was warming to this man. 'Good.'

Noah opened his bag and took out the newspaper. 'It's not going to help for long, though, is it? And I read the most recent letter that management sent to the newspaper. This strike doesn't look like it's going to be over any time soon.'

'There's a lot of backwards and forwards.' Ellen rolled her eyes. 'But I've got an idea. That's why I came to see Sadie, actually, to run it past her and see if she thought it could work.'

'You've got an idea to stop the strike?' Noah raised an eyebrow and Ellen bristled with annoyance.

'Yes, actually. And as it was my idea to start the strike in the first place, I think I'm the right person to sort this out, don't you?'

Noah let out a little chuckle. 'I suppose so.'

'In fact,' Ellen said, 'I'm going to go and run it past the strike committee.'

'What is it?'

'It's like a group of men who've put themselves in charge of the strike. They think they know everything about Wentworth and strikes, but frankly they don't know nearly as much as they think they do.'

Noah laughed again. 'No, I meant what's the idea?'

'Oh.' Ellen chuckled too this time. 'I'm just going to go and speak with one of the bosses. My sister works for him. He knows

212

me. Well, he knows who I am. At least I think he does. We're not getting anywhere with this collective bargaining business, so maybe a personal approach could work.'

'Maybe,' Noah said. He still looked faintly amused, but Ellen thought – at least she hoped – he looked a little impressed too.

She slid off the wall. 'I'll sort it out,' she said. 'Tell Sadie. And get that food.'

'I will.'

'Trust me, Noah,' Ellen said trying to sound confident, 'by this time tomorrow it'll all be back to normal.'

But she crossed her fingers anyway, just in case she was wrong.

The next day, Ellen was up with the lark. She wanted to walk into the factory when the bell went, among the few people who were still working, not try to get through the gates when they'd been closed for the day. And before then, she wanted to see Walter and Stanley to let them know what she was planning.

She'd been tossing and turning all night, worrying about Sadie. Knowing Noah was looking out for her made Ellen feel a wee bit better but there was no denying she felt awful about the whole thing. She knew that the strike was the right thing to do – it wasn't fair to expect them to work longer and harder for less money, that wasn't in doubt.

But she'd never really considered how hard it would be.

She wanted it over with now, and she knew that Sadie absolutely felt the same way. And so it was up to Ellen to fix it.

No matter what Walter said.

As she left home, she was determined to walk to the green where she knew Walter would be, but in truth she didn't feel confident. Her legs were a little bit shaky, and her stomach was churning.

'Stop being silly, Ellen,' she murmured to herself. 'This is your fight. It always was.'

'Morning, Ellen,' Walter called as she approached.

'Morning.'

She saw James was there with them and she was glad. He'd support her, she was sure.

'James says you want to go and meet management?'

A bit put out that James had been talking about her, she met his gaze and he gave her an apologetic shrug.

'I do, aye.'

'Aw, doll, it's a nice idea, but . . .'

'No buts,' Ellen said firmly. 'I don't want to hear them.'

'Injure one, injure us all,' said Stanley. 'You know the score. It's collective bargaining. We work together.'

'I'm not suggesting I go in there and only speak for myself,' Ellen said, beginning to get infuriated. 'I'm just saying my knowledge of Wentworth is one of our strengths.' She held her arms out wide. 'Use me.'

Walter and Stanley exchanged a glance.

'You know Wentworth well?'

'I've worked there since I was fourteen,' Ellen said. 'My sister works there, and so did my da once upon a time, and my gran.' She smiled, remembering Bridget's words at their sewing bee – how long ago that seemed now. 'Cut me, and I bleed Wentworth.'

Walter nodded.

'And you think Beresford will speak to you?'

'Last time we didn't get to see him because of blasted Malcolm,' Ellen said. 'But if I go in with the workers, and see him in his office, I know he'll talk to me. No gatekeepers. No letters to the newspapers. Just me and him.'

She stared at Walter and he stared back, and for a second she thought he was going to argue. But instead, he whistled. 'You know what you want, eh?'

'What I want is for you to take me seriously,' Ellen said.

'You'd do well to listen to her,' James put in. 'She doesn't like being ignored.'

Walter looked at her for a bit longer and then he laughed.

'I don't think he'll speak to you, doll. He's just a wee jessie – you saw how he ran away the other day. But have a go. What harm can it do?'

Ellen wanted to jump up and down and clap her hands, but she just nodded at Walter and Stanley.

'I'll walk with you,' said James.

They strolled across the green and Ellen felt their hands touching every now and then. Was it accidental? She wasn't sure. But then suddenly, she wasn't really sure how it happened, their fingers were entwined and they were holding hands.

Once they were into the trees at the edge of the green, sheltered from view, Ellen stopped walking so James had to stop too. She turned to face him, and took a deep breath.

'James?' she said.

'Yes?'

Ellen stood on tiptoe and kissed him quickly on the lips. He looked quite startled and, for a second, Ellen thought she'd completely misjudged the whole situation. But then he kissed her back so thoroughly that she felt more than a little light-headed.

'Walter was right,' said James, looking rather dazed as they drew apart. 'You do know what you want.'

Ellen giggled. 'It's important to be clear,' she said, which was something Walter liked to say. Then she sighed. 'I just want this strike to be over, James. It's too hard now. Poor Sadie's in a right state. She can't afford to feed her family.'

'Aye that's tough, right enough,' he said. 'Did you have any idea how far this would go that day when you stopped work?'

'No idea at all,' Ellen said. 'And to be honest, I'm not sure I'd have done it if I'd known.'

'I think you would have,' James said, looking at her with such affection that she felt sort of squirmy and warm inside. 'Because I think you're a woman with great principles.'

Ellen kissed him again, feeling the trunk of the tree pressing into her back.

'I have to go,' she said with genuine regret, glancing up at the Wentworth clock. 'I need to walk into the factory with the workers.'

'Come and find me as soon as you've seen him, yes?'

'Of course.' Ellen kissed him again.

'Aye, aye, what's all this?'

Ellen and James broke apart to see a young man, a few years older than James but similar in appearance, standing watching them, a little way from them, his hands on his hips.

'Oh shit,' James breathed. 'It's Frankie.'

'Frankie Briggs,' Ellen said in disgust, her heart thumping in fear. 'Just ignore him, James. He's got some sort of weird vendetta against my da.'

James's face was pale.

'You know him?' he said quietly. 'You know Frankie?'

'Well, not really, but he and his pals had a scuffle with my da at the football, and gave him a thick lip. My da was raging, James, and they've had a few run-ins since.' Ellen looked over to where Frankie was still standing still, glowering at them. 'He's a terror. We should go.'

She tugged at James's sleeve. 'C'mon, let's just walk away.' Her voice shook a bit because, despite her bravado, she was scared of Frankie Briggs.

But James didn't move as Frankie came towards them, his wasted leg dragging slightly as he walked.

'Hello,' Frankie said to him. 'Who's this, then?'

James had wrapped his arms round himself, almost like he was cold. He looked, Ellen thought, very uncomfortable.

'Aren't you going to introduce me?' Frankie said in a sing-song voice.

James stayed silent, looking at his feet.

'So rude,' tutted Frankie. 'I'm Francis Briggs.' He paused. 'James's big brother.'

Ellen's jaw dropped and she stared at James. 'Frankie Briggs is your brother?'

'Aye,' said Frankie. 'Frankie Briggs is his brother.'

He looked at Ellen through narrowed eyes. 'And what's your name, doll?'

'This is Ellen,' James said.

'Ellen what?' Frankie asked.

Ellen pinched her lips together.

'Ellen what?' Frankie hissed, putting his face close to Ellen's. 'Oh, wait. Don't tell me, because I know. I know who you are, and I know your stinking, bastard da.'

Ellen thought her legs might give way beneath her because she was shaking so hard.

'Frankie,' she said, trying to stay calm. 'Let's all just go and have a sit down and we can have a talk . . .'

'She's Catholic,' he spat at James. 'She's Catholic!' He was shouting now and Ellen was frightened by his aggressive stance as he stood in front of his brother.

'Yes,' said James, hanging his head.

Ellen realised with a sudden, cold understanding that all of this fuss about her being Catholic meant James wasn't. She'd not even thought to ask.

'You know she's Catholic and you're letting her do that to you?' Frankie spat on the ground. 'It's disgusting.'

'We were just . . .' Ellen began. James winced at her interruption and Frankie erupted.

'Shut your mouth,' he shouted. 'You disgust me. You Fenian . . .' he searched for the word he wanted. 'Fenian tart.'

Ellen felt the words like arrows, piercing her skin. She looked at James for support, but he was still holding himself, hugging his arms and almost folding in on himself. She wanted to go to him, comfort him, but she had a strong suspicion that would make everything worse.

'Do not talk to me like that,' she said to Frankie. 'And don't talk to your brother like that either.'

She took a step towards Frankie and then, suddenly, she was on the ground, falling heavily onto her behind as he shoved her out of the way to get to James.

'Stop it,' Ellen tried to shout, but she was winded, and she couldn't get her breath.

James, though, was unfolding. He was going from scared little boy to angry young man as Ellen watched.

And quick as a flash, he reached out and grabbed his brother by the front of his shirt. 'You leave us alone,' he growled. He drew back his fist and Ellen scrambled to her feet, not wanting the brothers to fight.

'That's enough,' she said, trying to insert herself in between them. 'Enough.'

Frankie swerved round her and this time it was he who grabbed James. 'You can't be courting a Catholic,' he said. And to Ellen's absolute horror, he swung a punch at James, who staggered backwards with the blow, holding his cheek.

Ellen drew herself up to her full height of just over five feet, and thrust both her hands into Frankie's chest.

'Stop!' she shrieked. 'Stop this!'

Frankie glared at her and she felt her resolve disappear as he towered over her. There was an odd look in his eyes, like he didn't really know who she was. Or that he didn't really know who he was. It scared her.

He reached out his hand towards her and she braced herself for him to hit her, but instead he yanked the crucifix she wore round her neck, pulling it so hard that her head snapped forwards, and the chain broke. She gasped to see it dangling from Frankie's fingers.

'How could you?' she said. 'Give that back.'

Frankie threw it into the nearby bushes. 'Get it yourself,' he said.

Ellen looked from him to James, not sure what to do next. Her heart was pounding so hard she thought it might burst from her chest.

And then the factory bell rang.

'Go,' James said, from where he sat on the ground, his eye beginning to swell. 'Go and speak to Beresford.'

Ellen absolutely did not want to do that right now. She shook her head. 'No, James, I can't leave you.'

James managed to get to his feet, and holding his arms out protectively to stop Frankie getting too close to Ellen, he nodded. 'Go on,' he said. 'I'll be fine.'

'But . . .'

James put his forehead against hers. 'This isn't the first time Frankie's lashed out, Ellen,' he said. 'If it wasn't you, it would be something else. Just go. I'll sort it.'

'Are you sure?'

James glanced round to where his brother was watching them, his face red with anger.

'Go.'

'But your eye . . .'

'Go!' he shouted. 'Go quickly, before the gates close.'

And, with her heart still thumping and her neck throbbing where the chain had bruised it when Frankie pulled it, Ellen picked up her skirt and ran.

Chapter Twenty-Eight

Ellen knew she was in no state to see Mr Beresford. Not with her skirt muddy from where she'd run across the green, and with her hair askew. And with her heart thumping so hard, she felt her chest jumping beneath her blouse, and her mind was racing.

But what choice did she have? She thought of Sadie, waiting beside the butcher's stall for a bag of scraggy ends of meat, and though she desperately wanted to turn back and check James was all right, she joined the small crowd of workers heading for the factory gate.

Carefully, she pulled her hat down over her eyes, and keeping her head lowered, she weaved herself through the people until she was roughly in the middle of the group. She spotted Janet just ahead of her, and turned slightly to the side so she was hidden behind a large man, to make it harder for her friend to spot her should she glance in her direction.

She carried on, feeling her palms sweating as they went through the gate and into the courtyard and the crowd began to disperse, with workers heading for their different departments. Ellen couldn't help wondering what they were doing just now – there couldn't be much work for them to do.

Up ahead, she saw Bridget and had to fight the urge to run to her and throw her arms round her and say sorry. She skirted the edge of the building, keeping a distance from her sister, and hoped she wasn't spotted.

'Ellen?'

Damn.

'Janet.'

'Is that you back to work, then?' Janet looked curious and, Ellen thought, a little disappointed.

Ellen, whose blood was already running hot and angry, scowled at her.

'It's not.'

'So why are you here?'

'I've a meeting with management,' Ellen fibbed. 'On behalf of the strike committee.'

Janet's brow wrinkled. 'Management?'

'Mr Beresford.'

'Ellen, he's not . . .'

'I know,' Ellen interrupted. 'He's a coward and he's the one who's behind all these changes. But I still need to speak to him.'

'He's not a nice man,' Janet said, knitting her fingers together. 'Are you going alone?' She looked round as if Walter and the rest of the IWS might appear at any moment.

'Yes, I'm going alone,' Ellen snapped. 'This strike happened because of me, and I am the one who's going to sort it out.' She tossed her head and went to walk on. Janet reached out and grabbed her arm, but Ellen shook her off and hurried away. How dare Janet try to stop her? Just because she worked in clerical with Mr Beresford, didn't mean she had the right . . .

Ellen's blood was up, but she carried on.

Bridget had gone now, up the stairs to the clerical department, Ellen assumed, and no longer caring whether anyone saw her or not, Ellen went the same way.

The factory was quiet. No hum of machinery or hiss of steam, so quiet that Ellen could hear her footsteps on the stairs as she pounded upwards, hoping she wouldn't bump into Malcolm.

On the clerical floor, things were even quieter. Ellen allowed herself a small flush of satisfaction that she – and Sadie, of course – had done this. They were the people responsible for shutting down this mighty operation in pursuit of fairness and equality. The thought spurred her on, heading for the offices at the end of the corridor.

She slunk past the door of Bridget's department, not wanting her sister to see her, but just as she went by, Bridget came out, wearing a hat and a coat that Ellen was sure she hadn't been wearing when she saw her just a few minutes ago, and walked straight into her.

'Oh!' both women exclaimed, and then Bridget said, in a shocked voice: 'Ellen?'

'Shhh,' said Ellen. She pushed her sister into the empty department so no one walking down the corridor would see them and Bridget tutted in annoyance.

'What are you doing?'

'Nothing,' Ellen lied. 'Nothing.'

Bridget scoffed. 'Och, Ellen, you're a terrible liar. What are you up to? Slinking about the clerical corridors looking guilty?'

'What about you?' Ellen said, suddenly realising that Bridget was leaving the factory, just five minutes after she'd arrived. 'What are you doing? Where did you get that coat?'

'It belongs to a friend,' Bridget said, not meeting Ellen's gaze. 'I borrowed it.'

Ellen looked from her sister to the coat stand at the side of the room where Bridget's usual outdoor wear was hanging. Her typewriter was uncovered, with a sheet of paper in it and her notebook was open on the desk. It looked for all the world as though she had just left the office for a moment. And yet, Bridget herself, with her unfamiliar coat and her hair tucked into a hat, and her bag clutched in her arms, looked like she was leaving for a while.

'Where are you going?' Ellen said, intrigued and a little annoyed that Bridget was doing something she'd not told her about.

She ignored the fact that she'd not spoken to her for more than a week. 'Are you doing something you don't want management to know about?' She gasped. 'Or Malcolm? Is it Malcolm you don't want to find out?'

'Shut up, Ellen,' Bridget said crossly, running her finger round the collar of the coat she was wearing. 'This is none of your business. Why are you here anyway?'

'None of your business,' said Ellen.

The women stared at one another for a second.

'If you breathe a word of this to Malcolm, so help me . . .'

'Ah ha!' said Ellen. 'So it is Malcolm you're hiding from!'

'Ellen.' Bridget's tone was stern.

'I don't speak to Malcolm,' Ellen said. 'I'm hardly likely to start now, am I?'

'Well, make sure you don't.'

Ellen grimaced. 'Fine.'

'I have to go.'

'Me too.'

Bridget gave Ellen a tiny nod. 'Good luck with whatever it is you're doing,' she said.

Ellen felt the corners of her mouth twitch upwards. 'You too.' She poked her head out of the doorway. 'All clear.'

Without another word to one another, the women scurried off in opposite directions. Ellen heard Bridget's footsteps fading away and headed towards Mr Beresford's office.

She'd never been in this part of the factory before. It was very nice – all wood panelling and shiny floorboards. No footsteps echoing around this bit of the corridor.

The managers all had their own offices, and Ellen knew from Bridget that Mr Beresford's was the first one she would come to.

She found it, with the door slightly ajar and his name on a metal plaque, and paused to gather herself. She was still edgy and anxious about what had happened to James, and unsettled by seeing Janet, but she was determined to get this done.

She pushed the door gently and went inside. The office was actually two rooms. The first was lined with shelves full of ledgers and was clearly where Mr Beresford's assistant sat. But her typewriter was covered and there was no one at the desk. Out on strike too, Ellen thought with pride.

At the far end of the room was another door, also slightly ajar and Ellen could hear voices.

She took a deep breath, wondering if she should wait for Mr Beresford to be alone. But if she waited too long, she knew there was a good chance she'd simply give up and leave – go back to the green to make sure James was all right.

So screwing up her courage, she took the few paces to the door of the office and knocked.

'Yes?'

The voices stopped and Ellen realised now it had been the wireless. She pushed open the door to see Mr Beresford leaning on the edge of his desk studying plans that were pinned to the wall. He looked dishevelled and out of sorts and she felt a brief – very brief – flush of sympathy for him. This couldn't have been easy for him. She almost understood why he'd run away.

'What?' he snapped, and Ellen's sympathy vanished.

'Mr Beresford? I'm Ellen Kelly.'

He looked at her. 'Kelly?'

Ellen nodded. 'Bridget's sister.'

'Right,' he said, without any real interest. 'Are you lost? Bridget's in the clerical department.'

'I know that. I didn't come to see her. I came to see you.'

'Did you, aye?'

'I'm with the strike committee.'

Understanding dawned on his face.

'Ellen Kelly?' he said. 'Cabinet polishing?'

'That's me.'

He pushed himself up from the desk and walked round to sit on the large leather chair on the other side.

'Get out,' he said.

'Please, Mr Beresford, could we just talk for five minutes?' Ellen begged.

'Is this that scum Walter MacDonald's doing? He thinks nothing of sending a wee girl to do his dirty work.'

Ellen was affronted. 'Walter didn't send me.'

But Mr Beresford wasn't listening.

'Or did he think you could win me over another way?' he said. 'That disgusting man, judging everyone by his own standards.'

'I don't know what you're talking about,' Ellen said. 'Walter didn't send me. I wanted to come myself and talk to you because I've worked at Wentworth for years. It's part of our family. I wanted to try to persuade you ...'

Mr Beresford stood up and walked back round his desk. Ellen was suddenly aware of how much taller he was than she.

'The thing is,' she began, feeling less confident. 'The thing is, Wentworth needs its workers ...'

She shut her mouth when, to her surprise, Mr Beresford reached out and ran a finger down her cheek. 'You're a sweet wee thing,' he said. 'Or at least you would be if you'd stop talking for one blasted minute.'

Ellen wasn't sure what to do. She'd got her speech all planned but it seemed for now it would be best to stay quiet.

She stood very still as Mr Beresford trailed his fingers down her jaw and her neck, then winced as he touched the spot where her necklace had scratched her skin.

He looked annoyed as she reacted.

'Take your coat off,' he said. Obediently, Ellen slipped it off and hung it on the hook behind the door. Feeling more than a little bewildered, she straightened her blouse and then stood a little way from her boss.

'As I was saying,' she began again.

'Have a seat,' Mr Beresford interrupted.

Awkwardly Ellen looked to see where she should sit, but Mr Beresford patted the edge of his desk. 'Up here.'

'Really?'

'Come on.'

She pushed herself up on to the desk. It was so large she could only just touch the floor with the tip of her toes.

'MacDonald really didn't send you?'

'No.'

'You thought you could . . .' he emphasised the word '*persuade* me yourself?'

'Yes.'

He was standing in front of her now and Ellen felt rather hemmed in.

'But if you're busy, I can come back another time,' she said.

Mr Beresford smiled at her. 'How are you planning to persuade me?'

Ellen swallowed. 'Well . . .'

Her words were lost as he launched himself at her and pressed his lips to hers. She could feel his moustache scratching her face and tried to turn her head away, but he wouldn't let her – he was too strong.

With horror she realised his hand was roaming across her front, squeezing her breast and making her gasp. She yanked her head away from his.

'Stop,' she said weakly. 'Stop it.'

'Don't pretend this wasn't what you intended,' he said. 'Coming in here, with your eyelashes fluttering, and your bosom on display.'

Ellen looked down at her blouse, which had been buttoned up to the neck, but wasn't now and felt sick.

'I didn't . . .'

Mr Beresford slapped her, right across the face. No one had ever hit Ellen before and she was so startled and shocked that she stopped talking immediately, putting her hand to her cheek in total disbelief. She felt no pain, just an icy numbness that was spreading through her body, causing her to freeze, stock still.

'That's better,' Mr Beresford murmured. He positioned himself in between Ellen's legs as she sat on the desk. Ellen could smell his breath, sour on her cheek as she turned her head away. He put his hands on her thighs and pushed them upwards, taking her skirt with them, and then burrowed his fingers up on to where her bare skin met the top of her stocking. Ellen couldn't move. She wanted to push him away, to tell him to stop, to scream for help but she was unable to move.

Mr Beresford's hands were cold, and Ellen breathed in sharply. And that moment, that shock of his icy fingers on her warm skin, woke her from her inability to move. She put her left hand on top of his, stopping him from going any further.

'No,' she said. She put her other hand down on the desk, feeling behind her for anything that could help. Her fingers closed round something metallic, a letter opener, perhaps? She didn't care. She picked it up and quick as a flash jabbed it into the flesh at the top of his arm.

Mr Beresford howled in pain and Ellen seized her chance. She wriggled away from him, out of his grip.

'You stupid girl!' he cried, his face twisted in anger as he lunged for her. Ellen brought her knee up into his groin and he buckled.

Ellen ran for the door, but Mr Beresford was on his feet and reaching for a bell Ellen hadn't noticed before, hanging from the ceiling in the corner of the room. He pulled on the leather strap and suddenly bells were ringing everywhere. Mr Beresford sat down on the floor, the letter opener still sticking out of his arm. Ellen paused for a second, wondering whether to make a grab for her coat, then thought better of it and fled.

She clattered down the corridor, past Bridget's door, towards the stairs and there, coming up the way she was heading, were two burly men she'd never seen before.

'She's one of the strikers!' Ellen spun round to see Mr Beresford standing at the door of his office, leaning against the frame. 'She stabbed me! Arrest her!'

Like a cornered rat, Ellen looked from Mr Beresford to the men coming up the stairs and back again. She had nowhere to go. But she wasn't going to give up without a fight.

One of the men grabbed her round her chest and lifted her off her feet.

'Get off me!' she shrieked. 'Let go of me!' She kicked out and wriggled, making it as hard as she could for him to take her where he wanted her to go, but he held on tighter.

'I think we shall need a policeman,' Mr Beresford called, a note of triumph in his voice that made Ellen want to scream in frustration. 'Make sure you warn them that she's aggressive. And I think I'll need a doctor. I'm bleeding.'

Ellen snorted. 'It's a wee cut from a letter opener, you big softie!' she yelled.

The man holding her squeezed her even tighter and she gasped for breath.

'That's quite enough from you,' he growled. 'You're going to jail, missy.'

Chapter Twenty-Nine

Bridget was having the time of her life. She'd never once thought she might sneak away from work, nor keep secrets from her husband, nor be hurrying to catch the train that would take her to see the Home Secretary, for heaven's sake.

But here she was, racing away from the factory, towards the station to do just that.

And she was loving every minute of it.

She'd found in the suffragettes a group of women who were exactly what she'd been looking for – except she hadn't even known she'd been looking.

Growing up, she'd always enjoyed the company of women – Ellen, their ma, and their gran – as well as the girls at the factory and the friends at the sewing bee. And these suffragettes were no different.

Yes, some of them were much more well-to-do than Bridget's friends in Clydebank. There were also a few factory girls among them. And some – like Ida – worked in shops, or in restaurants or hotels. Many of them didn't work at all. It was wonderful because everyone had a different take on things according to their own experiences. Ida had told her that sometimes their discussions got quite heated, but they all agreed on the fundamental belief that women should have the vote.

Bridget had found that the suffragettes and their work were

consuming her every thought. Today's trip to confront Mr Churchill was all she could think about right now, but in the back of her mind was the plan for census night. The thought that there was another fight coming gave Bridget a thrill. Like a thirsty man in the desert finding water, she just wanted to drink it all in. This rebellion. This malicious mischief.

And Ida. Oh, Ida was a revelation to her. She partly wanted to be Ida and partly wanted to be with her.

She saw Ida now, waiting for Bridget beside the station steps and her heart lifted. She waved and Ida waved back and Bridget skipped across the road to her.

Ida kissed her cheek and Bridget breathed in the smell of her scent, like roses on a summer's day.

'Was it all right?' Ida said.

Bridget made a face. 'Bumped into Ellen.'

'No!'

'Yes. She was creeping down the corridor towards Mr Beresford's office.'

Ida frowned. 'What was she up to?' She started walking up the stairs and Bridget followed.

'No idea,' she said. 'Perhaps a little malicious mischief of her own?'

Ida laughed loudly. 'I do hope so.'

'As long as she's all right,' Bridget said. 'I hope she didn't come across Mr Beresford. We usually make sure we're not alone with him because, you know . . .'

'Nasty man,' Ida said with a grimace. 'And so infuriating that everyone knows what he's like and yet nothing changes.'

The train puffed into the station and they stopped talking for a while as they let the passengers off before clambering aboard themselves.

They found an empty carriage and sat down. When they were settled, Ida took her hat off and shook out her hair.

'I tied it up too tightly,' she said. 'It's giving me a headache.'

'Let me,' Bridget said. She held her hands out for the pins and Ida dropped them into her palm. 'Now, let's go through the plan for today again. Just to be sure.'

She moved closer to Ida, who turned her back slightly so Bridget could pin up her hair.

'Yesterday Mr Churchill took the ferry from Belfast and got the train to Glasgow from Stranraer,' Ida said.

'And we know he definitely got to Glasgow?' Bridget asked, knowing ferries could be delayed or cancelled because of the weather.

'We do, because Vera stayed at the railway station all day yesterday waiting for him to arrive. She saw him.'

'Good.'

Bridget began combing through Ida's hair with her fingers, enjoying the feeling of it in her hands.

'And today?' she asked, though she knew because they'd been through this a hundred times already.

'Today, Mr Churchill will take the train to Clydebank, where he is going to visit the dockyard. His train leaves Glasgow at eleven o'clock.'

'And we'll be on it, too,' said Bridget. She gathered Ida's hair in her hand ready to twist it and as she was doing so, she rubbed Ida's neck gently. Ida wriggled.

'That feels nice.'

Bridget felt a strange sensation in her stomach, like the excited anticipation she'd felt the night before her birthday as a child. She looked at Ida's long, strong neck and had the oddest urge to put her lips right there on the nape, where the hair was soft.

Flustered, she shook her head, dislodging the thoughts.

'I imagine Churchill is enjoying his breakfast now,' said Ida.

'Pardon?'

'Churchill,' Ida repeated with a chuckle. 'Did you drift off there for a second?'

Bridget managed to gather herself. 'I think I must have,' she said. 'Sorry. So we'll be at Glasgow early so we can be prepared . . .'

'That's right,' said Ida.

'We will board the train and find his carriage, and outline our arguments.'

Bridget twisted Ida's hair round her hand and pinned it up, not so tightly that it would give her a headache, but enough for it to stay.

'There, you're all done,' she said.

'My head feels cold now you're not touching it,' said Ida, laughing. She turned to look at Bridget and they smiled at one another. The air in their carriage felt charged, like before a thunderstorm. Then the door opened and two men entered with suitcases and a blast of cold air, and the moment passed.

They spent the rest of their journey talking about silly things – Bridget being fed up that it kept raining, even though spring was here. Ida's desire to travel to the Highlands in the summer. A woman who'd come to Ida's shop asking for invisible ink. Nothing of substance.

The train puffed into Queen Street Station and they got out. Bridget felt fidgety and nervous.

'I can't believe we're doing this,' she said, pacing the platform. 'I can't believe we're going to speak to Winston Churchill.'

'It's a marvellous way to get our point across,' Ida said. 'Calmly and concisely. Gosh, here they come now. Ready?'

'Ready,' said Bridget. She took Ida's hand and squeezed her fingers. Ida squeezed back.

Coming towards them down the platform, emerging through the smoky air, was Mr Churchill. Bridget had seen photographs of the politician in the newspapers but she wasn't sure she'd have recognised him had he not been flanked on either side by men in dark suits in a way that made sure he looked important.

The women stepped back against the wall, letting him walk past them and watched to see which part of the train he boarded.

It was first class, of course. Bridget made a face at Ida because their tickets were for second class. She'd not considered that in all the planning she'd done.

'We'll get into second class, wait until the ticket inspector has checked, and then walk through,' Ida said.

Bridget had never once travelled in the section of a train that she didn't have a ticket for.

'Right,' she said, biting her lip.

Ida squeezed her fingers again. 'It'll be fine, trust me.'

Bridget found she did trust Ida. If she said it was fine, then it was fine.

'Shall we go?' she asked.

'Courage calls to courage everywhere,' said Ida quietly as they got on board.

Bridget felt a rush of adrenaline. The journey was just long enough to give them plenty of time to explain why they felt the way they did. Ida had written a little speech and had practised it over and over with Bridget listening to check she'd got it all right. They just needed a few minutes to get their point across.

Imagine if this worked? Imagine if Mr Churchill was so convinced by their speech that he threw his weight behind the campaign for women's suffrage? Why, she and Ida would be heroines. They would travel all over the country, and women would cheer as they went past.

They settled down in their seats, and almost straightaway the train's engine started up and they began to move.

Bridget stood up again, then sat down. Then stood up again.

'Relax,' said Ida. 'You're making me nervous with all that jigging about.'

'What if the ticket inspector doesn't come?' Bridget said.

'Then we'll simply walk down to first class anyway.'

'What if we get caught?'

'We'll say we got lost. Sit down, for heaven's sake.'

Bridget sat, shoogling her knees up and down until Ida put her hand on her leg to still her and left it there. Bridget took comfort from the warmth of Ida's palm on her thigh.

'Tickets please,' said a voice.

'Thank goodness.' Bridget's hands were trembling so much she could barely fish her ticket out of her purse.

They showed their tickets and waited for the inspector to pass them. Then, without a word, they got up and went out into the corridor, walking quickly along the train towards first class.

'Here,' Ida said, stopping so suddenly that Bridget walked into her back. 'He's in here.'

She turned to look at Bridget. 'Oh lord, what if he calls a policeman?'

'Now who needs to relax?' Bridget said, wanting to reassure Ida just as she'd reassured her. 'There's nothing illegal about sharing a railway carriage with a politician. We've got just as much right to be there as he does.'

'Except we don't have the right tickets,' Ida pointed out.

'We'll say we got lost,' said Bridget with a grin. She felt much calmer now it was happening. More in control.

Ida nodded. 'Right. You're right. I'm so nervous, goodness my hands are sweating.'

Bridget gave her a quick hug. 'Want me to go first?'

'Yes please.'

'Coats off,' Bridget said. They slipped off their outerwear to reveal the Votes for Women sashes they were wearing over their dresses, and taking a deep breath, Bridget opened the door to the carriage where Mr Churchill was sitting with another gentleman. He glanced up at the women as they entered and rolled his eyes. 'What now, Potts?' he muttered to the man next to him. 'What is this?'

Ida gave Bridget a little nudge to go further into the carriage and both women sat down opposite the men.

'Good morning, Mr Churchill,' Bridget began.

Mr Churchill snorted.

'It was a good morning,' he said. 'It is not now.'

Faced with such hostility, Bridget faltered and turned to Ida, who had recovered her normal confidence.

'Mr Churchill, may we speak with you?' she said.

'What on?' Churchill scowled. 'On votes for women?'

'Well, yes,' Bridget said, looking down at the sash she wore. 'We believe . . .'

'No!' Churchill barked, making both women and Mr Potts jump. 'No. I have had quite enough of votes for women. I was harangued by blasted suffragettes in Ireland and now this? I have work to be getting on with.'

'But, Mr Churchill, sir . . .' Ida said. 'What is the Government going to do for women?'

Mr Churchill stood up.

'Potts,' he said. Mr Potts stood up too, juggling briefcases and newspapers and documents. 'Let's find ourselves another carriage where we shall not be disturbed,' Mr Churchill continued.

Mr Potts slid open the door and Mr Churchill followed. 'For this behaviour, you women shall not get the vote now,' he said over his shoulder as he left. 'Mark my words.'

Ida and Bridget stared at him as he shut the carriage door with a clatter and disappeared off down the corridor behind the hapless Mr Potts.

'Well,' said Bridget eventually. 'That did not go quite as planned.'

'No, it did not,' said Ida in a rather good impersonation of Mr Churchill's gruff tones. 'I have had quite enough of Winston.'

The women dissolved into laughter.

'I really thought this would be it,' said Bridget. 'That he'd listen to us and change his views.'

Ida was laughing so hard she could barely speak. 'That we'd be the heroines of the suffrage movement?'

'Yes,' said Bridget, holding her stomach, which was hurting because of the mirth. 'Yes, that's exactly what I thought!'

They rolled around on the train seats like silly schoolgirls. Bridget's cheeks ached from smiling and she thought she couldn't remember when she was last so happy. So exhilarated and full of life.

'Will they be very cross, do you think?' she asked eventually as their chuckles subsided.

'The WSPU?' Ida said. 'No. They know it's a struggle.'

Bridget thought it was a struggle she was rather enjoying, but she didn't say so. 'They're meeting us at Clydebank Station?'

'They are. So it doesn't matter one bit that our attempt to speak to Mr Churchill was such a disaster. We've got another chance.' Ida smiled at her. 'And I've very much enjoyed spending this morning with you, dear Bridget.'

'I've enjoyed it too,' said Bridget. An image of the back of Ida's neck bared and waiting for her caress popped into her head and to hide her flushed cheeks, she peered out of the window.

'Here we are,' she cried, sounding a little unhinged. 'We're here, here we are!'

Ida gave her an odd look, but they gathered their coats and jumped off the train before it had properly stopped.

The rest of their suffragette friends were standing in a group beside the entrance of the station. They had banners and they were wearing their sashes and they all looked, Bridget thought, absolutely marvellous.

'How was it?' Helen called out. 'Did you speak to him?'

'We tried,' Ida said as she and Bridget took their places in the group, 'but he is a miserable curmudgeon.'

'Oh no,' said Vera, looking upset. 'I really thought this was going to work.'

'Me too,' Bridget told her.

'Then let's make it harder for him to ignore us now,' said Helen. 'Come on, ladies. We'll shout louder and make him listen.'

'I'll make him listen all right,' said Christina, the sour-faced woman who'd quizzed Bridget about the strike at her first meeting. 'We should follow the example of our sisters in London and throw some stones.'

'Potatoes,' said Vera softly. 'They threw potatoes at Mr Asquith.'

'Well either way, we need to act.'

'I don't really think . . .' Bridget began then stopped as Mr Churchill and Mr Potts emerged from the throng of passengers leaving the train. 'Votes for women!' she cried instead, her voice joining the others. 'Votes for women!'

Mr Churchill hurried past them, not even glancing in their direction, and headed for a car that was waiting for him.

Christina was standing next to Bridget, and now Bridget noticed her duck down to pick something up. To her horror, she realised Christina was clutching half a brick that had fallen from a nearby wall.

'Christina,' Bridget said in a low tone. 'Don't.'

'We have to make him listen.'

Mr Churchill got into the car, and Potts followed. Christina stepped forward, and Bridget went too. Christina raised the brick and Bridget dived for her hand, desperate to stop her throwing it.

But she misjudged it somehow, or perhaps she was a moment too late. Either way, instead of stopping Christina from throwing the rock, she somehow knocked it out of her hand and Bridget watched in horror as it arced through the air and landed with a sickening crack on the windscreen of Mr Churchill's car.

She turned to see the other suffragettes looking on in shock, Christina nowhere to be seen, and – she glanced down at her hands – brick dust all over her glove.

Chapter Thirty

Ellen was absolutely furious. Raging. At Mr Beresford. At the burly men who'd dragged her down the stairs and out of the factory gates. At the policemen who'd brought her here. At the whole world.

'He put his hand up my skirt,' she shouted as Beresford's men handed her over to a bored-looking policeman he'd flagged down on the street. 'He put his hand up my skirt, the filthy old . . .'

'Keep talking like that and you'll be locked up for longer,' the policeman said mildly, gripping Ellen's arms behind her back. He'd blown his whistle and another two officers had come running. Ellen spat and fought like an alley cat, but they managed to get her along the road to the police station.

'I'm just a wee woman,' she'd taunted them as they half carried her down the street, the tips of her toes dragging on the pavement. 'But it's taking three of you to get me to where you want me to go.'

She knew her anger was provoking them, making them more likely to throw her in a cell instead of less likely. If Bridget were here, she'd be contrite and polite, not lippy and aggressive. But, she thought, Bridget wasn't here. Nor was she ever likely to be.

The policeman at the desk took her details, though at first Ellen shut her mouth firmly and refused to talk. She stood at the desk, her hands planted palms down, and stared at the policeman asking the questions in silence. But when she wouldn't reply, he leaned forward, placed his elbow quite slowly and deliberately on her hand, and ground down. Ellen felt her knuckles cracking and gasped in pain, pulling her hand away.

'Name?' he said again, his face close to hers and leaving her in no doubt that there would be more of that to come if she tried to stay quiet.

So she'd given her name and address.

'What will happen now?' she asked.

'Now,' said the officer at the desk. 'You wait while we think about what to do with you. And believe me, missy, it could take a while. We're all otherwise engaged.' He stood up straighter with his chest puffed out. 'Mr Churchill's coming through town today and everyone's busy providing protection for him.'

'Well, not everyone,' Ellen pointed out. 'You're here.'

The man glared at her and she put her hands behind her back, just in case.

'You will wait,' he said.

Ellen looked round to where there was a wooden bench next to the wall. 'Here?'

He laughed.

'Oh no.'

And he'd brought Ellen down some stairs to the basement where there was a short corridor with two thick doors on either side.

'You'll have to share,' he said. He took a bunch of keys from his belt, opened the door on the right and pushed her inside. She turned to argue but he was too fast, slamming the door shut again. Ellen heard the key turn.

Inside, the cell was dim. It smelled bad – of sweat and urine – and the only light was coming through the small window on the door and another tiny opening high up on the wall. It was light enough to see now because it was the middle of the day but Ellen shuddered to think how it would be at night-time. Not that she'd still be here at night. Surely?

There were two wide benches on either side of the room, with a bucket at the end of one of them, which was obviously the source of the smell.

On one bench, a woman with matted reddish hair and muddy boots lay very still on her side, her hands under her head like a pillow. She wasn't asleep because Ellen could see that her eyes were open, but she didn't speak when she said 'hello' either.

Ellen sat down on the bench opposite, and swung her legs. She wasn't very good at waiting. Or at doing nothing. She wondered when Mr Churchill's visit would be over, and the policemen would all come back again and let her out.

'This is all a big mistake. I'm not supposed to be here,' she said to the woman opposite, who blinked but didn't answer. 'I should report him, really. Mr Beresford, I mean. What gives him the right to try to kiss me that way?' She had a sudden memory of the feeling of his lips on hers and tasted bile in her mouth. 'He put his hand up my skirt.'

The woman gave her a tiny nod of understanding and that small kindness made Ellen crumble. She began to cry. 'He touched me,' she sobbed in bewilderment. 'And now I'm here.'

Silently, the woman opposite sat up, reached into a pocket and offered Ellen a handkerchief. It was a bit grubby and tattered, but Ellen took it gratefully to wipe her eyes and blow her nose.

'You should sleep,' the woman said. Her voice was low and rasping, like she'd got a sore throat. 'It gets loud later when the drunks come. We willnae get any rest then.'

Ellen's eyes widened in horror at the thought of still being here later.

'I'm not tired,' she said, but she lay down anyway, feeling the wooden bench digging into her bones, and shut her eyes because she would do anything to make the time pass faster.

And she must have slept because suddenly she was woken by the clanging of keys. At last! Someone had come to get her!

She pushed herself upright, blinking in the sudden light from the open door. And for a second she thought she was dreaming because there, silhouetted against the brightness, was Bridget.

She almost looked like an angel with the light behind her. Ellen gasped. 'You came for me.'

But, no.

The police officer was shoving Bridget in the small of her back, pushing her into the room just as he'd done with Ellen. And Bridget – Bridget! – was turning to him and telling him in language Ellen had never heard her use in her whole life, that he should keep his hands to himself.

She had to be dreaming.

She pinched herself hard on the arm and shook her head, but when she looked up, Bridget was still there, staring at her in absolute astonishment.

'Ellen?'

Ellen was almost speechless with shock.

'What . . .? How?' She rubbed her eyes. 'Bridget?'

Bridget pulled a strand of hair off her face.

'It's me,' she said. Ellen thought she almost sounded proud.

The police officer sighed. 'Of course you know each other,' he said wearily, pointing from one sister to another. 'Of course you do.'

He prodded Bridget and she turned to him and hissed, like a cat, making him step back. Ellen hid a smile.

'No trouble,' he warned as he shut the door.

As soon as the key was turned, Ellen launched herself off the bench and flung herself at her sister.

'What on earth are you doing here, Bridget? Did you come to get me?'

Bridget hugged her briefly but then looked at her, bewildered. 'I had no idea you were here, Ellen.'

Bemused, Ellen pulled away. 'So why are you here?'

Bridget screwed her nose up. 'I threw a brick at a car.'

'What? Why?'

'Well, I was actually trying to stop someone else throwing it, but . . . well, you don't need all the details.'

Ellen was trying to make sense of this Bridget who stood before her, looking like her sister but sounding like a totally different person.

'Whose car was it?' she said faintly, because they didn't know anyone who owned a car – she hardly ever saw cars – but all the while wondering if it actually mattered. Apparently, though, it did because Bridget – much to her surprise – puffed out her chest like a peacock and pronounced: 'Winston Churchill's.'

Ellen sat down on the bench with a thump. 'Winston Churchill, the politician?'

'Home Secretary.'

Nothing about this was making any sense.

'Why did you . . . what . . . why?'

Bridget began unbuttoning her coat, the one Ellen had seen her wearing earlier on that day – oh what a lot had happened since then – and pulled it off her shoulders. And there, underneath, was a green and purple sash declaring 'Votes For Women'.

Ellen's jaw dropped. 'You're a suffragette?'

Bridget smiled. 'Yes.'

And suddenly everything made sense. Bridget was a suffragette!

'And you threw a stone at Churchill's car?'

'No, Ida and I . . .'

'Wait, who's Ida?'

Bridget's cheeks reddened and she sat down next to Ellen on the bench. 'She's my friend.'

Ellen nodded. 'So you and Ida?'

'We wanted to speak to Mr Churchill, put our point across in a civilised manner.'

'By throwing bricks at him?'

'No!' Bridget tutted. 'We got on the train he was on and tried to talk to him. But he was dreadfully rude. And when we got off at Clydebank, there were some other suffragettes waiting and Christina – dreadful woman – picked up a brick and I tried to get it from her but somehow I ended up propelling it into the windscreen instead.' She sighed. 'Just bad luck, I suppose.'

'For Mr Churchill,' Ellen said drily.

Bridget gave her a fierce stare. 'If we cannot vote, and we cannot get our voices heard, then how will we make our point? This is just another battle in the fight for equality – like the strike at Wentworth.'

Ellen bit her lip. 'Right,' she mumbled.

Bridget nudged her. 'Why are you here?'

Ellen had very much been hoping that she wouldn't ask her that. She put her face in her hands. 'I don't want to talk about it,' she said through her fingers.

Gently, Bridget prised her hands away. 'Is this something to do with Mr Beresford?'

'He felt her up,' said the other woman in the cell. Ellen jumped. She'd almost forgotten she was there.

'Shush,' she said sharply. But Bridget was looking at her with a knowing nod.

'Beresford? I wish you'd told me where you were going. He's a dirty sod.'

Ellen wasn't sure if she was more surprised by the news that Bridget knew about Beresford, or the way she'd said it. 'He's done this before?'

'More than once.'

'Course he has,' said the other woman. 'Men like him just get bolder. They don't stop.'

'That's true enough,' Bridget agreed. She slid along the bench nearer Ellen and put her arm round her shoulders.

'Ellen, did he . . . did he force himself on you?'

For a second, Ellen was back there in the office feeling so helpless and frightened in the face of Beresford's power and his desires. She swallowed, pushing away the memory.

'No,' she said. 'I stopped him.'

Bridget's eyes flashed with interest. 'Stopped him, how?'

'I stabbed him in the arm with his letter opener.'

This time it was Bridget's jaw that dropped.

The woman opposite hooted with laughter.

'Are you two sisters? Bet no one messes with you, eh?'

Ellen felt Bridget take her hand. 'No,' her sister said. 'No one messes with us.'

Ellen grinned. 'We're the Kelly sisters,' she told the woman. 'We run towards a fight, not away from it.'

'Good for you,' said the woman. She made a fist with one hand and punched it into the palm of her other. 'Good for you.'

'I'm sorry I was so horrible to you,' Ellen said. 'I understand why you couldn't stop work.'

Bridget's eyes gleamed. 'I'm glad you were horrible because it made me angry, and when I met Ida . . . well, she showed me how to use that anger.'

'Does Malcolm know you're a suffragette?'

'What do you think?'

Ellen giggled.

'He's not a bad man, you know,' Bridget said. 'He's not. He just thinks there's a way that things should be done, and he likes that because it makes him feel safe. This strike has left him very unsettled and unhappy.'

'That's clever of you to have seen that.'

'I know him better than he knows himself.'

'And yet, he doesn't know you at all, does he?' Ellen eyed her sister.

'No, I suppose he doesn't.' Bridget made a face. 'The other day he was telling me how he liked that I stayed the same while everything else changed and all the time I was thinking I was completely different and he didn't know.'

'Will you tell him you were arrested?'

Bridget rubbed her forehead. 'I'll have to, I suppose. Or perhaps the police will?' She didn't look as worried by that as Ellen had thought she would.

'Will we tell Ma and Da?'

They looked at one another.

'I don't know,' Ellen admitted. 'Will they be cross?'

'That both Kelly sisters ended up in a prison cell at the same time? I'd say so,' Bridget said, but she sounded amused instead of concerned.

Ellen looked at her curiously. 'You're completely different,' she said, in awe. 'Completely different.'

But Bridget shook her head. 'This is who I was all along,' she said. 'This is the real Bridget.'

A rattling at the door made them both look up expectantly.

There was a different policeman this time. Younger and fresh-faced.

'Kelly?' he said.

'Yes,' both Ellen and Bridget replied.

The policeman sighed. 'I've only got one Kelly. And a Walsh.'

'Oh blast, yes. That's me. I'm Walsh.'

'I'm Kelly,' Ellen said helpfully.

'You can both go.'

Both women let out little shrieks of happiness.

'What about her?' Ellen asked, pointing at the other woman.

'She can go too,' said the policeman. 'But she doesn't want to. Isn't that right, Morag?'

The woman – Morag – grinned at him. 'I'm still angry,' she said. 'If I go now, I'll just batter him again and I'll be right back here again. I need to calm down.'

Bridget took off her Votes for Women sash and handed it to her. 'Have you ever thought of joining the suffragettes?' she asked. 'We could do with fierce women like you.'

Morag looked pleased, running the sash through her fingers.

'Out!' the policeman shouted. 'I'm not running a boarding house, you know.'

245

The women scurried out of the cell, hand in hand, almost running up the stairs to the main entrance of the police station.

'You ought to be glad that someone came to vouch for you,' the policeman said as he followed them upwards. 'If it hadn't been for him, I'd have kept you locked up overnight.'

The sisters exchanged baffled glances. Who had spoken up for them?

'Da?' Ellen suggested as they rounded the corner at the top of the stairs.

Bridget shrugged. 'Maybe?'

But when they got into the front of the police station, it wasn't Da waiting for them. Nor was it Walter, as Ellen had half wondered, nor was it James, as she'd hoped.

It was Malcolm.

He was standing looking rather ill at ease, turning his cap round and round in his hands.

Both women stopped and stared.

'Will he be cross?' Ellen said under her breath.

Bridget looked at her. 'I don't know.'

Malcolm put his cap back on and looked at them. Ellen could see that he wasn't angry really. Not that red-hot burning anger she'd felt when the defect repairers were sacked. Instead it was ice that she could see in Malcolm's eyes.

'Hello,' he said.

Bridget went to him and put her hand on his arm. 'Malcolm,' she said.

'Aye.'

Ellen watched as her sister struggled for the right words and then simply said: 'Thank you.'

Malcolm simply stared at her. Bridget took her hand off his arm.

'A woman came to the factory to find me,' he said. 'Ida McKinley. She said you needed help and that you had been unfairly arrested for throwing a brick at a car.'

'I didn't throw it,' Bridget said. 'Ida was right.'

'She told me what I should say to make sure you were released.'

Bridget gave a tiny smile, barely noticeable. Malcolm's lip curled.

'She said she'd been arrested in the past.'

'Did she?' Bridget said mildly.

'Malcolm,' Ellen said, wanting to break the tension between her sister and her husband. 'What about me? How did you know I was here?'

Malcolm dragged his eyes away from Bridget and looked at Ellen. 'Sadie told me. But I knew. Everyone's talking about it.'

Ellen felt queasy. 'About what?'

'About Beresford . . .' Malcolm said. 'You know? And someone fighting back.'

Once again, Ellen was struck dumb. Today was definitely a day of surprises.

Malcolm looked weary. 'Beresford won't want any trouble,' Malcolm went on. 'He won't argue when he finds out you've been released.'

'Filthy man,' muttered Bridget.

Malcolm turned his attention back to his wife. 'I have to go back to work,' he said. There was a little pulse throbbing on the side of his face, but other than that he was perfectly still. Ellen thought he looked like a cat about to pounce on a mouse. 'I'll see you at home later.'

There was no question in his voice. Bridget nodded. 'I'll make tea.'

He looked at her with an expression Ellen couldn't read. 'You are not the woman I thought you were, Bridget,' he said.

'No,' said Bridget, 'I'm not. But believe me, it's as much of a surprise to me as it is to you.'

'I hope it's worth it,' Malcolm said. He looked from Bridget to Ellen, then back to Bridget. 'All this trouble and agitation. Will it be worth it in the end?'

He didn't wait for an answer. Instead, he gave Bridget one last lingering look, dripping with disappointment, then he turned and walked out of the police station without a backwards glance, leaving the women staring at him in surprise.

'Well,' said Bridget when he'd gone down the steps and along the street. 'I was not expecting that.'

'Me neither.' Ellen looked at her sister. 'So, tell me. What do you think?'

'About what?'

'Is this trouble and agitation worth it?'

Bridget lifted her chin and pulled her shoulders back.

'It most definitely is.'

Chapter Thirty-One

Sadie was sitting on the wall outside the police station biting the skin around her nails. She'd not done that since she was a little girl feeling nervous about going to school on her own. Not even after her father died. But since this strike had started, and the money had run out, she couldn't seem to stop.

She wondered where Ellen and Bridget were. It had been ages since Malcolm had gone inside and she was just hoping that he could make things all right again.

Sadie had found out almost straight away that Ellen had been arrested. One of the lads the strikers used to pass messages between divisions had come belting along the road, to where Sadie had been sitting with Walter. They weren't talking – Sadie, frankly, had had enough of talking. She'd brought some mending with her, so she was sitting against a tree, sewing a ribbon around the bottom of Rachel's skirt to make it longer, so she could wear it without flashing her underwear.

She thought Ellen's plan to speak to Mr Beresford was a mad idea. Mad but also brilliant. And she had a sneaking suspicion Ellen had come up with it to help her. Just as she had a sneaking suspicion that the bread and milk she'd found on their doorstep had something to do with Ellen. She felt wretched about shouting at her friend – that was why she'd gone to Clydebank today to see her, but she'd been too late. Ellen had already set off for the factory by the time Sadie arrived, so Sadie was planning to wait until she came back from speaking to Mr Beresford – hopefully with some good news.

But Ellen didn't come back.

She finished Rachel's skirt and turned her attention to some socks that needed darning. And then James appeared, his eye purple and swollen.

'Heavens,' Sadie said, putting her mending to one side and rushing to him. 'What's happened?'

'It's nothing,' James said. 'Just me being clumsy as usual.'

Walter got up and took James's face in his hands. Sadie felt a little emotional watching the paternal way Walter examined the bruises.

'Frankie?' he said.

James took a second to answer, but then he simply said: 'Aye.'

'He needs to stop taking everything out on you.'

'He's just angry at the world,' James said. 'It's not his fault.'

Walter gripped the back of James's neck in a strange, male version of a hug and for a second Sadie thought James might cry. But he didn't.

And then the lad came running across the green and broke the moment.

'Walter!' he shouted. 'Walter! Ellen's been arrested!'

James and Walter both hurried over to where the lad was standing, doubled over and trying to catch his breath. He'd obviously run as fast as he could, the whole way.

'Arrested?' Sadie gasped. Surely the boy had made a mistake? Ellen wouldn't have done anything to get herself arrested?

'She attacked Beresford,' he panted. 'Some folk are saying she stabbed him.'

'That dirty sod,' muttered Walter, and James's face reddened with anger.

'What?' Sadie asked. 'What am I missing?'

'I'd heard rumours,' Walter said, 'but I didn't think they were true.'

James looked grim-faced. 'Seems they are.'

'What?' Sadie demanded, confused by the way they were talking. 'What rumours?'

Walter rubbed his beard. 'Mr Beresford, it's said, considers the young women who work in the factory to be a . . .' he cleared his throat – 'a perk of the job.'

'You are joking?' said Sadie, glaring at James. 'You knew this and you still let Ellen go and speak to him on her own?'

'I didn't know for sure,' he muttered. 'I'd never have let her go if I'd known for sure.'

'Well, it's just talk, isn't it?' Walter looked uncomfortable. 'And you know how women like to talk. Rumours spread and they might not be true.'

Sadie glared at him, feeling hot and cold all at once. 'What if he . . .' she trailed off not wanting to put it into words. James looked as sick as a dog and even Walter looked upset.

'What should we do?' she said quietly. 'What can we do?'

There was silence – all three of them at a loss.

And then a woman approached them. She was nicely dressed, but she looked terribly worried, and her hair was falling out of its fastenings.

'Excuse me,' she said. Sadie noticed that she had a scar running down her cheek and over the edge of her mouth, which added to her frantic expression. 'I need to find Ellen Kelly. It's terribly important.'

'Ellen's . . . busy,' said Sadie, wondering why this strange woman needed her friend so urgently. 'Can I help? I'm Sadie Franklin. I'm Ellen's friend.'

The woman took a deep breath.

'I need Ellen,' she said desperately. 'I need to tell her that Bridget . . .'

Sadie felt a lurch of fear. 'Has something happened to Bridget?'

'She's been arrested.'

'Ellen?'

'No,' the woman pushed her hair off her face, 'Bridget, of course.'

Sadie exchanged a glance with the men.

'But . . .' she began.

The woman tugged her sleeve. 'Don't delay,' she said. 'Please take me to Ellen.'

'I can't,' Sadie said. This was becoming ridiculous. 'She's been arrested.'

'Bridget?' said the woman.

'No.' Sadie shook her head. 'Ellen.'

Once all the confusion had been sorted out, and they'd realised that both sisters had indeed been arrested, the woman had introduced herself as Ida McKinley. Sadie, still not quite believing it to be true, asked why Bridget had been thrown in jail.

'She threw a brick at the Home Secretary,' said Ida matter-of-factly.

'Pardon me?'

Ida sighed. 'We're suffragettes, you see? We were trying to make him listen to us. But one of our members got a bit carried away, Bridget tried to stop her, but she knocked the brick from her hand instead.'

Walter whistled in admiration. 'Who'd have thought it?' he said.

'Bridget's a suffragette?' Sadie said, bewildered. 'I didn't know.'

Ida shrugged. 'We need to get her out of jail. It's not fair.'

'Ellen, too,' said James, looking more worried by the minute.

Sadie thought about what they could do. 'We need someone to speak up for them. Make sure the police know this is all a big mistake. Someone with a bit of clout – Walter?'

But Walter shook his head sadly. 'I'm afraid I made a few mistakes myself back in the day. They know me down at that station.'

Sadie sighed and James spoke up. 'I'll do it.'

'They won't listen to you, son,' Walter said, clapping him on the back. 'Sad to say it, but it's true.'

James put his hand to his battered face and shrugged helplessly.

'Ida, then?' Sadie said, looking at her. But Ida was shaking her head, too.

'I've been arrested before too.' Ida looked half embarrassed, half proud. 'More than once, in fact.'

Sadie snorted. 'What a band of reprobates you are.'

'What should we do?' Ida put her knuckle in her mouth.

'I've got an idea,' said Sadie.

And so she'd raced to the factory gate and begged Ossy to get Malcolm. He eventually came down looking mutinous.

'Do not ask me to get involved,' he said before Sadie could even speak. 'Ellen has made her bed and now she's going to have to lie in it.'

'It's not Ellen,' Sadie told him. 'It's Bridget.'

Malcolm glanced round, up at the windows of the clerical department, as if he might see Bridget standing there.

'What about Bridget?'

'She's been arrested.'

Malcolm tutted.'No, she hasn't,' he said. 'Ellen was arrested.'

Sadie closed her eyes, briefly marvelling at the bad luck that had seen both her friends thrown in jail on the same day. 'Ellen was arrested here at the factory,' she said, clearly. 'Bridget was arrested at the railway station.'

'Bridget's not at the railway station,' Malcolm said, baffled. 'She's here. In the factory.'

'She's not,' Sadie said wearily. 'She's at Clydebank Police Station and so is Ellen, and I need you to go and speak to the police officers and get them out.'

'Bridget has been arrested?'

'Yes.'

'Why?'

'She threw a brick at the Home Secretary.'

Malcolm went pale all at once, like a light going off. 'She threw a brick?'

'Yes. Well, no. No, she didn't. She tried to stop someone throwing a brick. It's a misunderstanding.'

'Right. Good.'

'And it seems everyone knows why Ellen might have lashed out at Beresford?' Sadie said, wanting to know if Malcolm also knew. 'Did he . . .?'

'I don't know exactly,' Sadie said, all her suspicions confirmed. 'Lord, did everyone know about that filthy man? Why didn't anyone say anything?'

Malcolm shrugged. 'Gossip isn't the same as facts.'

Sadie stared at him for a second, then she said: 'Ellen wouldn't have attacked him without good reason.'

'No,' said Malcolm reluctantly. 'I suppose not.'

'So, let's go.'

Malcolm stayed where he was.

'Malcolm, you are the only person with enough . . .' Sadie screwed her nose up '. . . moral standing to persuade the police to let Ellen and Bridget go.'

Was she imagining it or did Malcolm stand up a bit straighter? 'Come on,' she said.

Malcolm shook his head and Sadie held up her hand.

'Don't,' she said. 'Do not tell me you're worried about how this might look to Beresford and the others.'

To give him his due, Malcolm did look a little shamefaced.

Sadie was simmering with anger. 'Bridget and Ellen are fighting for something they believe in,' she said. 'And you might not think they're going about it the right way, but surely you don't believe they should be in jail?'

There was a pause, and then Malcolm put his hat on and Sadie felt weak with relief.

'Come on, then,' he said.

'Do you need to tell anyone you're leaving?'

Malcolm looked back at the factory and then at Sadie. 'I don't think anyone will notice.'

Ida had caught up with them as they walked towards the police station, and Sadie had been impressed by her calm explanation of what Malcolm should say, despite Malcolm's short answers.

'Done this before, eh?' she said.

Ida had smiled. 'Few times.'

When they reached the police station, Malcolm had taken a deep breath, pulled his shoulders back then disappeared inside. Ida had hung back, further along the road.

'I'm not keen on getting too close,' she'd said with a wry smile. Sadie thought that was rather sweet because Ida was wearing a Votes for Women sash that was just visible, poking out of the collar of her coat and she herself had admitted she had a history with the local police. Sadie rather liked Ida.

Now Sadie was sitting on the wall, waiting to see if Malcolm had managed to get them out. She put her hand to her forehead, feeling a wave of exhaustion and hunger. She couldn't remember the last time she'd eaten. It wasn't today, that was certain, because Daniel had scoffed the last bit of bread and then looked so guilty about it, Sadie couldn't be angry.

It was getting later and the sun was beginning to drop down behind the tenement blocks. She had to get back to Glasgow and make sure the children were all right, though Noah had promised to look in on them, and Ma had been brighter this morning.

She looked up as Malcolm came out of the police station, and hurried down the steps.

Alone.

Sadie felt sick.

'Malcolm?' she called. 'What's happened?'

'Ask them,' he said.

Sadie stood up and watched as Ellen and Bridget came out of the building arm in arm.

'Ellen!' she called. Ellen looked thrilled to see her and came bounding over.

'I'm so sorry I shouted at you,' Sadie said, throwing her arms round Ellen and squeezing her tight. 'I was worried about things at home, but I shouldn't have taken it out on you.'

'Gosh, don't apologise,' said Ellen. 'I understand. At least, I want to.' She sat down on the wall. 'Tell me everything.'

'Here?'

'Why not?'

Sadie sat down again, and took a breath. 'I'm the only one working,' she said. 'And I'm not working, so there's no money. And the children just never stop eating. And Rachel's had the doctor . . .'

Ellen linked her arm through Sadie's.

'It's hard.'

'It is.' Sadie sniffed. 'Thank you for trying with Beresford.'

Ellen shrugged. 'It didn't work.'

'But you tried. Even though he . . . It means a lot.' She looked at Ellen closely. 'Did he do that?' she said, touching a hand gently to the angry red welts on her neck.

'No.' Ellen shook her head. Her eyes filled with tears. 'That was someone else.'

'Ellen? Who? A policeman?'

'No,' Ellen sighed. 'Let's just say it's been quite a day.'

Bridget had been arranging her coat and hat but now she came over to where the women were sitting.

'But the good news is, Bridget and I are friends again,' Ellen said.

'Less friends, more partners in crime,' Bridget joked.

'Malcolm looked annoyed,' said Sadie, and Bridget winced.

'He's having a hard time,' she said. 'I'll make things right, I hope.'

'We met your friend Ida McKinley.'

Bridget looked at Sadie with an odd expression on her face. 'When?'

'She's the one who told me you'd been arrested. She was terribly worried.'

'Was she?' Bridget's cheeks flushed. 'Where is she now?'

Sadie grinned. 'She's over there.'

Ida had been waiting a little further down, across the road.

'I'll go and speak to her,' Bridget said.

Sadie watched as Bridget darted over to see her friend and the two women engaged in lively conversation, with Bridget making all sorts of hand gestures. She'd never seen Bridget so vibrant, she thought.

Ellen was watching too.

'She's different,' she said. 'I like it.'

'Me too.' Sadie nodded. 'But I'm not sure Malcolm does.'

They both looked into the distance where Malcolm was no longer visible.

'Tell me who hurt you,' Sadie said, worried about her friend.

'James's brother.'

'Frankie?' said Sadie, remembering what Walter had said when he saw James's battered face.

'Yes. How did you know?'

'I saw James.'

Ellen's eyes widened. 'And is he all right? How is he?'

'He's all right. A bit battered, but he's fine. Walter was looking after him. He was worried about you, though.'

Ellen waved her hand, shooing away James's worries. 'Oh my goodness, I was frantic, Sadie. His brother is Frankie Briggs.'

Sadie looked blank.

'He's real trouble,' Ellen explained. 'He hates my da. He hates all Catholics. And he saw me and James kissing.'

'You kissed?' Sadie was thrilled.

Ellen grinned. 'Yes, but Frankie saw. And he knows who I am, and that I'm Catholic and he was furious. He's got such a temper and he shoved me, he punched James and he even pulled my crucifix off my neck. That's how he hurt me. He pulled the chain so hard it snapped and then he threw it in a bush.'

Sadie was annoyed. 'How dare he?'

'James says it's not his fault. He had an accident a few years back, and he's not been the same since.'

'That's no excuse.' Sadie folded her arms. 'I've got a good mind to go right into that police station this minute and report him.'

'Don't,' said Ellen. 'I've had enough of the police for one day.'

'So you and James?' Sadie said, wanting to change the subject. 'Tell me everything.'

But Ellen's face fell. 'James,' she said slowly. 'James's stepbrother is Frankie Briggs.'

'Aye, you said that.'

'James is Protestant.'

Sadie wasn't stupid. You couldn't live in Glasgow and not be aware of the tensions between Protestants and Catholics, but even so, she frowned at Ellen. 'And?'

'Frankie Briggs hates Catholics, and my da hates Frankie Briggs,' Ellen said. She sounded utterly miserable. 'This is never going to work.'

Bridget and Ida approached them and Sadie looked up.

'We thought we should go and have a cup of tea,' Bridget said. 'Ellen's got a plan.'

But Ellen shook her head.

'I do, but first I need to find James,' she said, sliding down off the wall. 'Shall I meet you back at the flat?'

Sadie stood up too and gave Ellen a hug. 'Good luck,' she said.

Chapter Thirty-Two

Bridget watched Ellen run off to find James. She knew that from the outside Ellen was trying to look calm but inside she would be a whirling swirl of confusing emotions.

She felt awful about Malcolm. Awful. Because he was so upset and sad, and she knew she'd let him down. But the truth was, none of this was about him at all. It was about her. The way she felt. The way she looked at the world.

The way the world looked at her.

'All right?' asked Ida.

Bridget nodded. 'I think so.'

She, Sadie and Ida began walking towards Bridget's parents' flat.

'It's been a very long day,' Sadie said. She looked quite pale and very tired, Bridget thought. 'A long week.'

'It has,' said Bridget. 'It feels like the strike has been going on for months, not weeks.'

'I suppose there were the changes before that,' Sadie pointed out. She gave a little smile. 'I started 1911 thinking it would be a good year. Better than last year, when my father died. More positive. You know, with my new job and everything. I expect you felt the same, Bridget.'

Bridget frowned. 'It was just a year like any other.'

'But 1911 is the year you got married,' Sadie said.

'Oh.' Bridget was a little embarrassed not to have thought of that. 'Yes.'

They crossed the road by the railway station and Bridget paused. She knew she should go straight home and speak to Malcolm but she really didn't want to. She was too tired. Too confused. She'd go back to her parents' flat now, just for a little while, she thought. Gather her thoughts.

'Actually,' Sadie said, 'I wondered if I could ask you something about that?'

'About getting married?' Bridget said. Decision made, she carried on, away from the road that would take her home to Malcolm.

Sadie sighed. 'How did you know?'

'Know what?'

'That you wanted to marry Malcolm? That he was the man for you?'

Bridget squirmed a little. She hated thinking about things like this.

'Well, I'd known him a long time,' she said carefully. 'Since we were children. And I admired him. His . . .' she searched for the right word – '. . . resilience.'

Sadie nodded, biting her lip. Bridget thought she looked a little disappointed.

'Why?' asked Ida curiously. 'Why do you ask?'

They were close to the flat now. Bridget felt in her bag for the keys she still carried.

'There's someone I like,' Sadie said. 'But like you and Malcolm, I've known him for a long time and I don't think he sees me in that way.'

'What way?' said Bridget.

Sadie flushed. 'You know? Like a woman?' She put her face into her hands, clearly embarrassed by what she was about to say. 'Because I can't stop thinking about him.'

Ida chuckled. 'As a man?'

'Yes,' Sadie groaned. 'I've known him my whole life and now when he so much as brushes past me, it's like my whole body is tingling. Like every sense is on alert. I can smell him, and feel him. I'm so aware of him.'

Bridget thought that sounded marvellous. And strange. She'd never felt that way about Malcolm. He was just ... there. A sudden image of the back of Ida's neck flashed into her mind, and how she'd wanted to put her lips to the soft skin, and flustered, she stumbled.

'Steady,' Ida said, taking Bridget's arm to stop her falling.

Bridget's whole body tingled at Ida's touch. She felt as if all her senses were on alert.

Oh Lord, she thought. *Oh my goodness.*

'Tell us more about this man,' she said, to cover her discomfort – or was it comfort? Because she was still holding Ida's arm and when she let go to open the front door, she felt cold.

'He's wonderful,' Sadie breathed as they made their way up the stairs and inside the flat. 'He's clever and funny. He knows me so well. He understands me. Sometimes he knows what I'm thinking before I know myself.' She sighed. 'I can't imagine ever feeling this way about anyone else.'

'Tea?' sang Bridget, who was feeling more out of sorts by the minute. She took her coat off and hung it up and went to fill the kettle.

Ida looked at Bridget curiously for a second, then turned her attention back to Sadie. 'Does this man ...'

'Noah.'

'Does Noah feel the same way about you?'

'No,' Sadie said.

'Are you sure?'

'He said he'd met the woman he wanted to marry.'

'What were his actual words?' Ida asked.

Sadie sat down. 'He was talking about a boy at school – he's a teacher – and he said the boy had asked why Noah wasn't married.

And Noah said he'd told him he'd met the woman he wanted to marry.'

'And then what did you say?'

Sadie thought. 'I didn't say anything because my brother came running over to tell me my wee sister was sick.'

Ida gave Bridget an amused glance. 'So he didn't tell you who she was?'

Sadie shrugged. 'I've no idea who she is. I don't know when he sees her because he spends all his free time with me and my family. She must be a woman from work, I suppose . . .'

Bridget smiled. Sadie was so sweet and so completely clueless.

'It's you, you goat,' said Ida.

Sadie blinked at her.

'What?'

Bridget laughed. 'It does sound like he meant you, Sadie.'

Sadie's cheeks flushed. 'No, I don't think so.'

Ida came over to where Bridget stood. 'We are older and wiser than you,' she said firmly. 'And we both agree Noah wants to marry you.'

'We do,' said Bridget, enjoying the feeling of being a 'we' with Ida.

Sadie sat back against the chair, looking thoughtful and, Bridget thought, rather happy.

She, on the other hand, was in turmoil as she poured water into the teapot. Sadie's questions had made her realise that her feelings for Malcolm were more than complicated – they were, perhaps, not the feelings of a wife for her husband.

And she rather suspected that the way Malcolm felt about her was not the way a husband should feel about his wife.

But she had absolutely no idea what to do about it.

Footsteps on the stairs made her look up. The door opened and in came Ellen.

'Hiya,' Ellen said. She looked a bit glum but she came straight to Bridget and gave her a hug.

'Did you see James?' Bridget asked her quietly.

Ellen nodded. 'He's all right. Physically, I mean. His face is looking rotten, but it'll heal.' She took a deep breath. 'I told him we can't be together.'

'Is that what you want?' Bridget frowned, confused.

'No,' said Ellen simply. 'It's absolutely not what I want. But his brother is Frankie Briggs, Bridget.'

'Frankie Briggs?' said Bridget shocked. 'His brother?'

'Stepbrother,' Ellen explained. 'Frankie's his brother, and his family are Protestants.' She shrugged. 'That's never going to work, is it?'

Bridget wanted to tell her sister that of course it could work. Of course they could be together if they really wanted to be. But she thought about her da's split lip, and the way Frankie Briggs was, and the way their da reacted, and she shook her head sadly.

Ellen breathed in deeply, blinking back tears. 'That's what I said to James.' She sniffed. 'That's what I told him.'

'That's horrible.' Bridget put her arms round her sister. 'I'm sorry.'

For a second, Ellen buried her head in the hollow of Bridget's collarbone and Bridget kissed the top of her head.

'I really like him,' Ellen sobbed softly. 'We really could have been something.'

'I know,' soothed Bridget, letting her sister cry. 'I know. It's rotten luck, it really is.'

When Ellen's sobs eased, she looked up at Bridget.

'You're so lucky to have Malcolm, even if he is a bit boring. You have no idea how agonising it is to be kept apart from the person you love.'

Bridget glanced over to where Ida was chatting to Sadie.

'No idea at all,' she said.

But that was a lie.

Chapter Thirty-Three

Ellen wanted something to think about that wasn't James or Frankie Briggs; fortunately the strike and what they were going to do about it was the perfect distraction.

Her parents had both come home, and Ellen had averted her eyes from where she could see the remains of Da's split lip. Gran, who seemed to have a sixth sense for when there was a get-together, appeared too.

And then there was a knock at the door and when Ellen went to answer it, she found James standing there.

'Why are you here?' she hissed, not wanting her da to hear.

'I've come to help with the strike business,' he said.

'But . . .'

He gave her a small, slightly sad smile. 'I understand what you said, Ellen. But I like you. I like spending time with you. And the strike's important.'

'It is,' Ellen said, feeling her heart swell with admiration for him. Which didn't help, frankly.

'I know we can't be together, properly, but we can still spend time with each other, can't we?' said James.

'I suppose so,' said Ellen cautiously. She looked over her shoulder at her father. 'Don't let on to Da, though. Don't tell him who your brother is.'

'I won't,' said James. 'And don't you be trying to kiss me or anything. I know what you're like, Ellen Kelly.'

Ellen rolled her eyes. 'I'll try my best,' she said. 'Come in. Everyone, this is James McCallum. He's on the strike committee.'

She watched her da carefully, hoping he wouldn't recognise the name but he didn't seem to. Ellen relaxed a wee bit and sat down next to James.

'What's going on, Ellen?' her ma asked, handing round some slices of bread and jam. 'Why's everyone in my living room? Not that you're not welcome, of course.' She beamed at James. 'Want a cold cloth for your eye, son?'

'I'm fine, thank you,' James muttered.

'Right,' said Ellen, sounding for all the world like she was calling a meeting to order. She almost didn't recognise herself and she was quite proud of it. 'I've been thinking. This strike shows no sign of ending any time soon.'

'You're right there,' said James.

'The strike committee are doing their best, and we can keep showing up on the picket line. But it's just going to drag on and on, by the look of it.' She took a breath. 'And in the meantime there are families struggling to feed their bairns. Families with no money coming in at all. They're getting desperate and that means they're more likely to want to go back to work – even for a reduced wage and longer hours – and that means all this work, all the effort we've put into the strike, will have been for nothing.'

James looked at Ellen with such pride that it warmed her heart.

'If we help the strikers with food and that, then we can keep going longer,' Ellen added. She looked around at the room, wondering what everyone thought.

'Och, Ellen, I'm not sure about that. Things are hard enough for us as it is,' her ma pointed out. 'It's the same for everyone.'

'I know that,' Ellen said, nodding. 'I don't mean for us to do it.' She spread her arms wide. 'It's collective, isn't. Collective bargaining and collective help.'

Sadie looked excited. 'You mean we all help each other?'

'That's exactly what I mean.'

'But what can we do?' said Sadie. 'How can we help?'

Bridget and Ida were standing at the edge of the room. Now Bridget spoke up.

'We can sew,' she said. 'That's what we can do. We can collect clothes and repair them, or alter them, and give them to families who need them.'

'Or sell them,' Ida suggested. 'To raise funds.'

'Yes!' Ellen clapped her hands. 'That's so clever.'

'And perhaps we could make big pots of soup,' Sadie said. 'And loaves of bread. And we can feed anyone who's really struggling.'

'I'll help with that,' Gert said.

Sadie smiled. 'I'll bet some of the women round our way will help too.'

'Wonderful,' said Ellen.

'Will we be fast enough?' Bridget said. 'With the sewing? There's only a few of us, and we're quick but we're not that quick.'

'We need machines,' said Sadie with a cheeky grin. 'Do you think Wentworth will donate some to the cause?'

Everyone laughed, except James, who was looking thoughtful.

'What if,' he said, 'we take them?'

'No, James,' said Ellen sternly. 'We can't do that.'

'I don't mean the good stuff,' he said. 'Not machines that are going to be sold. I mean the faulty ones. The broken ones. The ones they stash in Warehouse Twelve.'

Everyone stared at him.

'They throw those away,' Ellen said.

'Aye, they do. Once they've stripped them for parts. And they don't record what's in there, so they won't notice if anything's missing.'

'But broken machines aren't any use to us,' Ida said, biting her knuckle again.

'I can fix them.' James sat up straighter. 'Me and Walter and

Stanley. Lots of us. We can fix them. In no time at all, probably.'

'I can help with that.' Ellen's da had been hovering but now he came into the room properly. 'We can't have weans going hungry.'

Ellen grinned at her father.

'How will we get the machines?' she said. 'We can't just walk into the factory.'

There was silence for a moment.

'Imagine if the side gate was left open one evening,' Bridget said. 'Just for a quarter of an hour or so?'

'Imagine,' said Ellen. 'Who would do such a thing?'

Bridget glanced at Ida and then at the group. 'Me,' she said.

Ellen felt a shiver of excitement, fear and disbelief that they were doing such a risky thing. Despite James's assurances that the machines would be thrown away, it was still stealing.

'Is this the right thing to do?' she said. 'It's theft.'

Sadie rubbed her nose. 'Do you know what my father would say if he was here?'

'What would he say?' Ellen asked.

'He'd say "feed the children",' Sadie said. 'He'd tell us to look after the ones who can't look after themselves.'

There was a moment's silence in the room and then Ellen, feeling more than a little emotional, spoke.

'Are we all agreed, then?'

There weren't many of them in the sitting room, but the sound of agreement was loud and determined. Ellen smiled.

'James and I will get the machines,' she said. 'Ma, can you sort the soup?'

Her mother nodded.

'I'll get some pots from the canteen at Wentworth,' she said. 'Isobel works there.'

'She's not working there just now,' Ellen pointed out.

'Och, no, she's not, but she'll want to help.'

Ellen was impressed at her mother's enthusiasm to break the rules on behalf of other people.

'Go on, then,' she said to her mother.

'Noah and I will collect some donations of clothes,' Sadie said. 'And I'll call in the troops from Glasgow to help with the soup.'

'We've got a plan,' said Ellen in triumph.

'Except,' said Bridget.

'Except what?'

'Where are we going to do it?' She looked around the small room, which was already too full with just a few of them in it. 'We can't cook soup and mend clothes here.'

Ellen was immediately distraught. She'd had it all worked out – except that one thing.

'Oh, Bridget, I'd not thought of that.'

James sat up straighter.

'How about a church hall?' he said. 'Plenty of space and most of them have a wee kitchen area too with water and that.'

'Good idea, son,' said Da. 'There's no space at St Joseph's, mind. The roof of that hall blew off in that storm back in the winter and they've not mended it yet.'

'How about St Andrew's?' James said, speaking more quietly now.

Next to him Ellen stiffened.

Da scoffed. 'They won't help us,' he said.

But James hadn't finished.

'They will,' he said. He swallowed. 'Because I know the minister.'

Da raised his eyebrows. 'Is that your church?'

'It is, aye,' James said, slightly defiant. 'And my granddad, he's the minister.'

Da glared at him. 'Is he now . . .'

James squirmed under Da's stare. 'Uh-huh.' He swallowed. 'He'd let us use the hall. To help folk.'

'Och, that's so kind of you, James,' said Ellen's ma. She frowned, deep in thought. 'Is that Reverend Donaldson?' she asked. 'He's the minister at St Andrew's, is he not?'

'Aye,' said James.

'Right,' said Gert happily. 'Then I used to work with your ma, James. Nora, is that it?'

James nodded, but Ellen felt sick. Her ma knew everyone in Clydebank. Everyone. If she knew James's mother, then it was only a matter of time before she worked out who his stepbrother was.

She looked at her father, who was standing still looking at James silently and then at her ma.

'Nora McCallum, that's right,' Gert was saying. 'It was sad when your da died. He was so young too. But then I heard your ma got married again . . .'

Here it came.

'Ma,' Ellen said, trying to stop her, but Gert was too busy remembering.

'Who was it now, I heard she married?'

She looked at James and Ellen said again, more urgently this time: 'Ma.'

'Willie Briggs,' said Gert triumphantly. 'She married Willie Briggs and sure wasn't that a thing to be taking on, what with the trouble caused by that son of his.'

'Frankie Briggs,' said Da softly. 'Frankie Briggs is your brother?'

James shifted on his seat. 'Stepbrother,' he said. 'Sir.'

But his attempt at politeness didn't pay off. Da grew redder in the face.

'Ellen, what's this?' he said. 'What's going on here?'

'Da . . .' she began.

'No,' he said firmly. 'No.'

He looked at James. 'Get out,' he said.

Ellen got to her feet. 'No, Da,' she said. She was shaking but she wasn't going to let this happen. 'James is Frankie's stepbrother, and he is Protestant, but you know that's not his fault. It's just how it is. Sadie's not Catholic either and she's here.'

Her father glanced at Sadie but only briefly. 'That's not the point,' he said. 'That family are the scum of the earth, and I want nothing to do with them.'

'Allan,' said Ma. 'Calm yourself.'

James stood up now. 'I'll go,' he said. 'I'm sorry. I thought I could help.'

'You're going nowhere,' Ellen said firmly, gripping his arm. 'Listen to yourself, Da,' she said. 'James is a good man. He's been fighting for the rights of the workers and now he wants to help their families too.'

Da shook his head.

'Look at his face. Probably got those bruises fighting with some Catholics.'

'Frankie did that, Da.' Ellen was furious now, her anger matching her father's. She was aware of James next to her and of the others all still, watching them. But she wasn't going to back down.

'James is my friend,' she said, taking a deep breath. 'More than a friend. I like him and he likes me. And we're going to feed the workers at St Andrew's Church Hall.' She lifted her chin.

Her father looked at her in disgust.

'Then I'm afraid I want no part of this,' he said, 'You're on your own.'

And with Ellen watching in despair, he marched out of the flat, letting the door slam behind him.

Chapter Thirty-Four

Bridget and Malcolm were pretending nothing had happened. After the drama with Da and Ellen, Bridget had been nervous about going home because she really couldn't face any more shouting – not that Malcolm was the type to shout.

But instead, she'd gone home and found him sitting beside the fire, reading.

'Hello,' she said cautiously. 'Have you eaten?'

'Aye,' he said.

'Malcolm,' Bridget began. 'I really am sorry.'

'Aye,' he said again. Then he shut his book. 'I'm off to bed.'

And now they were walking to the factory, just like it was a normal day. Bridget remembered Janet saying the Kelly girls ran towards a fight and thought that Malcolm was the opposite. He hated confrontation. Avoided discord, whenever he could. That was why he didn't like the strike, she thought. He would always choose the status quo instead of upheaval or change.

But she still felt bad when they reached Wentworth and she told him that she had to stay late at work the next day.

'Will you be home for tea?' he said.

Bridget really wanted to go and see Ida. She told herself that it was because she wanted to discuss the plans that they were trying – and failing – to put in place for census night now they couldn't go to the bookshop. Every idea they had come up with had flaws, and so far there were obstacles in the way, no matter which way they turned. But she knew that wasn't the only reason and that frightened her a little bit so she nodded.

'I'll not be too late.'

'Right you are.'

He walked away and then paused and turned back.

'Bridget,' he said. 'Stay away from Beresford, won't you.'

Touched that he was worried, Bridget nodded her head.

'I will.'

'Right you are,' he said again.

Later, once the factory had emptied out the few people who were still working, and darkness was falling, Bridget hurried downstairs and out into the courtyard. Holding a clipboard so she gave the impression that she was working, she bustled across the empty space towards the side gate. Then she waited.

Wentworth had a few night watchmen who patrolled the edge of the factory once the bell had gone. Today's was a man called Paul. Bridget saw him coming and breathed a sigh of relief. She knew Paul. She knew his wife, too, who'd not long since had a baby.

As he approached, she gave him a cheery wave.

'Evening Bridget, you're here late.'

'Doing some overtime,' she lied, brandishing her clipboard. 'How's Sarah?'

'She's grand,' he said proudly.

'And the wean?' She couldn't remember if Sarah had a boy or a girl.

'Lynne,' said Paul. 'She's a wee smasher.'

'Send them both my love,' Bridget said, meaning it.

'Aye, I will.'

Paul waved again and went off to carry on his round. Bridget waited for him to get a little further, then she shrank back, into the shadows next to the wall, and gave a small gentle knock on the gate.

A knock came in response and Bridget swiftly unlocked the gate and opened it a fraction. Outside were James and Ellen, both dressed in black.

'You look like Ali Baba and the forty thieves,' Bridget whispered.

'Ali Baba and one thief,' said Ellen.

James shushed them.

'We don't have much time,' he said.

'Paul's just gone so you've got ten minutes at the most,' Bridget said. 'I'll keep an eye out. Go!'

She went back out of the shadows to the edge of the warehouse, pretending to check her clipboard every now and then, but really watching out for Paul to finish his circuit.

Behind her, Ellen and James silently carried several parts of sewing machines out of the storage shed and through the factory gate. Ellen had said that James had borrowed a bicycle with a cart from a friend who worked for a local butcher as a delivery boy, so they would take all the parts in that.

'That's us,' Ellen came up behind her and whispered in her ear, making her jump.

'Well done,' Bridget said, feeling her heart thump. 'I'll lock the gate behind you.'

Ellen and James slipped away into the night, and Bridget slid the lock along the gate. Then she leaned against the wood for a second, gathering herself. Breaking rules was becoming a bit of a habit.

'Everything all right there, Bridget?' Paul's voice made her jump.

'Oh yes, all fine, thanks.' She straightened up and smiled at him. 'It's been a bit of a long day.'

'Maybe you should get off home, now,' he said.

'I will.'

She walked past him and back into the factory, hoping he wouldn't think anything was odd. In the office, it was quiet, except for Mr Beresford's radio drifting along the corridor. Bridget put the clipboard away, picked up her hat and coat and left.

'Bridget?' Mr Beresford called. 'Is that you?'

As quietly as she could, Bridget ran along the corridor and down the stairs before Mr Beresford could find her.

Outside, Bridget thought about going home, and she thought about going to see Ida, but in the end she decided to walk to St Andrew's to see the hall. Perhaps there would be someone there and she could lend a hand with the sewing machines, or the soup or the clothes. She liked to feel useful.

St Andrew's was a redbrick church, with the hall built on the side. Bridget had never been inside, of course, but from the outside it looked very similar to St Joseph's. A church was a church, she thought, almost gasping at her insolence. Perhaps more Catholics should come here, and more Protestants go to St Joe's. Perhaps her father should come. That way he could see the similarities instead of the differences. She kept thinking about Ellen's face when Da had walked out of the living room yesterday. Her sad, stricken face. And their mother saying, 'He'll come round, doll,' but not really sounding like she believed what she was saying. Bridget couldn't quite understand why Da – who barely even went to church and wasn't what anyone would call 'God-fearing' – cared so much, nor why he was blaming James for his brother's mistakes.

It was funny, because in that moment, when he'd marched out of the flat, Da had reminded Bridget of Winston Churchill and his bloody-minded determination to ignore what she and Ida had been trying to say.

She shook her head at all the stubborn men in her life, and pushed open the door to the church hall.

She'd been expecting to see James and Ellen, but what she actually found was a buzz of activity. At one end of the hall James and another couple of men she didn't recognise had sewing machine parts and tools laid out on a dustsheet and were busily hammering and screwing.

On the far side, near the kitchen, her mother was speaking to a group of women in a very purposeful way. Bridget recognised

Isobel, who worked in the canteen at Wentworth, and some of the others. And she also knew that some of them weren't on strike. Which presumably explained the large pots that were stacked nearby.

And closest to her were Ellen and Sadie, surrounded by clothes.

'What's all this?' Bridget said, going over.

'The church had been collecting them,' Ellen said. She was sitting on the floor sorting short trousers into piles. 'James's grandad said we should have them, and Sadie brought some bits too.'

'Our doctor's wife donated a bag,' Sadie said. 'And the rabbi's wife, which was astonishing really because she's not normally so nice.'

Bridget chuckled.

'Ma looks like she's got the soup under control?'

'Aye, she's already got the butcher to give us some bones to use for broth, and Mrs McGinty's donated a load of potatoes.'

Bridget was impressed. 'Mrs McGinty did? She'd never give you so much as a smile usually.'

'Her son's striking,' Ellen said. 'She understands.'

'How are we going to let everyone know what's happening?' Sadie said.

Ellen grinned. 'Word will spread. You know what happened when we went out on strike? Trust me, people will come.'

'I hope so,' said Bridget.

Ellen stood up and dusted off her skirt. 'Shall I show you what we've planned?'

'Yes, please.'

Bridget followed her sister into the middle of the room. 'So,' said Ellen. 'Over where the men are tucked in the corner, that's going to be the workshop. James thinks we've got three machines for sure, but maybe four if a few of us get sewing – me, and Sadie and others – we can run up lots of clothes from what we've been donated.' She lowered her voice. 'Some of the bits Sadie's doctor sent don't even need washing – there are some lovely things in there.'

'I think it'll all be lovely once we've mended them, or altered them, or put two skirts together to make one,' Bridget said. 'We know what we're doing – we've been at this for years.'

'That's true,' Ellen said. 'And we don't want everyone to feel they have to pay, so we thought we'd have a box where people can leave a donation if they can afford to. But they don't have to.'

'That's a good idea.'

'I was going to ask Da to make the box,' Ellen said, her expression darkening. 'But now ...'

'Have you seen him?'

Ellen shook her head. 'I was in bed by the time he came back last night, and he was out early this morning.'

'I was surprised how angry he was.'

'Me too,' said Ellen. 'I'd persuaded myself that he'd be fine with it.'

'Maybe he just needs to calm down,' Bridget said.

'Maybe.' Ellen didn't sound sure. 'You know it wasn't just James who Frankie attacked?'

'What?' Bridget was horrified. 'When did this happen?'

'Before I went to see Beresford,' Ellen sighed. 'James and I were together and Frankie saw us and he went for us.'

'His brother punched you?'

'No, but he pushed me over and he broke my chain.'

'Your crucifix? Oh, Ellen, that's not right.' Bridget put her arms round her sister.

'James says he gets a bee in his bonnet sometimes, that's all. He had an accident when he was younger and he's not been right since.'

Bridget thought of Ida with that vivid scar across her face. 'Hmm,' she said. 'I'm not sure that's an excuse.'

'I don't want to upset anyone, Bridget. James took him home and he said he's all right with us now.'

'Is he, aye?'

Ellen shrugged, looking so miserable that Bridget gave her another hug. 'Show me everything else.'

'Soup over there,' Ellen said. 'No charge. We don't want anyone going hungry if we can help it.'

Bridget looked at her sister, immensely proud.

'You're a good person, Ellen Kelly.'

Ellen lifted her chin. 'I learned from the best,' she said.

Chapter Thirty-Five

Sadie could not believe how quickly everything had happened. Yesterday morning St Andrew's Hall had just been a big empty space. Now it was full of people.

She put her hand on her belly, which was full with the most delicious soup made by Gert and her pals. A thick broth that was full of vegetables and barley. Sadie couldn't believe how lovely it felt not to be hungry, though she had to admit, she wasn't feeling quite right. She was a little light-headed and – she touched the back of her hand to her forehead – quite hot. She hoped she wasn't coming down with something. That was the last thing she needed.

She'd brought the children with her today. She'd told them not to go to school and instead, she'd taken them with her on the train to Clydebank, not telling them where they were going. Daniel had been very perturbed and kept saying that he was missing an arithmetic test.

'Daniel, you're very clever at sums,' Sadie said. 'They can't teach you anything – you know more than the teachers.'

Daniel had looked pleased at that.

'Honestly, you'll be glad you came.'

They'd decided to open the 'Wentworth Welfare Centre', as they were calling it, when the factory bell rang that evening. Everyone in Clydebank lived their lives by the shift patterns at the factory, so it made sense. That meant there were still a few hours to go before – hopefully – some strikers arrived. But the women had been working through the night to make soup and bake bread and they were setting it up when Sadie and the children arrived, just as she'd hoped.

'Sadie and the weans!' Gert exclaimed as they entered the hall, looking in astonishment at the sewing machines set up in the corner and the women bustling around. 'Come and have something to eat.'

'Are you allowed to have soup for breakfast?' Rachel asked Sadie, her eyes huge as she looked around the room. 'Is it all right?'

Sadie gave her a hug. 'It's definitely all right.'

She and the children had eaten mugs of thick soup and already the little ones were looking healthier. Daniel was helping Ellen measure and cut cloth. And Eddie seemed to have joined a gaggle of children rushing around the hall, running messages to people. Rachel was attached to Gert's side, helping her lay out spoons and bowls.

'Where did this stuff all come from?' Sadie asked in wonder.

Gert tapped the side of her nose.

'Ask me no questions, I'll tell you no lies,' she said.

Wentworth, then. Sadie just hoped nobody in management stopped by the kitchen and noticed that half the equipment was missing.

They spent most of the day sorting and arranging. Sadie patched umpteen pairs of trousers that were worn through the knees, and a few jackets that had thin elbows, and then she and Ellen put all the clothes on long tables. And for a while she forgot about feeling off-colour, though as soon as she stopped she realised she still didn't feel right.

'I'm going to take the weans home,' she said. 'I don't like to leave Ma for too long.'

'Will you come back?'

'Of course!' Sadie said, crossing her fingers that she'd start to feel better. 'How could you cope without me?'

Ellen grinned. 'I hope people come,' she said. 'Even just to get some soup and bread. It would be a shame to waste what Ma's made.'

'I don't think it'll go to waste,' Sadie said confidently. 'People are hungry.'

'But not you.' Ellen reached out and touched Sadie's arm lightly.

'Not me,' Sadie agreed. 'And not the children. Not now.' She smiled at Ellen. 'Because of you.'

Ellen waved off her gratitude, and Sadie rounded up the children, promising she'd bring them back again on Sunday.

'Come on,' she said. 'We've got a train to catch.'

It was strange, actually, because Sadie hadn't said much to her mother about what they were doing at St Andrew's. She knew about the strike of course, and try as Sadie might to protect her from their money worries, she must have known about that too. But Sadie had been so busy rushing around and helping with setting up the welfare centre, she'd not had time to talk to Ma about it.

But the children were full of it, as soon as they got home. Babbling on to Ma about the soup pots and the clothes and how funny James was and how he made them laugh with his silly games. And Sadie was full of pride as she dished up some soup for her mother, made by Gert. She'd sent Sadie home with a whole pot saying they'd made far too much, and someone ought to take it off their hands.

Sadie hadn't argued.

Ma fixed Sadie with a stern look. 'You didn't mention what you were up to?'

'I've been busy, Ma.'

'You didn't think I might like to help out?'

Sadie actually had thought that her mother would want to help, but she was worried she might be too sick and too weak to really lend a hand. But there was no doubt she was on the mend – for now at least – and she seemed rather cross not to have been asked.

'Well,' she began but her mother shushed her.

'Go and get Miriam,' she said. 'We'll put our heads together. See what we can do.'

'Really?'

'Go.'

So Sadie went along the street to Miriam's, and found Noah there too, so they all walked back to the flat and Sadie filled them in on everything that was going on.

'It sounds impressive,' Noah said, as they reached the flat. Miriam went on ahead, up the stairs, while Sadie and Noah hung back a bit.

Suddenly feeling a little self-conscious, Sadie said: 'I'm going back there, now actually. Would you like to come?'

'To Clydebank?'

'Yes,' Sadie said. 'There might not be anyone there, you know? We've been spreading the word but we're not sure if anyone will come along. But I thought you might like to see what we've been doing.'

'I'd love to,' said Noah.

They left their mothers with their heads together, making plans and writing lists, and Sadie and Noah got on the train. It was quiet going to Clydebank at this time, and they had their carriage to themselves. Sadie leaned her head against the window and closed her eyes.

'Tired?' Noah asked.

'Very.' Sadie kept her eyes closed.

'You are a bit pale.'

Sadie was feeling even worse than she'd felt earlier. Her eyes were hot and her skin felt clammy. But she wasn't going to admit that. Not when it was the first day of the welfare centre and they needed all the help they could get.

With a bit of an effort, she lifted her head off the window.

'I'm fine,' she said. Trying to distract herself, she told him about Ellen and James.

'Ellen's da and Frankie have clashed a few times,' Sadie explained. 'Frankie's trouble and it's all mixed up in James being Protestant while Ellen is Catholic. It makes no sense to me.'

Noah shrugged. 'It's hard for us to understand when we're not in it,' he said. 'As far as I can tell, the only real clue about whether someone is Catholic or Protestant is what school they went to.'

'Or their name,' Sadie agreed. 'But even that's not always what you think.'

'Do you remember those boys?' Noah said with a chuckle. 'Years ago.'

Sadie nodded. 'That was funny.'

She had been cornered by a group of lads, a bit older than her, as she walked home from school.

'What's your name?' one of them had demanded.

'Sadie.'

He'd frowned.

'Are you Catholic or Protestant?'

Sadie had shaken her head. 'Neither,' she said. 'I'm Jewish.'

'But,' the boy had persisted. 'Are you a Catholic Jew or a Protestant Jew?'

Sadie remembered how Noah had come along just at the right moment. Two years older than her, and taller than the wee ragamuffins who were bothering her, he'd stood in between her and them and she'd felt safe.

'What's your name?' he'd asked the ringleader.

'Billy.'

Noah had looked at Sadie and then back at Billy. 'We're Protestant Jews,' he'd said.

And the boys had let them past.

'You're always looking after me,' Sadie said now, looking at Noah. 'I'm sorry to be so . . .'

'So what?' he said.

'Such a burden.'

He looked at her for a long moment, then he took his glasses off and rubbed his nose, before he spoke.

'Sadie,' he said, putting his specs back on. 'I've known you my whole life but still, every single day you surprise me.'

'Really?'

'Erm, yes!' Noah began listing things on his fingers. 'I'll take a job that pays better, even if it works me to the bone and annoys the rabbi's grumpy sister, because my family need me.'

'I did do that,' Sadie agreed.

'Oh, and I'll start reading seditious pamphlets about workers' rights.'

'Not seditious,' she said, beginning to chuckle.

'And then I'll call everyone out on strike. Not just one or two. Thousands,' Noah waggled his fingers in Sadie's face. 'Thousands!'

'You're being silly,' she said, laughing properly now.

'Wait, I've not finished. Then I'll lead all those thousands of people through the streets of Clydebank to get them the money they're owed. And get involved in the strike negotiations. And then set up a whole welfare centre to support the folk who've stopped work.'

He leaned back against the train seat, pretending to be exhausted. 'Every day,' he said. 'Surprises. So no, you are not a burden, Sadie Franklin. You are a joy.'

Sadie leaned her head against the window once more, pleased as punch.

Noah, for all his bookish nature and thoughtfulness, was a chatty sort as a rule, but he was stunned into silence when they arrived at the hall. He stood in the middle of the room gazing at the sewing machines – which were buzzing with activity as Ellen and some others busied themselves with alterations – to the soup pots and the volunteers waiting for someone to serve.

Sadie watched as Ellen finished a skirt and stood up to put it on the pile, shaking it out so it looked nicer. She waved at Sadie and came over to say hello.

'Is he all right?' she said, nodding towards Noah.

'Just impressed, I think.' Sadie beamed with pride. 'At least, I hope that's what it is.'

'He's really lovely,' Ellen said.

'I know.'

'I think you should tell him how you feel.'

Sadie thought about Noah listing all her good points on the train and she felt warm all over, as though someone had put a blanket round her shoulders. 'I know,' she said again.

Ellen looked a little sad and Sadie wondered if she was thinking of her and James, and the troubles they were having.

'Any sign of your da?' Sadie asked.

'Nothing.'

'He'll come round.'

'That's what my ma says.'

'You don't agree?'

Ellen shrugged. 'Och, he probably will.' She bit her lip. 'I hope so, anyway. He'll just make sure we all know he wasn't happy about it for a while.' She glanced around, checking to see if anyone was listening. 'I'm worried about James's brother though.'

'Has he been causing more trouble?'

'No.' Ellen shook her head. 'Well, not as such.'

Sadie took her friend's hand and pulled her to the side of the room where they were out of earshot of everyone. 'What does that mean?'

'It means . . .' Ellen sighed. 'I think he's following me.'

'WHAT?' Sadie's exclamation was so loud that everyone looked round and Ellen widened her eyes at her in warning.

'Sorry,' she said, quieter this time. 'What do you mean he's following you?'

'Just that I keep seeing him wherever I go.' Ellen looked tired suddenly. 'I've thought it for a while, actually, but I didn't know who he was then. But today, when I went to get some of the potatoes, I was on my way back and he was there, standing at the side of the road, just watching me. And last night when I walked home, I was on my own because Ma had gone somewhere with Isobel to pick up some things. So I went the long way round because I don't like going down the close in the dark, but even then he was there. Standing still, just watching. But not hiding. He wanted me to know he was there.'

'Like a warning?' Sadie said. Her legs felt a bit wobbly at the thought of the man, who'd blackened James's eye and ripped the cross from Ellen's neck, watching her friend.

'I suppose so.'

'What did James say when you told him?'

Ellen screwed her face up.

'Did you tell him, Ellen?'

She shook her head slowly. 'I don't want to worry him, Sadie. It's not his fault.'

'I know Frankie's had his troubles, but it's not right of him to scare you that way. You should tell James.'

Ellen sighed. 'I will,' she said. 'It's just . . .'

Whatever she was going to say was drowned out by the factory bell. Everyone in the room stopped what they were doing.

'This is it,' Ellen said. 'Good luck, everyone!'

Years later, Sadie would look back on that first evening at the welfare centre with a mixture of pride and admiration and exhaustion. But while she was in it, all she could think of was the next five minutes, because it was absolute chaos. Organised chaos, but chaos all the same.

She and Noah positioned themselves beside the table with the clothes. Sadie was glad to sit down because her legs were growing increasingly wobbly and she needed the rest, but she still wanted to be there.

On their table were piles of garments, from skirts to trousers and blouses and everything in between. There were hats and gloves at one end, plus a few pairs of shoes and boots.

Every single item had gone within an hour. Every single thing. There wasn't so much as a pair of woolly socks left.

But some people had brought things to donate too. One woman brought a few old tablecloths and sheets that she thought would make blouses, much to Ellen's delight. And an elderly man dropped off a roll of tweed he said he'd found under his bed. So the sewing machines were soon whirring away again. Bridget showed up at one point – without Malcolm – and immediately started cutting out patterns. And later her friend Ida arrived, too, with more supplies donated from her store – bars of soap and packets of tobacco.

The soup pots were flowing. Strikers had brought their wives and their husbands and their children and the women could hardly dish up fast enough. They ran out of bowls within minutes, but the word spread, and people were turning up with their own to fill. Ida went back to her shop and brought some enamel bowls, plates and mugs and they used them too.

The queue stretched out of the hall and along the street, and people were still coming, and to Sadie and Ellen's distress, they eventually had to turn folk away. Not the children – by then all the weans who'd come along had been fed – but some of the late arrivals.

'We'll need more food tomorrow,' Ellen said.

Sadie thought about her mother and Miriam and nodded. 'Definitely,' she said.

People were packing up now, the pots were washed and the sewing machines covered. Noah appeared next to Sadie and she leaned against him, all her energy gone.

'I'm so tired, Noah,' she said.

He smiled down at her, looking just as exhausted. 'Me too.'

'I'm half tempted to just curl up in the corner and sleep here for the night.'

'Nope,' he said. 'I'm taking you home.'

'Thank you.'

'For taking you home?'

'No, silly. For helping today and being so supportive.'

'My supportive nature might have its limits if we miss the last train,' Noah said.

'Come on.'

Sadie said goodbye to Ellen and quite forcefully reminded her to walk home with her ma and as many others as they could in case Frankie was lurking. Then she looped her arm through Noah's and they set off towards the station.

She slept all the way back to Glasgow. Noah woke her as the train pulled in, concern on his face.

They headed towards home, which wasn't far, thank goodness, because Sadie was finding it quite hard to walk. She was half tempted to simply lie down on the ground where she was and rest her bones.

'Sadie, you don't look well,' he said.

'I just need sleep,' she muttered. 'I'll be fine.'

And then everything went black.

She woke up in her ma's bed, though it took her a while to work out where she was. The sheets were damp with sweat and her head ached like someone had hit her with a brick. She opened her eyes and saw the outline of a person there, next to the bed.

'Da,' she said, starting to cry. 'Oh, Da. I've missed you so much.'

And then she must have slept again, because the next time she woke, it was light, and she could hear muffled voices, though she couldn't quite open her eyes to see who was there because her head hurt so much. Someone held a cup of water to her lips and she drank a little, then she was asleep again. Dreaming strange, bewildered dreams of Noah and factory bells and Frankie Briggs.

She woke for a while in the dark, and was frightened for a moment because she wasn't sure what time it was or where she was, but then someone took her hand and she felt better and slept again.

When she woke again, her head didn't hurt any more, and her skin was no longer clammy. It was light now and she opened her eye cautiously, but she felt all right.

Sitting herself up against the pillows, she saw that there, draped over the foot of the bed, sleeping peacefully, was Noah.

'Noah?' Sadie said quietly. He didn't stir.

'Noah?' she said again. She reached out a foot and prodded him gently. 'Noah!'

With a start, Noah awoke. He rubbed his eyes like a wee boy and then saw her sitting up.

'Sadie,' he said. 'Thank goodness.'

His face twisted and for a second, Sadie thought he might cry.

'Noah?' she said, confused.

'You've been so ill, Sadie,' he told her. 'And you were crying and talking to your da, and I thought . . .' He breathed in deeply. 'I thought you were going to die.'

'No,' Sadie said, shaking her head, but only gently because she still felt a little odd. 'I'm here. I'm fine.' She looked round, disorientated. 'What time is it?'

'It's ten o'clock in the morning.' He shuffled over so he was closer to her. 'You've been asleep for a whole day and two nights.'

Sadie was horrified. 'What about the welfare centre?'

Noah grinned. 'It's fine, my ma has gone and so has yours.'

'My ma?'

'Aye, she's doing great.'

'Ten o'clock?' Sadie said, suddenly realising Noah had somewhere to be. 'Shouldn't you be at work?'

'I told them I had to look after you,' he said. 'They were fine.'

Sadie stared at him. 'Have you been here the whole time?' she asked. 'A whole day and two nights?'

Noah crumpled the sheet in his fist then let go again. 'I have,' he said.

'Why?'

He looked at her, and she looked back at him.

'Do you really have to ask?'

'Yes,' said Sadie firmly, suddenly horribly aware that she'd been in the same sweaty sheets for two days and that her hair was stuck to her face.

She smiled at him. 'Remember when you said you'd already met the woman you wanted to marry and then Daniel interrupted us?'

'I do remember that.'

'Who did you mean?'

Noah took her hand.

'I meant you, you goose. Of course I meant you.'

Overcome with relief and happiness, Sadie leaned back against the pillow.

'Thank goodness,' she said.

Noah pushed a bit of her hair off her face. 'I love you, Sadie Franklin,' he said. 'And I can't believe it's taken me so long to tell you.'

'Me neither,' said Sadie. 'Now, are you going to kiss me or do I have to wait another two whole nights and one day?'

'No more waiting,' said Noah.

Chapter Thirty-Six

Ellen couldn't quite believe how busy the welfare centre was. They'd helped more people than she'd imagined they could. It made her proud, though a little sad, that there were so many folk struggling. And she felt bad that they'd ended up turning people away again when they'd run out of supplies.

The next morning, Ma had woken her early.

'You need to see this,' she said.

Bleary-eyed, Ellen had gone to the window in her bare feet, curling her toes up on the cold floor. Down below a lad called Donald, who delivered for Owen's Bakery up the road, was waving to her, standing next to his bicycle.

She opened the window.

'Was it me you wanted?'

'I've got some rolls and that,' he called up.

'What for?'

She looked round at her mother in confusion.

'For the welfare centre.'

Ellen shook her head.

'We can't pay for them, Donald. We've got no money.'

He'd grinned. 'Compliments of Mrs Owen,' he shouted. 'She says she'll do more for the evening.'

'Really?'

Donald swung his leg over the bike.

'St Andrew's, isn't it?'

'That's the one.'

He gave her a salute and wobbled off towards the church.

Ellen turned to Ma in amazement. 'Mrs Owen,' she said.

'Who'd have thought it?' Ma smiled. 'People really are doing their bit, aren't they? That's because of you. I'm proud of you, doll.'

Ellen ducked her head, embarrassed but pleased at the praise.

'Is Da still here?'

'Aye. He's just having something to eat.'

Ellen had barely seen her father since the other evening when he'd left the flat in anger at her romance with James.

'Should I speak to him?' she asked Ma.

Gert shrugged. 'You know what he's like, Ellen. Bloody-minded and stubborn.' A small smile played on her lips. 'Reminds me of someone else.'

Ellen made a face.

'He's not a bad man,' her mother said.

'You know Frankie Briggs pulled my crucifix off and scratched my neck?' Ellen said, tipping her head to one side. The welts were healing now but Ellen knew her ma would be able to see them.

'Oh, Ellen.' Ma put her fingers out and gently touched the marks. 'That's not right.'

'He was upset and angry,' Ellen said. 'And do you know why?'

Ma looked sick. 'Because you're Catholic?'

'Right.'

'That's enough, Ellen.' Gert's anger flared. 'Don't you dare compare your da to that man. Your father would never do something like that.'

'I know, Ma. But I just mean that it comes from the same place. Mistrust and mean spirits. And Frankie's got his problems – James says he's not been the same since he hurt his leg. But the way he's acted, judging someone without knowing them – that's the same as Da's done.'

'That's not it at all,' her mother said, but she looked thoughtful, and Ellen knew she'd struck a chord.

'Da is a good man,' she said. 'But him judging James because of where he goes to church, or because of who his brother is, isn't a good thing.'

Gert put her hand on Ellen's shoulder. 'Where's your necklace now? I'll get it mended for you, if you like.'

Ellen understood it was Ma's way of apologising for losing her temper and she was grateful.

'I don't know,' she admitted. 'Frankie threw it in one of the bushes at the edge of the green and I've not had time to go and look for it.'

'Aww, Ellen, that belonged to your gran.'

'I'll have a look when things have calmed down a bit at the welfare centre.'

'All right,' Gert said.

A noise at the kitchen door made them look up. There was Da, dressed for work. Ellen felt unsettled. How long had he been there? Had he heard their conversation?

'That's me off,' he muttered.

He gave her mother a kiss and nodded to Ellen then he went, clattering down the stairs in his boots.

'I have to go, too,' Ellen said. 'I'll get dressed.'

The second day at the welfare centre was even more successful than the first. They handed out Mrs Owen's rolls to children on their way to school, and Ellen felt so proud that those weans wouldn't be spending the day hugging their rumbling, empty tummies.

To her surprise, Sadie didn't come. But instead, two women arrived, introducing themselves as Bet and Miriam – Sadie's ma and her best friend.

'Sadie's sick,' Bet explained. 'I'm not surprised really. I don't think she's been eating properly and she works so hard. We were worried in the night. Noah was frantic. He thought she was going to die.' She looked a little shocked at the thought.

'She's all right now, is she?' Ellen said, alarmed.

'On the mend, doll. But we thought she'd be worried about you and the welfare centre, so we came to see you.'

'Noah stayed with her?' Ellen said. 'All night?'

'Aye,' said Bet. She and Miriam exchanging a knowing look. 'He did.'

Ellen beamed at them. 'Well, it's nice to meet you,' she said.

'We've come to help,' said Miriam. 'But not here.'

'Right,' said Ellen, confused.

'Miriam's got a pal who lives just across the green,' Bet explained. 'Mary Sylvester. Her husband works in the kitchen at the hospital, and he says they can use his equipment to make more soup.'

Ellen was almost speechless. 'That's so kind.'

Bet smiled. 'We all want to help.'

'Sadie said you've been under the weather too,' Ellen said. 'Make sure you take it easy, won't you?'

Bet nodded. 'Yes, I will. But let me tell you, I feel so much better for being out and about again.'

'Have you got ingredients?' Ellen said. 'I'm sure I can get some bits from Ma for you.'

'No need,' Miriam said proudly. She held up two big shopping bags, full to the brim with vegetables. 'And Ronnie Sylvester, Mary's husband, he's keeping us some chicken bones to use. He says we're doing him a favour. Mary's going to help us cook.'

'Wonderful,' said Ellen, clapping her hands. 'Thank you.'

With more soup provided by Sadie's mother and her friends, the extra bread from Owen's, and bits and pieces dropped off during the afternoon by local people keen to do their bit, the welfare centre's second day was even busier than the first.

The side of the hall where the sewing machines were had

turned into a bit of an exchange. People were dropping off bags of worn out, or too-small clothes, then browsing through the items the women had repaired or altered. Ellen, looking at the piles of fabric waiting to be tackled, wondered if they'd be able to sneak back into Wentworth and get another sewing machine. Or would that be pushing their luck?

As the evening went on, and the crowds of people waiting for soup began to dwindle, she found herself looking up every time the door to the hall opened. She'd not seen James all day, but she'd heard he and Walter had gone up to the factory to talk to management. It was the first time actual talks had happened – everything had been done through letters before now – and Ellen was cross that the Strike Committee had more or less taken over and she and Sadie hadn't been included.

She told herself that if they'd had to be up at the factory then they'd not have had time to start the welfare centre, but she was still annoyed at being left out. She just hoped an actual meeting meant an agreement was near. Despite the welfare centre helping people through these bleak, difficult days, she knew that they couldn't carry on with the strike indefinitely.

'That's us away back to Glasgow now,' Miriam and Bet said, coming over to say goodbye.

'Give my love to Sadie,' said Ellen. 'I hope she's doing better.'

They all hugged goodbye and the women went off, chattering nineteen to the dozen.

Ellen hadn't intended to walk home by herself, but actually, by the time she'd sorted out the clothes, tidied away all the bits of thread and helped wash out the soup pots, her ma was long gone – back to give her da his tea. She'd asked Ellen to leave with her when she'd gone, but Ellen had still had jobs to do and a part of her had been hopeful that James might pop in and walk her home instead.

The evening went on, though, and James didn't arrive. So Ellen had to go home alone.

It was dark when she left, of course, and the street lights cast long shadows. She locked the door of the church hall and dropped the key under the mat for whoever arrived first in the morning. Then nervous and jumpy, and wishing that James was there, she pulled her coat more tightly round her body and hurried towards the flat.

But as she emerged from the churchyard, she saw Frankie. He was standing watching her just as before, under one of the street lamps, his face glowing eerie orange in the light.

Ellen lost her temper.

'What do you want?' she yelled across at him. 'Why are you here?'

Frankie didn't speak, he just glowered at her.

'It's not all right, you know,' she shouted. 'It's not all right to scare women. You're just a big bully.'

'Leave my brother alone,' Frankie replied finally. His voice was rough and it sounded like he'd been drinking. 'Leave him alone.'

'Or what?' said Ellen recklessly. 'What will you do if I don't? Will you hurt me again? Like a big man, eh? Picking on a wee woman half your size?'

Frankie made a sound like a low growling noise, deep in his throat, and Ellen's bravado deserted her. She hitched up her skirt, and ran as fast as she could towards home, her heart thumping, and her breath fast and shallow.

In the flat, she checked and double-checked the doors were locked, then she went to the window and looked out into the street, frightened that Frankie could have followed her home. But the road was quiet and still. Ellen looked out for a long time and then, satisfied he'd not tracked her steps, she went to bed.

She even allowed herself a moment of satisfaction. She'd stood up to the bully. Hopefully Frankie had just needed someone to point out what an idiot he was being, tormenting a woman the way he had been doing, to make him see the error of his ways.

Feeling a bit happier the next day, she got up and dressed and went off to the welfare centre, hoping that Sadie might make it too. She was on her own because her ma was going to collect some more vegetables for the soup first thing, and there had been no sign of her father.

She felt safer on the bustling morning streets than she had done last night. And to her relief, there was no sign of Frankie. Perhaps she really had seen him off.

But as she went round the corner towards the church hall, she saw in the churchyard a small group of people, including one wearing long black robes – James's grandad, the minister, she assumed. She saw James was there too, and a few others, and she quickened her steps as she approached because she got the distinct impression that something was wrong.

'What's the matter?' she called.

James turned to her. He came out of the churchyard to meet her and caught her round the waist, stopping her going further.

'Hold on.'

'What?' Ellen said, worried now. 'Is someone hurt?'

'No.' James bit his lip. 'But the hall is . . .' He took a breath. 'It's wrecked.'

'Wrecked?' Ellen wriggled out of his grasp. 'What do you mean?'

She almost ran down the path to where the minister, along with a couple of other men, were standing.

Wrecked was actually a bit of an understatement.

The wooden doors to the hall had been torn from the hinges and kicked in. Ellen gasped in shock and recoiled as she realised that wasn't the worst of the damage.

'I didn't hear a thing,' the minister was saying. 'But I am a deep sleeper.'

'It's probably lucky you didn't hear it, Grandad,' James said. 'Because if you'd disturbed them, who knows what they'd have done to you.'

The sign that Ellen and Sadie had proudly put up outside to

296

tell people this was where the welfare centre was, had been torn down and was leaning against a gravestone. Ellen wiped away a tear. All their hard work.

'Can I go inside?' she asked.

The minister looked round at her. 'Are you Ellen?'

She nodded.

'I'm Reverend Donaldson,' he said.

'My grandad,' James added. But the minister didn't smile. He simply stood back to let Ellen enter the hall.

Inside it was even worse than Ellen could ever have imagined. The sewing machines, so carefully put back together by James and Walter had been pushed over. One of the wheels was half-way across the floor. Ellen bent and picked it up with shaking hands.

The tables where they served the soup had been overturned and some of the legs were broken off. The clothes – the clothes Ellen had left so neatly piled and sorted yesterday evening – had been torn and scattered all around the hall, and one of the windows had been smashed.

Ellen looked at it all with her hands over her mouth in shock. Her chest felt tight and it was hard to breathe.

James came to stand next to her, putting his arm round her waist. Ellen leaned her head on his shoulder.

'We worked so hard, James,' she said, crying properly now. 'So very hard. And we helped all those people.'

James's jaw was clenched. 'That's it now,' he said. 'That's it for the strike. People can't stay off work any longer if there's no help for them.'

'It's awful. I don't understand why anyone would do this.' A nasty thought occurred to her. 'Was it someone from Wentworth, do you think? Could it have been someone wanting to sabotage the strike?'

James shook his head vigorously. 'No, Ellen, come on. It's obvious who did this.'

Ellen hadn't wanted to consider that possibility. She began to cry again.

'Frankie?' she said. 'Was it Frankie?'

'I think so.' James looked wretched.

'He was here, last night,' Ellen whispered. 'Waiting outside. I shouted at him.' She breathed in sharply. 'Perhaps this is my fault? Perhaps he's done this because I lost my temper.'

'No!' James said. 'This is not your fault. There's only one person to blame, and that's Frankie.' He put his hands to his head, his face stricken with despair. It was as if all the fight drained from him in an instant. 'It was Frankie,' he said. 'Of course it was.'

'We should tell the police,' Ellen said.

'No,' James began, but Ellen stopped him.

'I know you want to protect your brother, but this isn't the way,' she said. 'If this was him . . .' she looked around at the damage . . . 'then he needs to suffer the consequences.'

James sighed. 'Let me speak to him before we do that,' he said. 'Maybe he can go away for a while – we have family in Dundee, they'd put him up.'

'Perhaps,' said Ellen.

'He could make a fresh start. Put all this behind him.'

'Do you think he'd do that?'

James looked doubtful. 'He might.'

'Well, if he agrees that he can't go on like this, then perhaps we don't have to speak to the police.' Ellen shrugged. 'But he needs to change, James.'

'I'll see if I can convince him,' James said. He sounded forlorn. 'What if he doesn't agree?'

'Then we go to the police. Make sure you tell him that. Either he goes away or he goes to jail.'

James sighed. 'All right. I'll go and find him.' He looked at Ellen. 'What will you do?'

'Clear up,' she said. 'Start again?'

'You're brilliant,' said James in admiration. Ellen felt a glow of pride.

'Go and find your brother,' she said. 'But be careful.'

'I will,' said James. 'I've just got something to do first.'

He wrapped Ellen in his arms and kissed her.

When they untangled themselves – eventually – he looked into her eyes.

'I love you, Ellen Kelly.'

Then he turned and walked out of the hall, leaving Ellen staring at him in pleasure and surprise.

Chapter Thirty-Seven

'We'll do you a parade,' Ellen said. 'We'll make you the best wedding parade Wentworth has ever seen.'

'Slow down,' said Sadie. 'It's much too soon to be talking about weddings for me and Noah. And don't forget that Noah doesn't work at Wentworth.' Sadie gave her a broad smile. 'How about we plan a wedding parade for you, instead?'

Ellen grinned, feeling her cheeks reddening.

'Maybe one day,' she said.

Sadie picked up a pair of trousers that had been ripped to shreds. 'I don't think we can save these.'

Ellen looked at them carefully, then screwed up her nose. 'Put them in the rag bag,' she said.

The rag bag was overflowing already and they'd barely started. Ellen didn't want to think too much about what an enormous job they had in front of them – clearing up the damage done by Frankie. If, of course, it had been Frankie, as they all assumed. James had gone off and not come back again.

'He must have been here ages,' said Sadie, sitting back on her haunches and surveying the room for the hundredth time. 'He's ruined every single bit of it.'

Biting her lip, Ellen followed Sadie's gaze. She was right. There were shards of broken glass from the smashed window on the floor and splinters of wood from all the ruined tables. There were muddy footprints everywhere, and the bread rolls they'd saved for this morning had been stamped into crumbs.

There had been a small amount of soup left over yesterday, which Ellen had hoped would do for some of the volunteers who were struggling to feed themselves too, but the pot had been pushed over and there was soup spilled all over. It was such a mess she was worried they'd never get it clean. There was even some paint splattered on the floor.

'There were pots of paint round the side,' Reverend Donaldson said, seeing them staring in despair at the mess. 'Whoever did this must have known we recently had the fence painted.'

Ellen thought that was more evidence against Frankie, but she didn't say anything.

'James tells me you don't want to involve the police?' the minister said.

Ellen and Sadie exchanged a glance but shook their heads.

'We just want to sort everything out and get up and running again.'

'Ah,' said the reverend.

Ellen's stomach sank. 'What do you mean by "ah" exactly?' she asked.

'The church wardens aren't keen on you running the welfare centre from here anymore.'

Ellen got to her feet, stumbling as the blood rushed into her toes and gave her pins and needles. 'Oh please, Reverend Donaldson,' she begged. 'We've been doing such a lot of good here. Feeding people and clothing them.'

'Ellen, I appreciate the effort and I can't say it isn't needed, but it just seems so risky.'

As if on cue, a wee boy – no more than four or five years old – appeared at the door of the hall, looking confused. His face was clean but the rest of him wasn't. He had a ring of dirt round his neck and his shirt was grey. And, Ellen noticed with a shiver, he had no shoes on.

'Where's the bread?' he said. He took a few steps into the building on his little grubby bare feet. 'Peter said there was bread.'

'Stop!' shouted Ellen. The little lad froze, looking terrified and Ellen felt awful. 'There's glass on the floor,' she said. 'I don't want you to hurt yourself.'

The boy's lip trembled but he didn't move. Ellen went to him and picked him up, feeling his little arms on her neck. He was light as a feather, bless him, and he smelled more than a little unpleasant. 'We don't have any bread,' she said to him. 'Someone broke in and trampled on it all.'

'That's not nice,' he said.

'No, it's not. What's your name?'

'Mikey.'

'Listen Mikey, I'm sure we can find you something to eat. Let's just get you out of the way of this glass and we'll go and get some food, shall we?'

Mikey nodded.

Sadie appeared clutching a pair of boots. She was just finishing lacing one up and she held it up to Mikey's foot.

'These might be a bit big for you, but we can put some newspaper in the toes,' she said. 'The shoes have been thrown all over the place and this was the only matching pair I could find. Shall we try them on?'

Still holding Mikey, Ellen helped him turn round so Sadie could slide the boots onto his feet. Then she gently let him down on to the ground again.

'Very smart,' she said. She bent down and tied the laces and watched as Mikey stamped his feet a few times in delight.

'Young man?' the reverend came over, his face less stern than it had been. 'Why don't you come with me and I'll see if I can find you some breakfast from my kitchen.'

'All right,' Mikey said. He took the reverend's hand and obediently trotted along beside him as he went to leave the hall.

Just before they got to the door, Reverend Donaldson turned back to Ellen and Sadie.

'Carry on,' he said. 'The welfare centre belongs here.'

All morning the women carried on with the seemingly never-ending task of cleaning up the hall. Ellen's mother arrived with her pals, ready for their soup-making, but instead had to turn their hands to picking up the pieces of wood and mopping the floors. Ellen and Sadie tried to fix the broken sewing machines but couldn't. They kept finding screws and springs and bits that Ellen didn't even recognise. She put them all carefully in a jam jar her ma found in the hall kitchen, and hoped that James would come back soon.

'Do you think Frankie will listen to James?' she asked Sadie again and again. Each time Sadie sighed and said: 'I don't know, Ellen.'

Ellen was almost driven mad with the torment of waiting. Until, finally, James came into the hall looking drawn and worried.

'You've done a good job,' he said, looking around.

The soup had been mopped up now, the broken glass swept away, and the torn clothes had been picked up and sorted out between the rag bag and a much smaller pile for the pieces that could be salvaged. Ma and her friend Isobel were on their hands and knees scrubbing the paint from the floor, while Sadie stacked bits of the broken tables at the side of the room.

Ellen went to James and put her arms round him. He rested his chin on her head and she thought how well they fitted together.

'We can't open this evening,' she muttered into his chest. 'It's just not possible.'

'Then we'll get it ready for tomorrow,' James said. He stroked her hair. 'There's too much hard work here to go to waste.'

'Did you speak to Frankie?' Ellen looked up at him hopefully but he shook his head.

'I couldn't find him.' He looked miserable. 'I went everywhere, but he wasn't in any of the usual places. I asked my ma and his da, but I didn't want to say too much.'

'You should tell them what Frankie's been doing,' Ellen said gently. 'You can't keep protecting him.'

'I know.' James rubbed his nose. 'I just don't think this is the real him, you know? He's been so angry since he hurt his leg. And the truth is, he's my big brother and he looked out for me when we were wee and our parents got wed. Now it's my turn to look out for him.'

'You're so kind,' Ellen said. 'But you know this is too big for you.'

James looked tearful. 'I know,' he said again. Ellen pulled him closer and they stood there, wrapped around one another for a minute, in the middle of the room.

'We should get cracking,' James said eventually. 'There's still a lot to do.'

'We should,' Ellen groaned. 'But I think we've done all we can do for now. We need to get the doors mended, and the tables are all broken. We can't pay anyone to do it for us – none of us have any money.'

'I'll ask Walter,' James said. 'He's bound to know someone. What about the sewing machines?'

'All broken. I was wondering if we could get into Wentworth again? Maybe take some more parts. I can ask Bridget.'

'Ask Bridget what?'

Ellen disentangled herself from James to see Bridget standing in the centre of the room, looking in horror at the hall.

'What's going on, Ellen?'

Ellen told Bridget everything, about Frankie and seeing him lurking outside, and coming to the hall that morning and seeing how damaged everything was.

'And he didn't even need to kick in the doors,' she said, beginning to cry again. 'Because I put the key under the mat.'

'Oh, Ellen,' Bridget said. 'Ida and I are here now. We'll help.'

'Can you mend the doors?' Ellen sniffed. 'Because we can't shut them and we can't leave everything here overnight with the doors hanging off.'

'Then we'll stay here overnight,' said Ida.

Ellen looked at her and the way she stayed close to Bridget in a sort of protective way. Not unlike the way James always stood a wee bit closer to her than he did to everyone else, and she decided she liked Ida a lot.

'Stay all night?'

'Why not?' Ida said. 'I'll go to my shop and get blankets and candles and we can camp out all night.'

'I can stay,' said Sadie. 'Ma's tired after yesterday but she'll cope with the weans this once. And Noah said he'd come by after work too, so I think he'll be here soon.'

'Are you feeling well enough?' Ellen asked Sadie.

'I am.'

'There you go,' said James, wiping a tear from Ellen's cheek with his thumb. 'We can stay and watch for any intruders.'

Sadie snorted. 'One intruder,' she said.

James turned to her. 'I couldn't find him,' he said. 'And nor could his da. He didn't go to work today either. Maybe he's gone.'

'I hope so,' said Sadie.

'Right, come along, Bridget, let's get those bits from the store and some food to share,' said Ida, chivvying Bridget along. Ellen was impressed. She loved her sister to pieces, but she wasn't the sort of person who you chivvied. Yet here was Ida, chivvying, and there was Bridget, letting her.

And in the end it was quite fun. Noah arrived with some bread and jam, and some cold meat, and Ida and Bridget came back with blankets and candles, a bag of apples and a bit of cheese. They lit the candles and ate the food, and as the sky darkened and night fell, they wrapped themselves in the blankets and curled up on the floor together.

'I've just had the most wonderful idea,' Bridget said, as they were quietly chatting together.

'What?' said Ellen.

Bridget sat up. 'It won't mean anything to you, Ellen, but Ida, listen. How about if we spent census night here?'

Ida was sitting on one of the few chairs that were still intact, a blanket over her knees. Bridget was leaning against her legs. She span round on the floor and looked at Ida.

'What do you think?'

Ellen had no idea what they were talking about, but she liked the way Ida's face lit up.

'I think that's brilliant,' she said.

'Explain?' Ellen demanded.

'Suffragettes all across the country have decided they're not going to be counted in the census,' Bridget said. 'If we don't count, then we won't be counted.'

Noah whistled. 'That's clever.'

'And illegal,' Sadie pointed out.

'Ach,' said Ida, waving her hand as though laws held no meaning for her. 'Some of our sisters in London are planning to walk round and round Trafalgar Square, and we considered doing the same in Kelvingrove Park, but the weather forecast is dreadful and there are no lights there. We thought we'd be counting broken ankles and wrists if we went there.'

'And then we thought we'd go to where we have our meetings in Glasgow,' said Bridget. The candlelight made her face glow and Ellen thought she'd never seen her sister so animated or happy. It warmed her heart to see this new side of Bridget and she wondered what Malcolm thought about it.

'But it's a flat, above a bookshop,' Bridget continued. And when we had all that rain the other day, the roof started leaking and then it collapsed, so we can't go there now.'

'And then we thought about my shop, but though a few of us could fit, we'd really want all of us to be together,' Ida put in.

'But could you stay here?' Ellen said. 'Wouldn't you have to be counted here instead?'

'In theory,' Ida said. 'But no one would know we were here, would they?'

Noah was gazing at Ida and Bridget in admiration. 'Civil disobedience,' he said. 'What a good way to make your point.'

Bridget looked pleased. 'That's the plan,' she said. 'Malicious mischief.'

'I reckon Walter and that could learn a thing or two from you women,' said James. 'About protest.'

'I reckon so,' said Ida. 'Maybe I'll give him a lesson.'

They all laughed.

'Well, this is nice,' said a horribly familiar voice. They all turned to see Frankie standing in the doorway. Ellen gasped and James jumped to his feet.

'Frankie,' he said. 'I've been looking for you.'

'Why? So you can get me arrested? Da told me you were trying to find me, and I knew you'd be after me so you could take me to the police station.'

His voice was thick with anger and in the dim light, Ellen could see James shaking. She stood up too.

'Frankie, please don't do anything hasty,' she begged. 'We've just cleared up.'

'Shut up!' he roared. 'You don't get to tell me what to do, you Catholic bitch.'

He lunged for Ellen but James was quicker. He flung himself in between his brother and Ellen.

'James!' Ellen shrieked.

James propelled Frankie across the room and pushed him up against the wall.

'Enough!' he roared.

Ellen felt rather than saw everyone else scrambling to stand behind her, protecting her, and she felt safe knowing they were there.

Somehow James had Frankie – who was much bigger and stronger than him – by the collar.

'I've lost everything,' Frankie said. 'Everything!'

'Not everything,' James said quietly. 'Not me.'

Frankie was still raging, but James gripped him tightly.

'Everything!' Frankie shouted again.

'My brother worked at the shipyard,' Ida said from just behind Ellen.

'No one cares about your bastard brother,' Frankie said.

Ida stepped forward, as though she'd not heard him. She held a candle up to her face, lighting the vivid scar that ran across her cheek. 'And one Friday, when I was eighteen, my ma asked me to go down and get his wages before he drank them all. You know how it is? Da's shop wasn't doing so well back then, and things were hard.'

Frankie snorted but he didn't interrupt. Everyone was still, listening to Ida's calm voice.

'And so I went,' Ida said. 'But the men were in one of those moods, you know how it is? When they all get a bit . . .' she paused. 'Silly.'

Ellen thought that threatening might be a better word for it. But she didn't say anything.

'I was the only woman down there that evening and they were teasing me, you know? Shouting things out and jostling. But my brother got angry and he started a fight with the lad who was being loudest. And I tried to stop him, and I got pushed.'

She took a deep breath. 'And I fell onto a beer bottle that some-one had thrown away. It shattered and, well . . .' she gestured to her scar.

'They thought I was going to die, but I didn't.' She smiled her odd lopsided smile at Frankie. 'But for a long time I wished I had. I bet you feel the same, do you?'

Ellen found she was holding her breath. Slowly, carefully, James let go of his brother's collar, though he stayed close, ready to grab him again if he needed to.

And then Frankie nodded slowly.

'Everything is ruined,' he said in a quiet voice.

'It seems that way now but it's not,' Ida said. 'It's just different.'

Frankie rubbed his cheek and Ellen thought he was crying, but she couldn't really tell in the candlelight.

'I was meant to be getting married,' Ida went on. 'A nice boy, called Hugh. But everyone called him Shug, of course. Except my mother.' She chuckled. 'I was working at Wentworth back then actually, in Department Eleven. My life was all mapped out.'

'What happened?' Frankie asked.

'I wouldn't go out,' Ida said matter-of-factly. 'When I was recovering, I stayed in the flat for so long that eventually I just couldn't go outside even if I wanted to. Every time I tried, I panicked so much I would make myself sick. I lost my job, of course, and Shug met someone else. And my brother, who I loved dearly, couldn't bear to look at me. He lives in America now. I've not seen him for years.'

'You lost everything,' Frankie said.

Ida shook her head. 'But I found other things. After a year or so, my father started coaxing me downstairs to the shop. One step at a time. Some days I couldn't do it. Others I made it further. He never forced me, just let me go at my own pace. And when I eventually got there, he began encouraging me to help customers. And one day – a few years after the accident – I realised I was serving all by myself and Da was just sitting down watching me. He left me the shop when he died.'

'Did you marry someone else?' Frankie said.

'I didn't.' Ellen saw Ida glance at Bridget. 'But I'm rather happy about that.'

'I'm sorry, James,' Frankie said. 'I'm really sorry.'

'I know, pal,' said James. Ellen felt tears in her eyes. 'I get it.'

'Will you tell the police?'

'No,' James said. He looked at Ellen. 'Will we?'

'No,' Ellen said.

'But I think I should tell Ma and your da, right?'

Frankie nodded.

'And,' James said thoughtfully. 'Maybe Walter.'

'Why?'

'So he can get the bosses at Wentworth to give you some money to compensate you for your accident.'

'They'd do that?'

'They might.' James put his arm round his brother's shoulders. 'Then you can think about what to do next.'

'Aye,' Frankie said. 'Right.'

'I'll take you home, pal.'

The brothers walked slowly towards the broken doors and Frankie stopped.

'Maybe I'll come back and help you mend everything,' he said.

'No!' Ellen almost shouted. 'I mean, no need. It's all in hand.'

James waved at Ellen and the men disappeared out into the night.

Chapter Thirty-Eight

'I think you're very brave,' Bridget told Ida as they walked back to the hall the following day. They'd all slept rather badly after Frankie's invasion, tossing and turning on their uncomfortable blankets on the floor, and Bridget felt her back aching. And they'd had to get on the first train to Glasgow in the morning to round up the other suffragettes, ready for this evening's census protest. 'You had no way of knowing whether he'd react violently or not.'

Ida shrugged. 'I recognised something in him.'

'I was scared he'd hurt you.'

Ida gave Bridget a look that she couldn't quite read. Half pleased, half quizzical.

'He didn't.'

'Well, I'm glad of that.'

They both smiled at one another as they walked. Bridget felt the rush of warmth she was getting used to feeling when she was with Ida. She liked it, just as she liked being with Ida. She liked the person she was when she was with Ida.

'So we're all set?' Ida said, startling Bridget out of her daydreams.

'We're all set,' she agreed. 'We're all going to be there at first. James says he and Walter can mend the broken machines, and he's going to try to find some of the other men who can mend the doors and the tables. Once that's all done, the others will go, because they need to be at home overnight ...'

'Because it's census night,' said Ida.

'Indeed,' Bridget said with a smile. 'So, it'll just be us suffragettes. We need to be quiet because we don't want anyone to know we're there. But I did think we could probably get away with doing some sewing.'

'Won't the minister hear the machines?'

Bridget shook her head. 'He says he's a heavy sleeper – he didn't wake up when Frankie crashed through the doors so I'm sure the hum of a machine won't disturb him. Frankie did such a lot of damage and Ellen seemed a little overwhelmed at the thought of putting it all right. There are piles of clothes that need repairing, and so many bits of fabric in the rag bag that I'm sure we could put to good use.'

'We'll be like the elves,' said Ida, tucking her hand into the crook of Bridget's arm.

'What elves?' Bridget frowned.

'The ones in the story, who made all the shoes when the shoe-maker was asleep.'

Bridget chuckled. 'Yes, we'll be just like elves. Green and purple elves.'

Ellen was already at the hall when they arrived, biting her lip and looking worried.

'Walter's gone off to see management again,' she said.

'It's Sunday,' Bridget said in surprise. The sound of the church choir was drifting over from next door.

'I know. They've never talked on a Sunday before. I'm not sure if it's good or bad.'

'Good, hopefully,' Bridget said.

'Has Malcolm said anything?'

Bridget screwed her nose up. 'I've not seen him.'

In fact, she'd hardly seen her husband for ages. She'd been at work, of course, and seen him around, but then she'd been with Ida or at the welfare centre. When she and Ida had gone to the shop for supplies before they'd camped out last night, she'd popped home and written him a note to explain what had happened. But she'd not actually spoken to him properly, not had a proper conversation, since he'd come to the police station.

Ellen raised an eyebrow.

'I know,' said Bridget. 'I know.'

'You're different, Bridget. I don't know if it's the strike or the suffragettes, or Ida, but something's changed and you're different.'

Bridget felt nervous suddenly. 'Good, different?'

Ellen smiled. 'Good, different.' She took Bridget's hand. 'But I'm not sure you're the same person you were when you married Malcolm.'

Bridget laughed, but it sounded nervous and shrill, because she'd had the same thought many, many times.

'We've only been married a little while.'

'I know.' Ellen shrugged. 'I just think you should speak to him, that's all.'

Bridget felt a little like she was standing on the edge of a cliff, about to jump.

She nodded.

'I will.'

'James is working on the sewing machines by himself but it's going to take him ages to get them all done. And, if the machines aren't mended, then we can't do anything with the clothes that got damaged. We can sew some bits by hand, I suppose, but it will take much longer that way. And there are still the doors to mend, and all the tables.' She rubbed her forehead looking tearful. 'I just don't think we're going to be able to open tomorrow.'

Bridget heard her stifle a sob, but she pretended not to notice.

'I feel like we've let everyone down.'

'I heard you could use a hand?'

The women turned to see their father standing behind them, his cap in his hands, looking contrite.

'Da?' Ellen sounded astonished and Bridget couldn't blame her. Their father was a stubborn thing.

'I heard what happened with Frankie Briggs,' he said.

'How did you hear?'

Bridget made a point of avoiding her sister's enquiring gaze and their father shrugged.

'I heard he went for you again and that James stopped him.'

'He did.' Ellen lifted her chin. 'James?' she called. 'My da's here.'

James looked alarmed, but he put down the sewing machine parts he was holding and came over, standing right beside Ellen.

'You put yourself in between your brother and my girl?' Da said.

'Aye,' said James. 'And I'd do it again.'

Da nodded. Then, to Bridget's astonishment, he held out his hand for James to shake.

'Thanks, son,' he said.

James shook Da's hand.

'No problem,' he said, which made Bridget smile because it was such an understatement.

Da put his cap on then took it off again. 'I've heard folk say Frankie's not been right since that accident he had.'

'That could be true,' Ellen nodded. 'But he still knows right from wrong.'

'Well,' said Da, 'sometimes we all have a bit of trouble with that. Maybe now he can get some help. Speak to a doctor or find somewhere to go?'

'That's what we're hoping,' said James.

'Good,' Da said. He fidgeted on his feet. 'I, erm, I brought you something.' He felt in his pocket. 'Now where did I put it?'

Bridget and Ellen looked at one another, not knowing what he was up to. And then he nodded.

'Here it is.' He pulled out something tucked in his fist. 'Hold out your hand,' he said to Ellen and she obeyed, looking confused.

Da opened his fist and dropped a chain into Ellen's palm. She gasped in delight.

'My necklace!' she said.

'Aye. Took me a while to find it, mind. And then Tam mended the chain for me.'

Ellen held the crucifix up and Bridget helped her fasten it.

'How did you know I'd lost it?' Ellen frowned.

Their father looked sheepish. 'I heard you telling your ma,' he admitted. 'And I heard what else you said, too.'

'I never meant . . .' Ellen began but Da held his hand up to quieten her. 'You were right,' he said. 'And so was your ma. I'd like to think I'd never lash out like that Frankie did. But I was wrong too.' He smiled. 'And I'm sorry.'

Ellen threw herself at her father and Bridget smiled to see them hug. For all their father's faults, he always admitted his mistakes and tried to put them right.

'Anyway, I've come to help,' Da said, flexing his fingers. 'It looks like you could use a good carpenter.'

'We really could,' said Ellen with a glint in her eye. 'Do you know any?'

Da laughed. 'Any more cheek like that, young lady, and I'll take my pals and go to the pub instead.'

'Your pals?' said Bridget.

'They're waiting outside,' Da explained. 'I didn't want them all watching me while I said what I had to say.' He raised his voice. 'Tam! Marty!'

His friends appeared round the door. 'Marty can help me with the wood, and Tam can give you a hand, James. He works on the engines at the yard.'

'Tam works at the shipyard?' James said with a raised eyebrow.

Da looked a wee bit embarrassed.

'Aye, he does.'

'I think I've seen you at church, Tam,' James said. 'You come here, don't you?' He looked straight at Bridget's da even though he was speaking to Tam. 'You come to St Andrew's?'

'That's right,' said Tam.

James squeezed his lips together and looked at Da, and Da shrugged.

'I was wrong, son.'

There was a pause and then James chuckled.

'Right you are, Mr Kelly,' he said. 'C'mon then, Tam.'

'Right, I'll get cracking on those doors,' Da said.

Ellen took him and his friends off to show them what needed to be done and Bridget went to find Ida. She found her in the churchyard with the suffragettes – most of them, at least. There was no sign of Christina, and Bridget was glad.

'This is exciting,' said Helen as Bridget approached. 'I think us all refusing to be counted, all across the country, will really make the Government sit up and listen.'

'I hope so,' said Bridget.

'And you'd like us to sew, I hear?'

'If you're willing?'

'Of course we are,' said Mary. 'And I brought us a wee something to help the hours pass quicker.'

She reached into her bag and pulled out a hip flask.

Helen chuckled.

'So did I.'

Several of the other women did the same and they all dissolved into giggles.

Helen opened her coat to reveal her Votes for Women sash.

'I wasn't sure if we should wear our colours,' she said. 'We're not always welcome.'

Bridget shrugged. 'Everyone here is protesting about something,' she pointed out. 'Working conditions. Pay. Women's suffrage. We've all got something to say.'

Mary and the others all unfastened their coats, too. Ida reached into her bag and pulled out her own sash, which she looped over her head. Bridget briefly regretted giving hers to Morag at the prison. She'd have to make herself another one, when she had time. Though it might not be something to make at the sewing bee.

But then Helen pulled another sash from her bag. 'I heard yours was donated,' she said. 'Some lass by the name of Morag?'

'You've met her?' Bridget was pleased.

'She came to a meeting.' Helen raised an eyebrow. 'Fiery one, that. Where did you meet her?'

'Jail.'

Helen hooted with laughter, holding out the sash. 'Here, I made you another.'

'Thank you!' Bridget put it on, feeling herself stand up straighter as she did.

'I knew you were up to something, Bridget Walsh.'

She turned, surprised, and saw Malcolm standing next to a gravestone. He looked sombre and – Bridget winced – disappointed.

'You take the others inside,' she said in a low voice to Ida. 'I need to speak to my husband.'

Ida's sharp eyes watched her carefully. 'Will you be all right?'

Grateful for the concern, Bridget nodded. 'I will.'

She waited for the other suffragettes to weave through the gravestones to the hall entrance and then she spoke.

'I should have told you that I'd joined the suffragettes.'

Malcolm sat down on a flat, raised family memorial. 'Yes.'

'I thought you might have worked it out when I was arrested.'

'Yes,' said Malcolm thoughtfully. 'I should have.'

'Are you angry?'

He shook his head. 'Actually, no.' He looked as surprised by that as Bridget felt. 'I've been doing a lot of thinking. Walking by the canal and thinking.'

'I've not seen you properly for days,' Bridget said. 'Is that where you've been?'

'Aye. I like being by the water. It calms me down.'

Bridget thought Malcolm was one of the calmest, stillest men she knew but she didn't say so. She just nodded and sat down on the memorial next to him.

'What were you thinking about?'

317

'You remember what it was like when I was wee?'

'I do.'

'I was just a lad, seven or eight years old, and caring for my brothers and sisters.'

Bridget squeezed her lips together. She knew how awful things had been for her husband, but she still didn't like hearing it.

'It was so frightening, Bridget. Like the ground had fallen away from under my feet.' He gave her a small smile. 'It's why I liked school so much. The rules, you know? I understood that. I didn't understand what was happening at home. And same as Wentworth.' He sighed. 'And I suppose with society. I like structure and routine, and this strike? Well, it's the opposite, isn't it?'

'I think so.'

'And the suffragettes – they're fighting to break the structure. To change the rules.'

'Yes,' said Bridget. 'Because the rules are wrong.'

Malcolm nodded. 'And the new working conditions at Wentworth are wrong too.'

'Thousands of strikers agree with that.'

'I thought about how sometimes things have to change,' he said. He turned to look at her. 'And I thought about me and you.'

Bridget took a deep breath. 'I do love you, you know.'

But Malcolm shook his head. 'Not in the right way. Not in the way a wife should love her husband.'

Bridget stared at him, astonished at his insight.

'No,' she said. 'Not in that way.'

'And if I'm honest, Bridget, I don't love you either.'

For a second Bridget felt offended, and then she was flooded with relief.

'Really?'

'I think what I loved was the idea of being married. It's that structure again, isn't it? The stability of having a wife who'd look after me, and who I could look after.'

The corners of Bridget's mouth twitched. 'And instead you got me.'

Malcolm laughed. 'I did.' He took her hand. 'I'm not sure what we do next.'

'Me neither.'

'We'll work it out.' He put her hand to his mouth and kissed her fingers, then he stood up. 'I'm going to go home,' he said.

Bridget nodded. 'I'm staying here,' she said. 'All night.'

'It's census night.' Malcolm looked worried.

'Aye, it is.'

There was a pause and then he gave a resigned shrug of his shoulders. 'You do what you have to do, Bridget.'

Bridget sat up a bit straighter and adjusted her sash. 'I will.'

Malcolm gave her a little wave and began walking towards the churchyard gate.

'Malcolm?' she called.

He paused and turned back to her.

'Are you going to stop work? Are you going to join the strike?'

'Are you?' he said.

Bridget thought for a second and then nodded. 'I think so.'

He smiled. 'Maybe I'll see you on the picket line.'

Bridget almost fell off the tombstone. 'Really?'

Malcolm laughed. 'Probably not,' he admitted. 'Perhaps next time, eh?'

Bridget watched him go, thinking that the men in her life were full of surprises today.

She sat there for a while, listening to the birds singing and the hubbub of chatter from the church hall. She thought about Malcolm and how strong he was and how he didn't even know it. And she thought about how he'd said she didn't love him as a wife should love her husband. She thought about that for a very long time.

And then, just as she was about to go back into the hall and lend a hand, Ida came to find her.

'I was getting worried,' she said. She came and sat down next to Bridget. 'Where's Malcolm?'

'He's gone home.'

'Is everything all right?'

She nodded. 'We had a good chat.' She looked down at her feet. 'He says I don't love him in the right way.'

'What does that mean?'

'In the way a woman should love a man.'

'Do you?'

'No,' Bridget said bluntly. 'And the thing is –' she paused – 'the thing is, I'm not sure I could ever love a man in that way.'

She looked straight at Ida, who was watching her very carefully. 'But I think I could love you.'

Ida smiled her funny crooked smile and Bridget felt her heart leap.

'Could love,' she said. 'Or do?'

Bridget took Ida's hand in hers and clasped it to her chest. 'Do,' she said. 'I do love you.'

'I love you, too.'

Gently, cautiously, Bridget leaned forward and touched her lips to Ida's. She felt as though the air around them was crackling with energy but kissing Ida felt absolutely normal. Like coming home after a long, hard day at work.

'Goodness,' said Ida. 'I'd hoped that might happen, but I thought it was impossible.'

Bridget laughed.

'And one can't believe in impossible things,' she said, just as Ida had said the first time they met.

They smiled at one another.

'I suppose we should go back inside,' Ida said reluctantly.

'I suppose so.'

Bridget got off the tomb and held her hand out to Ida. They shared a small smile, full of secrets, and then walked towards the church hall.

But just as they reached the door, Walter came hurrying down the path, rushing into the hall ahead of them.

'James!' he called as he went inside, followed by a curious Bridget and Ida.

Gradually the noisy chit-chat in the hall quietened down as Walter's arrival – and his worried, dishevelled appearance – registered.

'What's the matter?' James asked. 'What's happened?'

Walter ran his fingers through his hair.

'It's over,' he said. 'We can't win. The strike's broken – we're going back to work.'

Chapter Thirty-Nine

Ellen felt as if she was underwater. Walter was speaking but she couldn't understand what he was saying.

'Stop,' she said. 'Slow down.'

Next to her, James slipped his arm around her waist. Sadie came to stand on her other side and Ellen took her hand.

'Start again from the beginning,' James said to Walter.

Walter nodded.

'Right, well, you know management haven't been over the moon at having to negotiate with us,' he began. Ellen rolled her eyes. She knew that only too well. 'They've been digging in their heels.'

Sadie snorted. 'So unhelpful.'

'Aye,' said Walter. 'Anyway, the other day they said they'd only start proper negotiations if everyone went back to work.'

'WHAT?' Ellen was outraged. 'You didn't tell us that.'

'No,' said Walter looking mildly sheepish. 'We thought it might stir up trouble.'

'It would have done,' Ellen said. 'That's absolutely not on. As soon as they've got us all back, then what incentive would they have to pay us any attention?'

'I know,' Walter said. 'And we told them that. But they just wouldn't listen.' He threw his head back in frustration. 'When they called us in today, we knew it wouldn't be good news.'

'What did they say?' James asked.

'They said they want to make sure that everyone who's stopped work actually wants to be on strike,' he said with a sigh.

'Well, that's fine because we all do want to be on strike,' Sadie said with a shrug. 'We'd not be doing it if we didn't.'

But Walter was looking uncertain.

'How will they know?' Ellen asked. 'How will they know who wants to be on strike?'

'They're sending out forms,' he said. 'And the forms will ask if you want to be on strike or not. If they get six thousand people saying they want to go back to work, then the strike's over.'

'Doesn't sound too bad,' said Sadie. 'I really don't think that many people will want to go back.'

'And everyone will have to fill in their names and addresses,' said Walter. 'Everyone.'

They all stared at him. Ellen caught Bridget's eye – she was standing by the door to the hall with Ida, and she looked furious.

'I'm not typing any forms like that,' Bridget said.

'They're done already.' Walter rubbed his nose. 'Beresford's got some women up there now.'

'So, say for instance Ellen fills in her form, and says she's happy to be on strike,' said Sadie slowly. 'And she adds her name and address. But they get six thousand people saying they want to go back in.' She paused. 'What's to stop management punishing Ellen for saying she doesn't want to return? Giving her the sack, even?'

'Nothing,' said Walter. 'Nothing at all.'

They all looked at one another in silence. Ellen felt a horrible sadness. No, not sadness. Helplessness. They'd worked so hard, and the cards were stacked against them from the beginning.

'No one's going to vote to stay out,' she said, her expression grim. 'It's over.'

*

It was with heavy hearts that they all returned home that evening, knowing their forms would be waiting for them. Bridget and her suffragette friends all stayed behind, of course, and Ellen envied them the chance to continue their protest. Their fight wasn't over, but hers was.

'What will you choose?' Sadie asked, as they said their goodbyes.

'What can we do?' Ellen looked up at the sky as though asking for divine intervention. 'If we say no, and six thousand people all say yes, then I have a suspicion there won't be any jobs for us to go back to.'

Sadie winced. 'I think you're right.'

'We could still negotiate,' Ellen said. 'It doesn't have to be over. Or perhaps they won't get the numbers they need to force us all back to work. We could still change things at Wentworth.'

But she could tell from Sadie's face that she wasn't convinced.

'I'm going to say no,' Ellen decided all at once. 'What's the worst that can happen?'

Sadie screwed up her face, but then she nodded. 'I'm going to say no, too.'

In the end a couple of thousand workers voted to carry on striking. But they were far outnumbered by those who voted to return. The next day, Walter, James and Stanley went to management and conceded defeat. The day after that the factory gates opened once more.

Ellen met Sadie on the corner and together they walked up towards the factory, stopping to collect Bridget on the way.

'Remember that first day when we all walked out,' Ellen said. 'And there were so many of us?'

'And the day we went to get our wages, too.' Sadie sighed. 'We really did something important here.'

'It didn't succeed though, did it?' Ellen stopped walking and looked up at the factory gates ahead. 'Here we are, going back to the same pay and conditions we were working for before.'

Bridget tutted. 'Don't say that, Ellen. We might not see it now, but things have changed because of what you did. People have found their voices. Change is in the air, you mark my words.'

'Now you sound like Ida,' Ellen said, watching Bridget's cheeks redden and wondering why. 'You're spending so much time with her, you're starting to talk like her.'

'I don't think that's a bad thing,' Sadie pointed out. 'Ida's lovely.'

'Come on,' Bridget said, clearly having had enough of their teasing. 'Let's go.'

Ellen looped one arm through Bridget's and one through Sadie's and together they walked through the factory gates once more.

In the courtyard were some of the more junior managers, ticking off names on a list. Malcolm was there, but when he saw them, he buried his face in a clipboard and pretended not to see them. So it was another chap who asked their names and departments.

'Bridget Walsh, you're fine to go on up to clerical,' he said, writing something down with a flourish. 'Sadie Franklin and Ellen Kelly, you're to stay here in the courtyard.'

'Why?' asked Ellen. She had a bad feeling about this.

'I don't know,' the man said, but he was quite obviously lying.

They moved along a little bit.

'You can go up, he said,' Ellen told Bridget.

'I'm not going anywhere. I want to find out what's going on.' She folded her arms and planted herself in a spot at the edge of the small group that was gathering.

Ellen smiled to herself, liking this new, prickly Bridget.

She looked round and saw James standing with Walter and Stanley near the front.

Sadie tugged her arm. 'There's that Brody,' she said. 'And some of the Gorbals division.'

The uneasy feeling in Ellen's stomach began to grow. Everyone here had been a striker. Or one of the first folk who downed tools at least. The agitators, Walter called them. She saw the women from their department and gave a small wave. They stared back at her, stony-faced.

At the front of the group, Malcolm and another man were busy stacking pallets to make a platform, just like the one Ellen had stood on when the strike first began. It wasn't even a month ago, but it felt like a lifetime had passed since then.

'This isn't good,' she murmured to Sadie and Bridget.

Bridget frowned. 'They gave Walter a promise that voting no wouldn't affect someone's job.'

Sadie gave one of her snorts. 'When did they ever do as they said?' She glowered over at where management were gathering. 'They're just a bunch of liars.'

'They said that they couldn't be expected to employ anyone who was unfriendly towards Wentworth,' Ellen said dully. 'I see now that by "unfriendly", they meant anyone who organised the strikes.'

Sadie had gone a little red in the face with anger – or perhaps she was just upset – and Ellen couldn't blame her for feeling that way. She took her friend's hand.

'I will do everything I can to find you another job,' she said. 'My ma and da know everyone. They'll put in a word for you somewhere. We'll check the newspapers every day, and speak to everyone we can. And maybe you can take in mending for now. We've still got those Wentworth machines that James fixed.'

'Thank you,' said Sadie, with what seemed to be a great deal of effort.

'Shall we try to get a bit closer?' Ellen said. 'I want to look Beresford in the eye.'

'Really?' said Bridget. 'Are you sure?'

Ellen wasn't sure actually. Just the thought of being close to that horrible man was making her feel a little bit weak, but she very much wanted to show him that she wasn't scared. That he hadn't broken her.

She took Sadie's hand, and Sadie took Bridget's, and in a chain, they weaved through the waiting people right to the front of the crowd. Malcolm saw them there and came over.

'Bridget, you shouldn't be here.'

'I'm not going upstairs until I find out what's going on,' she said.

Malcolm gave her a look that was half exasperation and half pride, Ellen thought.

'Listen, I don't think—' But he was interrupted by the managers taking to the platform. They had loud hailers, just as the strikers had, and once more Ellen was struck by the similarities to that first day.

'Thank you for coming,' Mr Beresford said, his voice booming through the hailer. 'Sadly it has fallen to me to let you know that we no longer have a job for you at Wentworth. You have all proven that you are unfriendly towards this company and we cannot be expected to employ you. Please start making your way towards the gates. Thank you.'

A cacophony of voices broke out, people shouting questions and insults. Someone near Ellen began to cry and she turned to see it was Sadie, sobbing into her hands like her heart would break.

'Look after Sadie,' she said to Bridget and then, before she could even think, she pushed her way past Malcolm and the other managers and onto the platform.

Mr Beresford looked at her in horror, and Ellen shrank away from him, then gathered herself and grabbed the loud hailer from his hands.

'Excuse me,' she shouted, hearing her voice bouncing off the factory walls. 'Could I have a minute?'

Gradually the crowd quietened. Behind her she was aware of Mr Beresford gesticulating wildly but she got the impression he was a little wary of her. Which wasn't surprising really, but it pleased her. And it meant he was too nervous to make a grab for the loud hailer.

With a smile she looked over her shoulder at him. 'I've got a letter opener in my pocket,' she said quietly, and he backed off, looking shocked.

Ellen turned back to the crowd. 'I just wanted to say that I'm really proud of what we did here,' she said. 'I know it's not the result we wanted and I know things are going to be hard for us for a while. But we'll get new jobs. We'll move on. And perhaps Wentworth will know to look after their staff from now on.' She glared at the men who were all talking furiously, with Malcolm standing slightly to the side of them.

'Thank you,' Ellen said. She shoved the loud hailer back at Beresford. He took it with a glint in his eye, and as she was jumping down from the platform, he raised it to his lips.

'I would urge you all to spread the word about that woman,' he shouted 'She attacked me, unprovoked. She left me frightened and bleeding in my office, and then she manipulated her way out of jail.'

The crowd all swivelled to look at Ellen and she felt a rush of pure, white-hot rage. In a flash she was back on the platform and wrestling the loud hailer from Beresford again. He made a lunge for her, but Malcolm held him back.

Malcolm.

'I did attack Beresford,' Ellen said through the loud hailer. The crowd was so quiet, Ellen could hear her own heart thumping. 'I stabbed him in the arm with a letter opener.'

She paused. 'And I did it because he tried to kiss me, and then he put his hand up my skirt.' There was a gasp from the crowd. 'And I was scared and I didn't know how to stop him,' Ellen went on. 'And so I grabbed a letter opener from his desk and I jabbed it into his arm.' She let herself smile – just a tiny one. 'That stopped him.'

'Liar,' shouted Beresford. But Malcolm positioned himself in front of his boss so he couldn't get to Ellen.

'I'm not lying,' Ellen said to the other managers. 'And I'm not the only one.' She looked out into the crowd. 'Am I?'

There was a pause that seemed to go on forever. And then, right at the back of the crowd, she saw Janet. She raised her hand. 'He did it to me, too.'

Suddenly, Ellen understood that Janet had been trying to warn her when she tried to stop her seeing Beresford. She hadn't been jealous – she'd been caring.

Ellen put her fingers to her lips and blew her friend a kiss.

Next to Janet another woman put her hand in the air. 'He did it to me, too,' she shouted.

And then women throughout the crowd were raising their hands and shouting out that Beresford had done the same to them.

Beresford shoved Malcolm out of the way, then just as he'd done before, he turned tail and hurried away. Ellen knew that nothing would happen. She doubted he'd lose his job or even be disciplined. But she still felt better for exposing him. And perhaps the rumours would spread now and stop him doing the same to other women. She dropped the loud hailer and jumped off the platform.

'Well done,' said Sadie. 'He deserved that.'

Ellen grinned at her. 'It felt good.'

'I bet it did.' Sadie sighed and looked round at the crowd, which was beginning to stream out of the factory again. 'I suppose we should go home.'

Bridget was standing a little way from them, gazing up at the building.

'Bridget, I'll see you later?' Ellen said.

'Will you?' she said, sounding thoughtful.

Malcolm came over and nodded to them all in greeting.

'Thanks for keeping Beresford back,' Ellen said.

He looked at her, eyes wide with innocence. 'I didn't do anything,' he said. But Ellen knew he was fibbing.

'You should go upstairs, Bridget,' he said.

Bridget turned to them all and put her hand on Malcolm's arm. 'I'm sorry,' she said. 'But I can't.'

'I thought you might say that.' He sounded almost amused.

'That's me done with Wentworth,' Bridget said.

This time it was her who threaded one arm through Sadie's and one through Ellen's.

'Let's go,' she said.

So they went.

Epilogue

One week later

Ellen had a plan – she just needed a little bit more help and then it would all fall into place. Which was why she and James were here at St Andrew's again, looking at the sewing machines they'd left in the corner of the room when the strike had been broken.

'I'm not even sure we'd need all four,' she said.

James rubbed his chin. 'The way I see it, is you may as well have them all.' He gave her a sudden, cheeky smile. 'We can't take them back to Wentworth now.'

She stood on her tiptoes to kiss him.

'That's true enough,' she said.

James had a new job. Tam had put a word in for him at the shipyard and now he was working there. He said he liked being out in the fresh air, and Ellen could see in his face that he was telling the truth and she was glad.

Ellen, though, didn't have a new job. Nor did Sadie. Which was why she was here today, looking at the sewing machines that were a vitally important part of her plan

'Ida's got everything you need,' she told James. 'But you might have to do a few trips.'

'That's fine,' he said. 'It's nice to keep busy.'

She looked at him carefully. Frankie had gone away for a while to a special hospital that looked after people with head injuries because it turned out when he hurt his leg in the accident, he'd hit his head, too. James's ma and stepda had been terribly upset to realise that everyone had missed that his brain had been damaged – he'd had a bleed, apparently. But the doctors were hopeful they could do an operation that would help and Walter and the IWS were busy negotiating for Wentworth to pay Frankie some money to say sorry. It was a worrying time for James and his family and Ellen wanted them to know she cared.

'If you're sure,' she said.

He smiled at her. 'I'll be fine. Go and find Sadie and I'll meet you there.'

Ellen kissed him again and dashed off towards the station.

Sadie was on her way to Clydebank for the first time since the strike had ended and they'd all left Wentworth. Noah was sitting next to her on the train – he'd somehow managed to get some time off work and she was pleased he'd come with her.

'You've no idea what Ellen wants with you?' he asked, his brow furrowed.

Sadie actually had an inkling. The tiniest germ of an idea. But while the thought had crossed her mind in a 'wouldn't it be nice if we could . . .' way – in fact she and Ellen had even talked about it one day when they were sewing clothes at the welfare centre – she thought that Ellen had somehow managed to get things moving.

'You do know, don't you?' Noah said now, watching her.

'Maybe,' she admitted. 'But I don't want to say in case I'm wrong.'

'Is it a new job?'

'Stop asking questions,' she said with a chuckle. 'Tell me what the rabbi said. I don't even understand why you went to see him.'

'I went to see him to ask him if he'd marry us.'

Sadie's jaw dropped.

'You thought you'd ask him before you asked me?'

'Well, I thought he might be easier to win over,' Noah joked.

'And what did he say?'

'He said he thought us getting married was a terrible idea.'

Sadie's stomach lurched.

'Grr, that man is infuriating,' she said. 'I bet that sister of his has been dripping poison in his ear about me working on Saturday.'

Noah laughed loudly.

'I'm kidding,' he said, holding his hands up. 'He said we can get married in September.'

'This September?' Sadie said in surprise.

'Yes,' Noah said. 'If you'll have me?'

'Is that a proposal, Noah Spark?'

Noah grinned. 'Yes, it is.' He looked at her. 'Sadie Franklin, will you marry me?' He paused, looking a little worried. 'This September. If you want?'

'Yes, I want!' she said, throwing herself into his arms.

As the train pulled in to Clydebank and they got off, Sadie stood for a moment on the platform. She loved Glasgow, of course, and she didn't want to live anywhere else, but this town had something special too. Fighting spirit. She liked that. She had a feeling the strike at Wentworth was just the beginning of something. Something they'd started.

'Ready?' said Noah, taking her hand.

'Ready.'

Ellen was waiting for them at the bottom of the stairs, jigging about like an overexcited schoolgirl.

'I was so worried you weren't coming,' she said as they drew nearer.

'Why wouldn't we come?' Sadie said, frowning.

Ellen waved her arms. 'I don't know, I was just worried. And then the train was late and I started thinking that maybe I'd got the times wrong or perhaps I'd missed you and you'd gone wandering off somewhere, but you wouldn't know where to go because I'd not told you all the details, so I wouldn't know where to look for you.' She took a deep breath. 'But you're here now.'

Sadie put her arm through Ellen's.

'You'd better take us to where we're going, then, before you burst.'

Bridget was at Ida's shop, getting in her way as she tried to serve customers.

'Bridget, could you please just choose a spot and stick to it because you're always where I need to be,' Ida said mildly.

'Sorry,' Bridget said. 'I'll sit here quietly and wait.'

She went to the chair behind the counter, where Ida sat and read a book when it was quiet, letting her fingers brush Ida's as she passed.

'Have you got the keys?' she asked.

'James has them,' Ida said. 'He's putting the machines inside.'

'Good,' said Bridget. 'Good.'

She watched Ida sell a box of candles to a customer and then when the shop was quiet again, she said: 'I've got some news.'

Ida turned to look at her. 'Oh yes?'

Bridget pleated a bit of her skirt.

'Malcolm's impressed the bosses with the way he worked all through the strike and kept things going,' she said in a rush. 'He's been offered the chance to go and work at the factory in Manchester.'

'Manchester?' said Ida. 'Dreadful place.'

'You've never been to Manchester so don't be silly,' Bridget chided.

Ida gave her a small smile. 'Is he going?'

'He's pretty keen.'

'Right.' There was a pause. Ida picked up a cloth and began dusting the counter, not meeting Bridget's eyes. 'Well, that's lovely.'

'I'm not going to go with him,' Bridget said.

Ida turned back to her. 'You're not?'

'How can I?' Bridget said. 'I'm terribly busy. And my parents aren't as young as they used to be, they need my help. It's very impractical for me to move away.'

'Your ma's not fifty yet,' said Ida.

Bridget shrugged.

'You're really not going?'

'No.'

'People will talk.'

'Och, they might. But not for long.'

'Where will you live?'

Bridget had thought of that.

'Is there a flat? Next door?'

Ida nodded, slowly. 'There is.'

Bridget took a breath. 'Maybe I could move in?'

'Next door?' Ida's eyebrows almost disappeared into her hairline she was so surprised.

'Is it a terrible idea?' Bridget said.

Ida reached out and took her hand. 'I think it's the best idea you've ever had.'

Ellen led Sadie and Noah through the streets to Ida's shop. Bridget and Ida were waiting outside, looking happy and excited, and James was there too, leaning against the door of the shop next door.

'Where are we going?' Sadie asked.

'Nowhere,' said Ellen. 'Well, not nowhere. Here. We're going here.'

Sadie frowned. 'Ida's shop?'

'No.' Ellen shook her head and gestured for James to move out of the way. 'This shop.'

She flung her arms out wide at the shop next door to Ida's that had once been the greengrocer's. It had been closed for a while and the large window was grubby. Its awning was torn, and the paintwork needed sorting. Sadie looked at Ellen and Ellen grinned.

'There's a big space at the back where I thought we could set up the machines,' she said. 'And there's a back entrance too, so I thought perhaps people could drop off clothes donations there. And then we can line the front of the shop with rails to hang the clothes, and there's space for a desk for you. I wondered if people donate stuff, then we should pay them in coupons, which they can use in the shop, rather than just straight swapping old for new like we did at the welfare centre. Otherwise, we won't make any money at all. But I thought I'd let you decide that because you can do the sums.' She ran out of breath and stopped talking, watching to see what Sadie thought.

'A clothing exchange?' Sadie said. 'Like we did at the welfare centre?'

'Me, you and Bridget,' Ellen said. 'We can all sew. And Bridget can do all the clerical work, and you can do the money, and I'll deal with the customers.'

She looked at her sister and her friend.

'What do you think?' she said.

Bridget's eyes were shining and Sadie looked absolutely delighted.

'I think let's do it,' Sadie said. She held her hand out to Noah and he handed her the large bag he'd carried from the train.

'What's that?' asked Ellen curiously.

'Donations.' Sadie grinned. 'I had an idea we might need them.'

'You knew?' Ellen shrieked.

'I had an inkling.'

The women all stood back a little way, admiring the admittedly dirty and rundown shop front.

'I wish we had a camera,' said Ellen. 'It would be nice to have a photograph of the three of us on the day the Clydebank Clothing Exchange began.'

Sadie snorted. 'That's not what we're calling it,' she said.

'It is what we're calling it,' Ellen argued. 'It's simple and to the point.'

Bridget laughed. 'Shall we go and have a look at what it's like before we all fall out?'

With a flourish, James opened the door, and still bickering and laughing, the women went inside to start their new business.

Acknowledgements

This book would have been a whole lot harder to write if it hadn't been for all the help I've had from some brilliantly knowledgeable people, and I owe them huge thanks.

First of all, I need to thank Andrew Graham from the Clydebank Museum. He gave up a whole morning to give me a tour of the town and show me photos and memorabilia from the Singer factory, and to share his knowledge of the strike.

Harvey Kaplan, director of the Scottish Jewish Archives Centre, was so helpful and not only gave me wonderful insight into the lives of Scottish Jews at the time my story is set, but ideas for future books, too! Thank you too to my mother-in-law Faith Barrett, who shared her memories of growing up Jewish in Glasgow. Sadie's story about being asked if she is a Protestant Jew or a Catholic Jew came from Faith!

Author and friend Jim McCallum (who writes gripping spy novels under the name James Hume) was great at answering random questions about Glasgow when I emailed him in a panic, and that is why I named Ellen's sweetheart James McCallum after him.

Huge thanks go to my brilliant editor Sam Eades, who has the best ideas, my fabulous agent Amanda Preston, and my readers who have enjoyed my stories about Kew Gardens – I hope you like this one, too!

And, of course, thank you to my family – especially my Auntie Norma and her husband Robert who put me up when I was researching this story, and took me for cocktails, which is absolutely the way to this author's heart.